I0656418

THE JOURNEY'S END

Jane Woolfenden

First published 2013

© Jane Woolfenden 2013
Jane Woolfenden asserts the moral right to be identified
as the author of this work

Enquiries concerning these terms should be addressed
to *Blue Gecko Books*. bluegeckobooks@ymail.com

ISBN: 978-0-9575685-1-8

This novel is entirely a work of fiction. The names,
characters and incidents portrayed in it are the work
of the author's imagination. Any resemblance to actual
persons, living or dead, events or localities
is entirely coincidental.

Design and formatting by
Barbara Velasco (Papel Papel)

Printed and bound by
Lightning Source UK

All rights reserved. No part of this publication
may be reproduced, stored in a retrieval system,
or transmitted, in any form or by any means, electonic,
mechanical, photocopying, recording or otherwise,
without the prior permission of the publishers.

To Dennis, Jill and Robin

*C*ome, rest your weary head, my love
   The journey's done
It's time to sleep.
Don't shed another tear for me, my love
Your cares are gone
And you can lie, still warm,
Beneath the setting sun.

So long now since
We each were called by bright and far off shores,
And searched
For perfect islands in a dark and restless sea.
But look, oh look, the boat has come
To carry you back home at last;
You've reached your journey's end.

And though your day has turned to night, my love,
Our too brief sunlight
Changed to shadow by the turning of the world,
You should not fear the dark, my love:
For it is glowing with sweet memories.
And, quickly, look:
There is a new light, risen in another place.
It will be shining here tomorrow.

PROLOGUE

18 June 2001
London

The end is my beginning

∞

18 June 2001
Central London

6.56 pm

A woman grips the edge of her seat as the ambulance lurches first one way and then the other. Her name is Monica, but no-one else knows that.

The man sitting next to her takes a sharp intake of breath when her shoulder collides with his; then smiles, weakly, when she turns to apologize. He is wearing a dark blue shirt, she notices, and a bandage coiled in a rakish fashion around his head; a rosette of blood burgeons through the frayed cotton fabric.

She looks away, but the image swoops back into the darkened chamber behind her closed eyes. Blood, more blood, more than she has ever seen: glistening, viscous stuff, seeping out, seeping everywhere; seeping into places it should never have gone. Now everything inside the hollow of her belly starts to rise up, then flip over, before plummeting down: deep, deep down. She wonders if she is going to be sick. She opens her eyes and forces herself to look at the floor.

It helps.

She can see her toes planted on the metal step below her seat. Something is not right, she thinks. She examines her left foot, twisting it so that she can look at both sides. Her nails are painted: a shade of pink. But her feet are so very dirty. And why isn't she wearing any shoes?

She searches the area around her feet.

She is sure she must have some shoes. Hasn't she been at work all day? But she can't remember being at work. She can't remember anything much at all. And the effort of trying to remember makes her feel dizzy. Then her insides set off again: there they go – up and over. Perhaps she is going to faint, she thinks. She would be fine if only she could lie down; if only she could stop this horrible, high pitched whining in her ears. And it is so hot in here. Why is it so hot? She leans over as far as she can and presses her forehead against her knees.

When she looks up again she notices a woman sitting opposite her. Had she been there before? She isn't sure.

Monica looks at the woman's face. The colour is wrong: it is as if every last bit of blood has been drained from the veins and capillaries beneath the skin. The woman's eyes stare blankly into the space in front of her. She is clutching a copy of the *Evening Standard*. The newspaper is folded neatly in half, fresh from the news-stand; it is pristine, apart from the blood: dark red runnels of it, splayed out over the neat columns of text. The woman's pink linen skirt is also splattered with blood. Monica wonders whose blood it is.

She looks back at the newspaper, at the picture underneath the headline. There is a man, in a suit, and a little girl. But she, too, has a rivulet of blood splashed across her forehead.

Then, without any real understanding of why she is doing it, Monica starts to giggle; words are circling round and round inside her head: *Black and white and red all over – black and white and red all over.*

What's the rhyme? No, it isn't a rhyme, it's a joke. What joke? She can't recall. What's the punch line? What's the joke? Whatever it is, it's very funny and it's making her laugh. But she needs to know what it is, and now it's making her cross; she can't cope with all this forgetfulness. She turns to the man next to her – the man in the blue shirt – maybe he knows it. But he seems to be sleeping. She wants to scream out to them all, wake them up, tell them the joke. But she doesn't.

She is shivering now, and she tugs at the foil blanket someone has given her. She hadn't wanted a blanket; she hadn't wanted to come in this ambulance. She was fine, she had told them, just a small cut on her hand. But a man in a white coat had made her get in. And there they are now, on the other side, leaning over a stretcher; and someone is directing questions at it: sharp, urgent, questions.

'Can you tell us your name? – Sir? – Can you hear me? Sir?'

Monica can see a shape under a thin grey blanket. There is a foot sticking out from under one edge. No shoe, nor sock, just a foot. And an ankle. The skin is smooth, quite dark. Like the colour of biscuits, Monica thinks. She can't take her eyes off the foot; she marvels at how clean it is. How could it be so clean, when her own feet are so dirty?

Another voice now. 'His GCS is dropping. Sir? Sir? Can you hear me?'

Monica looks up at the narrow panel of window above the stretcher. She can see the tops of buildings, windows, a long green roof. There is nothing familiar. She doesn't know where they are going.

'We're losing him.'

'Sir?'

'Unrousable.'

A woman is leaning over the stretcher, pushing at the shape under the blanket, pushing onto it with both of her hands. Each time she pushes she makes a small noise in her throat.

There is another sound too: loud, rasping noises, animal noises. It is getting louder and louder. Monica looks across at the woman in the pink skirt. She is sobbing.

∞

Gordon Street, WC1

7.05 pm

A siren yowls in a nearby street; the sound wells up, melts away, becomes part of the whirr and grumble of city traffic. London noises, pulsing through the heaviness of a London summer.

A fan on the desk maunders its way round, stirs the brittle fronds of a potted fern, lifts the pages of an open book. Two more clicks and it will hesitate. Five clicks one way, five clicks back.

Isabel shifts in her seat, presents the other side of her face to the cooling stream of air. But she catches sight of the clock on the wall, so she turns her attention to the notebook in her hand; stares at the two lines of handwriting, and the shapes and patterns adorning the right-hand corner. This is all she has managed to produce in the last twenty minutes. She tugs at the edge of the page, disengaging it from the spiral metal spine, then crushes it with her fingers and tosses the paper ball into a waste bin by the side of the desk. Another moment passes. She picks up her pen, attempts to marshal her thoughts and send them in the direction they need to go: eighteenth century Yorkshire – according to the opening paragraph of the manuscript in front of her.

The fan judders on, unhurried, through its circuit.

Now she slams the pen onto the desk.

It's impossible, she thinks. Impossible to control her mind when it will keep sliding off in all directions; then, without warning, pull up at some fragment of memory – as yet fluid and lacking in definition, but enough to set her heart racing high in her chest, even before she is fully aware of what it is.

A voice, bright, female, breezes into her consciousness. 'Isabel I'm off now. Have a good evening. Don't work too hard.'

Isabel turns to her colleague. 'I'll try not to. But I need to finish

The Straw Bride by Thursday. And look at this pile of work that was waiting for me.'

Alice dips behind her own desk, emerging with a pair of trainers; they are grubby, well worn, the laces tied in neat bows. 'Tell me about it,' she says. 'When I went away in March, I came back to three weeks' worth of . . .'

She doesn't get to finish what she is saying. Another siren has sliced through the air, making them both jump. It is followed by a second, then a third. The sounds are unforgiving, time-stilling. The two women freeze and, for a split second, they become a tableau of themselves as they were just moments ago.

When the last siren has faded into the distance Alice speaks. 'That's the fourth or fifth in ten minutes. Hope it's not another bomb-scare.' She eases her feet into the trainers without adjusting the laces. 'I'd better get off. In case the tubes are up the spout.' She stands, shrugging a bulging leather briefcase onto one shoulder. 'God, I hope they're not packed. I'll fry in this heat.'

Weighted down by the bag, she takes a few lopsided steps towards the door. It has been wedged open with a couple of hefty hardbacks, in the vain hope of some cooler air from the corridor.

'Bye then.'

'Bye. See you tomorrow.'

Isabel turns back to her notebook and flicks it shut. She, too, should get going. *The Straw Bride* will have to wait until tomorrow. But she stays in her seat, continues to stare at the closed notebook. Her fingers slide over the cover, tracing round the script embossed onto the board, enjoying its texture. And while she is sure she wasn't thinking about him at that precise moment, now she finds she is incapable of thinking about anything else: the touch of his hand on her face, the searing agony of their kiss, the look in his eyes as she turned to leave. Then, of course, the rest of it pushes through with a vengeance: everything that has happened in the past few days.

How could it be otherwise? For while she has been working, talking, shopping, eating lunch, while she has been doing all the mundane things she would normally do in a day, there it has been, bubbling away in the furrows and convolutions of her brain.

It was about four o'clock when she decided.

And with her mind made up, there should have been some relief, euphoria even. But not quite yet. Before all that, there is something she must do. And for the moment this dampens any inclination to celebrate. And the sooner she gets home, the sooner it will be done.

She stands and walks to the window, remembering that she has to close it before she leaves. A pigeon shuffles sideways along the ledge and, once it is out of arms reach, coo-coos its disapproval at her approach.

She stretches up to push on the wooden frame, but is distracted by the motion of the street and so leaves off what she is doing to watch the people milling around below. There is a mother wielding a pushchair with three wheels, and a couple holding hands (students by the look of them; the girl's skirt is too long and it sweeps the floor as she walks). And Isabel marvels at how everything can appear so normal. The newspaper vendor is there on the corner, next to the flower man and his tubs of bouquets in cellophane wrappings; they are chatting, as usual, over a wall of *Evening Standards*, and looking out, as they always do, at the muddle of traffic edging towards the lights, and at the cyclists risking life and limb as they weave in between. And there is nothing – not a smile nor a wink, not an inclination of the head, not even a cursory nod – nothing to acknowledge the significance of the recent turn of events.

The pigeon, accustomed to her presence, takes another turn around the ledge. But Isabel doesn't notice it now as it struts by, first one way then the other, displaying its collar of shimmering purple feathers; she is still looking down at the street. She knows she should go home, but she remains at the window, staring at the people.

Isabel likes coming to this building. There is something thrilling, even now, about pushing on the studded black door with the huge brass knob in its centre. She doesn't need to come here; she doesn't need the money she earns from the odd bit of editing she does for her publisher; and most days she sits in her study, looking out over a haphazardly-tended garden in a pleasant segment of Belsize Park. But writing is a solitary process, and coming to this office in the centre of the city, seeing the words 'Tomaz & Sedamur' engraved on the metal plate attached to the railings, gives her a sense of belonging: something she needs to recapture from time to time.

From somewhere behind her comes a sound she recognizes, something she needs to respond to. She shifts her thoughts back into the room. Someone is tapping on the open door.

The man is vaguely familiar. He works in another suite of offices across the corridor and she tries to remember what is written on the sign attached to their door. Publishing? Travel? She's seen him before, passed him on the stairs, held open a door for him; they are on nodding terms but she doesn't know his name.

He is standing in the doorway, fidgeting with a paperclip he has produced from his trouser pocket.

'Hi there –'

He is tall, too tall. The top part of his body is leaning into the room but his feet seem determined to remain in the corridor.

'Mike Tully. From across the way.' He gesticulates behind him. 'Saw you were still here.'

'Yes,' she replies. 'I was just about to get off.'

'Ah,' he hesitates. 'Well, you may as well stay where you are for the time being.'

She makes a quizzical sort of noise in her throat.

'I mean, I thought you might not know. There's been a bomb – Oxford Street – on a bus as far as I know. Traffic's all messed up anyway. It's just been on the news. Happened about half an hour ago.'

Isabel has reached out a hand and is gripping the edge of a nearby desk; she doesn't notice how the underside of its smooth, lacquered top is surprisingly rough and grainy, nor is she aware of the indentations being formed on the palm of her hand by its bevelled corner. The blood has frozen in her veins, just for a fraction of a second; now it rushes to her head: an icy, thought-stopping, blast of it.

'Bomb?' she manages to get out. 'Where? Did you say Oxford Street?'

Fibre by fibre, cell by cell, her brain processes the information. Oxford Street. Who might be in Oxford Street? She scans the inventory of family and friends, her mind lunging from name to name – even those who couldn't possibly have been there – until, finally, it settles on one.

No. That's absurd.

She recalls a conversation.

His flight was at six.

She looks at the clock, makes a quick calculation.

The relief burns inside her chest.

He would be in the air by now, miles and miles away. And she remembers that it will be another twelve hours, at least, before she can talk to him, before she can tell him what she has decided to do. When this thought strikes her, it is more like a physical pain: the thought of him, high up above the clouds, hurtling across a darkening sky, not knowing that she has changed her mind and decided to . . .

'Where do you have to get to?'

She has forgotten that Mike Tully is still there. 'Get to? Er – Belsize Park. Up on the northern line.'

It seems a world away.

'You should be okay then,' Mike continues. 'As far as I know the tubes aren't affected. It's just the buses. I expect that . . .'

But all further words are crowded out by the sound of more sirens. Police? Ambulance? She can't be sure. She counts: one – two – three. This time they are close by, getting closer, bearing down on them: baleful, urgent sounds which seem to pierce through her skin and find their way into every nerve, every cavity of her body.

They both stand still, waiting for the noise to subside.

'It looks like they're bringing people to UCH,' he says.

Isabel shudders.

'And I'd best be off,' he continues. 'I've got to get through town somehow. Oh well. See you then.'

'Good night.' She turns away from the empty doorway and goes back to close the window. She makes sure that all the catches are secured then walks to her desk and stands for a moment or two, staring at the phone. She has remembered something. Didn't David say he had to come into town today? For a meeting? But where?

She tries to recall what he had told her, wishing she had paid more attention. Hadn't he said he would be home by lunchtime? Yes, that's right. And he had grumbled about having to do the shopping.

She should call him though. Just in case. He might worry about her. That is if he remembers she was due back in town today.

But she doesn't want to speak to David. Not yet. She isn't ready.

She chews on her lip while she decides what to do.

She lifts the handset and stabs her finger at 'nine'. The handset purrs back at her. She picks out the digits of her own number and waits, listening, picturing the phone at the other end ringing out through the house.

Ring-ring, pause, ring-ring, pause.

It is in the hall, on her grandmother's table, next to the soapstone cat (the man in the souk had sworn it was marble – on his mother's life, and the lives of his numerous children and, no doubt, Allah as well). Then there is another phone in David's study. If he were at his desk, he would have picked it up by now.

Ring-ring, pause, ring-ring, pause.

She examines the nail of her right thumb; part of it has broken off leaving a jagged edge. She opens the drawer of her desk, searches for an emery board.

Come on David, she thinks. Pick up the phone.

The ringing stops, there is a short pause, and then David's voice.

'Hello – '

'Hel . . .' she begins, but the other voice is still speaking.

'There is no-one available to answer your call. Please leave a message after the tone.'

The machine. Damn. She drops the handset back onto its cradle and starts to rearrange the papers on her desk, making two neat piles; she shovels up the larger of the two and stuffs the lot into a plastic bag.

She needs to get home.

But still she doesn't move. She continues to stand there, clutching the bag.

Should she go or should she try again?

'Shit.' She slams the bag onto the desk and glares at the phone.

'Where is he anyway?'

A few minutes ago she had been dreading going home, having to talk to him: now she is annoyed with him, because he isn't there. And she is beginning to worry about where he might be. A film of sweat has accumulated just above her top lip and she wipes it away with the back of her hand.

∞

At that precise moment, it was impossible for Isabel to appreciate the irony of her situation. She might, one day, at some point in the future: when she had learned to laugh again, or to smile at life's little jokes. But that was some way off and, for now, she had too many other things to concern herself with.

She wouldn't have realized, either, how strange all this might appear (had there been anyone there to observe) – this anxiety about her husband, this sudden need to reassure him that she was safe – when in little more than an hour, if all went according to plan, she would be telling him – may even have already told him – of her intention to take their four-year-old son and travel halfway across the world, to spend the rest of their lives with somebody else.

And there might be some who would say she was capricious: but Isabel was not capricious by nature. Those who knew her well would tell you she was level-headed, generous, loving, and loyal to the point of stupidity. The Isabel they knew cooed over the scent of babies' heads, and still wore the same perfume (Blue Grass) that she wore in the seventies (when she could get hold of it); could never pass an elderly man selling poppies for the British Legion (because they all reminded her of her granddad Raines); once wept at the futility of making melon balls (although she may have had a couple too many glasses of wine); had written two novels (with another almost completed); had never eaten an oyster, put out food every day for the birds in her garden, hated wearing a watch; and went on (at length) about the plight of the rainforests.

And this was the Isabel who had fallen in love again at the age of forty-two; the Isabel who had forgotten the joy of being in the arms of a man who loved her back.

And the thought of what she had to do, when she got home, was breaking her heart.

∞

She reaches under the desk and pulls out the battered red holdall she had borrowed from David for her trip to Edinburgh. She switches off the fan, picks up the plastic bag from the desk, and walks out of the office, closing the door behind her.

PART ONE

Malaysia and London
August - November 1993

∞

2 August 1993
Kampung Teluk, Malaysia

A lone macaque called out from a place deep inside the forest; on the beach, the machines droned on, incessantly. The Gula House was silent, deserted.

Set Yen was looking for Lee; Chen had arrived with the motorboat, to take him to the airport. She had already been to his house, to the staff quarters and to the one remaining chalet, now turned into a makeshift office, but she hadn't found him in any of those places. Someone said they had seen him walking towards the Gula House.

She started up the small flight of steps but stopped just before she reached the top. Lee was there, pacing around the edge of the room. His suitcase and a blue travel bag were standing in a corner by the reception desk. He had his back to her; his head was bowed towards the floor. He hadn't seen her approach, so she stayed where she was. It was clear that he was lost in thought. She would let him be for now.

When he had completed his circuit, he crossed to the reception area and toyed with the pages of a large, hard-backed book lying on the empty desk. She knew what it was: it was the old visitors' book, and she puzzled over why it was still there when everything else had been cleared away. She watched him flip over the pages before settling on one in particular. He stood for a while, looking at it, as if he had forgotten what he was doing. Then, with a sudden movement that made her jump, he ripped the page from the book, folded it into a neat square, and stuffed it into his pocket. Finally, he snapped the book shut and pushed it onto one of the shelves behind the desk. Without looking up, he stepped onto the verandah, leant on the wooden railing and stared out across the garden.

Set Yen also spent a moment or two looking around the room, amazed at how small it looked, now that all the furniture had been taken away. She had never understood why anyone would want to change Buah Lodge. She liked it the way it was. Small and friendly. It had been a good place to work too, and Lee had been the best boss she'd ever had. But now there were the new people, she wasn't sure about them. She didn't know where they were from – they definitely weren't Malaysian – but she didn't trust them. The man who had come to talk to them that day had promised her a job – she was sure about that – but she had found it very difficult to understand what he was saying and she wished, now, that she had asked for something written down.

She sighed and walked across the room. It was time to get him. Otherwise he might miss his flight. Poor Lee, she thought. He looked so sad, so alone, standing there, staring into space like that. It made her feel sad too. She knew how much he loved Buah Lodge, and how hard he had worked to make it such a special place. And now he had to see it all being ripped to pieces.

∞

Lee was conscious that someone had approached behind him. He turned round. It was Set Yen.

'Mr Lee?'

She had her hands clasped together in front of her and he could see her fingers feel for the jade bangle she wore around her wrist. She twisted it round, twice, before she continued.

'Mr Lee. Chen has come, with the boat. I think he wants to leave soon.'

'I'm ready to go,' he replied, nodding towards his luggage.

A cautious smile moved across her lips but she remained silent. Lee suspected that she was waiting for him to say something else, but he wasn't sure if he could trust his voice. He swallowed hard, then stepped across to his luggage and busied himself with that until he was confident he could keep his emotions inside – for now at least. 'I hope that you will still be here when I come back,' he said eventually. 'And maybe you will come and work for me again one day.'

'Of course I will, Mr Lee.'

It was true, she would. But he knew he shouldn't ask her to. Not unless he was able to pay what she would earn at the glitzy resort that would replace Buah Lodge.

But that was way off in the future. There was a long road ahead of him before he would be back to set up his new business. *Inshallah*. As his friend Hash always said.

'And are you sure they are going to give you a job when they open?' he asked.

She nodded. 'Yes, they have promised me.'

'And where are you going to stay until then?

'My village – in Johor. Just until it is all finished, and I can come back.'

'When do you leave?'

'In five days, when they . . .' She paused and looked down at the floor.

'When they are going to knock down the staff block,' he finished for her.

'Yes,' she said in a small voice. 'In five days' time.' She still didn't look at him, but made a move to pick up his travel bag. 'Let me help you.'

He got to the bag first and hoisted it onto his shoulder. 'No, Set Yen. Thanks, but it's too heavy. I can manage.'

She held out her hand. 'Have safe journey. And *Jumpa lagi*.'

'Yes, I will see you again.' He reached forward to take her hand, but changed his mind and gave her a hug. Then he picked up his suitcase and walked away from her, so she wouldn't see him blinking away the tears that were threatening to spill down onto his face.

Lee handed over his last remaining five-*ringgit* note to the woman behind the counter and waved away the change she was holding out to him. It would be a while before he needed Malaysian money again. His hand darted to his pocket where he had an assortment of fresh, clean, British banknotes folded neatly into his wallet. Still there; but the brief moment of panic had set his pulse racing.

The woman, clearly unused to receiving tips, flashed him a

broad smile before hastily stowing the coins in her apron, as if she thought he might change his mind.

He took the plate of food and looked around for somewhere to sit. The area that had been allocated to the café was a cramped and cheerless corner at the far end of the terminal. There were a few people eating and drinking, but most simply sat and stared at the abandoned drinks and food in front of them. A girl in a green overall was pushing a mop around the floor, skirting the tables, unmindful of people's feet, irritated by their luggage. Overhead, the departures board clicked intermittently through its reels of letters and numbers, before rearranging itself into orderly lists of flight numbers and destinations.

An elderly couple were occupying a table in the corner; the man had noticed something of interest on the board and was pointing it out to his wife. After a moment or two she stood up and started to gather together their belongings. Lee manoeuvred his way towards their table, hoping to get there before anyone else spotted it. He hovered nearby while the couple opened and closed bags, argued over who was going to carry what, lost and found their boarding passes. But, at last, they were ready to leave and Lee had the table to himself. He pushed aside the accumulation of crudely stacked crockery and slumped down. It had been a long day.

He studied his food without much interest. He wasn't hungry. And he certainly wasn't tempted by the dry-looking burger he now had in his possession. But he hadn't eaten anything since the plate of noodles he had forced down for breakfast, and he wasn't sure when he might get another opportunity. Joseph had said they would give him a meal on the plane, but it was already quarter past ten. Why would he want a meal in the middle of the night? With any luck he would be asleep.

He glanced up at the board, to check that his flight was still there: Malaysia Airlines flight 002 to London Heathrow, departing 23.45; the same flight she would have taken. Although it was almost two years ago, the events of that day still came to prod at him from time to time. And then he remembered something else. He reached into his pocket and took out the tiny square. It took three steps to unfold: the heavy paper soughed and cracked as his fingers moved round it; then it was done, and he could see what was written there, although he already knew what it said, he had looked at it so many times before. The date at the top of the page was printed in bold, black type – July 21 1991 – and underneath was the familiar handwriting: the large, looping *R*; a flourish on the final *S*; then, by contrast, four lines of neat, evenly-spaced letters and numbers.

Lee remembered copying that address onto a thin, blue envelope – the sort he used for airmail letters – and how careful he had been not to make a mistake. Looking at it now, he still couldn't imagine how he had got it wrong: that was a three, and a seven; the five was clear; and the street name, Green Lanes, that was straightforward enough.

The envelope had remained propped on his desk for two days, while he had tried to talk himself out of posting it. He was being stupid, he had argued. She had left without saying goodbye. Why would she want to come back? And he had pictured her at home, getting on with her life, having forgotten all about him. But each time he decided not to post it, he had thought about those precious few hours they had spent together, had relived them over and over in his mind, until they were as spent and worn as the bit of yellow cloth he used to clean his shoes. Then nothing made sense, not even when he had found out what happened that day. But no message? No attempt to make contact again? And so it had gone on, round and round in circles, until he was exhausted and, in the end, had lost all ability to make any rational decision. So he had posted the envelope.

And then the waiting began. He had worked out the time it might take for a letter to reach Britain (and he added a few more days, just in case), then the number of days she might take to reply (say three, or longer if she was busy), then five days for a letter to come back to Malaysia (maybe more, so he gave it seven); then there was the possibility that she was away, and he allowed for that. But the weeks had passed and eventually he realized that nothing was going to arrive. After a while he got used to the ache of being without her and he carried on with his life, trying to ignore the sensation that a part of him was missing. And sooner or later, when he tried to picture her face, he found that her features had lost their sharpness and the image was blurred.

A woman's voice burst into his consciousness, the words, first in Malay then in English, inviting the last remaining passengers to board a flight to Rome. He looked at his watch. He, too, should be making his way to the departure gate. He stood up and stuffed the piece of paper into his pocket. He wasn't sure what use it would be now, but it wouldn't do any harm to take it with him.

∞

4.25 pm

Isabel clutched the edge of her seat as the 171A swung into Newington Green. It was a long time since she had been this way – before the old 171 had acquired its suffix – but it all looked depressingly the same, if somewhat worse for wear.

She had not planned to do this. She had intended to change to the over-ground at Finsbury Park. But her meeting had ended earlier than expected and she had time to spare. So when the tube she was on had stopped at Manor House, she had found herself on her feet and darting towards the open doors; then she was standing on the platform, disorientated, watching her train disappear into the narrow tunnel opening.

Manor House: intersection of the Victoria and Piccadilly lines; ageing, inglorious, a little grubby, but familiar all the same. Of course, two years on things had changed behind her back: small things, like the brash new metal seats; and a screen where information slid by, largely unheeded. It seemed cleaner too, and brighter. Or was that her imagination? She felt like an interloper; she didn't belong there any more.

So she had hurried up the steps that led to the street and had walked down the hill to the bus stop, recalling that a 171 would take her to Islington, past the flat where she used to live. And from her vantage point at the front of the upper deck she had picked out the building, stared at the sitting room window with its dirty net curtains, and wondered if Susan Bailey (flatmate from hell) was still there, along with the boyfriend, and the bits of motorbike that used to find their way up and onto the kitchen floor.

Isabel was still thinking about Susan Bailey and the now nameless boyfriend, when she realized that the bus was no longer moving. She looked out. The bus had passed through Newington Green and was now at a stop just beyond. She found herself peering into someone's kitchen.

It was a tiny room, starkly lit by an unshaded bulb. Cooking paraphernalia (pans, plates, jars of herbs and spices, a bottle of oil, a tin with 'Pasta' written on it, two plastic colanders) filled three narrow shelves; there was a table, an abandoned mug, a couple of wooden chairs, a lone cactus on the windowsill and, through an open door, a girl, dancing, hugging something to her like an imaginary partner. When Isabel saw that it was a cat she smiled to herself, recalling the times she had swept an unwilling Charlie into her arms, dancing him round her own kitchen until he had decided enough was enough and jumped to the floor, skulking off to the safety of another room, leaving her to it.

A couple of men wearing caps and thin, mud coloured anoraks, had emerged from the metal stairwell of the bus; they were both breathing heavily from the effort of getting up the stairs. The bus was still stationary and Isabel hoped that the driver hadn't decided to call it a night. Half-expecting to hear a cheery 'last stop, everybody off', she turned round in her seat to see how many people were still on. The two elderly men were squeezing themselves into a double seat a few rows back. The rest of the deck was empty.

But no sooner had the men sat down then one of them was up again, drifting to the front of the bus, peering out through the windows as he went. 'Can't see a thing,' he shouted over his shoulder. 'Dunno what's holding it up.' With some effort he edged back, clutching at seats along the way as if he were steadying himself against the motion of the bus. Except it still wasn't moving.

Raised voices were coming from downstairs; it seemed that someone was having an argument with the driver. People in the cars behind were sounding their horns.

Isabel retrieved her watch from the bottom of her handbag and slipped it into her pocket. It wasn't yet quarter to five.

This was a time she liked: day turning to dusk, when lights were switched on but curtains not yet drawn, and a street would become a row of silent theatres – obscure, one-act dramas – or simple stage-sets, beguilingly devoid of actors who might, even now, be watching from the wings.

She relaxed into her seat and examined the shop fronts on the other side of the road. The large corner plot was a grocery-cum-off-licence, and next to that was a bookie's, and then a laundrette. Nebulous shapes drifted behind its misted windows. It wasn't until she looked again that she spotted the grandly-named 'Clock and Watch Emporium', a tiny establishment squeezed in between Ladbrokes and the convenience store. She could just make out a name above the shop door, 'Harry Bloomfield & Son'; the soft light slipping through the jumble of items in the window was the colour of old ivory, dimmed to near obscurity by the fluorescent brashness of the shop's two neighbours.

A bookies, an off-licence, a laundrette, a clock shop: an interesting combination, although not an entirely unusual one in these increasingly fading backwaters. Isabel found herself speculating on the type of person who could exist with nothing more than this on their doorstep. But then she was distracted. A ball of light had shot into the sky in front of her and was now bursting into a flurry of multi-coloured stars. Resisting the urge to call out 'ooh' and 'ah', she watched the bits of coloured light fall down to earth, gradually fading away into nothing in front of her eyes. Then the bus juddered into action and moved off down the hill, putting an end to the cacophony of blaring horns, which had started to get on her nerves.

The rows of buildings on either side of the road petered out as the bus crossed a railway bridge, giving its passengers a brief but extended view of the London skyline. It appeared that the bonfire-night celebrations were already well under way.

'Like bloody world war two,' grumbled one of the men behind her. 'I wouldn't mind . . .' he paused while a rocket skittered about overhead, '. . . but it all starts too soon nowadays. They've been letting the bleedin' things off since the beginning of October.'

Isabel looked at her watch again. Although she liked to be early, this was ridiculous; they weren't due to meet until six thirty, and the bus was now making excellent progress down Essex Road. She decided to get off at the next stop and cut through to Upper Street from there. That would kill a bit of time.

∞

4.20 pm

Lee sat on his bed and looked round the room, wondering what he could do next. He had cleaned the floor of the tiny alcove his landlord had advertised as the kitchen; he had taken his rubbish to the communal bin in the yard at the back; he had dusted all the surfaces that didn't have anything sitting on them; and he had even walked down the corridor to the shared bathroom, to check whether that needed a clean. It did, as always, but by that time he had run out of energy and decided not to bother. At least all the activity had warmed him up.

He moved to the window and rested his forehead against the glass, squinting out through his own reflection at the dismal buildings pressing in from across the street. But then a great lorry thundered by, causing the window to clatter in its frame, making him jump. He would never get used to the traffic in this city. It coursed past all day, it kept him awake at night: so many vehicles being driven round and round and round. Everyone in London going somewhere. And so many people. It was crazy, he thought. Back home he knew everyone in the village, but here, he didn't even know the people who lived in his building.

He had seen the assortment of names scribbled next to the bells outside, and once or twice he had seen someone emerge from the door to the street. There was one girl, bone-thin, with a face full of jewellery and poppy-red hair; that might be 'Maeve' he had once thought. And then there was the woman who spent her days in the laundrette downstairs, sitting amongst the washers and driers, filling the air and people's clothes with her cigarette smoke. He had passed her in the hallway a couple of times; she could be 'Maeve': unless she was 'Robinson' or 'Fahimi'.

He glanced up to see what the weather was planning to do, not that it was easy to tell from the meagre patch of sky at his disposal. It was solid with cloud and dark, like lead: heavy, oppressive. Until he had come to England, Lee had never imagined there could be so many different varieties of grey. It made him shiver to look at it. He moved across to the sink and filled a pan with cold water. He needed something to warm himself up.

It took a while for the pan to boil, without a lid. There hadn't been any lids amongst the muddle of items he had found in the cupboard when he had moved in. He pulled down the sleeve of his jumper, so it covered his hand, and lifted the pan of bubbling water from the tiny, two-ringed stove. The heat radiated through the thin fabric, but it was bearable. Just. He tipped the pan to let the water trickle over the dry flakes, then he watched them swell, as if by magic, into recognisable shapes: vivid green peas, shiny yellow corn, orange pieces of carrot. There were other bits too, floating about in the soupy mess, things he didn't recognize; he tried not to think about them too much.

He picked up the container, careful to keep his fingers on the rough plastic ridges that were meant to stop the heat getting through, and took it back to the window, taking a sip as he went, cursing to himself as soon as the hot glutinous stuff touched his lip.

Would he never learn?

He poked out his tongue and moved it over the part he had burnt; it tasted salty, the taste of MSG. He put the pot on the table so that he wouldn't be tempted to take another sip until it had cooled. The steam drifted up and formed itself into a ghost-like shape, hovering around for a while before disappearing off into the room. Lee sniffed at the air. It was supposed to be chicken; it didn't smell like chicken; it didn't smell like anything, much. But it was food, and he was hungry. The problem was that he was getting fed up with Pot Noodle: it had become a staple part of his diet – lunch, breakfast, and sometimes dinner. It was cheap, and warm, and that was about all there was to it. And he could buy it from the Indian store on the corner.

He looked at the clock by his bed; it was just half past four. He supposed he was having his 'tea' – a Pot Noodle, and an orange afterwards. Strange thing to do though, he reflected, naming a meal after a drink.

He knew he had messed up his budget somehow. It was only Friday, and he couldn't pull out any more money until Monday, the day he did his weekly shopping. He would just have to go through the red book, yet again, and find out where all the money had gone, and why his supplies hadn't lasted as long as they should have. Although he already knew the answer: everything was more expensive than he had planned for, especially if he shopped at the store on the corner. But the market was two bus-rides away –

Once more – and something he did on an almost daily basis – he cursed the fact that he had missed getting a place in a Hall of Residence; but his application had been late, and he was what they called a 'mature student'. This had counted against him for some reason. That's what he had been told, anyway.

He picked up the pot of noodles again and blew on it before taking a tentative sip. He cradled it in between his hands and waited for the warmth to permeate his skin and, with any luck, heat up the blood in his veins, which might then flow warm round his body like the water in the heating pipes he sat by at lectures.

From down in the street he could hear raised voices. A large red bus had pulled up at the stop on the other side of the road, its engine was still rattling and clouds of smoke spluttered and spewed from underneath it – great, thick, belchy globs of it, polluting the atmosphere. A long line of vehicles had been forced to a standstill behind it.

Lee studied the front of the bus and silently recited the list of places it stopped at on the way. He made a mental note of the number and final destination: 171A, Elephant and Castle. Odd name for a place, he thought.

Someone in one of the cars was sounding a horn; there was a more impatient blare from further down the line, then another, and soon everyone was joining in, as if it were some sort of a game, and the whole horn-pipping and honking thing was getting louder and louder, more and more frenzied. It was almost melodic, like an orchestra tuning up instruments before playing a piece of music.

Making all that noise won't get you moving any faster, Lee

wanted to tell them.

Then, suddenly, above all the blaring and hooting, came something else: a deafening crack; an explosion that reverberated around the sky. And far above the jagged roofs with their stained and decrepit chimneys, and their clutter of satellite dishes and masts and aerials, a volley of coloured stars came clattering to earth, leaving plumes of pinkish smoke to drift sideways across the sky.

'Waah!' The sound escaped out of him, and all of a sudden Lee wanted to laugh – which he did – but it was more of a squeak, which made him laugh even more, because it had been a while since he had heard the sound of his own voice.

Feeling elated by the sight of the fireworks, Lee stood and watched as the sky repeatedly lit up and fell dark again. He scooped out the last remaining bits of noodle then threw the pot into the bin. He didn't know what was happening out there but the urge to be in the midst of it took him by surprise. It was a way to feel connected to whatever was going on, he supposed, even though he knew that he wasn't.

He searched his pocket and pulled out a handful of coins: three heavy pounds and an assortment of silver ones. Almost four pounds, he reckoned. That should be enough for a bus, and maybe a bar of chocolate as well. He put the coins back into his pocket, grabbed his overcoat from the armchair and stepped out into the dingy corridor, checking the coat pocket for his bunch of keys before slamming the door behind him.

At the bus stop, Lee crossed his arms over his chest and hugged his overcoat closer to him. But this meant that his hands got cold, so he thrust them into his pockets, reminding himself to buy some gloves – preferably before he got frostbite. He had been in London for just over two months now, and he would swear that he hadn't been able to get warm since he arrived; the cold and the dampness of the place pierced straight through his clothes, his skin, and into his bones. But at least it wasn't raining. He was sure this was the first day in weeks that it hadn't rained.

A scruffy bird with grey feathers waddled over to where he was standing and started to peck around in the gutter in front of him.

Lee couldn't imagine what the poor thing was finding to eat down there; he felt sorry for it, and wished that he had something he could throw to it. While he watched the bird, he looked up every so often to see if there was a bus in sight. He had decided that he would get on the first one that came along and see where it took him; but he was quite pleased when it was a 171A that drew up, sending the bird flapping off to a spot further down the road. Maybe he would find out where Elephant and Castle was after all.

When the doors opened, he stepped on and offered the driver a pound coin, hoping for some change. Without looking up, and after what seemed like an excessive amount of rummaging in some sort of moneybox, the driver pushed two small coins at him.

'Thanks,' said Lee.

He wanted to say something else, something about the weather perhaps, or a comment about the fireworks that were still pounding away at the night sky, but the driver was already pulling on the huge wheel, eyes fixed on his mirror as he inched his bus into the stream of traffic. Lee took his ticket from the machine and made his way towards the metal staircase. That was the first person he had spoken to in three days.

∞

Upper Street, N1

Isabel took the slip of paper from her pocket and checked the name she had written down: 'Asiatic'. This must be it. He had said it was Chinese (well, his exact words had been: 'it's a nice Chinese-y place at the end of Upper Street'), but this was not at all what she had imagined. She pushed on the door and walked inside.

Two girls wearing skin-tight jeans and matching T-shirts broke off their conversation to stare across at her: that look of reproach, mingled with downright distaste, only teenagers are able to manage.

One of them eased herself off the bar stool where she had been sitting, picked up an enormous menu card, and strolled towards Isabel. 'For one?' Without waiting for a reply, she started off towards the vast interior – ranks of tables, starchy-white cloths; all fastidiously laid, but strangely forbidding.

Isabel stayed where she was.

'One? No . . .' The voice she heard was weak, pinched. She cleared her throat and started again, aiming for assertive over spineless.

'No, I'm meeting someone. But I'm early. Could I sit somewhere, and have a drink while I wait?'

The girl shrugged and gestured towards a small table nestled against the bar and cheek by jowl with the only other occupied table in the entire restaurant.

Isabel hung back. This was not quite what she had in mind. She wanted to sit where she could see the door and watch for him to come in; where she could be comfortable, and arrange herself in a way that said 'I'm relaxed and at ease with myself.' She pointed to the window area, which was set out with brown leather sofas and matching coffee tables. 'Can I sit here?' she asked.

Without changing her expression, the girl slid the menu onto the nearest of the low tables. 'Drinks are on the back.'

Isabel took off her coat and folded it in two while she worked out the logistics of where to sit. It would be awkward if he were to end up next to her, so if she sat on the two-seater, with her coat and her bag, then he would sit on the sofa opposite. Unless someone else got there first. As a precaution, she moved her coat to the other sofa. But now the fronds of a large potted palm obscured her view of the door, so she swapped places with her bag. Now she had a perfect seat, and a good view of the street outside; she could watch the world go by, and see everyone who came in.

She turned the menu to the side headed: **'........and from the bar'**. But this turned out to be a long list of cocktails with elaborate names. She wasn't a great fan of cocktails, and these were terribly expensive.

There must be something else.

She swivelled to face the bar, hoping for inspiration and taking the opportunity to look round the restaurant at the same time. The place was modern: all chrome and leather, and, very likely, expensive. It wasn't exactly buzzing with activity either; but she couldn't imagine it ever had much of an atmosphere. The exotic palms were a nice touch, though; it was sad that they had to exist in such tiny pots. She reached out to touch the smooth green fingers of the plant nearest to her. It was real.

When she looked up she saw that the waitress was watching her. She remembered that she was supposed to be choosing a drink, so she scanned the card, looking for something familiar. At the end of the list of cocktails was a section headed: **'........others'**. This appeared to be a selection of wines – although nothing by the glass, she noted (and it might seem presumptuous to order a bottle at this stage). Then, at the very bottom of the page, was a list of beers. She peered at the tiny writing and spotted something she hadn't seen for a long time: Tiger Beer.

As soon as she lowered the menu to the table, the waitress came over.

'Ready to order?'

Isabel smiled up at her, animated by the discovery of an old favourite.

'Yes, I'll have a Tiger Beer please.'

The girl remained stony-faced. 'Do you want to order your food yet?'

Isabel ignored the cutting remark poised on her lips; instead, she said: 'No thank you. I'm still waiting for my friend.'

This clearly wasn't the sort of place where they would be encouraged to linger, she thought, and in some cases that might be a good thing. But this time, she was certain, it was going to be different.

She pulled her watch from her pocket. It was just ten to six; still another forty minutes to go. And she wished, now, that she had spent longer browsing in that bookshop across the road.

She glanced over to where the two waitresses had been sitting, wondering where her drink had got to, but the bar area was deserted: just rows and rows of bottles, in all shapes and sizes, glinting back at themselves from the mirrors on the wall behind.

It was hard to tell what sort of place this was aiming to be. Isabel picked up the menu once more and scanned the long list of **•••••••mains•**, as they called them, with the increasingly annoying dots that introduced every heading in a 'look at me being all modern with my dots and my designer fonts, and my disregard for capital letters' sort of way.

There were some familiar Chinese and Thai dishes, a few Indian ones, and some with fancy French names that she didn't recognize – neither one thing nor another really – which was possibly deliberate. Wasn't there a name for it? But the menu was far too long –

The door to the restaurant rattled open, breaking into her thoughts. She looked up, to see who had come in, her pulse quickening in anticipation. Two people were waiting, unsure what to do.

It couldn't be him, yet, she told herself. It was far too early. But she knew that, soon, the door would open and it would be him, and that was the worst part: the moment you saw each other for the first time; when all hopes and expectations could be ripped away in one, dismal, heart-sinking second.

Someone else had opened the door now – a tall, dark-haired man, wearing a suit underneath a beige overcoat. And he was alone. But he wasn't wearing a scarf. He had said he would be wearing a red scarf.

Of course he could have forgotten the scarf, she mused, and she hoped that was the case, because he did look rather nice. And he had lovely, deep brown eyes.

Was he looking at her, in a purposeful sort of way?

She looked directly at him and smiled, just in case. But he had already turned away and was walking past her, into the restaurant area.

No doubt it would help if she asked for a photograph, she thought. It certainly would have spared her the numerous, wasted evenings she had endured over the past few weeks. But then, she didn't send out photos; it was more fun that way, at least that was her excuse.

Fun? Ha!

How much fun was it, struggling to find just one redeeming feature in a person, ignoring the fact that they made unpleasant snorting sounds when they laughed, or spent an entire evening talking about themselves, or turned out to be a good few inches shorter, or years older, than they had stated in their ad, or still lived with their mother? Yet it was amazing how desperation could make the disagreeable appear reasonably tolerable for a time. And maybe she could have put up with any of those things, if only they had proved to be sparkling, witty conversationalists, with a smattering of charisma. Was that too much to ask? And how much fun was it, returning yet again to an empty flat. alone, deflated, and bitterly disappointed. She had forgotten how wearying the whole experience could be.

And that was why she had vowed never to do this again; she had been having dinner with her friend Simon when she had said it – and she remembered her exact words – 'if I can't meet someone in the normal way, then I'm bloody well going to have to stay on my own'. And they had raised their glasses and made a toast: to Isabel's staying on her own.

Simon was the only other person who knew about her *Lonely Hearts* encounters. And she would never have considered it had she been able to meet anyone in what were regarded as more conventional circumstances. But there were just three men at Fromer Press, where she worked: two were over fifty and married; the other was Simon, who didn't count. Most of her girlfriends were decidedly attached or, worse, fixated on nappies, nursery places and school-runs. She was thirty-five and still living on her own.

Well, here I go again, she thought. Let's see what this evening will bring.

She had high hopes for this particular date, and her rarely-fading optimism which, even she had to say, had dimmed a little over the past few months, had gained a new lease of life. David Adamson's letter had been five pages long and, without doubt, the most appealing of the fifty-odd replies she had received to her insert in the *Lonely Hearts* section of *Time Out* (one joker had simply scribbled: 'I'm interested. Ring me' on the back of a postcard). David had come across as thoughtful – *we can just meet for coffee or something, if that would make you feel more comfortable* – and witty – *I'm looking for someone to share things with – walks in the countryside, trips to the coast, a Chinese takeaway, the bill (just joking). My friends tell me to get a dog – but a girlfriend would save on the vet's fees.* There had been no photo enclosed, but he had said that he resembled a somewhat darker version Richard Gere – *or so people have told me.* For a week she had carried the letter in her bag (he had apologized for not being able to meet her sooner, but he was taking his sister to Brighton– *she lives in Canada usually, well someone has to, but she has been visiting for a couple of weeks*), and she had read it so often that she felt she already knew him, even before she had spoken to him on the phone. She had contacted him the day after he got back, and they had talked for almost an hour; by the end of the call she had decided that he was definitely 'the one'.

She looked at her watch again. There was just enough time to go to the ladies and make a final check on her hair; she had spent a long time debating whether to wear it up or down, but now she wasn't sure –

'Excuse me, miss. You ordered Tiger Beer?'

It was something about the depth of his voice, or the gentle rise and fall of the syllables; or maybe it was the way he seemed to consider the words, one at a time, before allowing them to leave his lips.

She looked up.

He was young, no more than twenty-five; possibly Chinese, but he could have come from any number of other places. He was standing in front of her, holding a tray – her beer, an empty glass, a bowl of crisps or crackers – waiting, patiently, for her to reply. For a split second, their eyes locked together.

She looked away. 'Yes, that's for me,' she said.

He stooped to place the tray on the table then started to pour out her beer. His hair was long at the front and fell over his eyes as he worked. She knew that if she reached out to touch it, it would slip through her fingers like silk.

He straightened up, pushing the hair from his forehead in an achingly familiar gesture. 'Can I bring you anything else?'

She shook her head. She could have asked for something – a glass of water, a napkin, anything – just to make him stay for another minute; two or three at the most. But what would be the point? She watched him walk away, and waited for the emptiness to pass; then she turned her attention back to the window. She fixed her eyes on the procession of people passing in front of her: people hunched against the cold, hurrying home from work, tracking down their evening's entertainment; people in cars and buses, threading their way through the painfully narrow street; people whose lives would continue to unfold, long after she had stopped watching them. Sometimes, she had noticed, she could go for days, weeks even, without thinking about him. But then, out of the blue, something would jab into her mind and push out any contentment she had managed to salvage, leaving her to feel, as she did now, adrift and alone, like a shell washed up on the beach.

She saw that it had started to rain; people were pulling out umbrellas, struggling to get them up. An elderly man with a little white dog stopped outside the window and looked up at the sky, puzzled, as if he couldn't work out where the raindrops were coming from. He bent his back, slowly, deliberately, one vertebra at a time, and hauled the little dog into his arms before continuing on his way. They made very slow progress and Isabel felt sorry for them both. She hoped they didn't have far to go.

Another couple had come in; they were settling themselves into one of the sofas nearby. The man rested his arm along the sofa-back and as soon as his companion sat down, he leant in to kiss her. Now they were looking at the menu, discussing whether to have a cocktail or wine.

They seemed happy enough, Isabel thought; and she hoped that she, too, might find someone to love; or at least a bit of company, and some affection along the way. It would help, she concluded, if she stopped looking for Mr Perfect, and settled for Mr Eighty-per-cent instead. In fact she should know by now, there was no such thing as perfect.

But that wasn't true, was it?

The question hovered around for a while, challenging her to respond.

Yes, but *he* didn't want you either.

She closed her eyes for a moment. Images she had been striving to avoid now etched themselves onto the blackness behind her eyelids, and she wondered if anyone had watched *them*, or remarked on how happy they looked as they had talked and laughed and held hands. Just like the couple on the sofa.

Oh God! Not now.

She snapped open her eyes, reached for her glass and took a couple of swigs. It was madness to dredge up all this again – especially tonight. And she had been feeling so optimistic about tonight.

'Isabel?'

Her head shot up when she heard her name.

There was a man standing in front of her. He was tall and dark, wearing a beige mac and . . .

Shit! A long red scarf; wrapped twice around his neck. Him. David Adamson.

She couldn't believe she had missed him coming in.

But he was wearing glasses. He hadn't said he wore glasses.

'I knew it was you,' he was saying, 'well, I rather hoped it was anyway.' He allowed himself a brief smile. 'In fact, I feel as though I already know you. I'm David, by the way.' He held out his hand.

As she stood up to take it, all she could think was that he didn't look anything like Richard Gere.

∞

The bus was making very little progress as it jerked from one obstruction to the next. The snake of traffic extended all the way down the street, as far as Lee could see, and was hemmed in by an identical line of vehicles creeping sullenly in the opposite direction. Still, he didn't mind. He had nothing else to do.

He had often found himself riding around London on the top deck of these lumbering red buses; particularly in those first weeks, when he couldn't face any more books, or notes, or tables or graphs, and when his mind had been reeling with all the new and unfamiliar things he had to learn: cash flow distribution systems, principles of organization, pricing policies, leadership strategies, conflict management. And he had always thought that if he stayed on a bus long enough, he might eventually leave the confines of the city and reach one of those patches of green he had glimpsed from the upper windows of the library block. But his rides had only ever taken him through street after street of brick-built houses huddling beneath blocks of flats with graffiti daubed across their walls; or to wastelands beyond the periphery of housing; and once to an industrial site littered with the detritus of human existence, where abandoned fridges skulked amongst burnt-out cars and rusting trolleys from 'Tesco' and 'Asda', where he'd found a plastic bag full of rotting meat. For almost an hour, until another bus arrived to pick him up, he'd had nothing else to do but study the vulgar messages defacing the walls of the dingy, foul-smelling bus shelter.

Recently, though, he had hatched a plan. He would take a train somewhere – maybe to the north – when the weather had improved. If it ever did improve. Trains appealed to him in a way that cars and buses never would. Perhaps it was their speed, their elegance, or their promise of freedom and adventure. Most of all, he admired the way their tracks cut deep, iron gashes through the middle of the city, exposing its crumbling innards: derelict, shadowy, ignoble.

He rubbed at the fogged-up window with the sleeve of his coat and peered through the shape he had made. He had no idea where he was. The brightly-lit street below was teeming with people – stony-faced, bent double against the cold – all marching in the same direction, as if they had somewhere to go. And he knew that just beyond this street there would be another street, and another, and another; and each one would look very much the same as the last: clogged with traffic, and full of people going from one place to another. He couldn't see them but he knew they were there, moving around, going about their business.

Just like me, he thought. If anyone looked up and saw me sitting here on this bus they would think that I was going somewhere too. He sighed, and studied the knot of people at the bus stop, wondering how many of them had someone waiting for them, when they got to wherever they were going.

'Islington Green.' The driver's voice bellowed from the deck below; a voice that demanded to be obeyed.

Was this the last stop? Lee wondered, or was there something special about Islington Green? It didn't matter; he felt compelled to get off.

He leapt to his feet and clattered down the stairs, jumping through the exit door just as it was beginning to close, and almost colliding with an elderly man carrying a little white dog.

'I do beg your pardon,' said the man.

'Sorry,' said Lee.

The man clutched the dog closer to him and crossed the road, behind the bus.

It was an odd way to take a dog for a walk, Lee thought. But he already knew about the English and their pets.

It was raining now: that fine, persistent drizzle that he had experienced so much of since he had been in England. It was an unpleasant sort of rain too, he thought. Not the ostentatious spears of it he was used to back home, but the kind that invaded your bones, and seeped into your very soul, without you noticing. Until it was too late.

Lee paused for a moment while he looked up and down the street, trying to decide which way he should go. The traffic was still queuing behind the bus, each stationary vehicle casting a small pool of light over the one in front. Lee squeezed himself in between two cars and crossed the road, following in the footsteps of the old man with the dog.

∞

Isabel and David had been shown to their seats in the restaurant and were now looking at the menus they had been given. It was the same, over-sized card with the dots and the irritating typeface that she had read several times already; and she had already decided what to order. She lowered her menu, so she could see over the top of it. This was her first opportunity to study him.

She had to admit she had been a little disappointed at first; he wasn't at all what she had imagined.

Perhaps if he swapped those heavy glasses for some with a lighter frame - He had nice, bluish-grey eyes; it was a shame to hide them away. And perhaps if he smiled a bit more –

Her eyes were still fixed on his face when he glanced up and caught her looking at him. He put his head to one side, and she thought he was about to say something, but he looked away and appeared to be engrossed in the menu once more.

To cover her embarrassment she said: 'Have you chosen yet?'

'Yes,' he said, closing his menu and resting it on the table.

'What . . .'

'So how . . .'

They spoke at the same time.

'After you,' she said.

'How long have you lived in Finchley?' he continued.

'Oh, just over two years. I got fed up with flat-sharing and took the plunge – you know – bought a place of my own. It's tiny, but it's got a garden – and that's tiny too – but I like having my little bit of green space in the city – and it is handy for work – I'm on the Northern Line and I work in Bloomsbury so . . . yes, it's good. And I . . .'

She was aware that she was talking too much. That was far more information than he had asked for.

He was leaning back in his chair, arms folded across his chest, watching her.

'I'm on the Northern Line too,' he said. 'Different branch.'

'Yes, I know, you told me – Hampstead.' She didn't tell him that she had already found his street on the *A-Z*, already determined the best route from her flat to his; and from his flat to her office.

'So, you work in publishing,' he said.

'That's right. Academic publishing. We produce text books – books for schools – that sort of thing.'

'Sounds interesting. Is it interesting?'

'Yes it is – it must be – I've been there for seven years now. And apart from writing books of my own, it's the ideal job. I think I was lucky to get it.'

'Are you planning on writing books, then?'

She hesitated. The answer, of course, was a simple 'yes', but it wasn't something she found easy to talk about. She didn't even know why she had mentioned it. And she knew what the next question would be.

'What about?'

She and Simon were always thinking up pithy titles and blurbs for the so far unwritten novels. At the moment there were far more titles to hand than actual works in progress.

Luckily, the waitress had returned to take their order, and Isabel didn't have to answer David's question; not just yet anyway.

By the time they had finished their first course, and polished off a bottle of *Pinot Grigio*, Isabel had learnt the following about David Adamson: he had been born in Colchester; he had studied mathematics at Leicester University, then gone straight into the city to a firm of stockbrokers, and had been there ever since, working his way up within the company; he neither liked nor disliked his job – it was just something one had to do, he said – but he had never thought about doing anything else; he had spent his childhood in Ipswich; had one sister, unmarried, now living in Canada; his father had died when David was eleven and his mother lived in a village near Chelmsford, where there were some rather good pubs. 'We must drive out there some day,' he had added, reddening slightly when he understood the significance of what he had just said.

As the evening progressed, Isabel found herself enjoying his company. Looks weren't everything, she told herself, and at least he seemed reliable, at least you wouldn't be on edge all the time with someone like David; and he was steady (one of her mother's words, she noted with a flicker of concern – or was it annoyance?). He had a good physique too; and that would, most likely, be due to his daily visits to the gym. Perhaps he could be persuaded to get some contact lenses.

David had beckoned to the waitress and was now ordering a second bottle of wine. Isabel noticed that his dark brown hair had a pleasant reddish hue when it caught the light, and it twisted in soft curls around his ears and the back of his neck.

'You told me you came from near Manchester,' he said, as soon as the waitress had gone. 'But you don't have a Manchester accent. In fact, I could swear there was a hint of Scottish in there – just a tiny wee bit – it's very subtle.'

Very perceptive, she thought. 'I spent my childhood in Edinburgh,' she said. 'But when I was twelve we moved south – to Cheshire. After I left home, my parents went back to Edinburgh. They both have broad Scottish accents and they think I sound like a Londoner. I don't think I sound much of anything at all really.'

'No, that's not true. Your accent is rather BBC.'

'Hardly!'

'Yes, it is. It is lovely actually, with that bit of Scottish lilt creeping in occasionally.' He paused. He was gazing at her face so intently that she had to look away. 'Now I come to think of it,' he went on, 'you do look quite Scottish, with your long dark hair and pale skin.'

'My grandfather was a Benocci.'

He looked at her, blankly.

'Italian. That's where the dark hair comes from. Italian blood – from my mother's side. And I'm not always quite so pale. I do go dark when I've been in the sun.'

'Aha.' He pounced on this last piece of information. 'Yes, you said that you had recently got back from Malaysia. Last month wasn't it?' He was grinning at her, looking strangely pleased with himself.

'September,' she said.

'That's why I chose this place,' he gestured around the restaurant, 'I thought you would like Asian food, having been to those parts so often.'

'Only twice,' she replied. 'I've only been twice.'

'But you like it there?'

She hesitated. 'Yes, I did.'

'Did?'

'No, I do. I mean . . . I do like it. In fact . . .'

She looked at her glass, but it was empty; she bit on a piece of dry skin at the edge of her nail. Any distraction would do, as long as it kicked her mind away from where she feared it was going. She lifted the glass anyway, and stared into it. She really, really didn't want to think about this. But he didn't know –

'So what is it you like so much about Malaysia then?'

She glanced up, wary. But he was still smiling, waiting for her to answer.

'Oh, I don't know,' she replied. 'Being warm all the time. Never having to wear shoes. Not caring if you get rained on –' She rubbed at a mark on the side of her glass. That wasn't what he wanted.

Unable to resist any longer, she allowed herself to see it, as it once was: peaceful and serene in its jungle setting; a happy chaos of nature, dripping from trees, creeping over fences, sneaking into buildings, meeting, merging, everything becoming one –

'And how can you not love a place where you're woken every morning by monkeys crashing around in the forest?' she added, trying what she hoped was a laugh; not quite pulling it off. 'And where the only form of transport is a rusty old ferry.'

He looked perplexed.

He doesn't get it, she thought. And she wasn't being fair.

'It seemed different this time, that's all,' she conceded.

'What do you mean?'

She had tried to block it out, tried so very hard, but now, in it swept: the devastated forest, the mountains of rubble, the big house forever shuttered against the glare of the sun. These were the images that would stay with her now.

'The place is changing,' she said, at last. 'Changing in a way that isn't good. Too much building for one thing – and what they call land-grabbing. Everyone's out to make money, and no-one seems to care about the damage they are doing – to the environment, or to the people.'

'It's often the case,' he said.

'What is?'

'When you go back somewhere you've been before. It's never the same. You should never go back.'

'No,' she agreed, quietly. 'Not a sensible thing to do.'

'So you didn't get out in the sun much? I mean, you don't look as though you've just come back from the tropics.'

'No, not really – it was a business trip – I think I said. I hardly saw the outside of the hotel. You know how it is.' It was a lie, but it served its purpose. She seemed to be getting good at lying these days.

The business trip to KL had taken just four of the eight days she had been in Malaysia. As soon as she was able to get away, she had gone back to the island, back to Teluk. But there was no-one there. Instead, vast, ugly machines lumbered to and fro, like creatures from an alien world, humming and groaning, digging and churning, throwing up great clouds of dust to settle on each remaining bit of scrubby vegetation – a dull, grey film of it choking everything it touched – and in their wake an altered landscape, dry and barren, a jungle of steel and concrete. The once familiar buildings, now full of debris, were being ripped apart, piece by piece, even as she had watched; while her memories hovered like ghosts. Then there was the wind, picking it all up, bouncing it against the broken walls, blowing it about: litter and memories.

But no-one could destroy the memories.

'Anyway,' she continued, 'it was the start of the rainy season.'

Another lie.

'There wasn't much sun.'

∞

Now that he had got off the bus, Lee wasn't sure what he was going to do next. The rain didn't help – it seemed to be getting heavier – and there was no sign of the fireworks he had seen earlier. He walked up one side of the street and then crossed the road and walked back down the other side; there was very little to see: just one glittering restaurant after another, and the odd book shop or clothes shop thrown in for good measure. He paused for a moment outside one of the restaurants and inspected a menu attached to the door. The writing was thin and spidery and he had difficulty making out the words. But the prices were clear enough.

Fifteen pounds? For one dish? He couldn't believe it. That was almost half his weekly food budget. He peered inside. It seemed full enough, full of people talking and laughing, and eating; and the sight of them made Lee realize he was still hungry.

He decided that he may as well go back home. For one thing he needed to write to his sister. And he could pick up a bar of chocolate from the shop on the corner. The letter was something he had been putting off for a while. Above anything, he mustn't let her, or his mother, think that he was unhappy: but however he tried to hide the truth, she would, somehow, manage to guess at what he was really feeling; he had never been able to lie to his sister. Also, he didn't have any stamps; he had yet to find a post-office.

He started to make his way back towards the island of grass and trees wedged between the two main roads. This was where he had got off the bus so with any luck he should be able to find another to take him back.

The sweet smell of cooked onions reached him before he saw the large, white van parked in a side street. Hot dogs. He felt in his pocket and pulled out all the coins he had left, holding them in the palm of his hand while he counted: three pounds, and a little bit more; that should be plenty. He was looking forward to this.

Lee watched while the man loaded greasy slithers of onion into the middle of a bun and then topped the lot with a pale and disappointingly thin sausage. He had been hoping for something a bit more filling, but decided that he would enjoy it all the same.

The man thrust the hot dog towards him. 'Three pounds.'

Lee pulled back his hand; he had been holding out two pound coins. 'Three? Three pounds?' He must have misheard.

The man pointed to a large sign above his head.

'Ah.' That was stupid, he thought. He should have seen the sign. And now it was too late to change his mind.

The man was still holding out the bun and was peering down at him from the platform inside the van. Lee noticed that a few slices of onion – his onion – had dropped onto the counter. He wanted to pick them up and stuff them into his mouth, but when he looked at the man's face he decided it was probably best if he didn't. He dug into his pocket and produced the remaining coins. It was lucky he had enough. But now he would have to walk home.

Without speaking the man took the coins, put them into a large pocket in the front of his apron, and turned to the next customer.

Lee moved away and took a huge bite from his bun, sending bits of onion spilling down onto the pavement. He swallowed, then bit again, and before he was more than a few yards from the van he was popping the last chunk of it into his mouth. He chewed contentedly. That was good, he thought. But at a pound a bite, it should be.

'Gone,' he said to an abject-looking bird that had been showing some interest. He wiped his hands on his handkerchief then thrust them back into his pockets to keep warm. Now he had to work out how to find his way home. He supposed that if he followed the trail of bus stops he would get there in the end.

PART TWO

Malaysia
July 1991

∞

21 July 1991
Kampung Teluk

Isabel clung to both sides of the boat, to avoid being bounced from the wooden plank that was her seat. Sea-spray splashed up over her hands and arms; the wind tugged at her hair, whipping it against her face. In front of her, wedged between coils of oil-blackened rope, looking alien and ill at ease in its surroundings, was her suitcase. It had been an impulse buy and, although it might have been a touch more business-like than the holdall she usually took on her travels, the wretched thing seemed to have a will of its own; and she had come to despise it with a passion.

She smiled into the wind and tasted the salt on her lips. This was not at all what she had expected when she had stepped off the tiny plane and walked the short distance over the tarmac to the arrivals hall. She had been told that someone from the resort would be there to meet her, and that proved to be correct: the young man they had sent was positioned at the front of the waiting crowd, and was clutching a hand-drawn sign bearing her name. But when he hastened her past the scrum of bicycle-rickshaws, and the browbeaten Mercedes that served as taxis, to a small jetty just yards from the airport, then she had begun to wonder what she was getting herself into.

She had never done anything quite so spontaneous. Under normal circumstances she would have known precisely where she was going, would have planned out itineraries, spent hours daydreaming over maps. Yet now, here she was, without even a guidebook in her possession.

There hadn't been time.

It had all started with that phone-call, two days before she was due to fly home; and if she hadn't popped back to her room, to find some papers that her boss had mislaid, she would most likely have missed it. At this very moment, she would have been easing herself back to normality (collect cat, sort mail, unpack suitcase, load washing machine, buy milk, bread, eggs, maybe some fruit and a newspaper) still happily unaware that her life had already veered onto a course that was neither intended nor desired.

And at which point in all that contented banality, she asked herself now, would Ian have shown up to inform her that their two-year relationship had come to an end? But of course he wouldn't have, would he? He was too much of a coward to tell her to her face. Hence the phone-call.

Stunned and confused, the one thing that had been clear to her was that she did not want to go home, not just yet. She managed to negotiate two weeks leave, which, at such short notice, was more than she had hoped for; then, desperate to find a corner in which to hide, while she nursed her wounds and regained some self-esteem, she found herself walking into a travel office in the dingy backstreet behind her hotel. A solitary man sat behind a desk, staring into space, absently scratching the back of his head with the tip of a pencil. Despite the heat, he was wearing a thick woollen cardigan neatly buttoned to the neck; leaving visible only the clean but fraying cuffs and collar of a white, cotton shirt. She told him what she wanted.

'So soon- ah?' He had frowned as he reached for a battered cardboard file. He opened it and made the appearance of rummaging through the papers inside; then he put it down again, as if he had thought of a better idea. He peered at her and wagged his head from side to side. 'Definitely can find you very nice place. Just if you give me bit more time also.' But she had insisted that she didn't have more time, nor did she mind where she went, as long as it was quiet; and as far away from London as possible. He moved some more papers on his desk. 'Everything booked now,' he muttered to himself. It was clear that he found her request somewhat bemusing. He turned his attention to the fax machine, as if that might give him inspiration; she half-expected it to whirr into action at that very moment. But it was the leaflet propped against it that had caught his eye. He picked it up, studied it for a moment, and then beamed at her: an action that was both unexpected and mildly alarming as it required some considerable rearrangement of his features and resulted in the revelation of a perfect set of large, white teeth. He waved the leaflet at her. 'You take this one – very good – small-small place.' He squinted at the picture on the front, before handing it to her. 'Place very special, very natural. Definitely you will be liking it.'

He was still beaming when he stood at the open doorway to his office to watch as she made her way down the narrow lane towards Jalan Raja Chulan and the increasingly irrelevant world of her luxury, four-star hotel.

The boat ploughed on through the glistening expanse of sea, its prow slapping hard against each approaching wave. Lulled by the steady drone of the motor, and the soothing counterpoint of the water slapping against the side of the boat, Isabel closed her eyes and, as if in a state of reverence, tilted her face to the sun, relishing its warm touch, anticipating its healing balm. The wind snatched at her thoughts, and might have carried them away had they not weighed so heavy; so, for the time being, the conversation with Ian continued to tumble about inside her head, the words coming at her, over and over again, stabbing at the raw place just inside her chest.

'I'm really sorry,' he had said.

Really sorry, she thought now. Like hell you were.

'It isn't working, is it?'

'What do you mean?' She had asked him.

'It isn't working for me.'

What about me, she thought. And why now? His timing was appalling.

'What have I done?' she had asked.

'Nothing,' he said. 'It's nothing you've done. It's me.'

But she already knew.

'There's someone else?'

'No. No – really. There isn't. It's just . . . I just need some space for a while.'

Bullshit, she thought.

She had asked him to wait until she got back, so they could talk.

'No, Isabel, I'm sorry. I think we should call it a day.'

She had pleaded with him then. Why had she pleaded? Why hadn't she simply put down the phone? But she was convinced that whatever had gone wrong between them could be made right again.

In the end he had said it.

'Look – Isabel. I've met someone. I . . . We . . .'

'You bastard . . .'

He had hung up. She had dialled his number. It was engaged. She dialled again; the *beep – beep – beep* of the tone resounded inside her head. Even now.

At last, she had given up.

That night, curled in a ball on the edge of a king-sized bed that wasn't hers, surrounded by the impersonal and largely unwanted trappings of the executive hotel room, she had cried herself to sleep, the phone still pressed against her cheek. All this for Ian: the rat who had ended their relationship, four weeks before she was due to move in with him.

She realized that the noise of the motor had stopped and the refreshing breeze had disappeared. They had come to a standstill; the boat was gently rocking from side to side. She turned to see what was happening. The young man, who all this time had been sitting behind her at the stern, handling the outboard motor, now jumped out and proceeded to tie a length of rope to the jetty.

It was a rickety old thing: ranks of crooked struts, bits of wood nailed together or tied with fraying rope. Isabel eyed the precarious-looking steps she was expected to climb, wondering when she should make her move to get off. And what about the suitcase? The young man was steadying the boat, waiting. She noticed that his shirt was torn at the shoulder. There was a streak of green paint on the back of his hand. Cautiously, she stood up and stepped onto the narrow platform, still debating whether she should have attempted her case as well. But he had jumped back and was in the process of hauling it over the side of the boat. She wished it wasn't hers.

As there wasn't much room on the platform for two people, let alone an over-large suitcase, she made her way up the steps and onto the walkway. He followed with the case.

When he reached the top, he stopped to catch his breath. 'That is Kampung Teluk – Teluk village,' he said, pointing towards a haphazard collection of palm-thatched buildings which fringed, and in some cases occupied, the beach. 'Not far now – just the other side.'

It was the first time he had spoken since their tentative exchange of greetings at the airport, and she felt guilty that she hadn't at least tried to make some sort of conversation with him during the journey.

'It looks lovely,' she replied. 'Thank you.' She moved towards her case. 'Let me take that. You don't have to . . .'

But he had already picked it up.

It was a pity she hadn't left most of that stuff in KL, she mused, following on behind. If only she had been more organized.

The walkway ended abruptly; there was no choice but to walk across the beach. Isabel stopped to take off her shoes. He had paused too, and she realized that he was debating how to manage her suitcase over the sand: its stupid, plastic wheels completely useless now. She tried to read the expression on his face, but she couldn't. If he was annoyed he wasn't showing it.

Leaving the beach behind them, he made a right turn and led her across a bridge, and over a mangrove swamp. The foliage on either side of the path was becoming increasingly dense and bits of it brushed against her arm as she walked; it was as if they were heading straight into the jungle. But then they turned a sharp corner and, through a gap in the trees, Isabel saw where they were going.

She stopped in her tracks. 'Wow!' she exclaimed. 'It's beautiful.'

She hadn't meant to react quite like that, but what she had seen had taken her breath away. Contrary to all expectations, the man at the travel agency had been right: it was indeed 'very special, very natural'; and it was going to be her refuge for the next nine days.

The young man seemed pleased by her response. 'Yes, we are here,' he said.

They continued along a gravel path towards a pavilion-like structure with a low, rattan roof. Two sides of the building opened onto wooden verandahs, resplendent with bougainvillea: great, opulent swathes of it – orange, purple and the deepest of pinks.

When they reached the reception area, he put down her case, relief apparent in his face. 'Welcome to Buah Lodge, Mees Eez-o-bel.'

A girl appeared, as if from nowhere: silent, shoeless, pretty as a picture. She wore a crisp, bright sarong wrapped around her prim and delicate frame. She was carrying one single glass on a small tray.

With a slight bow she offered the glass to Isabel. '*Selamat datang* – welcome – to Buah Lodge.'

Isabel took the glass and downed the ice-cold juice.

'Er, excuse me . . .' The young man was hovering beside her; he had a book, and a pen, on another tray. 'Please can you write in here. Then I will take you to your room.' He disappeared, leaving Isabel to write in the visitors' book. She hoped it wasn't going to take too long; her clothes were sticking to her skin, she needed a shower.

It was the usual thing: name, address, passport number; and a scrabble through her handbag to find the passport (why didn't she learn the number by heart?). She had left the address section until last. Now she frowned at the page and its neatly ruled lines, wondering what to write, trying to ignore the unpleasant dragging sensation in her chest.

She had no address. She would be more or less homeless when she got back to London. Most of her belongings had been packed into boxes and she had already given notice to her landlord. But since she clearly wouldn't be moving in with Ian, she now had nowhere to go.

She had filled out many forms over the past two weeks; a tiny flutter of anticipation, each time she rehearsed her new address. Now, she supposed, she would have to revert back to her old one. What did it matter anyway? It would do for now.

When she had finished with the book, she sat back and examined her surroundings. A wooden fan turned languidly above her head, with a soft click-clicking sound. A tiny lizard scuttled across the ceiling; she saw its long, grey tongue flick out to catch some morsel to eat. A small hors d'oeuvre.

'Are you ready?'

The young man had returned.

'Please. Follow me.' With a wry grin, he stooped to pick up her case once again.

'Sorry about the case,' she muttered. 'I've been in KL on business and . . .'

'Don't worry,' he replied. 'I am used to it.'

Did she detect a touch of amusement in his voice? 'Thank you anyway,' she said. 'I don't normally carry so much. Usually I . . .' She tailed off. Who was she kidding? Once, she had Inter-railed through Europe with little more than a change of clothes and a rolled up blanket stuffed into a canvas bag. But just the once.

She followed him down the steps and onto the gravel path, hoping all the while that it wouldn't be too much further for him to carry the case and trying to recall what she had in it. Books, papers, but what else? Her business suit, two or three smart dresses, several pairs of shoes. Nothing that would be of use here. She would have to go shopping, she decided. If there were any shops to go to.

The path was taking them past pretty, wooden chalets; each one nestled between patches of lavish vegetation: palms with broad, shiny leaves; vast shrubs, heavy with fragrance and blooms; abundant ferns; and more bougainvillea, with its violent pink bracts.

'Here we are.' He had stopped in front of one of the chalets.

It had a deeply sloping roof, thatched with palm, and stood on thick wooden stilts, raising it several feet from the ground. A flight of steps led to a covered verandah. There was a huge front door with an intricate pattern etched into the timber; narrow wooden shutters stood to attention on each side of a single window.

He lifted her case, one last time, and heaved it up the steps. When he reached the top, he slipped his feet from the flip-flops he was wearing before pushing open the door and stepping inside. Isabel used the doorpost, to steady herself while she struggled to remove her own shoes.

The room was simple. White walls and a dark-wood floor; a bed in one corner, a wardrobe in another; a couple of rattan chairs and a small writing desk. Instead of glass, the window contained a panel of carved latticework.

He pressed a switch by the door and a ceiling fan juddered into action.

'Thank you.'

He inclined his head and shoulders towards her: almost a bow, but not quite.

'If you need anything,' he said, 'please ask me – or anybody else. I will be in the Gula House – where we were before.'

'The Gula House,' she repeated. 'Right. Thank you.' She was feeling tired, now, and wanted to be on her own. 'I don't think I need anything at the moment, thanks,' she prompted.

He seemed reluctant to move.

At last it dawned on her: he was waiting for a tip. But she didn't have any small notes or coins. She had meant to exchange some money at the airport. Embarrassed, she turned away and pretended to busy herself with her suitcase.

He left. The door shut behind him. *Click.*

It came without warning, welling up from inside: an awareness of being very alone, abandoned in an unfamiliar place without a friend in the world.

She moved to the bed and sat down on the spotless white cover.

The past ten days had been a whirl of meetings, dinners, receptions, clients; she had barely had the opportunity to be on her own. And then there had been that phone-call.

Was that only three days ago? It felt like a lifetime.

She stretched herself out, her limbs sinking, heavy, as the tiredness spread through them. Just before she closed her eyes, she noticed something move across the wall by the bathroom. It was a small, brown lizard. It stopped in its tracks and looked at her; then hurried away.

'Come back, lizard,' she whispered. 'I won't hurt you.' But it had gone. Back to wherever it had come from.

Even that thing doesn't want my company, she thought.

Soon, tears were rolling down her cheeks – just a few at first, then more, and more – and she buried her face into the soft, feather pillow, hoping that no-one would hear her crying.

∞

When she tried to open her eyes it was as if they had been glued together. The room was in darkness. She had no idea how long she had been asleep. She raised her head an inch or two but it was like trying to move a dead weight. The muscles in her neck and shoulders had stiffened, every part of her ached. She gave up and let her head sink back into the pillow. For a second, maybe even two, she lay still, her mind blank. Then she remembered. And a huge stone came plunging into the pit of her stomach.

With some effort she uncurled her body, tentatively, limb by limb, until she was sitting on the edge of the bed. Then she groped around for a switch to the lamp on the bedside table. She was annoyed with herself for falling asleep, and missing dinner as well. Although she didn't feel hungry, she would have welcomed a few drinks – and some company. She reached for her handbag and felt inside until she found her watch. She tried to read the time, but her eyes were gritty and her eyelids heavy and swollen. She rubbed them, then looked at the watch again. Twenty minutes to one: it was the middle of the night, and she was still wearing the clothes she had arrived in.

Her suitcase, still unpacked, was standing in the corner where it had been left. She stared at it for a while, focussing her eyes on the red padlock, then on the crumpled paper label that had been placed round the handle by the airline staff, then on a dark stain just below the outside pocket that she hadn't noticed before.

Uninspired by the case, her gaze moved to the door. A needle of light showed through a crack in the wood. Puzzled, she turned to the window. Sunlight glinted unevenly through the closed shutters. Intrigued now, she walked across and reached through a gap in the latticework to push at the wood. The sudden burst of light was dazzling but exhilarating. It was still day.

She was certain that the shutters had been open when she arrived, yet she didn't think she had closed them. She scanned the room. Everything seemed to be in order. She went back to the bed and picked up her watch, but this time it said ten minutes past six. She shook it, to see if it had stopped, then realized what had happened.

'Stupid! You had it upside down'.

Now she knew that it wasn't the middle of the night, she strode to the door and pulled it open. A wedge of evening sunlight washed over the floor and mounted the bed, bathing the cover in shades of pink and orange. The air was thick with heat and exotic scents; the sounds pulsing through it were otherworldly, incorporeal. Although the sun was low in the sky, it was still bright – incredibly bright – and she stood, spellbound, as it sank into the horizon, turning from orb to ellipse in front of her eyes. She found herself smiling. Maybe life wasn't so bad after all. Somehow – and she couldn't quite believe her luck – she had ended up in the most perfect spot imaginable.

And if she could get a gin and tonic from somewhere, she thought, it would be even better. It was time to explore the bar.

'Drink?' she asked herself.

'Yes please,' she replied, heading back into the room and to her abandoned suitcase.

'Oh God!'

Isabel had removed the padlock, unzipped and lifted the lid, and now she was staring at the mess inside the suitcase. She had packed in haste.

Now she pulled things out one by one, chatting to herself as she worked, finding comfort in the sound of her voice.

'Dress – no use, jacket – no use, skirt – maybe, toilet bag – yes (but why unfastened?). Great, that accounts for the stain. Shoes – no use, shorts – yes.' It had been a stroke of luck putting those in, she thought.

'Dress –' She held a plain, blue cotton dress at arm's length before adding it to the maybe pile. 'Bikini – yes.' That had been for the hotel pool but she'd never had the time.

'Right – that lot can go back in.' She bundled up the items forming the largest pile and pushed them back into the case.

'Doesn't leave much. Will definitely have to go shopping.'

There was a gentle tap on the door.

'Come in.'

No-one entered. The tapping was repeated.

She shouted louder this time. 'Hello – come in.'

The door moved and a head appeared. It was the guy who had met her at the airport.

'Miss Eez-o-bel. Sorry. Sorry to disturb you. I . . .' He ran a hand through his hair, pushing it back from his face. 'You were not sleeping.' This was more of a statement than a question.

'No.' She stood up quickly, hoping to hide the mess on the floor behind her.

'I . . . We wonder if you would like to have some dinner.' He pronounced this as *dee-nar*.

'Ah. What time do you serve it?'

'Well, around now, but . . .' He looked at his watch. 'Tonight there is just you, so . . .'

Her sleep-fuddled brain wasn't up to this. She felt she should say no. But she was hungry now –

'Well, yes, but . . .'

'Good. So, maybe you would like curry chicken – Malay style? Or would you like something else? Maybe . . .'

'No,' she interrupted him. 'Chicken would be great. Thank you. So, shall I come now, or . . .?'

'Maybe half an hour? Or if you need more time . . .' He had spotted the open suitcase, and the piles of clothes on the floor.

'No, half an hour will be fine.'

He was still hovering by the door. Then he spoke again. 'Er, I hope that you don't mind but . . .' He hesitated. 'I closed your shutters – I think you were sleeping – I came by earlier.'

At least now she knew she hadn't been imagining things.

'It will be better for you,' he went on, 'if you close them when you are sleeping. Keep out insects and stuff.'

She nodded.

'So, we will see you in half an hour?'

He stepped back and closed the door behind him. There was a pause; then she heard the sound of his flip-flops on the steps, and the scrunch of gravel as he reached the path below. She listened to the sound of his footsteps until they had faded away and she could hear them no longer.

The only person here? That wasn't at all what she had imagined.

So much for a bit of company. The only people she had seen so far were him – the driver-porter-whatever he was – and the young girl with the drink; she was alone, in the middle of nowhere, and some guy had been creeping around her room, or chalet, or whatever they called it. And what did he mean by 'insects and stuff'?

She slumped onto the bed and stared at the two remaining piles of clothes: the yes pile and the maybes.

She shouldn't blame him. He was only trying to be helpful. In fact, he couldn't have been more charming.

'But you always have to think the worst of people, don't you?'

'Yes,' she replied, scooping up the things from the floor and transferring them to the bed, 'because they are unreliable bastards the lot of them – men the world over – every last one of them.'

She thought she had no more tears left to cry, but now she could feel them welling up again. She shook her head violently. 'Right,' she said, addressing the pile of clothes, as if it she were expecting it to argue back at her. 'I'm going for dinner. And I'm dammed if I'm getting changed – if it's only going to be me there.'

He was waiting at the entrance to the Gula House. He had changed his clothes, and was now wearing a batik shirt, teamed with plain black trousers. A pair of black leather sandals had replaced the flip-flops. Somehow, she wasn't surprised to find that he was also the waiter.

With a touch of formality, he showed her to a table – the only one set for dinner. Someone had set out one knife, one fork, one spoon, a glass, a jug of water, a napkin, and a small vase of flowers: beautiful pink flowers. There was music playing: a female voice, a melancholy Chinese song.

Plates and dishes arrived, and she delved her spoon into a bowl of steaming rice, piling a generous amount onto her plate; she popped a forkful of it into her mouth before lifting the lid from a second dish – pieces of chicken in a creamy sauce. A third, contained dark green leaves bathed in a rich, brown sauce.

The food was simple but good, and Isabel ate with relish; but she felt uncomfortable sitting on her own in the otherwise empty room, and a touch guilty that all this had been prepared just for her. And she wished that she had brought something to read.

She didn't see him approach.

'Is everything good for you?'

She tried to speak but had a mouth full of food. 'Mmm –' was the best she could do.

'I hope I haven't made it too spicy for you?'

'No –' She swallowed and cleared her throat. 'Thanks –' She gulped some water from her glass.

She had intended to say more, but he had moved away. It was a pity, because she wanted to tell him how much she was enjoying her meal. Well, he'll be back, she thought.

But by the time she had finished there was still no sign of him. She sat at the table for a while, contemplating the empty dishes, wondering what she should do. The Chinese songs were beginning to get on her nerves and she wanted to go back to her room. It had only been hers for a few hours but it was all she had. And the thought of it was comforting.

She wondered if she should let someone know that she was leaving, but there was no-one about – just a few muffled sounds coming from the kitchen.

She had dragged a chair from her room and was sitting on the verandah. The outside light was switched off, but her eyes had become accustomed to the darkness around her and she could make out the alien shapes of nearby plants and trees and the shadowy forms of the neighbouring chalets. Every so often a light would wink through the blackness as a branch was stirred by the breeze, and from time to time she could hear the whoosh of the waves breaking on the beach beyond the mangrove swamp.

The calm was interrupted by the sound of voices. German?

Or Danish? Then, 'Anyone fancy a beer?' The accent was unmistakable: Australian. She didn't catch the reply, but there were muttered 'g'nights', and the sound of flip-flops tailing away in the direction of the Gula House.

So there are more people here after all, she thought. And she wished that she had stayed at her table for a while longer; she was clearly missing out on some company.

Then, out of the gloom, two figures appeared. These two were clearly locals, more likely staff; they were both carrying trays of empty plates and glasses.

One of the men spotted her on the verandah and shouted up, 'Goodnight mees.'

'Goodnight,' she replied.

∞

22 July 1991

It was seven thirty. The fresh morning sun cast a sharp and brilliant light over the Gula House; all around was the buzz of early morning activity, which would inevitably wind down once the searing heat of the day had seeped into the earth. The sound of soft, singsong voices coming from the kitchen could just be heard over the trills and twitters of the birds as they fluttered from tree to tree and jostled for perches. Deeper inside the jungle, monkeys clattered around in the highest branches, their shrill calls piercing the forest canopy. A few foraging lizards scratched and rustled beneath the building; others pattered along the wooden beams that supported the roof, before scurrying across the palm-thatched ceiling in pursuit of a meal. In the dining area, two young women worked. They wove between tables like a pair of busy hummingbirds, visiting each one to set out spoons and forks, bowls and plates; then back into the kitchen – a burst of melodious chatter, a giggle or two – and out again, with a jug of freshly squeezed juice, or a basket of fruit. The shot of blue in their sarongs mirrored the colour of the morning sky.

Isabel hadn't needed a wake-up call. The moment the sun had put out its first, tentative rays, the whole garden, the jungle, and everywhere around, had begun to babble and hum. It was as if all the creatures on the earth had been waiting patiently for a sign. Now, as she wandered down the path leading to the Gula House, she pondered over how a place could seem so calm and peaceful, yet at the same time so incredibly noisy.

She was the first to arrive for breakfast but was relieved to see that all the tables had been set out. She chose the one where she had eaten dinner the night before; there were no flowers now but in their place was a basket of fruit covered with a crisp white napkin.

When she looked up again, there was a girl standing by her side.

'Good morning Miss. You take coffee, or you like tea?'

Before Isabel could reply, the girl continued: 'You arrive yesterday Miss Isabel.' The statement was turned into a question by the lilt of her accent.

'Yes, I did.'

'Ah.' She paused. Then: 'I had day off yesterday. 'My name is Set Yen. You can call me Sally. What is your name?'

'Isabel,' she replied, and added: 'I'll have tea please – Chinese tea?'

'Yes, Miss Isabel.'

'Wouldn't you prefer to be called Set Yen?' Isabel asked. 'It's a lovely name.'

'I don't mind.' Set Yen giggled. 'But I think it is better for you to remember Sally. One guest told me it is an English name.'

Isabel tried to think of some response but couldn't come up with anything other than 'Aunt Sally'. In any case, Set Yen had glided off towards the kitchen. Perhaps she would think of something else before she returned.

While she had been talking to Set Yen, Isabel had noticed two other guests approaching from the garden. She watched as they climbed the steps and strolled into the dining area. The man was tall and fair, with long, athletic limbs; his straw coloured hair was short and tightly curled. He wore small, round glasses with gold coloured frames. The young woman was taller, by at least a couple of inches; her hair was loosely tied into a ponytail, but that didn't stop it gleaming like burnished gold whenever it was caught by the sun. The couple were deep in conversation, but they were speaking a language that Isabel didn't immediately recognize. They were making their way to the opposite corner. As they passed Isabel's table, the woman smiled shyly.

Once they had sat down, the man pulled a bright red handkerchief from his pocket. He took off his glasses, and started to polish them. It was clear the two of them had just shared a joke. They were both laughing.

'Here you are, Miss Isabel.' This was Set Yen, back with a pot of steaming tea. She had also brought a basket of bread and a dish of honey. She had a white card tucked under her arm. She handed this to Isabel. 'If you like warm breakfast,' she said, 'please, can choose from here.'

Isabel scanned the menu. As well as the usual egg dishes, and something called 'beef-bacons', there were several Chinese and Malay dishes on offer. Was it too soon to be adventurous?

'How you like Buah Lodge? Very nice-*lah.*'

Not sure whether this was a statement or a question, Isabel nodded. She let her eyes roam once more around the room and to the garden beyond. The colours seemed even more vibrant in the sharp morning light.

'It's lovely,' she replied.

She settled for boiled eggs, and Set Yen returned to the kitchen, leaving Isabel to herself again. She wondered where the young man from yesterday was. It must be his turn to have a day off, she thought.

As Isabel was finishing her breakfast the blonde woman arrived at her table. She stretched out a lean and tanned arm.

'Hello,' she said, shaking Isabel's hand. A collection of heavy silver bangles clashed and jangled as she moved. 'I am Els.' She gestured towards the table where her companion was still sitting. 'And that is Pieter. Over there.' Pieter grinned and gave Isabel a wave. 'You arrived here yesterday?'

'Yes, that's right,' Isabel replied. 'And it was deserted. I thought I was the only person here.'

'No, there are people here. We are here. For five days more. So you are from England, I think?'

'Yes. Have you been there?'

'Of course! We have travelled to London many times, and to Birmingham one time – for a concert – yes – and to Scotland also.'

'I was born in Scotland.'

'It is very nice there. Ah, and we are from Amsterdam.

'Oh, I . . .' But Isabel's reply was cut short.

'Here they are.' A man had come into the dining area, dropped the rucksack he was carrying, and bounded towards them. He had flung his arms around Els and now he was lifting her off the floor, swinging her round. 'Hellamgonna miss you guys.'

A second young man had appeared, and was standing by, watching what was going on. Both of them were tall, fair, their skin tanned to a dark, golden brown. These must be the people she had heard last night, Isabel decided. The Aussies. Pieter, too, had stood up and was coming over to join them, still clutching a slice of toast.

Finding that her table was now the centre of so much activity, Isabel wasn't sure whether to stand, and try to join in, or remain where she was. She picked up her teacup and examined the contents. There was a mouthful left. When she lifted the cup to her lips she could feel that the tea was stone cold, but she drained it anyway, for want of something better to do.

'You the mystery Brit who arrived yesterday? We were hopin' to catch up with you last night. So hi! How you goin'? I'm Steve by the way.'

Isabel stood up and found herself looking into the deepest, bluest eyes she had ever seen. And they were gazing back at her from under thick, long lashes.

Steve gestured towards his friend, who still had his arm around Els. 'An' that's Luke.'

Luke retrieved his bag from the floor. 'Hey, you guys – s'a real shame – but we should move or we'll miss our flight. Good to have met you, Isabel. Shame we godda go.'

'Well, it's obviously hello and goodbye then,' she said, taking Luke's outstretched hand, wishing she had come up with something a bit more original.

Steve turned to Pieter and Els. 'C'mon on you two, if yer comin' to town with us. The others are at the jetty.'

'See you at dinner.' Els shouted back over her shoulder.

Isabel raised her hand in acknowledgement, before sitting down again. All of a sudden it seemed very still and quiet.

So what next? A whole new day stretched ahead of her; a blank canvas, waiting to be filled in whatever way she pleased. It had been so long since she'd had time to call her own, now she wasn't sure what she was going to do with it. She wondered whether to stay at the table for a while longer, to see if anyone else would turn up, but decided that she had been sitting there long enough. It was time to get out into the sunshine.

She needed something to distract her mind; and yesterday, when she had been looking through some leaflets, she had read about a waterfall somewhere nearby in the forest. She decided to find it. But the one pair of shoes she had that were sturdy enough for a walk through the jungle, had cost a small fortune in Fenwick's. She put them on anyway, accepting, with a touch of regret, that they would never look quite so pristine again: yet a few days ago, she didn't know she would be on a tropical island – or walking through a rainforest.

She set off past what she imagined were the staff quarters and through a gap in the shrubs, towards the jungle at the back of the compound. Ahead loomed the great rainforest trees with their festoons of moss, ferns and long, trailing stems, and their leaves mottled with light and shade. And as far as she could tell, there was just one track leading into the forest. It would be impossible to get lost, she concluded, if she stuck to that.

Insects lurking in the undergrowth chirred unceasingly, the sound becoming more intense with every step she took, and soon she was surrounded on all sides by thick, luscious jungle, everything vying for its own space to grow; now a flash of colour – startling shades of red and orange – a mass of iridescent plumage, a flock of tiny birds swooping into and out of the sunlight. She watched them streak into the forest then stood still, to look about her. A plant brushed her shoulder and she reached out to touch one of the delicate cream petals; it was fleshy, succulent. A dark stripe moving across the path in front of her became a battalion of giant ants, filing to and fro with their macabre trophies: an insect's wing, a head, the hollow corpse of a dead beetle. Carefully, she stepped over the undulating line. At this rate she was in danger of getting nowhere fast. But it was enchanting; it was as if she had raised the lid of a treasure trove and stepped inside. She couldn't resist a theatrical twirl. 'My first rainforest!'

The track appeared to be well used. Some of the vegetation had been cut back and as far as she could make out there was still only one possible way to go. Even so, she was relieved when she saw the sign. It was a piece of wood nailed to the trunk of a tree, with an arrow, and 'TO THE WATERFALL' painted in black ink.

She continued in the direction of the arrow, stepping out briskly now that she was sure she was going the right way. The loose stones moved beneath her feet, crunching out a mesmerizing rhythm as she walked. Then it started: the demons inside her head, poking around with their spiny little fingers until they found what they wanted; pulling out thoughts, one by one, in time with every step.

No more Ian – want him back? – find someone else – he doesn't want you – no more cricket matches – (where had that one come from?) *– you didn't like them anyway –*

'Yes I did,' she said out loud. 'They were fun. He said I inspired him.' She glanced over her shoulder, embarrassed, in case someone had heard her talking to herself. And in any case, who were these people inside her head, arguing with her like this?

Not ready for commitment (Ah – that one was definitely Ian's voice) *–not to you, anyway – wonder what her name is? – it's getting too serious* (Ian's voice again) *– heard that one before –*

'But it was his idea to move in together,' she remarked.

Shouldn't have been so eager – too clingy! – he called you that – didn't he?

And so it went on. And on. The ritual unravelling of the last two years. Had it been her fault that it had gone wrong? Was she too 'clingy'?

She thought about the times she had waited in (hair washed, clothes ironed) just in case he called; and the times she had wiped away the make-up, put away the clothes he never had chance to admire, gone to bed in tears. Of course when he did call she would be turning out a cupboard, or doing her laundry, or watching a video with an early dinner on her knee; and she would have to clear stuff from the radiators, vacuum the sofa where the cat had been sitting, check there was nothing untoward lying around in the bathroom, put on make-up, get changed – all in the half-hour it took for him to get to her flat. On more than one occasion she had ended up having two dinners in one evening. No wonder she was putting on weight.

It's because you're too fat –

She ignored that one.

Maybe he was right, though. Maybe she had put too much pressure on him.

No you didn't, you were just being you – the you he didn't want – his loss – he didn't think so – if only you hadn't been away. If only . . .

'For God's sake! Isabel!' She stopped, shocked by the sound of her voice ringing though the forest. A bird, high up in the branches, shrieked and fluttered its wings.

'It isn't your fault,' she said, quietly this time, noting also that she was out of breath.

It was then she noticed that the track had been climbing steadily upwards and that the undergrowth had become more and more entangled, making the path narrow and difficult to negotiate. In fact it was hardly a path at all. She spotted the remains of a fallen tree and sat down, wishing that she had brought some water, wondering how she had managed to lose her way.

All around her, the trees soared skywards, pushing higher and higher, competing to be first through the canopy; creepers and vines entwined the narrow trunks, clinging to them, choking them, in their own struggle to gain a place in the sun high above.

The canopy itself was a rich mosaic of browns and greens and glinting daubs of silver where the sunlight filtered through, and of bright patches of blue where a tree-fall had left a gap in the vast, leafy roof. And there, below, the light-starved saplings had responded with flurries of fresh new shoots, unfurling themselves into spiny green fingers, or pushing up from clumps of leaves rotting on the forest floor.

Isabel closed her eyes and let the heat wrap around her, wishing it could cleanse her mind of unwanted thoughts, draw them out through her pores, just as a sauna would draw the impurities from her skin. But her mind wasn't ready to give in – not just yet – it was on a roll: Isabel's relationships with men.

Her friends told her she went for the wrong types – so where, then, were the right ones? And what was right and what was wrong? And who made the rules? No, it was clear that she was doing something wrong (because hadn't the same thing happened with Martin – who spent all of their five months together telling her that he 'didn't do relationships').

Perhaps it wasn't too late. Perhaps she could convince Ian that she could change –

A loud thud, as if something had fallen out of a tree, and the sound of something moving around in the bushes, forced Isabel to abandon this particular train of thought for the time being.

That was when it struck her: she was in the middle of a forest; she had strayed from her path; she had no idea what might be lurking there, and she wouldn't have a clue what to do if anything appeared. Also, no-one knew where she was. And who cared anyway?

She jumped from her seat and brushed herself down – more for the need to do something practical than to remove what may or may not have been stuck to her clothes. She should go back, she thought, but all traces of a path had disappeared. She began to pick her way through, skirting the broken branches that now looked like snakes, and the fallen brown leaves that resembled any number of slimy reptiles. She continued walking downhill, in the direction she thought she had come.

Crash.

There it was again. She stopped, waiting for the next sound but all she could hear was the pounding of her heart. She walked faster, and then she was almost running, stumbling over roots and stones, oblivious to the scratches that were appearing on her bare legs. At last, she could see sky again, big blue chunks of it; and the sun, lighting up great patches of the forest floor. She felt relieved to be out in the open, but also rather foolish. She hadn't been deep inside the forest at all, she had barely ventured beyond the fringes. No wonder she hadn't found the waterfall.

Crunch – crunch.

She froze.

The sound came again. This time it was more regular, like footsteps on dead leaves. It was getting louder. Whatever it was, it was getting closer. She could already see the newspaper headline. *British tourist found dead in Malaysian rainforest.* How long would it take before someone discovered that she was missing? And how would they trace her parents?

She glanced towards where the sound was coming from. A man

was approaching; she could see his dark, muscular legs pushing out from below the hem of his sarong. Above the sarong he wore a grubby white vest and on his back was a bundle of wood, tied in a length of cloth. His face was gaunt, browned by the sun. He carried a long, curved knife.

Isabel continued to walk, striding out in long, measured paces, hoping to appear confident.

As they drew level, she kept her eyes on the ground; she could hear the sound of his breathing. She quickened her pace, but her foot slid on the gravel and she had to clutch at a nearby branch to steady herself.

'Berhati-hati!' he called out to her

∞

Isabel's speedy exit from the forest had led her straight to what she assumed was Teluk village; it was clear, now, that she had taken the wrong path: this was nowhere near where she had started out.

It was difficult to tell where the village ended and the beach began, for one seemed to merge into the other, and gaps in between the hotchpotch of buildings offered enticing glimpses of a sparkling sea. But every house had its shutters tightly closed; the only movement came from the occasional string of laundry swaying in the breeze; the only sound was the soft swish-swish of the waves rolling backwards and forwards on the beach. The place appeared to be deserted.

Judging by the position of the sun, it was well past mid-day. Isabel wasn't hungry but she was desperate for some water.

The first wooden sign announced 'M. K. SEA FOOD'. The letters were unevenly spaced, the brushwork thin and shaky; and underneath, five Chinese characters, most likely saying the same thing. There were some plastic tables and stools set out on the sand under a ragged canopy of thatch, but there was no other sign of life. No doubt Mr M. K. was inside, snoozing away the hottest part of the day.

But in due course she came across a shop: a ramshackle affair, thrown together from little more than bits of corrugated iron. Hanging from this patchwork of metal was a rusty placard advertising 'KENT 14's', tempting the onlooker with a giant pack of cigarettes. The sign was missing most of its fixing screws, and looked as though it would come crashing to the ground in the next high wind. There was a child-sized bike propped against the open door and a few sun-bleached chairs arranged beneath a nearby tree. A tin awning shaded the front of the shop and beneath this was a counter. And here, arranged in a neat line and in a rainbow of colours, were bottles of drinks.

Isabel approached and peered towards the shadowy interior. In a corner, partially hidden behind a stack of empty crates, was a fridge with a glass door. She could see bottles of water, tucked in amongst cans of drink and what might have been pieces of chicken covered in plastic wrapping, but she couldn't very well walk in and take what she wanted, so she stayed there for a while, pushing the fine, apricot-coloured sand into small mounds with her foot. Then, because she couldn't think of anything else to do, she wandered down the gently sloping beach to gaze out at the sea.

The smooth expanse of water glistened invitingly back at her. The tide was out and the beach swept round in an arc, becoming narrower and narrower, until it disappeared altogether into a segment of jungle that had tumbled down to meet it; a wood-fire was burning nearby – wisps of smoke rose from behind the straggle of buildings at the far end of the village – and she could just make out the thatched roofs of Buah Lodge nestled amongst the palms. In perfect silence, an eagle soared above the tallest of the forest trees, its wings spread, its head tilted towards the ground.

It was when she looked back at the village that she noticed a small, round face peeping out at her from behind one side of the shop. The little body emerged a moment later and she saw that it was a boy of about three or four, dressed in a blue pyjama suit. He stood with one bare foot resting on top of the other and examined Isabel with wide, brown eyes. When he had done, he turned and scurried away.

Isabel waited for a while and soon she heard the familiar scuff-scuff-scuff of flip-flops, then two figures appeared: the little boy and a young woman. The woman was pulling her long, black hair into a ponytail as she walked; by the time she reached Isabel, she had secured it with a pink elastic band.

'Yes? What you like?

'Water – cold – please –' The words came out at random, one at a time; it was the first time since breakfast that Isabel had spoken to anyone – other than to herself.

The woman went into the shop and emerged with a large bottle of Bleu. She held it to her cheek. 'Cold-*lah*.' She handed it to Isabel. 'One *ringgit*.'

Isabel wedged the dripping bottle under her arm so that she could reach into her pocket for some money; the sodden paper label slid from the plastic and clung to her skin. 'Thank you,' she said, handing over a coin.

'Wel-come.'

Isabel opened the bottle and put it to her lips; the water wasn't very cold but it would serve its purpose.

The woman continued to stand in front of her, watching her every move.

'Thank you,' Isabel said again as she replaced the cap on the bottle.

The woman nodded.

The little boy had wrapped his arms around his mother's leg; he stared up at Isabel with huge, unblinking eyes. 'Bye-bye,' he shouted, as soon as she had turned and started off down the path.

She was eager now to change into her swimming things and plunge into the sea to cool down. Without slowing her pace, she took another gulp of water, letting some of it slide past her mouth, over her chin, and down inside the neck of her T-shirt. This resulted in a fit of coughing, and she had to pause for a moment while she recovered her breath.

She had stopped outside a pretty house, with a tiny front garden: a row of tin drums, each containing a flowering shrub. The walls of the house had been freshly painted and splodges of green paint still dotted the wooden verandah. Lined up in front of the closed door were five pairs of flip-flops. Isabel glanced at one of the windows. Two dark eyes stared back at her from under a pale blue headscarf. She moved quickly on and, once past the house, she turned to look back at the shop. The woman, with the child nestling against her legs, was still standing outside, still watching.

*

On her way out to dinner, Isabel scooped up her novel. It was a satisfyingly thick paperback, bought especially for the trip, but so far she hadn't managed to get beyond the first chapter. She was looking forward to a good read.

She could hear the buzz of voices coming from the Gula House and she wondered, not for the first time, where everyone got to during the day. That was something she could ask Els and Pieter, she thought. She scanned the room for them, but they weren't there.

She was heading for her usual table, but she soon saw that it was already occupied. A young man with pale, skinny legs was twisted round in his seat, talking to a couple at an adjacent table. She quickly changed direction and made for another table passing a group of four, in animated conversation. One of them glanced up as she went by.

'*Guten Abend,*' he said.

She sat down near the bar and placed her book in the space where her plate would eventually go, carefully lining it up with the pattern on the tablecloth. When the kitchen door flew open, she saw the guy who had met her from the airport; he was carrying two bowls of food. He grinned at her.

Set Yen was next to emerge.

'Chinese tea, Miss Isabel?'

'Ah – no – not this time. I'll have a beer please.' She had spotted the bottles in a fridge behind the bar.

Set Yen melted away, and Isabel opened her book at the page that was marked with her London-KL boarding pass. But she soon realized that she had no idea what was going on; she would have to start it again from the beginning. She put the book face down on the table and turned her attention to the people in the room.

The skinny guy had taken his chair and joined the man and woman at the next table, his heavy, mud-caked boots splayed out in front of him. Isabel couldn't hear what he was saying, but he was clearly excited about something and was waving a fork around in the air, revealing a dark bloom of sweat underneath his arm. The other two were nodding, enthusiastically – one, pink and dewy as if fresh from the shower, the other mopping his brow with a handkerchief; his stiff cotton shirt still bore the creases from where it had been folded into a suitcase.

'Tiger Beer, Mees Eezobel?'

The voice took her by surprise. She had not seen him approach. She had been expecting Set Yen.

'Er, yes . . .' she stuttered.

He placed a glass and the bottle of beer on the table, before speaking again.

'Did you have a good day?

'Yes – thank you. I had a walk, and a swim – you know – the usual things.' Not usual for him, though, she thought with a stab of guilt.

'I can see that you have been out in the sun.'

Isabel raised a hand to her cheek. It was burning. She was annoyed with herself for having fallen asleep on the beach.

He had removed the bottle top and was carefully pouring beer into the glass. He was leaning towards her and she noticed a segment of gold lying against the smooth skin at his throat; she wondered, vaguely, what was attached to the chain around his neck.

'Actually, I tried to find the waterfall,' she added, glad to have thought of something else to say. 'You know – there's a waterfall at the back of here – in the forest.' But of course he knew. And she was exasperated by her sudden inability to make conversation.

'Yes. I know it.'

'I tried to get there but . . . well, I wasn't sure. Is it safe to walk in there?'

'In the forest? Yes, of course. If you keep to the track.'

'It's just – I thought, maybe, there might be animals – snakes – or something.'

He laughed. 'No snakes.' Then: 'You didn't see any did you?' He seemed concerned.

'I don't think so.'

'That's good.' He looked down at the empty bottle he was holding, and started to twist the glass neck to and fro between his fingers.

She broke the silence once more: 'But in the end, I didn't find the waterfall. I think I took the wrong path.'

'You got lost? That's strange. There should be some signs. It should be easy –'

'No, I didn't really get lost, I gave up, I was worried about . . . well, snakes and things.' She reached out to touch her glass. It was icy cold and she longed to take a sip from it. She wished now that she hadn't mentioned snakes; he would think –

But why did she care what he thought? She pulled back her hand and flicked at the pages of her book. 'Anyway,' she went on, 'I'm sure all sorts of things live in there.'

He nodded.

'And I heard some strange noises too.'

'Yes, it is home to many different creatures. You will hear them at night, I am sure.'

'I did,' she laughed. 'They woke me up.'

'I, er . . .' He hesitated. He was still toying with the empty bottle. 'I . . .'

She gave him what she hoped was an encouraging smile. He appeared to be struggling with his English.

'I can show you, if you would like to go – I mean – to the waterfall. I can take you there.' He stopped, abruptly.

Had she known that was coming?

He was waiting for her to speak.

She knew she needed to say something.

'Okay. That's kind of you.' Her voice sounded calm, offhand almost, and not in the least affected by what was going on in her stomach.

Why on earth had she agreed to that?

He also appeared taken aback by her reply. 'Ah – good. So how about eight o'clock, tomorrow? After breakfast. Before it gets too hot.'

She nodded.

'I will see you at breakfast then.'

She watched him walk towards the kitchen. When he had disappeared through the swinging door, she picked up her glass and took a long swig of beer. She wasn't simply concerned about what she had got herself into, she was angry with herself, too. Why – honestly – had she mentioned the waterfall in the first place? And to him – a waiter, at her resort! Hadn't it been obvious what would happen? Perhaps she should call him back, she thought, and tell him that she had something else to do. The truth was, she had planned to spend the day on the beach, and that was certainly what she would rather do. So how could she get out of it? Without offending him.

She shook her head, silently chastising herself for being so stupid.

She saw him just once more that evening, while he was serving drinks to the four Germans. He hadn't even raised his head to look in her direction. Set Yen had brought her dinner, and a young man she hadn't seen before had cleared away her plates and brought her another beer, as well as telling her that his name was Amir, that he came from Indonesia and was the youngest of five brothers.

She drained her glass and sat back in her chair. It was a shame that Els and Pieter hadn't shown up, she had been looking forward to seeing them. On the other hand, at least she wouldn't have to explain to anyone what she was doing tomorrow.

Most of the other guests had moved through to the lounge area. The guy in the boots was sprawled over one of the sofas, reading aloud from a copy of *The Rough Guide to Southeast Asia*. The other two were seated squarely in their armchairs, listening intently. On the table between them were three bottles of beer, a book and a large, brown leather handbag.

Isabel pushed back her chair, picked up her own book from the table, and walked towards the exit. As she passed by the three of them, the woman looked up, expectantly, her flushed cheeks lifted by a broad smile. She was wearing bright pink lipstick, freshly applied by the look of it, possibly without the aid of a mirror. Her hair clung in damp strands around her neck.

Isabel smiled back, and walked on by.

PART THREE

London
August 1994

∞

1.10 pm

I sabel knew that David would cut it fine, but now he was ten minutes late. Perhaps it had been unwise to try to squeeze this into his lunch break.

To make matters worse it had started to rain. She had already felt the odd drop of it land on her bare arms, and caught the scent of wet dust that accompanied a summer rain shower; now the paving slabs were gradually darkening as the random globs began to merge. Directly overhead, livid clouds had turned the sky the colour of old slate; yet, to the south, a different day was unfolding: great patches of white scudded over the city, leaving dabs of blue to glare through the gaps in between.

She decided to stop looking in the direction of the tube station and, instead, walk towards the pillar-box on the corner: by the time she had got there, and turned round to come back, he would have appeared – she was sure; he would be hurrying towards her, very likely studying his watch, with that puzzled expression on his face as if, somehow, it had misinformed him. He might even give it a shake for good measure.

Her walk to the corner and back took exactly one and a half minutes; then she was back where she started: 'Rosehaven'. But there was still no sign of David.

She stood by the gate and studied the façade of the building, taking in the way the bricks had been laid to form an intricate pattern just underneath the eaves; the satisfying shapes of coloured glass in the window above the front door; the exotic-looking lantern hanging in the porch. And the more she saw, the more she wanted this to be her home. A whole house! With an upstairs, and a pantry, and a cloakroom, according to the estate agent's blurb (a real one too, where people could hang their coats, and not just a few hooks in a downstairs toilet). And, unlike many of the other houses along the street, it even had a small front garden, with its own family of blackbirds by the look of it; she had already seen a female pecking around under the hedge, now she could see the male, perched on the low wall separating the garden from next door's. He had his head cocked to one side, watching her. Was that a sign, she thought? A good omen?

She looked at her watch again.

'God, where's he got to?'

She really didn't want to have another argument. She had already snapped at him on the phone this morning, and then felt guilty about asking him to take time from his busy schedule. But when he had suggested that she might go and look at the house on her own, she couldn't quite decide whether to feel hurt (because wasn't looking for your first home together something that should be shared?) or put out that he was leaving her to do all the running around.

She looked over to where the estate agent had parked his car; he had his head turned away, and was talking into a mobile phone. He had already offered to let her into the house, but she had said that she would wait for David. In fact, the exact words she had used were, 'I think I'd better wait for my partner', and then he had looked at her with that 'oh so they're not married' expression, which had made her feel even more self-conscious. She had been trying out the word 'partner' for the first time. Given that she was approaching the wrong side of thirty-five, and had been speaking to someone who couldn't be much older than nineteen, the word 'boyfriend' hadn't seemed quite right somehow. But the English language was pitifully inadequate when it came to such matters.

Just as she was debating whether to attract his attention, and ask him to let her in after all, she spotted David. He had just turned into the street and was walking towards her. She noticed that he was carrying a large, unopened umbrella.

As soon as he lifted his head to inspect the houses, she stepped away from the gate and waved. He raised a hand in response.

'Hello,' she said, once he had pulled up beside her.

'Sorry I'm late.' He leant forward to kiss her cheek. 'Had to wait ages at Camden. 'Where's the chap?'

She gestured towards the red Fiesta parked on the opposite side of the road.

'Why didn't you go in?'

'I thought it would be nice if we went in together.' She smiled at him, so it wouldn't seem like an accusation. 'So, what do you think? It looks perfect, doesn't it?'

David glanced towards the estate agent, who was now getting out of his car. 'We haven't seen inside yet,' he warned, 'and don't sound too enthusiastic. We might want to get the price down. Don't think much of the garden,' he added, his voice louder now. 'It makes the place look untidy – but we could always pave it over. There isn't a garage at this one is there?'

'Good afternoon. Kevin Warren.' The young man handed David his card. 'And you're absolutely right, sir. Many of these properties have been updated in that way. It is a popular choice in this area to convert a front garden into a parking space, and there is enough room here for up to four cars.'

Isabel looked down the street, and at the ugly patches of concrete where hedges and trees would once have been. What a shame all those gardens had been destroyed, she thought. And why would they want four cars anyway? Their house – she was already thinking of it as theirs – looked much better with its garden intact. An oasis of green. And that was something she was prepared to fight for if necessary.

Once inside, Isabel was even more convinced that this was the house she wanted. She hoped that David felt the same although so far he hadn't given anything away.

'So,' she said, when David had finally disengaged himself from Kevin and had popped upstairs to find her, 'what do you think?'

'Yes – um – it's not bad. Bit more than we had budgeted.'

'I know. But don't you have that feeling about it?' She paused, trying to think of a way she could put over what she felt, without annoying him. 'They say that you always know straight away – within the first couple of minutes – like with people.'

'Well it's probably the best we've seen so far.' He perched on the windowsill and took a calculator from his shirt pocket.

She crossed the room and stood beside him, staring out over the lawn, and listening to the tap-tap-tap of his fingers on the keypad. It would have been good to see him get excited about something, she thought, just for once.

A rainbow had arched its way over the treetops; the colours were starting to leach away, like a painting that had been left out in the rain. Isabel could just make out the red and the orange, and the blues that were fast disappearing into the blue of the sky.

'I used to believe in that pot of gold at the end of a rainbow,' she said. 'I remember, once, going to look for it with my father. We walked and walked, but the rainbow just kept getting further and further away.' She laughed. 'I think I cried because I was so disappointed.'

'Well, there's no such thing is there? It's an optical illusion. Didn't they teach you that at school?' He still hadn't looked up.

'Well, I know that now – '

He had taken off his tie and she could see the end of it sticking out from his trouser pocket. It was blue with white dots, one that she liked. She worried that it would be crushed by the time he got back to work; she thought about taking it from his pocket and folding it, carefully, into a neat roll, but he would tell her to stop fussing. So she didn't. He seemed tired, and she felt sorry for having a go at him earlier. She reached out her hand and rested it on his shoulder, letting her fingers stray to the hair at the back of his neck. He had let it grow again and it was curling over the edge of his shirt collar. She picked up one of the curls and twisted it round her finger; it felt dry, brittle.

She cast back to the day they had decided to buy a house. It had been a Sunday morning, they were at his flat, sitting up in bed with the newspapers; she remembered that much. But whose idea had it been? However many times she had been over it in her mind, she couldn't recall what had been said – or who had said it first. The next thing she knew they were discussing mortgage arrangements, filling in forms. She was amazed at how easy it had all been and how quickly, it seemed to her, they had come to this life-changing decision. She had thought there might be a certain amount of angst about whether they were doing the right thing, or at least some sort of serious discussion about 'the relationship'. But there had been none of that. The moving-walkway that they each, for their own separate reasons, had been so keen to step onto, had taken them, surely and swiftly, to the very next stop.

David had stopped tapping on his calculator. He stood up, leaving her arm to dangle idly by her side.

'Well –' he began to pace up and down the room, 'we know we can get a bigger mortgage than we need, and we know we can pay it back – as long as neither of us has problems getting tenants. But it is a risk – that's all I'm saying.' He turned to look at her. 'Are you prepared to take the risk?'

'David – if all else fails we can sell the flats.'

'Er, I don't think . . .'

'Well I can sell mine.'

Neither of them had ever said as much, but Isabel did wonder whether their decision to hold onto their own flats for the time being was less about being financially astute and more about being cautious – in case things didn't work out. But she knew that she would gladly sell her flat, if it meant getting this house.

'At least we know we have that option anyway,' she said. 'Therefore it isn't much of a risk at all.'

'Well, that's up to you, of course.' He looked at his watch then back at her. 'This isn't a bad room, you know.' He glanced round once more before going out onto the landing. She saw him peer through the door into the bathroom.

'Good size,' he shouted over his shoulder. 'Beth says it's something to . . .'

'Beth?' she echoed. The thought of him having discussed it with his sister knocked hard against her earlier enthusiasm. What the hell had Beth got to do with this? She willed herself not to react.

'Yeah – I faxed over the details last night. She was asking how we were getting on. Says it's always a bonus to have two decent bathrooms – a useful feature when you want to sell on.'

Isabel turned her back on his voice and concentrated her thoughts on the garden instead. A tree at the far end was starting to bear fruit; she couldn't tell what it was, but the thought of owning her own fruit tree made her feel very grown-up all of a sudden. She wished she didn't get so irritated whenever David mentioned his sister. She rested her forehead against the window. It was too tall for an apple tree – maybe it was a pear. It wasn't that she didn't like Beth – they had got on perfectly well together on the couple of occasions they had met – but why did he still have to consult his big sister about everything he did? Wasn't it time he moved on?

She straightened up and took a final look around the room. This one would make a perfect study, she thought; and she could see herself sitting at a desk placed just where she was standing, in front of the window, writing her novel. It was so peaceful here, at the back of the house. The garden's lush greenness seemed to reflect back onto the walls, giving the room a serenity all of its own. The recent rainfall had washed away all traces of city dust from the plants and trees; everything looked refreshed and new. A new beginning.

They left Kevin to lock up, and set off together towards the tube station. Isabel had hoped to stay a while longer; she wanted to wander around, maybe have a coffee somewhere, get a feel for the area. She linked her arm through his. 'I loved it. Didn't you?'

He was walking quickly, his footsteps tapping out a steady beat on the pavement. She was having trouble keeping up with him.

'And did you notice?' she went on, struggling to get her breath, 'that was the first one we've seen where they haven't ripped out all the original features – you know – like the sash windows and dado rails and . . . Hey, I wonder if there are real floorboards that we could strip down. I don't suppose you noticed did you? I didn't think to look.'

At last, they were forced to come to a stop while they waited to cross the road. David pulled a tube pass from his pocket.

'Do you have time for a quick coffee before you go? she asked.

'No, I've got to get back.'

'But don't we need to talk about it?'

'We'll talk tonight.' He looked at his watch and frowned. 'Look, I've really got to be going.' He leant towards her and kissed the top of her head. 'You're coming round to mine tonight aren't you? Don't forget your key, I might be a bit late.'

He turned to go, but Isabel caught hold of his hand. 'I think we should go for it – don't you?'

'Yeah – okay – if you want. Whatever you decide – it's fine by me.' He took his pass out of its red plastic wallet and started to move towards the ticket barrier. 'But if you do want it, you should ring Kevin this afternoon – let him know – before anyone else goes to see it. And that damn name will have to go. Can't stand houses with names.'

She waited in the station foyer until he had got into the lift and the doors had closed behind him. Then she turned and walked back towards the house.

As soon as she got back to her flat, Isabel rang Kevin to tell him that they wanted to make an offer on the house. She then dialled the number for David's office. While she was waiting for someone to pick up the phone at the other end, Charlie jumped onto her lap. She smoothed down the fur on top of his head, feeling the vibration of his purr against the palm of her hand.

'Hello – David Adamson's phone.'

The female voice was unexpected.

'Oh – hello – is he there?'

'No, David is in a meeting right now. Could I take a message?'

Isabel cupped her hand over Charlie's skull and flattened down his ears, and suddenly she was looking at David's Uncle Peter – wide, benign face; broad nose; bald as a coot – but minus the glasses. She had to stifle a giggle.

'No, it's okay, thanks. I'll speak to him later.'

She replaced the receiver and swept Charlie into her arms, pressing him against her cheek. 'You are going to have a lovely new garden to explore, and lots of rooms to hide in,' she whispered into his fur. But as soon as she loosened her grip, he jumped to the floor and, with a nonchalance that was his own speciality, launched into his washing routine.

Isabel wandered into the kitchen. She had bought a bottle of Champagne at the shop next to the station. If she didn't get it out of the fridge now, and put it by the front door, she would probably leave it behind.

∞

7.15 pm

L ee sat on his case to see if that would make a difference. It
didn't. He would have to leave something behind. He pulled
open the lid and caught one of the books that slid out, before it
hit the floor.

'Chi Wan – '

His friend was busy extracting cubes of ice from a tray he had
found in Lee's freezer compartment.

'What?'

'Want some of these books?'

'Yeah – okay,' Chi Wan replied over his shoulder. He continued
bashing the ice tray against the side of the fridge.

'What about some sweaters?'

'Yeah – yeah. Everything gratefully received.'

A piece of ice flew out and skidded across the floor. Chi Wan
picked it up and chucked it into a glass.

'Hey, I don't want that one,' Lee shouted. 'I know what's been
on that floor.'

'Tough,' Chi Wan replied. 'It's in your glass.' He extracted a
couple more cubes, put them into a second glass, then splashed in
some whisky. 'I'll put yours here then.'

'Good – good.' Lee was zipping up the case again. 'I've finished
now. I can close it.' He picked up a padlock from the floor and
fixed it to the case. 'Let's hope I can lift it.'

He straightened up then walked to the table to get his drink.
'Yam seng,' he said, raising his glass towards his friend. 'And
thanks for bringing this round.'

'It's your going home present. Can't let you go without a good
send off. Cheers.'

They clinked glasses.

Lee took a large swig. It was a while since he'd drunk whisky. The liquid burnt his mouth and made him cough.

Chi Wan laughed. 'Can't take your booze?'

'Oh yeah – I can drink you under the table.' But the effort of speaking made him cough even more and he was in danger of spilling the contents of his glass.

'Hey, don't waste it,' Chi Wan said. 'That bottle was expensive.' He picked up one of the books that Lee had taken out of his case and started to leaf through it. 'Mmm – this is a good one. Are you sure you don't want it?'

'No, not sure – but it won't be any use where I'm going.'

'True – but what about when you come back?'

'Well, you can give it back to me then. I know where you live.'

'Ah – but I might have shifted.'

'I'll find you.'

Chi Wan picked up two more books and studied their covers. 'Hey, these are great. Thanks.'

'Welcome.'

'So what are you going to do when you get there? Have you decided?'

Lee scratched his head. 'Dunno. Get a job in KL. Work in a restaurant.'

'What? A waiter?'

'No! Cooking.'

'Cooking?' Chi Wan sounded incredulous. 'A chef?'

'Why so shocked?'

'Don't you need to be able to cook first? You can't just give them pot noodle you know.'

Lee grinned at his friend. 'I've done it before.'

'Hard work.'

'Don't care – just need to save enough so I can come back.'

Chi Wan stood up and reached for the whisky bottle. He topped up their glasses. 'Can't you get a job here? You'd earn more.'

'Can, yes, but what's the use? If I can't afford to eat.'

'True.'

'And in KL I'll stay with my mum, and my sister. Anyway, I don't think I'm allowed to work here.'

Chi Wan shrugged. 'Allowed? Who cares? You know Benny Liu? He got a job at Poons.'

Lee pulled a face.

'And Jefferi Tan – he works in this club in West End. So how long do you think it'll take?'

'What?'

'To save enough.'

Lee studied his glass for a moment, swirling the remaining whisky round and round until it moved on its own: a miniature whirlpool. 'A year? Maybe. They'll keep my place for a year. Don't know if I can have longer. Just need to make sure I've enough for three more years, without using up all my savings. I've got plans for those.' He rubbed at his forehead, distracted for a moment by the sound of a car stereo blasting though the open window. 'I didn't know it would be so expensive to live here. And I hadn't planned on this extra year.'

'Yeah – that was a bummer.'

'But you knew you were going to be here for four years – before you got here.'

'Guess so.'

'It was a big shock for me. No-one had told me about any foundation programme. I thought I was going straight to the degree course. Some agent in KL said my high school certificate was okay.'

'Poor show.'

'Then when I got here, they told me it wouldn't transfer, or something. I suppose all the grades are different now. It was ages ago when I left school.'

'Yeah – I forgot – you are the granddaddy in our class.'

'Ha-ha. Very funny.' Lee downed the rest of his whisky and put the glass on the table.

Chi Wan immediately filled it up again. 'How old are you anyway?' he asked, laughing. 'You still look good, for someone so ancient.'

'Thirty-three,' Lee replied. 'And you're too young to drink this stuff. Shouldn't you be in bed by now?'

'Nah – she's out with her friends tonight.'

'So what happened with you, then?' Lee continued, when

they had both stopped laughing. 'Didn't your school do British exams?'

'Yeah. I did A-levels. But not the right ones.'

'But it's alright for you, you've got rich parents.' Lee smiled at Chi Wan to let him know that he was joking.

'No I haven't. I . . .' He stopped when he noticed that Lee was grinning at him. 'No – really. My gran and my auntie put in for me to come to the UK. That's why I have to work hard. I can't let them down – specially my gran.' He picked up the books Lee had given him and put them on the floor next to his rucksack. 'Before I get too drunk and leave them behind,' he explained. 'Funny, isn't it, how back home they all have this thing about UK education being so bloody wonderful. But we know better, don't we?' He banged his glass onto the table making Lee jump. 'It's load of bollock.'

Lee looked away trying to keep a straight face, amused by his friend's choice of words.

'You're lucky anyway,' Chi Wan went on. 'I'm not going anywhere for at least another year. Fuck this place. They only want our money. It's all a big swizz if you ask me.'

Lee hoped that Chi Wan wasn't right; but it was a popular theme amongst some of the students in their class. And he had to admit that he, too, had been disappointed so far. He wasn't sure if he had learnt anything that he didn't already know – apart from some useful jargon. It was all just common sense. But he needed the bit of paper at the end, so he could move on through the system and get another bit of paper. Those bits of paper were what counted – particularly with the people he needed on his side. 'Well,' he said, 'it should be better at LSE. That has a good reputation.'

'Let's see,' Chi Wan replied. 'Don't bank on it.' He ran a hand through his hair, leaving tufts of it standing upright, making him look as if he had had a shock. 'Hey, when you have stopped messing around in the kitchens of KL – poisoning everyone – I'll be a year higher than you – your senior.'

'True. Then you can help me with my assignments.'

'Ha-ha. If you want to fail.'

'So what are you going to do for the next couple of weeks? Laze about on your backside?'

'No. Me and Ginny are going to Birmingham to stay with her mum and dad for a few days.'

'Ah. Be careful,' Lee shook his head in mock disapproval. 'Sounds serious. Do they approve?'

'What? Of me? Of course. I can be charming when I want to be.'

'But their daughter's boyfriend, a Chink!'

'Nah – they like me. Every time I go, I take flowers and chocs for the mum, and a bottle of booze for the dad. And I get fed like crazy. Ah – it's the good life.' He poured himself some more whisky and pushed the bottle towards Lee. 'Come on – we've got to finish it.'

'Oh God,' groaned Lee.

'I'm not taking it back home with me.'

'Ha – then it will stay here, for the next poor sod who gets this room.'

Chi Wan took back the bottle and poured Lee another measure. 'Anyway,' he said suddenly, 'did you ever find that girl you were looking for? You know, when you first came here?'

Disconcerted by this unexpected turn in the conversation, Lee shot his friend a glance – to see if he was joking around – then immediately wished that he hadn't moved his head so quickly.

He was puzzled by the question. He didn't remember telling anyone about her. But Chi Wan looked completely serious for once. The problem was that Lee could see two of him: two Chi Wans, two heads bent to one side; both looking at him, both waiting for a reply. He picked up his glass to take a drink, then thought better of it and pushed it to one side, slumping in his seat. Suddenly he felt very weary. All he wanted to do now was to go to bed. He had a very early start in the morning.

He toyed with the circle of jade he wore around his neck. 'No,' he replied. 'I didn't. I tried – but I gave up in the end.'

It was almost two o'clock in the morning by the time Lee got to bed. He wasn't even sure it was worth the trouble. He had to be up by six the next morning. As soon as he lay down and closed his eyes, the room started to spin. He had to sit up and switch on the light to stop himself being sick.

He wasn't aware of falling asleep – only of waking up the next morning with the worst headache he had ever had.

He made a promise to himself that he would never drink whisky again.

PART FOUR

Malaysia
July 1991

∞

23 July 1991
Kampung Teluk

I sabel finished her coffee then carefully folded her napkin and placed it by the side of her plate. It was probably a good thing he hadn't shown up, she thought. He had either forgotten about their excursion to the waterfall, or maybe someone had given him some job or other that he couldn't get out of. She pushed back her chair and stood up. She could have her day by the sea after all.

It was as if he had been watching, and waiting: he appeared from nowhere.

'Good morning, Miss Eezobel. Are you ready to go?'

Ah. The beach would have to wait, she thought. 'Please – just call me Isabel,' she said.

'Is-a-bel.'

She saw the way his smile reached his eyes, creasing them at the corners.

He opened the fridge behind the bar and pulled out two bottles of water; he thrust them into the rucksack he was holding.

'After you.' He followed her down the steps and into the shimmering morning heat.

She was conscious of his presence behind her, the sound of his feet on the gravel path in time with her own. She could hear dogs barking in the distance; the air was spiced with wood smoke.

It didn't take long to reach the edge of the forest and just ahead of them now were the majestic trees with their huge, buttressed roots looking like long, pale limbs. As they approached, Isabel was reminded of entering a cathedral for the very first time, taking in its awe-inspiring vastness, being humbled by its magnificence. The air hung still and heavy, and the musty-sweet scent of rotting bark rose up from the forest floor. And for a moment everything was silent. The whole jungle cacophony had ceased, as if the inhabitants of the forest were holding their breath in anticipation.

The path was just wide enough now for the two of them to walk side by side, and Isabel wondered if she should try to make some sort of conversation. But as the minutes unfolded, the silence threatened to become too wide a channel to cross. She glanced sideways at him. He was looking down at the ground, seemingly lost in his own thoughts; his straight, dark hair had formed a curtain across his eyes. The top two buttons of his shirt were undone and as he leant forwards she saw what was attached to the chain around his neck: it was a pale green circle of jade, with a single Chinese character at its centre.

She had taken her eyes from the path for a second; the next thing she knew she was stumbling forward. Her foot had caught in a piece of root protruding from the forest floor.

An arm shot out to steady her.

'Careful!'

She would have fallen had he not reached out to stop her.

'Are you all right?' His hand was still on her arm. It lingered, for the briefest of moments, before moving away.

'Yes – sorry. I mean – yes, thank you.'

He carried on walking.

'I'm too clumsy,' she added, falling back into step with him.

He didn't reply. But what did she expect him to say? It was true. She was clumsy. It was because of her height, they had told her. She had grown too fast. 'Will ye never stop growing?' her mother used to say (she would be kneeling on the floor busy with her tape measure and the red Oxo tin where she kept her pins, as she lengthened yet another of Isabel's skirts). Of course, she had stopped growing, eventually. But she was still tall, and she had felt it keenly these last two weeks. Apparently, her bones were too big as well – or so her mother had told Mrs Mackie (Isabel had heard them chatting over the garden fence). 'It's a shame,' she had said. 'Isabel's big-boned, you know. Got it from her father.'

They were getting deeper into the forest now, and the canopy had become a dense, green roof; just a few flecks of light managed to penetrate through, dotting the ground with tiny pools of sunlight.

Isabel recognized the point where the path started to slope, gently at first but she knew it would soon get steeper. She needed some water, and thought she might ask for some. Then she realized that she didn't know his name.

She rehearsed the sentence in her head before breaking the silence.

'I'm sorry, but I don't know your name.'

'My name?' He sounded surprised that she had asked. 'It's Lee.'

'Lee?'

'Yes. Lee Kim Cheng.'

'So, Lee is your family name?'

'That is correct.' He tipped his head to one side, evidently amused by what she had just said. 'But everybody calls me Lee. Only my mother, and my sister, call me Kim Cheng.'

She tried to picture him with a mother and sister: two dainty Chinese women, one young, one older, and Lee towering over them, his arms around their shoulders.

'And you are Is-a-bel Waines – Raines,' he corrected himself. 'I should improve my English,' he said, laughing. 'But I keep on practising. I . . .'

He had stopped walking and was holding out his hand, as a sign for her to stop too. He put one finger to his lips. Isabel looked down the path to where he was pointing, but she couldn't see anything. What had he seen? There was nothing there.

Then, there was movement and something ran into the undergrowth; she caught a glimpse of its thin little legs and bony rear end as it trotted away. It looked like a small dog, no more than a foot high.

'What was that?' she whispered.

'*Kancil*,' he replied. 'A mouse-deer.'

'A deer?' she queried. It was too small; she couldn't believe it had been a deer.

'Yes, they are common here, but not easy to spot. They usually don't come out in the day.'

'But it was so tiny.'

'It's true. So they are not deer – not really.'

Just as she had suspected. He had been joking. That couldn't possibly have been a deer she had seen.

'They are from the camel family,' he added.

She laughed. 'Camel? No, I don't think you mean camel!' He was mixing up his animal names. She looked at him. He was grinning.

'You don't believe me do you?' He shook his head and carried on walking. 'But it is true.'

'I . . . Er, I don't know.' Was he making fun of her? 'I've never heard of such an animal.'

'We have a story here in Malaysia about this animal,' he continued. 'There was a prince who was out hunting with his dog. They came across a *kancil* and the dog tried to chase it. But the little thing was not afraid. In fact, it turned around and chased the dog instead. The prince was very impressed by its bravery, and he decided to build a town, right there, on that very spot. And . . .' He stopped speaking and looked at her. 'What's wrong? You don't believe me again?'

'No, no it's not that. Your English is incredibly good.' She had blurted it out before she could stop herself.

'You think so? Hmm, that's good.' He was rummaging in his bag now. 'Funny story isn't it?' He handed her a bottle of water and opened another for himself. 'You know that town,' he went on, 'in the story – it's called Malacca. That's where I was born.'

'Oh, I've been there,' she said quickly, glad of the opportunity to switch topics. 'Well, sort of. I went for the day – from KL. It's nice, I liked it.'

'I haven't been there for a long time. My mother lives in KL now – with my sister.' He held out his hand. 'Shall I take it?'

She gave him back the bottle and they continued walking.

The track had veered to the right and was getting progressively steeper; the soft matting of dead roots and leaves had given way to loose stones and smooth rock. There was no option but to walk in single file, with Lee leading the way.

Isabel kept her eyes fixed on his feet, watching where he stepped and making sure she took the exact same route over the rocks, aware, also, of his sun-browned legs and the well-used muscles which tightened with each step he took.

She paused for breath. 'I don't recognize this. I don't think I came this way yesterday.'

He had just taken a giant step up onto a platform of rock. He stopped now, and turned to face her. 'This used to be a small waterfall once, but the water goes another way now. We need to follow this track to the top. It's not far. Are you okay?'

Isabel wiped sweat from her face with the back of her hand. She looked up to where he was standing. She wasn't sure if she could make it in one go. 'Yes, fine – thanks.'

'Need help?' He leant down, and held out his hand.

She reached up, and felt his skin beneath her fingertips as their hands locked together. And then, before she had time to think about anything else, she was there, standing next to him, shoulder to shoulder, on the rock.

He loosened his grip and their hands moved apart.

'Can you hear it?'

Isabel listened. It was the sound of water crashing down from a great height. As they climbed on, the noise became louder and louder until there it was, in front of them, long silver ribbons of it pouring over the glistening rocks, then pausing to form a natural pool before cascading off again into the shadowy green depths of the jungle. The waterfall.

Lee dropped his bag onto the ground and sat on a large stone, his feet inches from the eddying water. Isabel chose a spot nearby. As the cooling spray hit her skin, she couldn't help thinking about the effect it would be having on her hair.

Lee took out the bottles of water and stood them upright in the pool, propping a stone against them so they wouldn't fall over. 'Chilled water. Ready in five minutes.'

Isabel stretched out her hand and let the stream of water flow over her fingers.

'The air is fresher up here,' he said. 'Easier to breathe.'

'It's lovely,' she replied. 'And thank you for showing me the way. I would never have found it by myself.' She pressed a cold, wet palm onto her burning shoulders. 'I hope it didn't cause you any problems,' she went on, 'taking the morning off work, I mean.'

He was looking at her, his head tilted to one side, his eyes wide, enquiring. Then his face relaxed into a broad grin.

'No. Not a problem,' he replied. 'I think it will be fine.'

*

They sat in silence for a while, both focussed on the relentless torrent of water plunging over the rocks and splashing into the pool in front of them. From time to time, a lone bird would call out, its cry ringing through the trees; sometimes the notes would be echoed in another part of the forest, and then something would flap about, hidden within the frenzy of greens that made up the jungle. After that there would be silence once more – apart from the sound of the waterfall.

Soon another noise started up, gonging out from amongst the branches above their heads. Isabel looked up, trying to spot what it was.

'That's a hornbill,' said Lee. 'You won't see it, it will be high up – high in the trees.'

As if in response, the goose-like sound came again, becoming faster and faster until, finally, it degenerated into a strange and manic cackle which reverberated around the canopy. Isabel found herself laughing back at it. She couldn't resist; its gaiety was infectious.

Lee seemed amused. 'You should come back next month,' he said. 'When the forest will be full of them. Ah, look –' he had spotted something else now. 'There goes a minuvet.'

Isabel looked to where he was pointing and saw a bird with luminous red feathers. It had found a tiny spot of sunlight and had perched there to preen itself, before flying back into the shelter of the trees. When Isabel turned back to Lee, she saw that he had stood up and was making his way over a bridge of rocks to the other side of the pool. She watched him crouch down to fish an object from the water, and then another. He carried the two rusty cans to where he had been sitting and dumped them next to his bag.

'They should take their rubbish back with them?'

'Yes, it's a shame,' she said. 'Such a beautiful place, and then tourists come along and spoil everything.'

'It's not always tourists,' he said, shaking his head. 'It's local people too. They don't care either.' He pulled a crumpled plastic bag from his rucksack and put the cans inside, along with their own empty water bottles.

'But I'm a tourist too,' she added.

'And if there were not tourists, I wouldn't earn any money,' he said wryly. 'But here, it is not so bad. In some places, like the big national parks, it's lot, lot worse.' He picked up his bag and slung it over his shoulder. 'All those people tramping everywhere – they will destroy it. Hai – but I could go on about this all day.' He pushed a hand through his hair and grinned at her. 'Don't worry. I won't.'

As she strolled back from the beach later that afternoon, Isabel found herself looking out for the different types of trees Lee had shown her in the forest. She hadn't realized how old some of them were, and how precariously they survived. She stepped onto the bridge that crossed the mangrove swamp, and studied the mass of roots twisting and pushing themselves into the mud. She watched a tiny crab scuttle sideways and disappear down a hole – body first, claws last.

What was it he had said? That thousands of plant and animal species were lost each year, because of the logging? She tried to pin down the conversation – but her mind was already wandering elsewhere. Perhaps she could ask him tomorrow.

'Oh God,' she moaned. 'Tomorrow.'

He had caught her off guard. She had asked if there were any shops tucked away in Teluk, or whether it was an easy walk to the next village. An innocent question. Then what? Hadn't he laughed at her? Not unkindly – but with that amused look on his face – the one she had noticed before – when his eyes sparkled mischievously, and the dimple appeared in his cheek. That was when he had told her that all the shops were in the town. And as there was one road on the island – which didn't go anywhere, except to some big resort – the only way to get there was by boat.

And then he offered to take her. Tomorrow.

∞

Later that evening, Isabel made her way to the Gula House. As she arrived, Els and Pieter were getting up from their table.

Els beckoned her over. 'Come and have a drink with us when you have had your dinner. We are going to sit in the lounge.'

Pleased to have caught up with them at last, Isabel set off towards her table, acknowledging the three people she had seen yesterday.

The woman beamed back at her. 'Hello there,' she said. 'Did you have a good swim? We saw you down on the beach, on your own.'

'Yes. It was lovely. I . . .'

'You must come with us next time. Mustn't she Rob?'

Rob set down his fork and nodded enthusiastically.

'We've found a nice beach, down the way there,' the woman continued. She gesticulated vaguely in the direction of the sea. 'It has all the facilities – you know?'

Rob was still nodding.

'It was in the book.' The young man sitting with them tapped on the cover of a book parked on the table next to his plate. 'The bible.'

'And this is Phil,' said the woman, beaming at Phil. 'He's from . . . Where's it again dear?'

'Brockport. Upstate New York,' replied Phil.

'And I'm Sandra, and this is my husband Rob. We're not from New York.'

'How do you do?' said Rob, holding out his hand. 'Robert Wilkes.'

They wore matching silver rings.

'Hello, I'm Isabel,' she replied, shaking his hand. It was large and moist. She was anxious to get away before they asked her to join them. 'Better go and eat, I think. See you later.'

As she crossed the room, she glanced around to see who was serving dinner this evening. Set Yen was there, and Amir, but there was no sign of Lee.

After dinner she joined Els and Pieter.

'Isabel! Hi!' Els jumped up to greet her. 'Come and sit.' She patted the jewel-like cushions on the sofa then turned towards the bar where Set Yen was standing and waved an empty beer bottle, holding up three fingers of her other hand at the same time. Set Yen nodded demurely.

Els bounced onto the sofa next to Pieter. 'Oh God – I hope that isn't a rude sign over here.' She re-attempted the three-finger gesture, screwing up her face as she manipulated her fingers into different permutations.

'I'm sure it isn't.' Isabel reassured her.

Els slipped her feet from a pair of white moccasins and curled her long legs under her, snuggling against Pieter's arm. 'So – we haven't seen you around. What have you been doing?'

'Oh, not a lot. Just exploring, and swimming. It's lovely here isn't it?

'Yes, it is very peaceful,' Pieter replied. 'We like it very much.'

'I had the whole beach to myself this afternoon,' Isabel continued.

'Perfect,' said Els. 'Have you been to the tiny island?'

Isabel had secretly hoped that no-one else went there. 'Yes, I walked across when the tide was out,' she replied. 'I was hoping to get marooned, so I'd have to stay there for ever.'

'Aha, sounds good,' remarked Pieter. 'Do you snorkel?'

Set Yen arrived with the beers and put them on the table between the two sofas.

'No, I've never tried it.' Out of the corner of her eye, Isabel could see Sandra, Rob and Phil. They had picked up their drinks and were drifting towards them.

'Oh, you should,' said Els. 'There is this place called Coral Island. If you can get up early to catch the boat . . .'

'May we join you?' Rob was hovering behind an empty armchair.

But Phil was already on the sofa, next to Isabel. She moved up, as if to give him more space, even though there was plenty of room for two. Sandra took the remaining armchair, leaving Rob stranded. He wandered out to the verandah and found a wicker chair, which he proceeded to drag across the room.

'Hello. I'm Sandra and that is my husband Rob.' She raised her voice on the word Rob and Rob, who had his back turned and was still grappling with the chair, lifted a hand in response. 'And this is Phil, from America. Did you arrive today?' The entire introduction, and this last question, had been addressed to Pieter.

'No, we have been here for four . . .' Pieter looked towards Els for help, but Els had found something of interest on the back of her hand. 'No. Five days now,' he went on.

'Oh. I thought . . . well, we didn't see you at dinner last night.'

'No, she had done too much shopping.' Pieter put his arm around Els and gave her an affectionate squeeze. 'We had to eat in the town,' he went on, 'until I had recovered. Then we had to wait for the last boat.'

'Oh, do tell us if you know any good places – to eat, I mean,' said Sandra. 'We like to have a change – you know. But you should have called them – here – they would have sent a boat for you. Wouldn't they Rob?' She turned to her husband for confirmation.

Isabel missed Rob's reply, if there had been one. She had been distracted by some activity at the far end of the Gula House: someone was coming up the steps; she could hear voices. A large hibiscus plant was blocking her view, but in a moment she would be able to see who it was. She leant forward slightly, sensing that Phil had followed her gaze and was also looking towards the steps.

The two German men were settling themselves at a table in the dining area.

'You don't want to wait for that late boat.' Sandra was saying. 'You'll never know if it is going to come.'

The kitchen door swung open. But it was Amir. He walked over to speak to the Germans, and now the three of them were laughing about something. Isabel watched as he turned and walked back towards the kitchen, smiling to himself. The door snapped shut behind him.

'– and we did try to talk to them yesterday, didn't we Rob?'

Rob nodded.

'But they don't seem very friendly. Well, that's the problem if you go away with friends, isn't it? You never get to meet anyone else. I was telling Isabel here, we've found this other beach – it belongs to another resort – but it's much nicer than the one they have here –'

Isabel found it difficult to believe that there could be a more idyllic beach than the one on which she had idled away the afternoon, picking up shells, watching the crabs, day-dreaming, until a glorious setting sun had turned the sea a shimmering, coral pink.

'– and it's a bit more upmarket. There's more going on, more facilities and what-not.' Sandra was still talking. 'See, when we got here, and I saw that there weren't a swimming pool, I said to Rob, there's no pool. Of course there's a pool, he said – there must be. But there isn't, is there? Anyway we got the manager here to take us to the other place in their boat. He'll do that, you know. What's his name, love? Mr Yow?'

'Yo, dear. It's Yo. Gilbert Yo.'

His wife looked at him askance.

'He *told* me his name was Gilbert,' Rob protested. 'Don't they give themselves some queer names?' he added, looking round at the group, his west-country accent endowing the occasional word with long, deep burrs.

'Well they must think we can't cope with their real names, darling. It's quite sensible really.' Sandra turned back to Els. 'So, anyway, this Yo fellow took us in the boat to this other beach – we just slipped him a few whatsanames.'

'*Ringgit*,' offered Rob.

'Anyway, why don't you come along with us tomorrow? Isabel's coming. Aren't you?'

Isabel knew that all eyes were now on her. She glanced up and caught Els's raised eyebrow.

'Well, er . . .' she stuttered, 'not tomorrow. I have something arranged for tomorrow.' She hoped no-one would ask what it was.

She looked away and concentrated on her drink. She took a couple of sips; she attempted to fill her glass – although the bottle was already empty – she balanced the cap back on the top. What was she doing tomorrow? He had offered to take her to the town, that's all. They hadn't made any precise arrangements.

For the umpteenth time her eyes strayed towards the kitchen door.

And was it sensible to go off somewhere with him? Again? Mightn't he get the wrong idea?

She turned her attention once more to the conversations taking place around her. Phil was explaining how to catalogue a book. It sounded as though he worked in a library. Els was describing something they had seen on the reef yesterday. This evening, her blonde hair was free from its ponytail; as she spoke she wound strands of it round her fingers. Pieter looked on, admiringly. Their voices soon receded, and merged with the general clatter and chatter coming from the jungle behind the building; and Isabel's mind wandered back to where it had been seconds before. She did need to go to the town, it was true. But Els would certainly have offered to go with her – or even Sandra – if she had mentioned it.

'No, I don't think I could do it,' Sandra's voice now. 'I'm not a very strong swimmer, am I Rob? Anyway, what happens if the water gets in your – you know?'

Isabel could hear the sound of laughter. She spun round. There was a woman standing by the reception desk. Her tailored outfit and matching luggage hinted at money, or a penchant for designer labels. A man was struggling up the steps with another large suitcase. As he reached the top, he thudded it onto the floor. The woman giggled and clattered off a string of unintelligible words.

'Japs have arrived.' Phil had leant towards her. She felt him hiss the words into her ear; she pictured the tiny droplets of spit landing on her hair. She grimaced.

Phil took this to be a sign of assent, and started to carp on about tourists – Japanese tourists in particular; it sounded like a speech he had rehearsed many times. 'They're like fuckin' sheep,' she heard him say. But she was trying to listen to what was going on at the desk. She could hear that the Japanese woman was speaking in broken English now, speaking to someone else.

Was it Lee? It had to be.

Phil was now in full flow. 'Travel in packs. Don't have the sense to go anyplace on their own. I don't get it.'

Isabel nodded. She didn't want to be rude, but he really was a bit of a bore. Still, all it seemed to require was an occasional nod or 'aha'.

She moved her head so she could just about see what was going on behind her. Lee was in the dining area; he was showing the couple to a table. She hoped Phil would notice that these two Japanese people were travelling alone. Somehow she doubted it.

'It's not like being in the city,' Els was saying, 'always chasing time. Here, time just follows you around, at your own pace.'

Now Lee was handing out menus; he was saying something; the other two were nodding their heads.

'Where do you live Isabel?' This was Rob.

She relaxed back into the sofa's cushions. 'In London,' she replied. 'North London – do you know it at all?'

He shook his head. 'We don't get up there very much.'

She watched Lee walk towards the bar. So far he hadn't looked across to where they were sitting.

'It's a large hotel, just down the coast,' she heard Phil say. He had his guidebook open in front of her and was stabbing with his finger at one of the pages. 'We should go there for a drink – it says there's a nightclub. If we all went together, we could get Yo to bring us back.'

Lee was still at the bar, pouring out drinks. Should she go and speak to him? To let him know that she hadn't forgotten about tomorrow. Unless he was hoping that she had.

She kept her eyes fixed on him, waiting for him to look up, so she could at least acknowledge him. But he didn't look up – not even when he had finished at the bar and taken the drinks to the Japanese couple. He stood at their table for a few moments more, then turned and disappeared into the kitchen.

Sandra had told them that she had a headache, and had gone to bed. After escorting her to their chalet, Rob returned and insisted on ordering another round of drinks.

'She's 'ad too much sun,' he said, walking back from the bar with two bowls of nuts. He put the bowls on the table, picked out a large nut and examined it. 'She likes these does Sandra.' He chuckled, then popped it into his mouth. 'Oh well,' he said, chewing vigorously, 'she'll be right as rain tomorrow – all set for another day on the beach.'

Isabel was deep in conversation with Els when she heard the approaching rattle of bottles. She looked up, smiling.

It was Amir. He grinned back at her.

Rob had certainly become more talkative since Sandra had left, and was keeping them entertained with stories of his delivery business in Devizes.

'You should go on the stage,' Isabel told him, clutching her stomach which was aching from having laughed so much. 'You'd make a brilliant stand-up comedian.' She reached for her drink and eased herself back into the cushions. As she lifted the glass to her lips she spotted Lee. He was relaxing against the back of a chair, arms folded in front of him, talking to the four Germans. She had a feeling that he'd been watching her; but when she looked towards him he glanced away.

∞

It had rained heavily during the night and droplets of water continued to fall from the trees, striking the vegetation beneath with the rhythm of a slowly ticking clock, making the leaves shiver and jerk like the mechanical displays in a toyshop window. The warmth of the sun had not yet dispersed the dawn mists, but the sky was almost ready to turn a perfect, picture-book blue. It was going to be a hot day.

Somewhere nearby a cockerel crowed, and further off, perhaps in the village, a dog was barking. Concealed in the undergrowth, countless cicadas yammered and droned; their volume turned to its highest level.

By the time Isabel reached the steps to the Gula House, the thin cotton of her blouse was clinging to her back. She dabbed at the fine layer of sweat that had formed at the back of her neck, under her hair.

She spotted him straight away. He was standing on the other side of the room, with Set Yen. Their heads were bent together over something he was holding; they were both laughing.

She paused, embarrassed, thinking she should turn and go back, wishing her sandals didn't make such a noise on the wooden slats. But he had looked up. He had seen her.

She saw him speak to Set Yen, before crossing towards her. He looked anxious, she thought. He was going to tell her that he hadn't managed to get another day off, after all. And yet he didn't look as if he was dressed for work; he was wearing shorts and flip-flops, and a bright blue cotton shirt. Perhaps he had other plans. She was glad she hadn't brought her bag or purse with her. At least it didn't look as though she were expecting to go somewhere.

As he approached, a cautious smile spread across his face.

'Good morning, Isabel. I wasn't sure if . . . If you were going to come.' His eyes were sharp, alert, like a bird's, darting over her face, looking for clues. 'You still want to go shopping?'

She half-nodded, half-shrugged. It was all she could manage.

'It's just . . . We should leave quite soon. To catch the boat. But come and have some breakfast first.'

'I'm sorry, I didn't realize – about the boat, I mean.' She had assumed they would be going in the motorboat, the one that belonged to Buah Lodge. Wasn't that why he had offered to take her? 'I don't need breakfast – really. If we have to go now. It's okay.'

But Set Yen had already appeared with a basket of bread and some coffee.

'Thanks,' Lee said to Set Yen, before turning to Isabel. 'I'll be back in about fifteen minutes.'

She ate a piece of bread and gulped down some coffee; now she needed time to go back to her room for her purse.

One day, she told herself, I'll stop making my life so complicated.

A rusty, but doughty ferry had arrived and was in the process of turning round: it bobbed and clunked, irritably, and belched out thick, black smoke as it laboured to reverse in. Lee and Isabel had just arrived too, but they still needed to walk the length of the jetty. Isabel was out of breath. It was too hot to rush around like this, she thought.

The jetty shambled across the beach then stretched out precariously over the water. Standing at its end was a cluster of people waiting for the boat: four or five women with headscarves pinned at their throats, their heads together in quiet conversation; a couple of men pulling contemplatively on thin, hand-rolled, cigarettes. A handful of children, unimpeded by what looked like their party-clothes, were running around the women's legs, playing hide-and-seek behind the ankle-length skirts. As Lee and Isabel approached, one little girl abandoned her friends and bounded towards them, her small head and nut-brown limbs poking out from a somewhat impractical white dress, replete with nylon frills and bows and several sizes too big by the look of it. She caught Lee by the hand and pulled him to the edge of the walkway where they remained for a few minutes, crouched down, heads bent over some mysterious treasure. Isabel saw him dip into his pocket and then press something into the tiny hand. Shrieking with pleasure, the girl ran back to the group of women, palm held out, to show them what she had been given.

Abandoned now, Lee stood up and returned to where Isabel was waiting. 'One of my neighbours,' he said, shaking his head. 'Too much energy.'

The boat had moored and was rising and falling in the water, creaking and groaning each time it made contact with the jetty. It was time to get on.

Isabel approached, hoping she could manage it, without making a fool of herself. She hung back and watched the others board. The children went first, bundled up and lifted over the side, into the obliging hands of some passengers already on the boat. Next went the women. In a stately fashion, they gathered their skirts around their legs and picked their way down the steps leading from the jetty to the boat, before being heaved on by the waiting crew. Baskets and boxes followed. Then it was Isabel's turn. She negotiated the steps and, ignoring the outstretched hands, leapt onto the boat, colliding with the person waiting to help her. Lee followed, swinging himself down and into the boat, in one swift movement.

'Let's go up,' he said.

They climbed the narrow iron staircase and emerged on the upper deck. It was full, and noisy with the yattering of so many conversations happening at once and the occasional crate of squawking chickens. Most people had managed to find seats – on benches, on boxes, on bundles – some carried baskets of fruit or vegetables, others nursed paper-wrapped packages held together with knots of string, and in amongst this medley of animated faces, which seemed more like a social gathering and nothing like a daily commute, were four, pale-skinned young men, conspicuous by their height – the only other westerners on the boat. With their backpacks stowed between their feet, they stood at the rails, looking on, bemused.

Lee pushed his way through the crowd, checking every so often that she was there behind him, heading for a space on a bench at the front of the boat. A man wearing a white, crocheted cap edged up to make room and Isabel sat beside him on the hard seat. Smiling broadly, and exposing a couple of shiny gold teeth in the process, he reeled off a stream of singsong Malay, motioning to Lee to sit down as well. But Lee grinned and shook his head, and said something back to him, before leaning up against the rail of the deck.

Renewed activity below was a sign that the boat was about to depart. Whistles were blown, ropes were untied and flung onto the deck, where they landed with a slap. Chains clanked against the side of the boat as the anchor was hauled in and, with much yelling and shouting, the boat pulled away from the jetty. The hubbub on the top deck gathered pace too as the passengers' voices competed with the noise of the engines. Isabel leant back and closed her eyes; she emptied her mind of everything else and let the sounds fill her head, thrilled by the foreignness of it all. She knew Lee was standing nearby, and could make out his voice above the rest as he chatted with the man sitting next to her. As the boat swung round, it brought her out of the shade and into the full morning sun; she could feel the touch of its rays on her upturned face and with it came a twist of excitement. She had no idea what to expect from the day ahead, but she had a good feeling about it. Cocooned by the warmth, the gentle motion of the boat and the hum of unintelligible conversation going on around her, all the things that had been weighing on her mind began to recede and a wave of contentment spread through her.

'Dua di Batang.'

She recognized Lee's voice and, sensing some movement around her, she opened her eyes. Lee was rummaging in his pockets. He pulled out some coins and held them in the palm of his hand.

'Oh – let me – please,' she offered, struggling with the zip on her purse.

'No. No, it's done. It's nothing anyway.'

A man in a navy blue uniform tore off a couple of tickets and handed them to Lee.

'Terima kasih.'

'Sama-sama.'

'Tree-ma kasser?' Isabel tried to mimic what Lee had just said. 'What does it mean?'

'Thank you,' replied Lee. 'It means thank you.' He laughed. 'Your pronunciation is good.'

'Can I give you some money?' Isabel held out a twenty-*ringgit* note.

'Of course not,' he replied. 'Put it back. That is far too much anyway.'

She hesitated.

'It's nothing,' he went on. 'And anyway, I should have taken you in our boat, but someone had already promised it to another guest – I didn't know until this morning.'

Isabel was concerned that he'd had to go to so much effort on her behalf. 'Ter-rima-kasih,' she said, hesitantly.

'Sama-sama,' he replied. 'You're welcome. And this way, you can be like a local.'

He was right, she thought. And it was much more fun like this.

'Everyone uses the ferry to travel between villages,' he went on, 'because they are not joined together by roads. And our boat is always in demand. Your friends have it today. I thought you had gone with them.'

'My friends?'

Then it dawned on her. He was talking about Rob and Sandra, and Phil.

'No – no . . .' she stuttered, 'I only met them last night. They're not . . . I mean, they did ask me but . . . I think they've gone to another beach. But that wasn't what I wanted to do. I . . .' She wanted to explain that this was exactly what she wanted to do. She looked up. His eyes were fixed on her, waiting.

'I'm much happier doing this,' she went on. 'I don't need to be with other tourists.'

He smiled and handed her one of the tickets he was holding. 'Good. So, now we are going to Batang, a small town, near to the airport. It is the main town on the island. I hope that you will find what you want to buy.'

What did she want to buy? she asked herself now. Casual

clothes? Something to wear while she was here? And would she find anything to fit? She had tried to buy a pair of shoes in KL last week and her request for a size six and a half was met with barely-masked amusement. She hoped, too, that when they got there he would leave her alone to shop by herself. And she did wonder now why he was here at all, given that they weren't using the motorboat. He probably had an arrangement with some stall that sold tacky souvenirs? Or worse, a brother or a cousin with a shop she had to visit – 'We give you good price' – and she would end up paying silly amounts of money for things she didn't even want –

The man sitting beside her was tapping on her arm and pointing up at the sky. Four large birds, their outstretched wings glowing a deep tawny red, were circling around overhead.

'They're eagles,' said Lee. 'He wants you to see the eagles.'

The three of them watched the birds swoop and wheel and soar above the tree-covered slopes until they had disappeared from view.

The man started to chat to someone else, so Isabel got up from her seat and stood at the rail, next to Lee. The shoreline slipped by in front of them: an expanse of forest rising steeply from the water's edge or, occasionally, a long, green finger of jungle that would creep into the sea, causing the waves to lap at the tentacle-like roots protruding from the sand. Sometimes, when they rounded a corner, a beautiful cove would come into view – they were passing one now, its beach deserted; just a couple of large, black birds pecking about in the sand. A curl of wood-smoke hinted at a village, and this was revealed a few minutes later: a cluster of graceful palms; a few simple, wooden houses and an accumulation of lean-tos. A group of children were swimming nearby; they shouted and waved at the boat as it passed, squealing with delight when it sent a ripple of waves to disturb the otherwise tranquil water. And all the time, constantly in view, shadowy and imposing, was the island's one mountain, forming a striking backcloth to the fascinating moving picture show.

Isabel looked on, enthralled, while snatches of island life were played out in front of her eyes, always aware of Lee standing close by. She still couldn't understand why he had given up so much of his free time, but . . .

She jumped, as she felt a light touch on her arm – like the brush of silk against her skin.

'You were dreaming,' he said. 'But we will soon be there. We should go down now, to avoid the squash.'

Most of the other passengers had had the same thought. The upper deck was emptying, and the two of them joined the noisy throng of people making their way to the deck below. It was hot in the stairwell. The air was dense, pungent; Isabel tried to hold her breath as she was pushed along by the mass of moving bodies. A stray elbow dug into her arm, the filaments of a basket scratched against her bare leg. Now someone was pressing up against her back, as if they were steering her towards the exit; she could feel the warmth of the other body through the thin cotton of her blouse. She twisted round, ready to make some amusing remark: a pair of salt-reddened eyes squinted back at her. Lee was nowhere to be seen.

She emerged into the sun, blinking, until her pupils had adjusted to the bright light. He was waiting on the quayside. As soon as he spotted her he lifted his hand in greeting.

'Are you okay? Shall we go?' Before she had chance to reply, he was ushering her through the crowds.

There were people everywhere: unloading crates; stacking things onto trolleys, onto bicycles, and onto small, motorized scooters that sounded like lawn-mowers as they phut-phutted away with their wobbly cargo. As she followed Lee down an alleyway leading away from the bustling seafront, she glanced back at the boat. The four tourists she had noticed before were still there at the rails of the upper deck, watching the commotion down below. They would have seen her get off, she thought, might even have watched the two of them walk off towards the town; and she tried to see herself in their eyes, and wondered if they had been curious about her and Lee.

The alleyway was shady and cool, and appeared to be empty – apart from the large, yellow baskets, filled to the brim with rubbish. Open doorways revealed dimly-lit stairwells, mailboxes and electricity meters: a treacherous filigree of antiquated wires and rusting pipes. The heavy musk of burning joss sticks permeated the air, mingling with the smell of fish and rancid vegetables.

Isabel tried to keep pace with Lee. But he was striding out, as if he were in a hurry to get somewhere. At last, he slowed down to step over a large dog, asleep and stretched across his path; it had something clasped between its paws and was nuzzling it, like a child with a soft toy. A dead rat.

Lee turned. 'Sorry about that. Short cut.'

They emerged from the alleyway into a lane crammed with narrow, open-fronted shops.

'This is the shopping street,' announced Lee, pausing to look left and right before turning left into the lane.

Like the seafront it was busy with people going about their chores, but here the pace was slower, more sedate. Elderly Chinese women scuffed along in dainty slippers, some bent almost double over ancient handcarts, others carrying their daily shopping in black plastic bags; their skin, stretched like parchment across wide, angular faces, was thin, almost transparent: thin enough to see the delicate, aging bones beneath. A couple of school-girls, in crisp, clean uniforms, giggled over a bag of sweets, and veered to avoid a young woman with a baby strapped papoose-like on her back; its black, beady eyes stared out at Isabel from its inscrutable, doll-like face. Then there were the bicycles. There was one now, ridden by a young man in flip-flops, and with a baseball cap on his head; Isabel stepped aside to let him negotiate the confusion of objects spilling from the fronts of the shops. It was hard to imagine how anyone gained access to those dim, overcrowded interiors, how customers managed to squeeze past the crates of bottles piled to the roof, then the cans of paraffin and sacks of rice that littered the floor, or avoid the rows of dried fish strung up in lines, and the bunches of green bananas dangling from the ceiling.

Each establishment had its own signboard, sometimes two, and these covered a variety of languages and scripts: 'Pusat Penukaran' was wedged between 'Hiap Tai Trading Co' and 'Wong Electrical Sdn. Bhd.' (which, intriguingly, sold Chines medicines).

This was quite likely where his mother shopped, Isabel thought, unkindly, as they passed yet another place selling rolls of gaudily-dyed fabrics and dull, cotton trouser suits, along with buckets and brooms, and beach balls wrapped in plastic bags to keep off the dust. It was difficult to imagine that she would find anything here.

Most of the shops were two-storey buildings, with what seemed to be living accommodation up above. As they paused outside one to watch a man buying spices shovelled from a large, dusty tin and into a twist of newspaper, Isabel could hear the click-click-click of *mah-jongg* tiles and the clamour of raised voices coming from an open window.

'Someone's been cheating,' Lee informed her.

They had almost reached the end of the street, when Lee stopped; they were outside one of the few shops which had a glass window. Arranged on a rail next to the door, was an assortment of sarongs and brightly coloured scarves.

'We are here,' he said. 'I think this is what you want. Shall we go inside?' A wind chime jingle-jangled as he opened the door.

Worried about what she was going to find, she followed him in and closed the door behind her. With the soft click of the latch, the heat and smells and sounds of the street disappeared, as if by magic, and while her eyes adjusted to the dim light inside, things began to take shape around her. It was like an Aladdin's cave, packed full with wonderful things: sumptuous fabrics, draped over surfaces or stacked in neat piles; all sorts of clothing, in silks and cottons; bags and belts, jewellery and scarves – all in a mesmerizing array of colours. In one corner stood an electric fan, cooling the shop and stirring the dresses hanging on rails nearby.

How did he know?

A woman emerged from the dark interior behind the counter. Lee greeted her warmly in Chinese, then said to Isabel: 'This is my friend, May Ling.'

He and May Ling chatted for a moment or two, then he turned back to Isabel. 'I hope this is what you were looking for,' he said. He looked concerned.

Isabel wanted to tell him that it was exactly what she was looking for. But he had already carried on speaking.

'She says please look around – and you can try anything you like.'

While Lee was explaining this, May Ling smiled and nodded. She was tiny: slender and fragile as a little bird; her perfectly straight, black hair encased her head like a polished jet helmet. In a nearby mirror, Isabel caught sight of herself. She had scraped her hair into a ponytail, but bits of it had escaped and were hanging in tendrils around her face. Her blouse was damp with sweat and her heavy linen shorts felt tight and uncomfortable.

'You just go in there,' Lee continued. He was pointing towards a long green curtain near the back of the shop. 'I am going to disappear.' He looked at his watch. 'Would half an hour be enough for you?'

Isabel nodded.

'Don't worry about the prices,' he went on. 'Everything is negotiable.' He opened the door, letting an arc of sunlight sweep in from the street; but then he appeared to think of something else and he turned to May Ling, speaking once more in Chinese.

Isabel heard her name – 'Eez-a-bel'.

May Ling nodded energetically. '*Hăo – hăo,*' she said, before disappearing into the back of the shop.

Isabel was grateful that Lee would not be standing over her while she shopped. Even so, she felt a twinge of regret as the door closed behind him and she was left alone. She wondered where he was going.

She turned her attention back to the shop. Cautiously, she reached out to touch a dress hanging on display in the window. The blues and turquoises in its pattern reminded her of the sea and she longed to slide it over her head and feel the smooth, delicate material cool against her skin.

Feeling now like a child in a sweetshop, she flitted around, gathering up dresses, sarongs, blouses and skirts, moving from rail to rail each time something caught her eye. It was not long before she was ready to slip behind the green curtain, with an armful of things to try on.

She was standing in front of a mirror propped in the middle of the shop, when she heard the click of the door handle and the soft tinkle of wind chimes. It was Lee. She could see him, standing behind her own reflection, watching.

When she didn't turn round, he knocked softly on the back of the closed door. 'I am back again,' he said. 'How are you getting on?'

'Very well.' She turned to face him. 'And thank you. Thank you for all your help.'

He was looking at her, but he didn't speak; his face was expressionless, impassive. Now, she felt self-conscious. She wondered if she had offended him somehow.

'*Sama-sama*,' he said, eventually. And then: 'You look . . .' He paused, tugging on his ear. 'It's very . . . pretty. Yes. Very nice.'

May Ling had heard his voice and emerged from the back of the shop. They spoke together in Chinese.

'Have you chosen anything else?' Lee asked.

Isabel gestured towards a small mound of clothing draped across the counter. 'Just these.' She couldn't help laughing. 'I have never bought so many things all at once.'

May Ling was carefully picking through the clothes, folding each item, before stacking everything in a neat pile, and all the time chattering happily to Lee. Isabel was grateful that he was there to negotiate; although she would have gladly paid any asking price.

'We have agreed one hundred *ringgit*,' he said at last. 'Is that okay for you, Isabel?'

She nodded and pulled her purse from the pocket of the shorts she had been wearing. Okay? It was incredible. According to her rough calculations, that amounted to around twenty pounds.

May Ling disappeared for a moment and came back carrying a small bag. It was soft and velvety, and closed with a drawstring tie; it was the same colour as the pale apricot sand they had seen from the boat, and perfectly matched the dress Isabel now had on. May Ling said something to Lee in Chinese.

'She is going to give you the bag – as a gift,' he said.

'No – I can't take that,' Isabel replied. She had already paid so little for the clothes, she couldn't accept the bag too. On the other hand, it was just what she needed. 'I must pay for it.' She opened her purse again.

Lee placed his hand on her arm to stop her. 'It's fine. It's the normal way – really. Because you have bought a lot of things.'

Isabel wished she could thank May Ling in her own language; but all she could do was nod and smile and say 'thank you' in

English, hoping that she would be understood. May Ling smiled and nodded back.

Isabel loved the little town, the extraordinary shops, the unusual smells, the torpid heat of the narrow lanes and the constant clamour of people. She also loved the way the cool, delicate cotton of her new dress skimmed her body and brushed against her legs as she walked. Not long ago, she had wondered if she would ever be happy again; now, the world seemed like a very good place to be.

They took the long way back to the quay and as they walked Lee talked about the town, telling her something of its history, explaining how it was populated mainly by the Chinese, who ran most of the businesses there.

'This is where I come when I want a good Chinese meal. One that I haven't had to cook myself,' he added. 'You should come back on Thursday – when it's market day.'

'Ah – yes. I love markets.'

'I can believe it,' he said.

If he had offered to bring her back on Thursday, she would have agreed. But he didn't pursue the matter. In fact, he seemed distracted.

He was silent for a while then looked at his watch. 'I need to call in somewhere before I go back,' he said. 'There is a resort, just north of here – I have some business there. Then we can get the boat to Teluk. Would you mind?'

'No, of course not. It means I'll get to see more of the island.' She was pleased that the outing was going to be prolonged. She wondered what sort of business he had to attend to.

They continued to walk, side-by-side, occupied with their own thoughts. Isabel was aware of a lightness inside her heart, something she hadn't felt for a very long time. She had to admit that she was enjoying herself, wandering around with Lee – not as a tourist, but as if she were part of the real life of the island. She was surprised, too, at how easy he was to be with. He had a quiet intelligence that made her feel safe and comfortable; but above all, she sensed that, with him, she could be herself – really herself – and he wouldn't be judging her, or waiting for her to slip up.

And for the moment she was quite happy not to return to Teluk. At Buah Lodge everything would be different: Lee would go back to being the shy young man who waited on tables, and met guests from the airport; and she would have to endure the well-meaning but unwelcome interrogation from Sandra and Rob. Where had she been? What did she do? Who did she go with?

How could they possibly understand any of this?

∞

The Mayang Palace, Batang

Isabel sank into the chair, and flinched when her bare arms met the cold leather upholstery. It felt wrong being there.

She looked around the vast lobby, loathing its phoney Orientalism, breathing in its dry and insubstantial air. Despite the elegant marble pillars, the tall ferns in bronze pots, the extravagant wall hangings, it reminded her of an airport lounge: stark, impersonal, a place where people sat to pass the time. The scrupulously co-ordinated chairs and sofas were clustered around glass-topped tables, each adorned with a single, flawless orchid. And there people sat: alone, or in twos or threes, but all finely dressed, manicured and Rolexed. Some had heads bowed towards plates of food, others reclined, drink in hand, or stared into space, faces rigid with the mask of nonchalance affected by the wealthy and privileged. Voices were muted, barely audible over the genteel clink-clink of porcelain against porcelain, and the quasi-Asian music issuing from speakers hidden somewhere in the fabric of the building.

Isabel took a menu from the table in front of her. She suspected it was well past lunchtime and she was beginning to feel hungry; but the cheapest thing on offer was a sandwich – at around four pounds – that was almost as much as she had paid for the dress she was wearing. She placed the menu back on the table. Lee had said he would be back in twenty minutes. Perhaps he would want to eat something too. Not here, though.

She had spotted an arcade of shops on the other side of the lobby so she wandered over to look at the displays in the windows, amazed at the abundance of designer logos and relieved that Lee hadn't brought her here to do her shopping.

There was a T-shirt with an elaborate butterfly motif picked out in beads, its garish colours presumably a nod towards holidaymakers. She peered at the price tag. It was ludicrously expensive, and that was before the dry-cleaning bills. In fact everything on sale seemed oddly impractical for a holiday on a tropical island – unless, of course, you never left the hotel grounds and, judging by the people in the lobby, it was unlikely that any of them did venture very far.

It was sad to think that the most they would see of this beautiful island was the short ride in an air-conditioned limo on the one road between here and the airport; and, if they were lucky, they might get carted off to a 'cultural show', or some 'traditional' village and its ubiquitous souvenir shops. But they would all go home, happy that they had seen Malaysia. And the following year, somewhere else would be ticked off the list.

Isabel lowered her bags of shopping to the floor and rested against a pillar. She felt strangely detached from everything going on around her: it was like watching a film, but one that could scarcely hold her attention. Her mind kept skipping elsewhere, although she could never quite chase it down. She hugged her arms across her body and rubbed at her skin. It was far too cold in here; she longed to get outside and into the sunshine. She wondered what Lee was doing and hoped he wouldn't be long.

It was as if her thoughts had conjured him up because at that same moment she saw him step out of one of the elevators.

He spotted her almost immediately and raised a hand.

'Hi. Hi. Sorry I was long.'

'No, you weren't. I've been fine.' She gestured towards the middle of the lobby. 'It's very comfortable.'

'Would you like to have a drink, or something to eat?' he asked, 'I forgot the time.'

She hesitated, wondering if he had any idea how much things cost. 'I'm not . . .'

'Come on.' He had grabbed the shopping bags from the floor. 'Let's sit down and order something. Can we have two glasses of water please? With some ice?' he added to a passing waiter and then, to Isabel: 'You need to catch them when you can. The service here is pretty bad.'

He made his way to an empty table and she followed, taken aback by his assuredness.

'Do you like the shops here?' he asked, as soon as the waiter had left. 'They don't have anything I want.'

'Phew! That's a relief.' He touched his forehead with the back of his hand, in a mock gesture. 'But I should have asked what you were looking for, before I took you to the town.'

'To be honest, I couldn't even afford a T-shirt here,' she said. 'But I'm not sure I would want one.'

'Ah – I was right, then. Not your style.'

She didn't know quite how to respond. It was disconcerting to think that he had considered what may, or may not, be her style. She sipped at her water.

They sat in silence for a moment or two, then he picked up the menu. 'Are you sure you don't want anything to eat? You must be hungry. I am.'

'No – really.'

He glanced at her, uncertain. 'Just have a look.' He passed her the menu, then leant across to grab a second one from an adjacent table.

She watched him as he read, trying to guess what was going through his mind. But his expression gave nothing away. She was curious. He didn't seem at all uncomfortable in this environment, even though, apart from the staff, his was the sole Chinese face in a room full of affluent westerners. But it was clear that he had been here before, which was strange. It certainly didn't seem like his sort of place, and it certainly wasn't hers.

Then, in a flash, it occurred to her. He had come to look for a job. Somewhere like this was bound to pay more than Buah Lodge. She looked around at the gaunt, expressionless faces of the waiters filing to and fro with trays held above their heads. She couldn't bear to think of Lee working here; she tried to envisage him in the starched white uniform, responding politely to the commands of the frosty-faced tourists. She knew the sort of people who came to a place like this: the sort who would look straight through him, as if he didn't exist. To them he would be just another waiter, in another luxury resort. They would never bother to find out anything more.

'Lee –' She spoke his name, softly.

He looked up with a start.

'I would much rather go somewhere else. Somewhere more . . .' She thought for a moment. 'You know – somewhere more local? Perhaps – Malaysian, or Chinese food? Do you know anywhere like that?'

'Of course. Are you sure?'

'Yes,' she replied, and stood up, certain that she had spotted a trace of relief in his voice.

'Come on then. I know a place. Shall we walk?'

She nodded.

'Let's get out of here then.' He snatched up her bags of shopping and headed for the door. She made an attempt to grab back the bags but he dodged away and collided with a chair; its feet scraped along the marble-tiled floor. Without needing to look, Isabel could sense that heads had swung round to peer in their direction. She gathered up her skirt and skipped after him, embarrassed by the flapping noises made by her loose, leather sandals.

Suddenly, Lee stopped in his tracks and turned to wait for her. He was smiling – the wry, lopsided smile that crinkled his eyes and lit them up, so they resembled slivers of jet.

'Sorry,' he said meekly.

'What for? Come on, let's eat'

As they crossed the lobby together, she felt a certain buoyancy in her limbs. Those people could look down their elegant noses as much as they liked, but all their money couldn't buy happiness – or friendship – and it was she, Isabel, who was having a good time, not them, by the look of it. And this last thought made her want to laugh out loud, but she contented herself with beaming back at a cheerful concierge who was holding open the door for her.

Then it was like colliding with a wall of steam. After the air-conditioned hotel, the atmosphere outside seemed thick as a blanket; it was difficult to breathe and she had to squint against the intense, afternoon light that cast a harsh, silver glow over everything in view. But she was glad to be outside.

They walked through the grounds of the resort and out of the main gate. The sea was just visible through a row of manicured shrubs.

Lee turned to her with a grin. 'It's a pity we didn't eat there, you know – we could have got a free meal.'

She looked at him, but he was now staring intently at the ground.

What on earth did he mean? She didn't dare ask.

Twenty minutes later they were settled at a table, each engrossed in a plate of steaming noodles.

'Are you sure this is a restaurant?' asked Isabel, looking pointedly round the small verandah, and at the three other tables laid out with batik cloths. They were the only people there.

'Of course it is,' he replied, laughing. 'What do you think? That I have brought you to someone's house?'

'Well it looks like it,' she said. 'But this is delicious – just what I wanted.'

Lee leant back in his chair nursing a glass of beer. 'You didn't like the Mayang? – The Mayang Palace. The place we have just been to,' he added when she didn't reply.

'Ah.' Isabel sucked on the large piece of ginger she had just put into her mouth. If she told him how much she disliked it, she risked hurting his feelings – especially if he wanted to work there. 'It's not my kind of place,' she said, eventually. 'And it's just too expensive. For me anyway,' she tailed off.

'Resorts like that one are being built all over Malaysia.' He studied his glass for a moment before continuing. 'And the government encourages it – more development – they want more tourists to come. Good for business.'

'Well, I prefer smaller, quieter places.'

'Aha? Like Buah Lodge?'

'Exactly like Buah Lodge.

'That's good then.' He smiled at her. 'The trouble is, more money comes from the big, luxury resorts – ones with conference rooms, swimming pools, golf courses – you know – for business people. Those are the sort of tourists our government wants.'

Isabel looked away. 'Actually,' she said, meekly, 'I'm here on business too.' Now he would think that she was just like the rest of them. 'Well, at least I was when I was in KL. I was at an exhibition. But then I came here to get away from it all. And I really hope that this island doesn't get over-developed too.'

'It is a pity you were not here last year,' he said. 'It was Visit Malaysia Year. Ah, you should have seen our government's wonderful advertising campaign – come and see leatherback turtles laying their eggs on our beautiful beaches.'

There was a touch of irony in his voice. But he was still smiling.

She put down her fork. 'No I didn't see that.'

'Everybody welcome,' he went on, 'to come and disturb their peace and quiet. And by the way, do, please, help yourself. Take some eggs back home for souvenirs.' He shook his head. 'Really, it was very bad. Our government is so desperate, you see. And money talks. But the turtles? Ah! They don't have any comment.' He downed the rest of his beer. 'Another one for you?'

Isabel picked up her glass and emptied it.

He was already on his feet. 'I'll get two more. Is local beer fine for you?'

She nodded, still thinking about what he had just said and how bitter he had sounded. He seemed to really care about these things. She didn't think Ian had ever cared about anything much. Except perhaps himself.

When he returned he was clutching two bottles in one hand and in the other was a plate, piled high with fruit. He set down the bottles with relief. 'Wah – cold,' he gasped. 'And some fruit – a present from the chef.'

'Wow. Looks great. Thanks.' She took a spiky red fruit from the plate and examined it. 'So,' she continued, turning the fruit around in her hand, 'are you saying that you don't approve of tourists?'

'No, of course not. Here, shall I help?' He held out his hand. 'It's a rambutan – you peel it like this.' His narrow fingers worked their way round the fruit, pulling off pieces of hard, red shell and dropping them onto his plate. He handed back the glistening white centre. 'Be careful for the stone.'

'Thank you.' Isabel popped it into her mouth and bit on something hard. 'Ouch.'

'I warn you,' he said, laughing. 'Try this.' He was cutting into a large, green-skinned fruit, revealing dark, orange flesh and a mass of small, black seeds, which he expertly removed. He cut off a segment and handed it to her. 'In answer to your question – of course, we need tourists. And they can bring benefits.'

She bit into the juicy flesh, surprised at the taste – something between pumpkin and melon. 'What benefits can busloads of tourists and swanky golf courses bring to a lovely place like this?'

'Well –' He studied his hands for a moment. 'I think that tourism can provide jobs for local people.' He picked up another rambutan and began to peel it while he spoke. 'The problem is that in many cases the local people don't benefit at all – if staff are brought in from other parts of the country, if foods are imported from overseas –' he paused to grin at her, 'to meet the strange tastes of the westerners.' He put the peeled fruit onto a plate and began another. 'If some of the money from tourism was given to local communities, it could be put to good use.' He stopped peeling fruit and looked at her. 'That is my too long answer to your question. And anyway, if there was no tourism, you would not be here now.' He held out the plate of rambutans he had peeled. 'And you would not be enjoying our local produce. I hope you are enjoying it.'

She glanced up at him, wondering whether he was making fun of her. He was still smiling but as she caught his eye, he looked away. She turned her attention to her plate, not sure what to say.

'Tourism is not a bad thing,' he added, almost to himself. 'But it needs to be controlled. Carefully.' He was prodding the empty rambutan shells with his finger.

'What do you mean?'

'People are greedy. If they can see quick money to be made, they will want to make it. That is obvious. But they should look ahead, and see what damage they are doing, in the long term.' He let out a dramatic sigh. 'One more beer?'

She watched him as he walked back towards the restaurant. How could he go for a job at that awful place if he hated everything it stood for?

For the second or third time that day, Isabel found herself

having to re-think her opinion of Lee. And she was ashamed of the way she had stereotyped him. Why had she been surprised by his knowledge of the issues, by his thoughtfulness? Because he was a waiter? That would teach her to make snap judgements about people, she thought. There were all sorts of reasons why he might have chosen the job he had. Or maybe he hadn't chosen it at all. Whatever his story was, it was certainly a talent wasted. She wondered how old he was. Older than he looked, probably. It was hard to tell.

She took a piece of pineapple from the plate and bit into it. The juice ran down her wrist and she wiped it away with a tissue. When she looked up again he was walking towards her, carrying two more bottles of beer. The familiar spring was back in his step.

She pulled at a strand of hair that had fallen loose, regretting that she hadn't sorted it out after she had finished trying on clothes. Lee was standing behind her, filling her glass from the new bottle. Just as he would if they were back at Buah Lodge, she thought. She realized that her hand was still clutching the stray bit of hair; she let it drop and picked up a piece of fruit.

'Tell me about your work,' he said when he had finished with the beer and had taken his place at the table. 'What was your exhibition about?'

'The exhibition? Hmm. In KL.' She rooted around in her mind for the information she needed. It seemed a long time ago: work, the exhibition, the phone-call, Ian. 'It was a British Council exhibition,' she replied.

'Ah, the famous British Council.'

'You've heard of it?

'Of course. They have a good library in KL – where you can read British newspapers.'

'We – I mean, the company I work for – we produce some of their publications. I work for a publisher. As an editor. We publish all sorts of books – not just for the British Council. Actually, I'm not sure why they sent me to KL, it wasn't even my project.' She glanced up at him. 'But I'm glad they did.' Then quickly: 'Is that where you learnt your English? At the British Council?'

'No, I studied it in high school. And from my dad. He was a

teacher.'

'Ah – so that's why your English is so good.'

'No it isn't – not really.'

'It is – I was impressed by how good it is.'

'Thank you very much. My dad thought it was important that we – me and my sister – should be able to speak English well.' He paused and looked away for a moment; he picked up a rambutan and put it down again. 'There was a time, once, when English was the language used in schools. Then things changed. When I went to school everything was in *Bahasa Melayu* – that is the language of Malaysia. But at home we usually spoke Mandarin or sometimes even Hokkien or Cantonese.'

'Chinese dialects.'

'Correct. My mother's family came from Johor – they were Cantonese speaking – but my father grew up speaking Hokkien.'

'So now you speak four – no – five languages. That's impressive.'

'Many people in Malaysia do. It's normal. But me, I don't speak so many languages – just a little bit of each. Just enough.'

She decided not to tell him how she had just scraped through French 'O' level, the only foreign language she had ever attempted to learn.

He was reaching over now, to take some fruit, then, abruptly, he drew back his arm and examined his watch. He stood up and ran both hands through his hair, pulling it back to reveal a wide sweep of forehead. 'Sorry, but we should go. I didn't know what time it was. We must not miss the boat.'

Reluctantly Isabel pushed back her chair and took her new bag from the seat-back where it had been hanging. So what if they did miss it? There would be another. She would much prefer to carry on talking, find a cosy bar by the sea, maybe –

Trying to ignore where her mind was galloping off to, she reached into her bag for her purse. And, of course, he would be worrying about getting back to work. 'We haven't paid the bill yet,' she said.

'I have paid.'

'Oh,' Isabel selected some notes and held them out to him. 'I didn't know. Well, I must pay you back.'

'No – today you are my guest.'

She wasn't sure what to say. She couldn't let him pay for all this. It was unlikely that he earned very much. 'But you . . .'

He interrupted her. 'It was my pleasure. I enjoyed it.'

She gave up, resolving to find another way to repay him. 'Thank you,' she said, wishing she could think of the word he had taught her. It began with 't' – or was it 'r'? She was too embarrassed to ask him again.

In the deserted lanes, the shops had their shutters closed and were slumbering in the velvety afternoon heat. But the quayside had burst into activity once again: the boat was in.

Amidst a flurry of shouting and whistle blowing, wooden crates and baskets were being hauled from the jetty, then manhandled into the rusty viscera that was the lower deck. The smooth faces and sinewy limbs of the crew glistened with sweat and oil. On the deck above, people had already settled themselves onto the wooden benches and were now swapping tales with their neighbours, or busy sorting through the bags and baskets of shopping arranged around their feet.

Isabel stepped cautiously onto the moving gangplank and made her way across. When she reached the other side, one of the crew caught hold of her arm and guided her onto the boat.

'*Berhati-hati*,' he shouted over the din as he deposited her on the deck.

Where had she heard that before?

Lee was close behind and jumped aboard just as the ropes were being untied.

'That was lucky,' he said. 'Just in time. Shall we find a seat?' He began to make his way up the iron staircase.

'I hadn't realized that it would be so crowded,' remarked Isabel, still out of breath from the rush to the boat.

'This one always is.'

'This one?'

'The last boat. For a while anyway.'

That explained why he had been in such a hurry, she decided.

They had reached the top now and he was looking around for a seat. 'The next boat is the night boat,' he went on. 'It goes the other way round. Slowly. Stops at all the villages along the way.'

They managed to squeeze themselves into a couple of spaces on opposite benches and sat in silence as the boat pulled away from the jetty. Isabel was still trying to remember how to say 'thank you' in Malay. What had the man downstairs just said to her? *Berhati-hati.* That couldn't be it, could it? She looked at Lee but he was staring at the floor.

She broke the silence. 'Lee?'

He turned and smiled at her.

'What does *berhati-hati* mean?'

'It means be careful. Take care.'

'Ah.'

He was still looking at her. His eyes soft, patient.

'And – I know that you have already told me but I've forgotten – how do you say thank you?'

'*Terima kasih.*'

'Right. Thank you. I mean, *terima kasih.*' She laughed, then tried to think of something else to say – something to block out the irritating sound of her laugh still ringing out in the air between them.

'Doesn't your . . .'

'Isabel – I . . .'

They had started speaking at the same time.

'Sorry,' he faltered, 'I interrupted you. Go on.'

'No – it's okay, it wasn't important.'

'I was . . .'

'*Maaf.*' The woman who had been sitting next to Isabel had stood up, and was trying to squeeze her ample figure between the two of them, preventing any further conversation for the moment. The green stalks protruding from her basket brushed against Isabel's arm as she pushed by.

Isabel relaxed back into the additional space she had gained then looked across at Lee. One of her bags of shopping was propped against his legs. He had reached down and was pulling at the handle, twisting and untwisting the black plastic until it had started to tear.

She broke the silence again. 'Doesn't your boss mind you taking all these days off work.'

His head jerked up. 'My . . .' For a moment he looked puzzled. Then: 'Ah – my boss.'

Did a smile pass across his face? Perhaps. But it was impossible to tell what he was thinking now as he was looking down at her shopping once more. And she wished she hadn't asked him the question. For some reason, it seemed to embarrass him.

She opened her bag and concentrated on fishing out the paper napkin she had picked up at the restaurant. She wiped away the sweat that was stinging her eyes. When she looked up again she was perturbed to find he was staring at her. She used the napkin to dab at her forehead.

At last he spoke, but he was laughing now. 'It is not a problem. My boss is very happy. He tells me I should take every day off, if I am enjoying myself so much.'

Isabel frowned. She had no idea what he was talking about. Or why he was making fun of her. 'What do you mean?' she said. 'How . . .'

He leant across, and touched her arm, briefly. 'I'm sorry – I am teasing you. But I didn't know it was what you thought. Honestly I didn't.' He was laughing now. 'My boss? That's me. I gave myself the day off.'

She shook her head, still not understanding what he was saying.

'Buah Lodge – is my place. I am the boss.'

∞

Kampung Teluk

It had rained again: a heavy downpour with drops as hard as grains of rice. It had beaten down onto the rattan roof and it had driven into every lush corner of the garden, releasing an exotic mix of perfumes, making the scents rise up out of the darkness and trickle into Gula House. Then it had stopped, as suddenly as it had begun: as if someone had turned off a tap.

Isabel was sitting at her table on the far side of the dining area, the place where outside and inside seemed to merge into one, where graceful strands of bamboo could reach in and brush against her body, and where the air, hot and heavy, remained undisturbed by the ceiling fans at the centre of the room. With her arm on the sill, she gazed out towards the black void behind the building, listening to the gentle tap-tapping of rainwater dripping onto the broad, waxy leaves of the nearby banana trees. Somewhere out there, melting into the blackness, and pulsating with nocturnal life, was the forest: the towering primeval monument which, according to Lee, might one day disappear. Just a few more generations, he had said. That's all it would take.

She pushed back her chair and wiped her mouth with the napkin; a faint trace of lipstick adhered to the white linen. Now she had finished her meal, she wasn't sure what to do. She looked around the room, wondering where Els and Pieter had gone this evening. The Japanese couple were there, peering at each other across their meal. The Germans were there too. As she stood up from her table, one of them inclined his head in a half-bow. The door from the kitchen opened and she looked up, expectantly. But it was only Amir, come to clear away her empty plate.

She made her way to the lounge area and sank into one of the armchairs near the reception. She stared blankly at the wall in front of her, then at the tapestry hanging behind the desk. She studied the patterns woven in gold, red and orange thread, and wondered if Lee had chosen it; and she imagined him standing at a market stall, picking it up, caressing the fabric with his fingers, smiling to himself, oblivious to the mayhem around him. She took a deep breath and opened her book at the page she had marked, but the words simply floated in front of her eyes. She closed the book and put it on the table beside her, almost toppling the carved wooden elephant she had forgotten was there. She reached out to run her fingers over the animal's smooth, broad back, lingering over a patch of faded colour – just a hint of the reds and greens that had once embellished it. A rattan blind knocked against a wooden frame and her hand sprung back.

Perhaps she should go back to her chalet, she thought, or at least move to another chair, so it didn't look as if she were waiting for something – or someone.

Was that what she was doing? Waiting?

No, she decided, not waiting – simply relaxing in the lounge after dinner. But she needed a drink, to complete the picture; and glad to have found something to do she stood up and crossed to the bar, hoping that Amir would appear from the kitchen again so he could get her drink, maybe chat for a while.

But no-one came.

The Japanese man looked across, nodded. She nodded back. Seconds passed.

This was crazy, she thought. All she had to do was put her head round the kitchen door, to see if there was anyone around, just as she had done so many times before.

She wandered back to her chair. The ceiling fan click-click-clicked above her head.

It was just over two hours since they had arrived back from Batang. He had left her at the fork in the path leading from the jetty – he had to go to the village, he'd said. But then what? No 'see you later'? Or 'see you at dinner'? This was where her mind was a blank. He had been in a hurry, everything had happened so quickly, and she had been left to walk back to Buah Lodge on her own, still reeling from what he had told her.

Once more, her skin crept with embarrassment at the recollection. Of course now she knew the truth about him, it was obvious. But how could she have thought otherwise? And what must he think of her? He had seemed amused at the time, but he could have been insulted. She had made herself look foolish, too.

The only way forward was to apologize.

And thus, finally, she had come up with a reason to stay.

The shrill of the cicadas crescendoed as Isabel stepped outside onto the verandah. Now the rain had passed over, the air was still and heavy with the scents and sounds of night. She settled herself into a wicker armchair and closed her eyes. If she tried hard enough she could just pick up the rhythmic swoosh-swoosh of the waves sweeping the sand, somewhere beyond the edge of the garden.

When she heard footsteps, she flicked open her eyes but willed herself not to turn around. The steps came closer and then someone spoke.

'Miss Eezobel?'

She looked up. It was Amir.

'A gin-tonic for you.'

'Thank you.'

He set the drink on the table in front of her. He had brought a bowl of nuts as well. 'Just in case you are still hungry.' He grinned and turned away.

A fraction of a second: she heard herself calling out to him; she had called him back.

'Amir.'

'Yes?'

It was too late now. She plunged in. 'Is Lee here tonight?'

'Er, no. Lee not working today.' He paused. He looked worried. 'Is there any problem?'

'No, nothing. Don't worry. Thank you.'

He nodded and left.

She allowed herself a breath. Let her pulse slow a little.

Damn! Amir would almost certainly tell Lee that she was looking for him.

She sipped her drink and stared out towards the garden. It was lit by a half-moon; softer light pooled under tiny lamps dotted along the path. The wicker creaked as she moved in her chair.

Lee must have gone out, she thought. And she wondered where he went on his evenings off. She tried to envisage a house, but she didn't know where he lived, nor whether to picture him alone, or with someone else – a girlfriend? – Set Yen? – or a wife – maybe some children as well. The thought had never occurred to her before, but it seemed her mind had raced ahead, and to somewhere she didn't think she wanted to go. She shook her head, as if that might put a stop to it all. It was none of her business where he was or what he was doing. And as soon as she had finished her drink, she was going to go back to her room.

She heard the sound of his feet on the gravel before she saw him; he was some distance away, walking across the garden, walking towards where she was sitting. Her heart was still drumming inside her ribcage when he bounded up the wooden steps and stood at the top, facing her.

'Hello Isabel. You are here.' He looked fresh and neat, as if he had just come from a shower.

'I'm just having a drink.' She picked up her glass as if to prove it.

He pulled a dead flower from an overhanging branch and inspected it for a moment, holding it in the palm of his hand. Then he looked up again. 'May I join you?'

'Of course.'

'You see –' he spread out his arms and gestured towards the room behind her, '– I'm not a waiter this evening.'

She took a sip of her gin and tonic. It made her cough.

'It is very quiet tonight,' he said, pulling up a chair. 'Your English friends have gone to the town – to a bar or club or . . .'

She made what she hoped was a disapproving face; she was still coughing.

'Are you all right?' He looked concerned.

She nodded and put down her drink. 'Not my scene,' she managed to get out at last.

'I think they find it very quiet here.'

'Yes, I think they do. But I don't,' she added. 'It's perfect. Here

– I mean. Exactly my sort of place – peaceful, quiet, and . . .' She stopped. Her words had tumbled out but now she had no idea what she wanted to say.

He was waiting for her to continue.

'I mean – not everyone likes brash nightlife do they? Some people prefer to get away from it all.' She took a deep breath. She was talking too much. She scratched idly at the back of her hand. 'Don't change it, will you?'

'I'll try not to.'

He was smiling, but he seemed to be gazing over her shoulder, in the direction of the garden. She looked down at her hand, to see what was causing it to itch. A large white bump had formed on her skin.

'I've been bitten,' she said, examining the lump. 'I forgot to put mosquito stuff on.'

'They didn't bring anything for you?' He jumped up. 'Wait here. I will come back.'

When he returned a few minutes later he was carrying a lit mosquito coil. He placed it on the floor by her feet. 'I hope they have not bitten too much,' he said as he returned to his chair.

'I'm afraid they like me,' she replied, then wished she hadn't. She looked down at the green coil and watched the smoke curling around her legs. It gave off a pleasant, musky odour. She needed to fill the silence. 'So, how long have you had this place?' she asked.

'It always belonged to my mother's family and then it came to my uncle, but . . . Well, then he brought in a business partner. I started working here about twelve or thirteen years ago – something like that. When my uncle died, four years ago, he left his share of the business to me, and so his partner is now my partner. You have met him, I think – Mr Yeow? Gilbert?'

Isabel nodded. Gilbert, or 'Yo' as Sandra and Rob called him, was the one everyone thought was the manager. She had seen him a couple of times. He didn't seem to be around very much.

'He usually does the pick-up from the airport,' Lee continued, 'but the day you arrived he was busy. That's why it was me who came to collect you.'

She wished she could remember more about that day; she had

been too bound up in her own troubles to notice anything much.

'I'm sorry I thought you were . . .'

'Nothing to be sorry for.' He stood up. 'Good. Here's Amir.'

Amir lowered the tray he was carrying and put a bottle of Tiger Beer and an empty glass onto the table. 'Your usual Mr Boss.' He was laughing.

Lee glanced at Isabel; she smiled back at him. She couldn't blame them if they were making fun of her.

'And a drink for Miss Eezobel.' He had brought her another gin and tonic.

'Thanks Amir,' said Lee. He sat down again. 'By the way,' he said to her, 'I saw your other friends in the village.'

She thought for a moment. 'Els, and Pieter?'

'The two from Holland. They were at the seafood restaurant. They had been looking for you. I think they wanted to invite you – to join them.'

She visualized the three of them standing together, talking about her. She wondered if he had told them about their trip to the town.

'They had waited for you,' he went on, 'but . . .'

'I had dinner here.'

'Yes, I know.'

There was nothing to read into that, she reminded herself. He was bound to know who was having dinner in his restaurant. 'Don't you mind if your guests eat somewhere else, instead of here?' she asked.

'No, of course not – why should I mind? It is good for the village.'

'Yes, but not for your business.'

'Well . . .' He picked up the bottle of beer and started to fill his glass, then he stopped for a moment and looked at her. 'You see, I don't think it is exactly like that.' He finished pouring and set down the empty bottle. 'Buah Lodge is part of the community. It was built on village land after all. We should not take something away, without giving something back.'

Isabel nodded; but she had never thought of it like that.

'We are lucky to be able to bring people to stay here. If they eat in this village, or the next one, and if they buy things in the town, then it is good for everyone, for the whole island. We all help each other in different ways.' He took a sip of beer from his glass before going on. 'You see, that is the difference between here and the Mayang. A big resort like that gives nothing back to the community – they just take. And the people who stay there don't need to go outside the gates if they don't want to. Even the beach was moved there – and now it is private, which means local people can't use it.'

There was a coconut-shell ashtray on the table. He picked it up and turned it over in his hands. 'Even the stuff in their shops is imported, including what they call the local crafts. They are probably mass-produced in China – not even in Malaysia.' He frowned and put the ashtray back where it had been.

It was unusual not to see him smiling and Isabel wished she could think of something helpful to say. 'We're not all bad, you know,' she said. 'Us tourists, I mean.'

He looked up, quickly. 'No, I didn't mean . . .'

'I know you didn't. Anyway, you must like some tourists, otherwise you wouldn't be doing all this,' she gestured around her. 'You have made it very beautiful.'

At last, he smiled. 'I am glad you like it.'

'I do. It's lovely. And I know what you mean about those big resorts. I don't like them either. And they attract some awful people – who complain all the time – especially if things aren't quite what they're used to back home. I don't know why people like that bother to come away at all – it's just so they can boast about all the exotic places they've been to.'

He laughed.

'And I think you've got one or two like that staying here at the moment.'

He raised his eyebrows. 'Have I?'

He had leant forward and was looking straight into her eyes. 'So you are not like that?' he said. 'You have had your *nasi lemak* every morning? Or was it eggs and bacon?'

'Well . . .'

'And your gin and tonics.'

'I can live without those if I have to.'

'And if your beach has some rocks – and sand flies – you won't complain?

'No.'

'And when the electricity fails, you don't mind if you have to take a cold shower.'

'Not at all. I never complain.'

'Then you are the perfect guest.'

Isabel knew he was teasing her. She looked away, but could sense that he was watching her. She licked at her lips, feeling for traces of the lipstick she had put on earlier, hoping it had gone. She rubbed her mouth just in case. 'I hate places like the Mayang,' she said, breaking the silence. 'Everything about it is artificial. Man-made Malaysia – a snap-shot of a country, all in one place, so that people can go home and say that they've done Malaysia.'

He smiled wistfully. 'That is true. And real Malaysia is being destroyed – to make space for places like that.'

'God – how can people get away with it?'

'Very easily. When money is involved.' He put down his glass. 'If you knew how much forest was cleared away to make room for that resort – '

'I can imagine.'

'Something which took thousands – no – millions – of years to evolve. All destroyed. Just like that.' He banged his hand onto the table. The glasses jumped and rattled. 'Sorry.' He laughed. 'I get a bit excited sometimes.'

'I can see that.'

'But I wish people would understand that this . . .' he gestured into the darkness beyond the garden, 'that nature is not . . . What is the word?' He rubbed at his chin. 'Exhaustible? – no, not that. In-ex-haust-ible. Hmm – long word. That's what I mean. When it's all gone, it's all gone.' He shrugged. 'But who needs the real thing as long as they have – how did you say it? Man-made Malaysia? Yes, that is a very good way to describe those places. Man-made.'

He had placed his hands together, as if he were praying. Now he studied his fingertips. 'They bring in stuff – from who knows where – to make what they think the tourists will want. But that is their first crime. Because almost everything they need could be found here – if only they tried harder.'

Isabel sighed and looked down at her empty glass. Then she remembered something from earlier. 'So, if you hate that place so much, why did you want to eat there this afternoon?'

He laughed. 'Only because it was free.'

She looked at him, puzzled. 'Yes, you said that before but . . .'

'I know the manager. They owe me something.'

'I see,' she said, uncertainly.

'You didn't think . . .'

'Well, when you said we wouldn't have to pay . . .'

'Hey! First you think I am a waiter, or the gardener maybe. Then . . . Hmm, I'm surprised you are still sitting with me now.'

Isabel felt the heat rise to her cheeks. When she looked up again he was beaming back at her. She laughed. 'I'm sorry I didn't mean to imply . . .'

He stood up and touched her lightly on the shoulder.

'Don't worry. I'm joking with you. Anyway, I am a bad boy, just like you think, because your glass is empty and I haven't offered you another drink. You will have another gin and tonic?'

She hesitated. Perhaps she should ask for something else. A local drink. But she had no idea what. 'How about your local speciality then?' she said.

'Ah –' He scratched his head. 'Are you sure?'

'Not all us tourists are the same, you know. Despite what you think. And I do like to try out new things. In fact, I've got a cupboard full of *ouzo* and *raki* –'

'Ra-ki?' he repeated the word slowly. 'Sounds a little bit like *arak*. That's a local spirit.'

'Is it nice?'

'You need to get used to it. How about Chinese liqueurs? Have you tried them?'

She shook her head.

'How about snake wine?'

She pulled a face.

He laughed. 'Good for men.'

She was about to ask why, but thought better of it.

'But we do have nice drinks. Let me go to see if I can find something that you will like.'

Lee went off in search of drinks and Isabel was left alone with the sounds of the jungle and the distant rat-tat-tat of Malay coming from somewhere inside. She sat back and peered up at the sky; it was alive with thousands and thousands of shimmering stars, all mingling together above the outline of the canopy trees.

She couldn't quite believe that she was here, in this wonderful place, having a fascinating conversation, with the man who owned it.

She rubbed at her bare arms, and then hugged herself tight, as if she could curb the giddy feeling that was welling up inside her. Was this what happy felt like, she wondered. And she had to lean back in her chair, and push her head hard into the cushion, to stop herself shouting out the words – to the stars, to the forest, to the world – *I'm happy! For once. I'm truly happy!*

She looked at the sky once more, but the millions of tiny, silver pinpricks were starting to blur; and she had to screw up her eyes to prevent a few, warm tears from spilling over.

'It's the Southern Cross.'

She hadn't heard him return. Now he was standing beside her, a glass in each hand, gazing up at the sky. She poked at the corner of her eye with a finger.

'The Southern Cross?'

'Yes. What you are looking at.' He put the glasses on the table and knelt beside her chair. 'Look. There.'

Her eyes followed his outstretched arm. The skin was smooth, the colour of cinnamon; she wondered how it would feel, if she touched it.

'See – just above that tree – the one in the shape of a   ah, how to say?' He rubbed his forehead as if he were trying to make the word appear. '*Xiēzi* – in Mandarin – Shee-dzi. You know? The insect with the tail that bends over? Stings you. Ah, how do you call it in English?'

She smiled. She knew exactly what he meant. There it was in front of her, looming black against the inky sky: a tall tree with a long, looping branch. Just like the tail of a scorpion.

'A scorpion?'

'Yes – yes, that's it. Just above the scorpion. Do you see it?'

There were four stars, brighter than the rest, forming the shape of a cross.

'Yes, I can see it now.'

He was still kneeling by her side, still looking up at the stars. She could sense the rise and fall of his chest as he breathed, slowly, in and out.

The stars continued to glitter back at them.

'I've never seen that before,' she said.

He stood up, using the arm of her chair to balance himself.

'Let's see if you like this.'

He handed her one of the glasses he had brought from the bar. It was full to the brim with a colourless liquid. She put it to her lips. The scent of rose petals. She took a sip and swallowed. The liquid burnt as it hit the back of her throat.

'Turkish Delight,' she spluttered.

He looked puzzled.

'Turkish Delight. That's what it tastes like. It is a sweet that tastes of rose petals.'

'Yes – that is exactly what we are drinking. Rose liqueur. Do you like it?'

She took another sip. The liquid was thick and sticky. 'I might get used to it.'

He laughed.

'But one glass will probably be enough.'

'It is a Chinese liqueur,' he said, downing the entire contents of his own glass. 'But I can't take too much. I find it a little bit sweet.'

Isabel took a larger sip and swallowed quickly. It was not a drink to linger over. But the fire, now in the middle of her chest, was emitting a warm glow through the rest of her body, and she settled into her chair, feeling very much at ease with the world.

So how come she had got it all wrong so far, she mused. Hadn't things started to go downhill ever since she moved to London? For without stopping once to think, she'd been caught up in the whoosh and whirl of the merry-go-round that was life in the city. And all she had done was lean over the side and snatch at bits of this and that as best she could, while the music jangled away in the background, like some soundtrack to her life. But now, here she was, as far from all that as she could possibly be. By sheer good fortune she had found herself in this remarkable setting; and she felt calm and still and at peace with herself.

She concentrated on finishing the drink, a sip at a time until it was gone. Beyond the garden the forest creaked and rustled, and from time to time a call rang out through the darkness.

The air had become heavier, hotter.

'My partner, Gilbert, thinks we should provide some entertainment in the evenings,' Lee said suddenly.

She studied his face. Was he joking again, or serious now?

'What sort of entertainment?' she asked.

'I don't know. Music. Maybe karaoke'

'That would be awful.'

'Karaoke is very popular in the big resorts – especially with the Japanese tourists.'

'But not here, surely? It would be terrible.'

'I agree. I don't think that we should offer that sort of thing. I am not sure everyone would want it. But Gilbert says we should provide more to do in the evenings.'

'So, he has been talking to some of your other guests,' she said.

'Afraid so.'

As he spoke, she heard a soft whistle coming from deep inside the forest.

He held up a hand. 'It's a nightjar. Listen, it will come again.'

It did – pitched on a higher note this time.

'See, I told you it would.'

He put his head to one side, waiting for it to sing out once more. But now there was a different sound – the clink of glasses – and it was getting closer and closer. Then Amir appeared; he was carrying a tray of drinks.

'I got us some more – in case you didn't like the liqueur,' Lee said. He looked at the empty glass she still had in her hand. 'Or would you like another one of those?'

She shook her head. 'It was lovely, but quite strong. I'll be sozzled at this rate.'

'Sozzled?'

'Drunk – you know – too much to drink.'

'I don't think so.'

Amir began to load the empty glasses onto his tray.

'Thank you,' said Isabel. She passed him her liqueur glass.

'I think you are very English,' Lee said as soon as Amir had moved away. 'Very polite.'

Isabel looked at him, smiling.

'Set Yen thinks so,' he went on. 'She is always talking about you.'

She continued to smile.

Sweet, charming Set Yen.

She wondered when they had discussed her. Over a drink? While they were cooking a meal together? In bed? The thought landed heavily.

'You would be surprised how impolite some of the guests can be,' Lee continued.

'I wouldn't be surprised at all,' she answered.

Of course, they made the perfect couple. And Set Yen deserved to have someone like Lee. Even so, she couldn't help feeling a tiny bit jealous.

He was still speaking; his voice, deep and mellow, cut across her thoughts.

'I think that some of the visitors we have to this island set a very bad example,' he said.

She visualized them working together, laughing together; they were in each other's arms, they were kissing –

'I'm sorry – I don't mean people like you.'

He had stopped talking and was looking at her.

She grappled around for a suitable answer. 'I know that,' she said. 'It makes me cross as well, when I see how some people behave. And you are right, they show no respect for the people who live here.'

'Yes, that is true.' He sighed, and ran a thumb over the condensation on his glass: first one way then the other, making the shape of a cross.

Isabel watched the movement of his hand, focussing her eyes on the neat white crescent at the base of his nail, her elation of moments ago trickling away as the spectre of recent events started to bear down on her once more, plucking at her skin with its long muggy fingers: her boyfriend had dumped her, she had no idea what she was doing with her life, and every time she met someone remotely nice, she found that they were already attached to someone else. But there was nothing she could do about any of that at the moment.

'I do agree with you,' she said. 'About the tourists, I mean. I bet the locals really dislike them?'

'Sometimes, but there is another problem too – especially amongst the younger people. You can't blame them, I suppose. They see a different way of behaviour to the one they have been taught. And they think that it is better. So they copy it – the clothes, the language, everything – which isn't always a good thing. I am sorry, I don't mean to offend you, but it is a different way of life here in Malaysia.'

She nodded, but remained silent.

'And they also see an opportunity to make money – so they can have that lifestyle for themselves.' He paused to drink. 'It starts off with small-small things. The coral for example. They see that tourists like to take pieces of coral, so they decide to take it themselves, to sell. And then they see that people like to do snorkelling, and suddenly . . .' he swiped at a passing insect, 'they have found an old boat, and they are taking people out to the reefs. But most of the time they don't know what they are doing and they cause too much damage. As I said, you can't blame them. They just want to make a quick buck like everyone else.' He laughed. 'Like me. I guess that is what you are thinking. I am also making money from the tourists.'

'No I wasn't.'

It was true: she hadn't been thinking that at all. Far from it. She had been watching his hands, turning and twisting, punctuating the air as he made a point, sometimes straying towards his eyes to push back the unruly lock of ink-black hair. She had been thinking how different he was to anyone she knew. And all these things mattered to him, she could see that.

'I wasn't – really,' she said, 'I think what you say is interesting.'

'It is something I think is important. Perhaps you can guess.' He smiled. 'But you see, I think, tourism is a good thing. As long as it is managed well.'

'You think so?'

'Yes, I do. But education is important too – educating the local people. My uncle taught me this. He was worried about the way things were going.'

'So how do you educate them?'

'You must get them to open their eyes, to look around, and teach them that what they can see is their greatest asset. Once they realize that this can be used – to make money – which is what everyone wants to do – isn't it? – then you have to show them how to do this carefully, to explain the importance of looking after it, and that it isn't only about making money quickly – it is about the future. But in some cases it is too late.' He spread his hands in front of him, his long, slender fingers tapping on the table top as if it were a keyboard. 'It is very sad but many of the world's coral reefs have already been destroyed – not just by stealing the coral but by polluting the water also. But coral provides food and shelter for creatures. It also protects the coastline from being worn away. So if we destroy the coral we are causing too many problems for the future. This is what you must teach people.'

'Let's hope it really isn't too late,' she said.

He shook his head and looked down into his glass. 'There are many such problems and it is very difficult when you are up against the big boys.'

She felt sorry for him. She wondered if the large resort was taking away his customers.

'The competition must be a problem. From the Mayang, I mean.'

He shrugged. 'It's a different place. They attract different people, they offer different things. We are small. I think that we should stay small – there is less damage that way. But I have many ideas to make it an even better place to come to.' He looked up again, his eyes shining. 'Lots of ideas.'

'You want to change Buah Lodge?'

'Not to change. But I can make it special.'

'It already is special.'

He looked pleased. 'More special, then. I want it to be different. Not like the other resorts. I want people to feel where they are, to enjoy the environment as it is, naturally. And if we are not owned by some big, foreign company, then we have the freedom to do just what we want.' He sighed. 'Another large resort would be a disaster for this island. There would be more tourists here than locals. It would unbalance everything.'

'What do you mean another resort?'

'The Mayang – actually the company that owns the Mayang – they want to take our land, to swallow us up. They have made an offer.'

'No! Will you let them?'

'I will try not. The problem is Gilbert. I am working very hard to persuade him to say no.'

'But what about all your plans, doesn't he care about Buah Lodge?'

'He cares but, you know, this is only a job for him now. Not a project – like it is for me. He tries to be interested, but he will retire soon. And he is thinking about money. Being comfortable. If I could buy him out, that would be the best solution for everybody. But I don't know if I can afford it. I am working on it.'

'That's awful.' She didn't know what else to say.

'But I think I can persuade him to stay on a little bit longer. And then, maybe, by then, I will have saved enough money.'

She was horrified at the unfairness of it all. Why did everything in life have to come down to money? It was wrong that someone with such positive ideas, someone a bit different to the others, couldn't do what he wanted to do. All because of money, or politics, or both.

They sat for a while immersed in their thoughts. She knew he was thinking about Buah Lodge and she wished that she could think of something useful to say.

A waft of fragrance, powerful and sweet, swept in on the night air.

'What's that smell,' she asked. 'It's amazing.'

'*Trompet tree* – those white flowers – over there.' He pointed to a spot further along the verandah where a mass of white, funnel-shaped flowers shone out through the darkness. 'They flower at night only. Come and see.'

He sprang from his chair and moved away, without looking back. She supposed she should follow him, so she stood up and walked to where he was standing. He had stopped at a point where the tree was almost close enough to touch.

'Some insects love it, said Lee. 'Like the moths. They feed from it in the evening.'

She stood by the rail and looked into the semi-darkness, conscious of the jungle pressing up against the perimeter fence as if, one day, it might creep through the gaps and claim the garden as its own.

From somewhere behind the lodge came an unearthly wail.

Isabel looked up, startled.

'Don't worry, it's just an owl,' he said.

It came again. *Woo-woo. Woo-woo.*

They listened as the sound echoed around the forest.

'How could anyone wish to spoil the peace and tranquillity of this place?' she asked.

As if on cue the owl hooted once more.

Lee laughed. 'Peace and quiet? Listen.'

She listened. It was as if the place had come alive; there were noises coming from every corner now. 'I suppose it's true,' she said. 'The forest is never completely peaceful is it?'

'Ah, but a different kind of peace. Never quiet but always peaceful.' He leant over and broke off a flower from a nearby bush. He held it out to her. 'This one smells good too. A bit more subtle. It is Gardenia.'

She took the white flower from him and held it to her nose, taking in the sweetness of its scent. The petals felt waxy against her skin.

They stood in silence for a while, both leaning on the wooden balustrade, both looking out over the garden, listening to the sounds of the forest beyond. He was standing close – so close that the tiny hairs on her arm could sense his presence next to her; and she willed herself not to move. She stood as still as was possible, until every muscle in her body ached with standing so still.

It was late when she got back to the chalet, but she wasn't ready to close the door on her day, not just yet. As long as she stayed outside, there was a sense of being connected: to the forest, to the garden, to him.

The chair she had brought out yesterday was still there, so she sat down, still holding the fragrant, white flower he had given her, and let the night air embrace her. The undergrowth buzzed and hummed beneath the wooden boards.

Bits of their conversation floated into and out of her mind. While they had walked in the garden, he had pointed to plants and trees, telling her their names, what they were used for, what creatures liked to eat them. Then he had asked about her life back in England, and she had found herself telling him things she had never told anyone: almost as if she were just discovering them for herself.

And he had listened.

She understood now. Ian had never asked such questions, had never shown interest in her past, or in her plans for the future; their conversations had always been about him, and about what he wanted from life. And she knew that she had never been a part of his future; she supposed that, deep down, she had always known it – if only she could have admitted it to herself.

She had told Lee about the novel she wanted to write, told him that she had already sketched out a plot, but never had enough time to work on it. And he had said: 'You should come here – to Teluk. It would be a perfect place to write.'

Was it foolish to see that as some sort of invitation? she wondered now. 'I can't afford to give up my job,' she had told him. 'Yes you can,' was his reply, 'if it is so important to you to write your novel. And anyway, you can live very cheaply here.'

And he was right, of course. If only she had the courage to give up her life in England. What would she be giving up after all?

He hadn't said anything else after that, because that was when Amir had arrived. The two of them had spoken in quick, urgent bursts of Malay, and Amir had apologized to her, in English, for interrupting them. Then Lee had turned to her and said he was needed, and had to go. 'Shall I walk with you back to your chalet?' he had asked. And she had told him that she would be fine walking by herself.

I must put the flower in a glass of water before I go to bed, she said to herself.

PART FIVE

London
July 1995

∞

1.00 pm

Her two friends were already there, perched on stools in front of the bar. Isabel could see Lynn's trademark mass of red curls bobbing above the crowd. She pressed through the fray, wondering why on earth they had decided to meet in this particular pub on a Friday lunchtime. It was packed at the best of times.

'Here she is.' Emma jumped down from her stool and stepped forward to give Isabel a hug. 'Congratulations. You sly old thing.'

'Come on, let's see it then,' said Lynn.

Isabel held out her hand.

'Ooh,' Emma cooed, 'it's gorgeous. Are those sapphires?'

Isabel nodded.

'Look at the size of that diamond,' Lynn said.

'So tell us all about it.'

'There's nothing really to tell.'

'Didn't he get down on one knee?' Lynne asked.

Isabel laughed. 'Shall I get a drink first?'

Emma waved to the barman. 'What are you having? G and T?'

Isabel nodded.

'Come on then,' Lynn said, as soon as Isabel had a drink in her hand. 'Let's have all the details.'

Isabel thought for a moment. 'Well, it just happened.'

'What do you mean?' Emma asked.

'He just came out with it. Quite suddenly. We were talking – about children, for some reason – God knows why – and he said, did I ever want to have children. And I said, maybe, one day, if I ever got married. And he said, well we'd better get married then.'

167

She laughed. 'Very romantic, wasn't it? And the next weekend we went out and got a ring, and here it is.' She held up her left hand and wiggled her fingers.

'And he wants children?' Lynn asked.

'Looks like it,' Isabel replied. 'Although he's never mentioned it before. Not that we've ever really discussed it before.'

Emma took hold of Isabel's hand and studied the ring. 'You're so lucky –'

'Quick – there's a table. C'mon let's grab it?' Lynn had launched herself at a nearby table and was now busy clearing away empty bottles and glasses. Emma and Isabel rescued their drinks from the bar and threaded their way towards her.

'So how did it feel?' Emma asked, once they had sat down. 'You know – when he actually said it.'

'Don't know really. Bit scary I suppose. Because that's it, isn't it? The rest of your life. All mapped out. But we are living together, so I suppose . . . well, it seems like – you know – the next thing to do.'

'Yeah, I keep hinting to Terry,' Lynn said. 'But it doesn't work. He thinks commitment is just a word you get in women's magazines. Two and a half years – and we don't even live together. How did you manage it? You and David had only been together for about six months when you got that house together.'

'Eight.'

'Well, whatever it was, you didn't hang about did you?'

'I think David thought it would be cheaper if we ran one place instead of two.'

'That sounds like David,' said Emma, laughing.

'We'd never even talked about moving in together,' Isabel continued. 'And then one day it just came up in conversation – out of the blue – and the next thing, we were looking in estate agents' windows. It was all very sudden.' She looked down at the shiny new ring. 'A bit like this, I suppose.'

'Well, however it happened,' Emma said, 'I'm very happy for you.' She caught Isabel's hand and gave it a squeeze. 'You are so lucky to have found *the one*. It only ever happens once.'

'What does?' Lynn asked.

'Finding your person. The one. Everyone has that one person

that they're meant to be with.'

'What, only one?' Lynn shook her head. 'Shame.'

'Yes, your soul mate,' Emma replied.

'So what if you never find him?' Isabel asked. 'You know, this special, right person that's meant for you.'

'You have to put up with all the Mr Not-So-Rights while you wait for him to turn up,' Lynn said. 'I wonder where mine got to. He must be hiding.'

'Shush. You've got Terry,' said Emma.

Lynn snorted.

Isabel picked up her glass and tilted it, watching the wedge of lemon slide to the opposite side. If Emma's theory was correct, how could you be absolutely sure when you *had* found your true soul mate? Wouldn't it be obvious? She lifted the glass to her lips. And what if you did find them?

She took a gulp of her drink; but the question floated into her head regardless.

What if you did find them? Then lost them again? Did you really have only one chance?

She took another sip, then returned her glass to the table. Anyway, she had David now, and *he* did want to be with her. Emma was right – she was lucky to have found him. He was a good person. He was reliable, clever – and she was going to marry him next year.

'I don't think I'm ever going to find *my* Mr Right,' Emma was saying. 'I think I'm destined to stay single for the rest of my life.'

'Don't be silly,' said Lynn. 'Someone would be very lucky to have you. They don't know what they're missing. You know what your problem is?'

'No, but I'm sure you're going to tell me.'

'You're putting everything on hold while you wait for your so-called Mr Right to come waltzing through that door. Instead of sitting around, waiting, you should get on with your life. Believe me, doing things on your own is no bad thing anyway. And I bet the minute you stop looking, he'll turn up – just like that.'

'Well let's hope I've had my roots done then.'

'And your legs waxed,' Isabel laughed.

'Oh God! Yes. Wouldn't it be awful, if the day our paths finally crossed, he ditched me, because I had hairy legs?'

'If he is your *one*,' Lynn scoffed, 'then he should want you whatever your legs look like.'

'Bit risky though,' Isabel said. 'Best be prepared – just in case.'

Lynn shook her head. 'Too much like hard work, if you ask me. They have to take me as they find me.'

'I don't think I'd ever want a man to see me not looking at my best,' Emma said.

'Well, you'd better not start having babies then,' replied Lynn. She turned to Isabel. 'Talking of which – is that what's coming next? Babies? – Oh my God, you're not, are you?'

Isabel laughed. 'No I'm not. Though I suppose I should hurry up. Before it's too late.' She continued sipping her drink while her friends looked on, quizzically.

'Well, Mother Nature hasn't caught up, has she?' she went on. 'I don't feel old, yet, and by twentieth-century standards I'm not old – but my body is. And it's deteriorating fast. A few hundred years ago someone my age would have had about ten children by now.'

Lynn grimaced. 'Thank God we live in the twentieth century then.'

By the time Isabel got back to her office, it had gone three o'clock.

Simon put his head round the door. 'Hi, sweetie. Had a good time?'

'Yes, thanks.' And it was true, she thought, she *had* had a good time. She had forgotten how much she enjoyed going out with her girlfriends. It had been a long time. In fact, now she thought about it, it was a while since she had been out anywhere at all (trips to Brent Cross with David didn't count) and she remembered that they hadn't even been out to celebrate their engagement.

She walked to the open window and stared up into the flawless blue sky, until she was dazzled by the light of the sun glinting from the windows of the building opposite; when she closed her eyes the shimmering white orb continued to float behind her eyelids. It would be a shame, she thought, to go straight home after work. Not that she was going to get much more work done today; she was feeling pleasantly tipsy, what with the gin, and the intoxicating warmth of the summer sunshine.

She went back to her desk and perched on one corner, pulling the phone towards her. She dialled the number and waited, while the ring tone shrilled in her ear.

Four rings.

'David Adamson.' His words were cropped, businesslike.

'It's me.'

'Hello, me.'

She could sense him relaxing, possibly shifting in his chair.

'Are you having a good day?'

'Not too bad,' he replied. 'Busy. Nothing I can't handle.'

Silence. He was waiting for her to speak again.

'I fancy going out somewhere tonight. Do you want to meet me after work?'

'I thought you were meeting your friends.'

'That was lunchtime. I've already met them.'

There was a pause. 'You said it was this evening.'

'No I didn't.'

Another pause. 'I've arranged to have a drink with Tony Symonds.'

'Oh.' She tried to put a face to the name. 'Boy's night out?'

He laughed. 'Not exactly. He's a new partner.'

Had he mentioned it before? She couldn't recall.

'Got to be seen,' he went on, 'so they can't talk about me behind my back.'

'So you'll be late.'

'Quite.'

'And drunk.'

'Possibly.'

She gathered up a small pile of paperclips and started to arrange them in a straight line, as if they were carriages on a train.

'Okay. Have fun then.'

'I won't, but it's got to be done. Did you have a good lunch?'

'Yes, thanks.'

'Good. You can tell me about it later. Got to go. Late for a meeting.'

'Bye then.'

'Bye.'

She heard a click as he put down the phone. She scooped up her train of paperclips and poured them back into their container. She sighed.

She thought about asking Simon if he fancied going out. But that would only annoy David. In any case, she didn't much feel like clubbing these days; they were all noise, and smoke, and scrums of young people drinking themselves insensible.

Must be getting old, she told herself.

She slipped from the desk and sat in her chair, swivelling it round so that she faced the window again. From there, she could just about see the elaborate cornice and attic storey of the terrace opposite. Someone had opened one of the squat dormer windows and was leaning out to smoke a cigarette.

Perhaps she should make the most of having the house to herself, she thought, and get on with some writing.

She turned the chair back towards her desk, pleased to have come to a decision.

Isabel re-tuned the radio to *Jazz fm* and stretched out on the bed. She had been sitting at the desk for too long and her back was aching. To make things worse, all she had to show for the last couple of hours were the balls of screwed up paper filling the waste bin. Where had it gone? That hunger to write, that used to be her constant companion?

A breath of air pushed at the curtains, billowing them into the room before letting them fall over the open windows. Swathes of white voile. The sun had dropped low in the sky and was burning with a fierce, orange glow, coaxing the room into a demure, rosy blush.

Isabel closed her eyes, listened to the wistful tones of the saxophone coming from the radio, let her mind wander. There was a room, starkly furnished; a thin, white curtain dancing in the breeze; a soundtrack of soft, smouldering jazz. There was a man kneeling beside a bed. He was reaching out, putting his hands behind her head, drawing her close; slowly, he leant forward, kissed her.

She jerked open her eyes. No, not this –

Slowly: back to the familiar contours of her current surroundings; and here she was, all by herself. She swung herself round and sat up, rubbing at the place in her back where it ached.

PART SIX

Malaysia
July 1991

∞

25 July 1991
Kampung Teluk

Lee yawned and stretched his arms above his head, one hand still clutching the pen he had been using. Sheets of paper marked with scribbled notes were cast around his chair, looking like lily pads dotted across a temple pond. He picked one up, stared at it for a moment then screwed it into a tight paper ball and tossed it across the room. Next, he picked up a cup from the nearby table; he peered into it. It was still half-full, but an oily film had formed across the liquid inside. He wondered what time it was and whether he needed to muster his weary limbs and start his day.

The forest was resonant with the grunts and cries of awakened beasts, and the sun was up – a fiery ball just visible through the haze. Soon the damp, early-morning mists would be burnt off, to reveal the familiar shape of the jungle-clad hills in the distance.

It had been dark when he had got out of bed to make his tea; and when he had come out onto the balcony there had been no more than a hint of light leaching into the dawn sky. He must have fallen asleep in the chair.

At least he had had some sleep.

Last night, after he had been to see Gilbert, he had gone straight to bed. But his mind had been troubled by what his partner had told him; and all he could do was lie there, wide-awake, watching the hands of his clock drag themselves round the hours. He knew that he shouldn't blame Gilbert for his decision – he was just an elderly man who wanted to retire in comfort. But the Mayang people knew that too. They also knew that *he* didn't want to sell – he had made that quite clear yesterday. What made him angry was the way they had gone behind his back and made Gilbert an

177

offer that he would find impossible to refuse.

He bent down and started to pick up the papers littering the floor. These bits of paper, he thought, ruefully, represented his life – a life reduced to columns of figures, added this way and that: income, outgoings, savings, loans. And however many times he did the calculations the answer was always the same. He didn't have enough. Not yet.

His only hope now was to persuade Gilbert to hang onto his investment a bit longer.

He stared up at the nearby *mangga* tree and was distracted for a moment by the birds, busy with their whistles and calls before they fled for cover from the heat of the day. Then he had an idea. It was true that he couldn't afford to buy out Gilbert, but he could afford to pay him something – like a monthly salary. He reached down, rooted amongst the papers, then brought one to the front, flattening it out with the palm of his hand while he stared at the notes he had made. Yes, that might work. He could offer to pay him to stay on – a sleeping partner.

He put the piece of paper onto the table, stood up, stretched again and tightened his sarong before walking to the balcony rail. He loved this time of day and often came out here, into the cool morning air, to drink his tea and listen to the forest as it woke. But this morning, the perfect view of the sea glinting through the ranks of slender palms failed to have the usual effect. And the musky aroma of wood-smoke meant that the village was well into its morning ritual. He, too, should get dressed and get going; he had a busy day ahead. But his fingers remained pressed onto the rail. There was something still churning inside his head, making him feel off-balance, and it was nothing to do with Gilbert, or Buah Lodge. He knew exactly what it was, and there was no point in trying to ignore it any more.

He moved to the other side of the balcony and peered through the trees which shielded his villa from the rest of the compound. He listened to the pulsing of the insects on the ground below, letting the sound roll round and round inside his head, until it seemed to keep time with the beat of his heart. He was looking in the direction of the garden. He couldn't see it from here but he didn't need to, it was all there, sealed away in his mind: the garden, alive with night sounds, and rich with all those perfumes it kept tightly locked away during daylight hours; the garden where they had walked yesterday evening. Walked and talked; talked about so many things. And he didn't think he had ever felt as comfortable with anyone before. Before Isabel. There, he had done it. He had said her name. He couldn't put off thinking about her any longer.

And if Amir hadn't come to find him last night –

He shook his head, as if he could shake away what was beginning to take shape.

What was he playing at? This was against all the rules. His rules. But what was he supposed to do? He couldn't get her out of his mind.

He tried to think when it had started. Was it that time in May Ling's shop? When she had been looking in the mirror, at her new dress? She had turned round, and smiled – such a radiant smile – although he didn't believe for one moment that it had been for him. She had looked happy then, and so different to the young woman he had met at the airport; and so beautiful. The dress she had on was the colour of saffron, made of something so delicate that it seemed to float over her body as she moved.

He closed his eyes. He wanted to make sure the image was firmly printed in his mind, so that he could call it up again whenever he needed it. When she had gone.

He could hear the swish-swish of a broom; the sound was moving closer and closer. He opened his eyes and looked over the balcony rail.

It was Jalil, one of the garden boys, sweeping the terrace underneath. He looked up and waved. '*Selamat pagi*,' he called out.

'Good morning,' Lee shouted back, thinking once more that he really must get going. He had a lot to do today. Set Yen's mother was ill – that was something else Gilbert had told him last night. He would let her go home for a couple of days, and he would have to find a temporary replacement. There was a girl in the village – Su Pei. She had worked at the Mayang, so she did have a little experience. He would do that straight away; he would go and see her this morning. He would also call in on his friend Joseph, if he had the time. Joseph was sensible. He would advise him what to do.

He went inside to see what time it was. The tiles on the floor were cold against his bare feet and he shivered when he noticed that the fan was set to its highest speed. A thin white curtain, swollen with air, moved behind him. He turned down the fan, then grabbed his watch and went back outside. It wasn't as late as he had thought; there was still some time. Time to close his eyes and let his mind wander for a while.

He returned to the wicker chair and relaxed into the cushions. Now he had acknowledged his feelings, he didn't want to stop thinking about her; and the thoughts came tumbling out of his head like stones down a mountainside, picking up momentum as they went. So, was it then – in the shop – or was it even before that? Was it when they had walked to the waterfall?

He still couldn't quite believe what he had done and he wondered when he had become so brave. Even now, he could see himself standing at her table, talking to her – 'the English girl' – in the same way as he chatted with all of his guests. And then, suddenly: *I can take you*. His face burnt with embarrassment as he heard his own voice ring out through the warren of memories.

He certainly hadn't planned that. And all along she had been thinking that he was one of the staff! He chuckled to himself, recalling the look on her face when he had told her the truth. He had longed to put his arms around her, there and then, and kiss away whatever pain he sensed she was carrying with her. But, of course, he hadn't, and he couldn't. However much he wanted to. In any case, he would be a fool to imagine that she would be interested in him.

So why did he go looking for her yesterday evening? He wouldn't blame her for thinking that he was pestering her.

Ah, but there would be no chance of that happening this morning. He had work to do and he should get on with it. Most likely he wouldn't even see her today.

He stood up and shook his head. He hadn't had enough sleep. That would explain why he was feeling so light-headed. He turned and reached for the iron latch on the shutters; as he did so, a series of whoops and cries rang out from a nearby tree. The song hung in the air for a few seconds; he waited, and listened; then came the reply, resounding through the forest. He lifted the latch and went inside, leaving the gibbons to continue their haunting duet.

He may have been caught off-guard by the realization of what he was feeling, but deep down he knew that it hadn't begun last night, nor had it begun when they went to Batang, nor even when he took her to the waterfall. It had started the moment he had first laid eyes on her; when he had seen her walking towards him at the airport: the girl with the sad, dark eyes, the reluctant smile, and the massive suitcase. That was the moment he knew he was going to fall in love with her.

∞

The hum of voices grew louder as Isabel approached the Gula House. She could see people moving about inside. Was Lee there amongst them she wondered? She reached the top of the steps and paused; it seemed unusually crowded. She willed herself not to look towards the kitchen door.

Just because he had been friendly last night, didn't . . .

'Yoo-hoo! Isabel.'

It was a woman's voice. Isabel looked round.

'Over here.' It was Sandra. She had got up from the table and was flapping her hand in the air. 'Why don't you join us?'

Isabel hesitated.

Now Rob was attempting to stand, still clutching onto his napkin; his chair made a scraping noise as he pushed it back. Several heads turned in his direction. And there was Phil too, lounging in the corner, one arm on the sill of the open window. Their table was strewn with the remains of breakfast: egg-smeared plates, empty cups, pieces of toast, an abandoned sausage. There didn't seem to be space for anyone else.

She had no choice but to go over.

'Good morning,' she said clinging to the back of the chair Rob had pulled up for her.

Sandra was fussing about, trying to make room: picking up plates, putting them down somewhere else, brushing at crumbs; none of which had the slightest effect on the state of the table.

'So. Isabel!' This was Phil. 'What happened to you yesterday? Thought you were comin' to the beach.' He sucked noisily at his coffee cup. 'You gonna come today?'

'Yes, dear,' Sandra cut in, before Isabel had the chance to reply.

'You come with us. It's the Mayang Palace – the place where we go – much better. And your friends have gone diving again. They go every day don't they? I think you said you don't dive. Well, anyway, you can come with us. You don't have any plans do you?'

'No. Nothing. I was just . . .'

'Well, that's all right then. We've to be at the jetty for ten. You've plenty of time.' She turned to her husband who was still hovering at the edge of the table. 'Rob, get Isabel some breakfast.'

Rob waved towards Set Yen. 'Hello! Miss! Could we have another place laid? Over here.'

Isabel felt herself flinch, and hoped no-one had noticed. He meant well – they both did – but she had been caught off guard. This was going to be impossible to get out of. And thank goodness she hadn't bumped into them yesterday.

'They're ever so slow this morning,' went on Sandra. 'Anyway, you sit here with Phil, while we go and get our things sorted. We'll be back in a jiffy. Phil's all ready – aren't you Phil?'

Phil raised and lowered his eyelids in response. He was like a huge bullfrog, Isabel decided, sitting under his stone, watching, languidly, as Rob and Sandra fussed around the table.

She glanced over to where Set Yen had been standing. But she had gone.

'So we'll see you in about half an hour then, shall we?'

Isabel realized that Sandra had asked her a question.

'Mr Yow is taking us in his boat, isn't he, dear?' continued Sandra, not noticing that she hadn't had a reply

'It's Yo,' said Rob.

'Oh well, if you say so dear. Yo – Yow – it's all the same isn't it? Right-o then.' With this, Sandra gathered up a novel, a pair of spectacles and the pink cardigan that had been hanging on the back of her chair, and marched towards the steps.

'Bye for now,' muttered Rob, scuttling after her.

Isabel was left with Phil.

He had turned in his chair, his bare legs thrust out in front of him, his rucksack propped against his feet; a corner of buttered toast had fallen down and was wedged in the folds of the material.

Isabel looked at Phil's watch. It was twenty to ten. When she looked up, she saw Amir crossing the room towards her.

'Sorry – Miss Isabel.' He was out of breath. 'Bit busy today.' He smiled nervously.

'That's okay, Amir,' she replied. 'I'll have some jasmine tea and some . . .' She hesitated, looked around for inspiration: anything but toast and jam.

Just at that moment Set Yen appeared from the kitchen with two plates of food: mounds of rice on dark green leaves; pieces of hard-boiled egg; something covered in a rich red sauce. Isabel had no idea what it was.

She pointed. 'I'll have that please.'

Amir looked at the tray and then, with a gentle clatter of Malay, said something to Set Yen.

Isabel watched, smiling, waiting for the usual amicable beam from Set Yen.

But she didn't look her way.

Amir turned back to Isabel. 'You want *nasi lemak*?'

'Yes, please.' She was watching Set Yen, and the tray, disappear down the steps of the Gula House. Something gnawed at the back of her mind. Where was she taking it? It was only half a thought, but it continued to churn around until it had formed itself into something more substantial. Was she taking it to Lee?

'Sit down, please.' Amir was piling the empty plates onto a tray.

Reluctantly, Isabel sat down opposite Phil.

'Jesus! The staff here are slow,' he said, before Amir was out of earshot.

Isabel glanced at him, then away, her eyes fixed on Amir's back as he hurried towards the kitchen door. When he opened it, she might be able to see inside.

'I don't think they are slow at all,' she said. 'In fact I think the staff work very hard.'

Phil licked his finger and poked around in some crumbs on his plate.

'Well, you know . . . Huh, back home, in the States . . .' He transferred the crumbs to his mouth. 'I guess yer get what yer pay for.'

Out of the corner of her eye, Isabel saw him shift his weight from one buttock to the other.

'D'you get to the States yet?' he asked.

'No, I . . .'

'You should. You'd love it.'

Isabel studied her fingernails. How the hell did he know what she would, or wouldn't, love? She was cross with herself for agreeing to go to the beach.

'Mees Eezabel?'

Her head shot up.

Amir placed a plate of food in front of her. She looked at it warily. As well as the rice, egg and cucumber pieces there were four or five large prawns bathed in a thick, red sauce. It was clearly going to be very, very spicy. Without hesitating, she ladled a spoonful into her mouth. She was determined that Phil should think this was what she had for breakfast every day.

As soon as she tasted the first mouthful, she let out a loud 'Mmm.' She hadn't meant to, especially as it sounded a touch theatrical, but she had been taken by surprise: it was, in fact, incredibly good.

'You like that stuff?' Phil asked.

She nodded, trying to ignore the fire at the back of her throat. Her eyes were beginning to water.

Phil watched while she took a second spoonful. 'Jeez,' was his only comment.

∞

The Mayang Palace, Batang

I sabel let her arm flop over the side of her chair. She plunged her fingers into the hot sand.

'– and it's very quiet. There isn't much to do is there?'

She realized that Sandra was speaking to her; she opened her eyes. Sandra seemed to be waiting for some sort of response.

Isabel hadn't a clue what Sandra had been talking about. She scooped up a fistful of the sand and let it slip out between her fingers. She had been thinking about Lee, wondering why he hadn't appeared at breakfast time, and whether he had been avoiding her. 'Hmm, that's true,' she offered.

The reply seemed to satisfy Sandra; she moved round in her chair so she was facing Rob. 'Isabel agrees with us – don't you dear – about the place – not enough to do.'

Isabel glanced at Rob, but his eyes were fixed on the book he was reading.

But why should Lee be avoiding her? she thought. There was nothing to avoid. He was just being sociable last night. That was all. And today he was probably busy. And, as it turned out, it was a blessing that he hadn't been there to see her go off to the Mayang Palace – after everything they had talked about yesterday.

But of course he would know. Gilbert would tell him.

'And you know . . .' Sandra had turned to her again, 'we don't even have a TV in our room. Do you have one? We did complain – to that young one – what's his name?'

'Amir?'

'No. The other one.'

'Lee?'

It was almost a relief to say his name out loud; to release it

186

from the confines of her thoughts. One single, simple, syllable, but loaded with such significance that she was afraid it might show in her voice.

'Yes, him,' said Sandra. 'He isn't quite as friendly, is he? Well anyway, we'd expected there'd be more going on – you know – organized like. That Yow's all right, though isn't he? He's been ever so helpful.'

Isabel made an appreciative noise.

It had been Gilbert who had brought them here this morning, and it was the first time that Isabel had caught more than a fleeting glance of Lee's partner.

Squeezed onto a bench at the back of the boat, alongside a stack of grubby tarpaulins, she had watched him manoeuvre them round jagged promontories, past deserted coves and perfect white sandy beaches; she had watched his hand work the rudder, had stared at the calluses which stood out from the darkened skin on his bony fingers, despising him for all the things she knew about him. She couldn't help it. This man had been close to Lee's family; he would have laughed with them, eaten a meal with them, clinked a glass, shared a confidence. And now he was betraying Lee, turning his life upside-down. Just to get what he could for himself. But when Gilbert had dropped them off at the rather grand jetty belonging to the Mayang Palace, and unloaded their bags – and a packed lunch from Buah Lodge, because Sandra had not wanted to pay the prices at the Mayang – Isabel had felt a sudden sense of loss. It was an odd emotion – heightened, possibly, by the uncharitable nature of her earlier thoughts about him – for much as she disliked him, Gilbert had been a link to Lee. And while Sandra had fussed around the various bags that had been deposited on the wooden pier, and bickered with Rob about where he had put the sunscreen, and why it should have been wrapped in a plastic bag, Isabel had watched Gilbert reverse away and set off back in the direction of Teluk. He had looked small and frail in the empty boat: just an elderly man who hoped that, one day soon, he could retire in comfort.

'– and last year we went to Antigua.' Sandra was still talking. 'On one of those cruises. We got in with a very nice crowd and the food was smashing – eat as much as you want – you know

– one of those all-in places. Not like here. We don't think the food at Buah –' she pronounced this as Boo-a '– is very good, do we Rob?'

Rob looked up from his book. 'Not as good as in Antigua – eh love?'

'They can't seem to do a decent breakfast here, can they?' Sandra went on.

'No, not to our liking,' said Rob. He sighed and closed his book, leaving a finger inside to mark his page. 'The locals aren't so friendly either, are they? Bit standoffish, we think.'

'Not like Antigua,' Sandra replied.

It was like watching a double act, and Isabel was glad that she wasn't required to participate. She stood up and stretched. 'I think I'll go and have a paddle.'

'Yes, that's nice dear,' said Sandra. 'You'll see it's lovely here – no nasty rocks and things.'

No, Isabel thought, as she surveyed the meticulously raked sand, and the row of white, plastic sun-loungers where Sandra had installed them, that's because it's all man-made.

She marched towards the sea, glad that the tide was out so she could get as far away from them as possible, be on her own for a while. When she arrived at the sea edge, she stopped and let a trickle of soft, warm water run over her toes; she stepped forward and felt it play around her ankles. The mud-like sand gave way beneath her weight and her feet sank down into it; she giggled to herself as she freed first one foot then the other, then jumped back onto the firmer sand at the water's edge. Only then did she turn back to look at the resort: a vast expanse of painted concrete; a vulgar white blot on the landscape. Behind it was a beautiful swathe of forest, forced to stop short at a line of spindly, alien trees, which she knew formed the perimeter of the newly laid out golf course. The whole complex left an ugly, bald patch in the otherwise luscious green landscape.

She stood there for a while, contemplating the scene, until something knocked heavily into her arm. A young boy stumbled alongside her.

'Soz,' he mumbled, before picking up the ball and speeding away.

A second boy was chasing after him. He stopped when he

reached Isabel and yelled at the retreating figure: 'Pig. I'll fucking get you for that.'

Isabel winced: not so much at the language, or the volume of his outcry, but at the recognition of his accent. British. Absently, she smoothed the sand that the boys had scuffed up with their feet. She could still hear them shouting at each other, and although she had her head down, concentrating on the sand, she sensed that there was someone else there now, someone behind her. She spun round. It was Phil.

'What's up?' He moved towards her and placed two fingers on the back of her shoulder. 'Hey. You got burned. Just there.'

'Ow!' Isabel jerked away. 'That's sore,' she added. It was a poor attempt to mask her reaction to his touch.

But he seemed oblivious. 'Got any cream? I'll rub it in for you, if you want.'

When he laughed she could see a row of narrow, butter-coloured teeth; a couple of them looked as though they had been filed to a point.

She adjusted the ties of her sarong. 'No it's fine, thanks. I'll be fine.' She turned over some shells with her foot; she knew he was watching her. She tried to pretend he wasn't there.

'How long yer here for?'

She tugged on her fingers, using them to count back the days. 'Another five days.' She did the calculation again. 'Four and a bit. I've got the afternoon flight back to KL –' She stopped to consider the significance of what she had just said. Back home, in less than five days. So soon.

'I've got another week,' said Phil.

'That's nice.'

'Dunno.' He kicked at one of the shells she had been looking at. 'I'm a tad bored. Thought there'd be more to do. Might cut loose an' do a few extra days in KL.'

Isabel was tempted to ask why he had come here in the first place, as it was so obviously not his scene, but she had caught sight of Sandra advancing towards them, one hand clutching at her neon-pink sarong, the other clamped over the crown of an impracticably wide-brimmed hat – no doubt a fine specimen of the Antiguan craft industry, thought Isabel, unkindly. Behind

Sandra, Isabel could see Rob. He was waving a couple of bottles in the air.

'I think we're wanted,' she said, glad of the distraction. She turned to walk back but Phil had grabbed at her elbow.

'Hang on a sec.'

She shook off his hand and gave a quick wave to Sandra, who was still picking her way across the sand. What with the sarong and the hat, she wasn't making a great deal of progress.

Phil leant in towards her; she could smell the stale nicotine on his breath. 'There's this thing here, tomorrow night. Worth checkin' out. Free drinks and all.'

'Is there?'

He had stepped back and was waiting: legs planted wide apart, hands on hips.

She needed to think. Quickly.

'So how about it? You wanna come?

'I don't think I can. I promised to go for dinner with Els and Peiter tomorrow – you know, the two from Holland?'

'Dinner with those guys?' He scratched at a spot on his chest. Isabel noticed that his nails were bitten down beyond the tips of his fingers. 'Nah, it wouldn't be their sort of thing.'

'Hello you two.' Sandra had finally pulled up beside them. Thought you would like –' she was struggling to catch her breath and talk at the same time, '– some lunch – and a beer – oh – I'm out of breath now,' she gasped. 'The boy came round – and we ordered – for you both. You'd best come and have it – while it's cold.'

Lunch time. That meant it must be about one o'clock: three more hours to go before they were due to be picked up. Isabel wondered if she would get the chance to read her book in peace for the rest of the afternoon. Somehow she doubted it.

Back from the beach, Isabel hurried to her room and searched through her clothes, trying to find something to change into. All of a sudden, nothing seemed quite right.

She showered quickly, washing the sand and the sea from her skin. When she had finished, she wrapped herself in a towel and moved to the mirror, to deal with her hair. She felt refreshed and clean, and glad to have washed away all traces of her afternoon on the beach, and the ride back to Teluk.

In the boat she had found herself wedged between Phil, on one side, and a skein of rope, on the other. She had spent the journey trying to avoid contact with Phil's knee – which would keep gravitating towards her leg – and the rope, which was dark and viscid with oil.

'Ugh.' She shuddered at the thought.

She snatched a towel from a nearby rail and rubbed vigorously at her head.

∞

Kampung Teluk

It was seven o'clock by the time Isabel opened her door to step outside. The heat closed around her and, in an instant, her skin was damp, clammy. Within minutes her carefully dried hair would have surrendered itself to the humidity and would be hanging, lank and sticky, around her neck and face.

The sun had just dipped below the horizon and had left, in its wake, strand upon strand of wispy pink cloud: a reminder that it was still shining brightly on some other place.

She walked towards the Gula House, slowing down when she was close enough to hear voices coming from inside. More than anything she didn't want to get caught up with Rob and Sandra again, and Phil of course. But would Lee be there? She took a deep breath and continued on.

As soon as she stepped inside she spotted Els and Pieter. They were sitting at a table near the bar. She steeled herself and marched across the room towards them, not daring to glance at any of the other tables, nor beyond, towards the kitchen.

Els jumped up from her chair. 'Hello stranger! Where have you been? Every day we have missed you. What have you been doing? Come – Pieter get a chair – come sit with us.'

Pieter pulled over a chair from a nearby table and held it while Isabel sat down.

'So. What have you been doing?' Els asked for the second time.

'Oh, not a great deal,' Isabel replied. 'I have . . .' What should she tell them?

'I've been lazing around on the beach,' she continued, 'did some shopping. But today . . . Well, today wasn't much fun.' She went on to explain how she had been roped into going to the Mayang Palace with Sandra and Rob, and what an awful place it was. She had just told them about Phil inviting her to go with him tomorrow night, when Els gave her a nudge.

'Oh, you know, we saw you yesterday. With Lee.'

Isabel felt the blood rise to her cheeks.

Els flashed her a smile. 'You were going somewhere together?'

'Were we?'

Els seemed amused by something; Isabel felt like laughing too. She took a deep breath, trying to contain a sudden rush of pleasure.

'Yes,' Els said. 'You were running off together down the path.' She put her head to one side. 'Going somewhere very quickly –' She stopped, leaving the sentence hanging in the air as if it were a question.

'Oh, then?' Isabel said, as casually as she could manage. 'Yes. He was showing me where to do some shopping – I needed a few things – you know – and he took me to the town.' She stopped.

Els was still beaming at her. 'Very nice? No?'

'Of course, you've been there too, haven't you? I forgot. Yes, the shops are . . .'

'No,' Els interrupted, 'I mean Lee. He is a very nice guy.'

'He is.' conceded Isabel. 'Very nice.'

'Ah, yes,' Pieter joined in. 'That is true. The other night, we talked together. And we had some drinks. Many drinks.' He laughed. 'He told us of his plans for this place. I hope that he has success. We will come back very soon to see what he has done.'

'I hope so too,' said Els. 'His ideas are good.'

Isabel nodded, not daring to speak. It felt very strange to be sitting here with Els and Peiter, discussing Lee, when she had spent the entire day thinking about little else.

'He's a very clever guy,' Els went on. 'It's a pity he has had so many problems in his life.'

'Has he? I didn't know.'

'You know, his father died, when he was going to finish high school, and so then he was the head of the family. He was just seventeen or eighteen when he came to work here.'

'Yes, for his uncle,' Isabel was able to add.

'But he wanted to go to the university – in KL, he told us – but his family couldn't afford to pay for it. His dream was to study.'

'Study? Study what?' asked Isabel.

'Ah, I'm not sure. Something about conservation.'

'What, with animals?'

'I don't know. I don't think so. The land, I think. The forest.'

Before Isabel could ask any more questions, Amir had arrived to take their order for dinner.

While Els and Pieter were debating what to have, Isabel took the opportunity to scan the room. Sandra and Rob had yet to arrive, and Phil was nowhere to be seen. Neither was Lee. But there was a girl she had not seen before, serving drinks to the two German couples. There was something about the way she held her head, and her long, straight back, that gave her an air of confidence. She was pretty too, and she had a bright pink flower tucked behind one ear.

Isabel could hear Pieter's voice and she realized that she had missed some part of the conversation. He was talking about Lee's house.

'You know, that high one, at the edge.'

'The one with green shutters,' Els added.

She nodded. She had noticed it. But she didn't know that was where he lived. It was a big house too, far too big for one –

The girl had finished serving the Germans and was approaching their table.

'Do you like any more drinks?' she asked.

'Who's she?' Isabel whispered to Els, as soon as the girl had left to deal with their order.

'Don't know,' replied Els.

'Very pretty,' added Pieter. 'Hey, what . . .'

Els had kicked him under the table.

The food took a while to arrive but was as good as ever, and Isabel ate her enormous helping of curry chicken and rice with relish. She wondered whether Lee had cooked it. She was sitting with her back to the kitchen door and she ached with the effort of not turning round whenever she heard it swing open. A drink might calm her nerves. 'Didn't we order some more beers?' she said, staring at her empty glass.

'Yes, that's true,' replied Pieter. 'What has happened to them?' He stood up and wandered into the centre of the room. Under cover of watching Pieter, Isabel allowed herself to look around once more. She noticed that Rob and Sandra had finally arrived. They were sitting near the bar.

Sandra waved when she saw Isabel looking over, then she nudged Rob. He looked up from the magazine he was reading and raised his beer glass. Isabel returned the greeting with her empty glass, feeling guilty about her earlier attempts to avoid them. It wasn't their fault that they irritated her; they were perfectly harmless, and kind at heart. There was no sign of Phil though. She shifted round in her chair to see if he was lurking elsewhere. It was then that she happened to look beyond the bar and out towards the verandah – to the exact spot where she had sat with Lee last night.

She saw the girl first, slumped in one of the wicker chairs.

'She's supposed to be getting our drinks!'

'Who is?' Els looked up from her meal.

'That girl, and she's just . . .'

That was when she noticed Lee. He had his back to her but she knew it was him; he was leaning towards the girl, showing her something written on a sheet of paper. Pieter must have spotted them too, because now he was striding to where they were. Lee must have sensed Pieter approach and raised his head. Although she immediately glanced away, Isabel knew that he had seen her looking at them.

When Pieter returned, he seemed amused. As he passed behind Els's chair, he bent to kiss the top of her head, then said something to her in Dutch. Els nodded in reply. Minutes later, the girl arrived with a tray of drinks. Isabel watched as she arranged fresh bottles and glasses on the table. As her hand came down to collect Isabel's empty glass, Isabel saw the gold ring on the fourth finger of her left hand. The realization punched her hard. So this was Lee's wife.

Els and Pieter were leaning across the table, exchanging forkfuls of food. Els caught Isabel's eye. 'Are you okay?' she asked.

'Yes, fine, thanks.'

'You are very quiet.'

'No. I'm always quiet. Just a bit tired, maybe.'

It would have been easy to confide in Els, and she was tempted to tell her everything. But she was afraid that it would all sound very foolish; she barely understood it herself. She knew nothing about Lee, had known him for less than four days, and yet, for some reason, she couldn't seem to get him out of her mind.

As she scraped up the last spoonful of rice from her bowl, she resolved to stop behaving like a teenager with a crush, and concentrate on enjoying the rest of her holiday. Without any more fantasies about Lee.

After their meal, the three of them took their drinks onto the verandah. Els proceeded to tell her stories of their life in Amsterdam; as Isabel listened, she gazed out over the moonlit garden where she had strolled with Lee the night before.

'People always find it very funny when I tell them that Pieter is a doctor and I am a nurse,' Els said. 'But it makes a lot of sense. Or we would never see each other.'

'Always busy,' Pieter added. 'It was as if I didn't leave the hospital. And so I didn't have the time to meet anyone in the outside world.'

'Ah, he doesn't know it – but I had already decided that we should be together – even from the first time I saw him.'

'Yes. I did know that.'

'No, you didn't. I let you believe it was your own idea. But I had planned it all – right from the start.'

Pieter shook his head and winked at Isabel.

It turned out that they both worked in the same hospital in Amsterdam. Els was in the paediatric section, Pieter was an anaesthetist.

'I still make an excuse to go to her ward,' said Pieter, 'so that I can catch sight of her.' He smiled shyly at Els.

Isabel smiled too, trying not to feel envious. It was a shame that all her own relationships seemed to fizzle away into nothing.

It was as if Els had read her thoughts. 'So, Isabel,' she said. 'Do you have a boyfriend?'

Not even a glimmer of one on the distant horizon, Isabel thought. But not wishing to bore them with the ongoing saga of her unsuccessful relationships she replied: 'No, not at the moment. Just ended one actually – or he ended it for me – just before I came here. So I'm free, and single, and . . .' She stopped, not having anything further to say.

'Well, I am sure that you will meet someone else very soon,' said Els. 'You are too nice to be on your own for long. Don't you think so, Pieter?'

Pieter nodded.

Els stood up and leant her back against the wooden balustrade. 'There is a lovely smell, somewhere here. I wonder what it is.'

'Oh, that's the trumpet tree,' Isabel replied, straight away.

'Yes? You are very clever to know that.'

'No, not really. I . . . Anyway, it has that smell to attract the moths. They like its pollen, or something, I don't quite remember.'

'I am impressed.' Els looked at her quizzically.

'Actually it was Lee who told me,' she confessed, feeling the hint of a missed heartbeat when she said his name.

'Aha.' Els was nodding. 'See, Pieter, our friend Lee has been giving botany lessons as well.'

Pieter laughed.

Isabel would have been happy for the conversation to turn back to Lee – in fact she longed to talk about him – but she feared what they might tell her: that he lived with Set Yen in the big house – *ah, didn't you know?* – or worse, that he was married, with three children – *you know, to the girl we saw this evening; yes that is his wife.* Quickly, she changed the subject. 'Do you like being a nurse?' she asked Els. It was a fairly inane sort of a question, but it served the purpose.

They talked for a while about work and careers. Els, still gazing out over the garden, revealed that if she wasn't a nurse then she would like to be a gardener. 'I like to watch things grow,' she said. 'It is very satisfying. And it is even better if you can eat what you have grown. So I would like to have a little piece of land of my own, where I can grow my vegetables. And I would like to have chickens, and children running around my feet.'

Isabel told them about her own dream of giving up her job, so she could write novels.

'Yes, you should do it,' enthused Els. 'You should always go for what you feel in your heart.' She drained the last few drops of beer from the glass in her hand and walked back to the table. 'After all, you have just the one life,' she added. 'Hey, Pieter – maybe we will appear in one of her books.' She turned to Isabel. 'You know, I don't think I could write a book. I don't have self-control. And I think maybe I need the security of my work too – so no chickens for me. Not just yet.'

'Yes, me too,' said Isabel. 'I am probably too much of a coward to give up my job – even if it was so I could do what I really wanted.'

'So who is your favourite writer?' asked Pieter.

Isabel thought for a moment. 'I have lots of favourites. I like Jane Austen, and Virginia Woolf.'

'Ah,' said Els. 'I have read one of her books once, but I didn't understand any of it.'

'Which one?'

'It was about . . . Ah, I'm not sure what it was about. But it was in a lighthouse.'

'*To the Lighthouse?*'

'Yes. Maybe.'

'Have you read any of her others?'

'No, I haven't.'

'You should try. Honestly. Read her early ones first. It helps.'

'I read detective stories,' Pieter told her. 'I like a murder.'

Els held up the book she had with her. 'What I am reading now.'

Isabel squinted at the title. She couldn't make it out; it was in Dutch. But then she recognized the name of the author – Thomas Hardy. 'Oh – depressing,' she said.

'Yes, it is very dark, this one.' said Els. 'But I enjoy it.'

Pieter shook his head. 'I don't understand why she reads it. It makes her sad.'

They talked about books for a while, and then films, and Isabel felt her spirits reviving. She was on familiar territory again, and Els and Pieter were good company. She soon began to wonder if she had been getting everything a little bit out of proportion; she had let her imagination run away with itself. Tomorrow, she decided, she would forget all about Lee – and who he lived with

– or was married to. It was none of her business after all. And she would spend the entire day on her favourite beach. And then she would work out what she was going to do with the rest of her life.

The new girl came over to take their empty glasses. 'Any more drinks for you?' Her face no longer looked sulky.

Isabel decided that the two of them must have had an argument; and now they had made up.

'Another beer?' Pieter's voice cut in.

'Actually I won't if you don't mind.' She stood up. All three of them were looking at her now.

'I'm feeling a bit tired. I think it's time I went to bed. Long day.' She pulled a suitable face. 'Will you be around tomorrow?'

'Yes,' replied Els. 'We are going for snorkelling in the morning, but we will be here later.'

Pieter was nodding, enthusiastically. 'I am sure we will be sitting right here, in this same place, having some more beer.'

'Well in that case, I'll definitely see you tomorrow. Good night then.'

Isabel felt their eyes on her as she turned and walked away. The quickest way to her chalet was through the restaurant and down to the path at the back of the Gula House, and she had intended to go that way, but instead, she made for the steps leading to the garden. She knew that they would still be watching her, wondering why she was going the wrong way. She wasn't altogether sure herself. What she did know was that, now she was outside, she wasn't feeling tired at all. In fact she felt incredibly wide-awake.

She had taken this same path many times before – before she knew it would lead her past Lee's house. But, all of a sudden, it felt wrong to be there. What if he spotted her? Would he think she was looking for him? An innocent walk had been tainted by the information she now had in her possession.

She made an abrupt U-turn and went back in the direction of her own chalet. She would sit on her verandah, she decided, and read her book.

∞

Lee made one final tour of the kitchen, checking that everything had been left in order. It had been a busy night; he was tired. He stared at an untidy pile of dishcloths that had been left on top of a workbench, and without thinking about what he was doing he started to re-fold them, one by one, until he had formed a new, slightly neater pile.

Su Pei had been disappointing, he reflected. More than disappointing. He was beginning to wonder whether it had been wise to take her on in the first place. She had worked at the Mayang Palace for just a few months and yet her head was full of it: 'they do it like this at the Mayang, they don't do that at the Mayang'. Well she could go back to the Mayang for all he cared – except that he needed the extra pair of hands. Still, it was only for a couple of days, until Set Yen's mother was better. Even so, she had already upset Amir, and the boy who came in to do the washing-up. He'd had to take her to one side and talk to her – something he hated having to do – and worse, he had seen Isabel look over, while he was doing it, then he had been about to acknowledge her but she had turned away, suddenly – too suddenly – and without even a smile. That was what had truly unsettled him.

He had finished sorting out the cloths; now he spotted a stray knife next to the sink. He inspected it. He wondered if the three of them were still there, at the table, or whether they had gone. He had planned to join them for a drink once he had finished in the kitchen, but the clearing up had taken far longer than he'd expected. He washed the knife and dried it with one of the cloths he had just folded. He wiped his hands on a yellow towel and put his shoulder to the kitchen door, then stopped. What would he say to them? He stood there for a while, trying to think, but his mind had gone blank all of a sudden.

'*Celaka*,' he swore, under his breath – not that there was anyone around to hear. This woman was seriously unnerving him. He took a deep breath in and pushed on the door.

As the door swung back behind him he scanned the room. They weren't there. He cursed again, this time not so quietly; and Amir, who had been standing nearby, put his hand over his mouth and started to giggle.

'Sorry,' muttered Lee.

Amir grinned back at him.

Embarrassed (and since when had he started swearing in Malay, he wondered), Lee walked swiftly though the restaurant, not letting his eyes focus on anything in particular. Then he caught a glimpse of Els's golden-blonde hair.

They were still here after all. They were out on the verandah.

He waited for his pulse to slow, then walked on. But as soon as he reached the open doors he saw that she wasn't there. Els and Pieter were alone.

He hesitated, not sure that he should interrupt them. They had their heads close together, they were laughing at something. He started to move away but Pieter had spotted him and was waving him over.

'Hey, how are you?' Pieter shouted. 'Exhausted?'

'You can say that, yes.'

'You were very busy tonight. Sit down. Have a drink with us, please.' Pieter stood up and slipped his feet into a huge pair of canvas shoes. Before Lee had chance to reply, he had set off towards the bar.

'Bad night?' asked Els.

Lee moved towards the empty chair and sat down heavily. He shook his head. 'What a day. I am glad it's all over.' It was then that he noticed the empty glass in front of him. This was where she had been sitting, he thought.

'Am I disturbing you?'

'Of course not,' said Els. 'You look tired.'

He nodded.

'Pieter told me you were having some problems today.'

Lee picked up the empty glass and swivelled it round with his fingers. He wondered when she had left, whether he had just missed her. 'Bit short of staff,' he said eventually. 'Set Yen has gone home to look after her mother. And one of the kitchen boys didn't turn up. I had to run to his house to find him. And there he was with his arm bandaged up to here.' He chopped at his arm to illustrate. 'He had cut it when he was cleaning a fish for his mother.'

'Don't you have a new girl working?' Pieter had arrived back clutching three bottles of beer and a glass for Lee.

'Yes,' replied Lee, 'but she is giving me a big headache.' He laughed. 'Anyway, it's just for a short time. Until Set Yen comes back.'

'Let's hope her mother gets better quickly then,' said Els, raising her glass. 'Cheers.'

'*Gān bēi*,' replied Lee. The beer was icy cold and felt good as it slid down his throat. He took another, smaller, sip and put down his glass, next to Isabel's abandoned one. 'Where is Isabel tonight?' The question had jumped out before he had the chance to stop it.

'She went back to her room I think,' replied Els. 'She was feeling tired too.' She grinned mischievously. 'She went to that resort today – with the English couple.'

Lee nodded, trying not to show any reaction. He already knew about the excursion to the Mayang. He had been quite surprised to hear that she had gone with them.

'I don't think that she wanted to go,' added Els waving her arms around in the air. 'They captured her.' Her words were punctuated, as usual, by the sound of her silver bracelets. 'I think, if Sandra says you have to go somewhere – you just go.'

Lee laughed.

'You know, tomorrow, it is our last night here,' she went on.

Lee nodded. 'Yes, I know that.'

'Of course. Silly me.' She shook her head. 'We will miss all this when we are back in the city.'

'Maybe you will come back one day.'

'For sure, we will. It is a paradise. This place, and . . .' She lifted an arm and made a wide gesture towards the garden and the sea beyond. 'Ah, everything.' She reached out for her drink then seemed to change her mind and left it where it was on the table. 'Hey, I have an idea,' she said. 'Why don't we go to the village tomorrow night – for a goodbye drink? It will give you a rest too.'

Pieter looked over to Lee. 'Are you free?'

'Well, I would like a night off but . . .' He hesitated. 'I don't know. At the moment it is a little bit difficult for me. I have to . . . Er, let me think about it.'

He knew he shouldn't – not while things were so unsettled. But he had to. Because he was certain they would ask Isabel to join them too.

'It isn't fair,' Els was saying. 'You are in charge.'

'Yes, but he is having some problems at the moment,' Pieter replied. He turned back to Lee. 'How about if we don't go to the village? We will have our drink here, then you can find us when you are free.'

Lee was about to reply but was distracted by the sight of the American guy poking his head through the open doors, peering round as if he were looking for someone.

Lee downed the last of his beer. He had come to a decision. 'No – I need to get away from here. Gilbert can be in charge tomorrow. I shouldn't have to work every night. I will stay to check that everything is fine, and then I can join you later. How about that?' He was beginning to like the idea more and more. He wished he had thought of it himself. 'And I'll take you to Coconut Café. As my guests.'

'No, we won't accept that,' said Pieter. 'It was our idea. We are buying for you tomorrow.'

'And we will invite Isabel too,' said Els.

Although Lee had been thinking of little else, the sound of these words sent a ripple of excitement down his spine. He closed his eyes for a second then flicked them open and looked at Els. 'Will you see her tomorrow?' he asked. 'To tell her.'

'Ah, maybe not. I am not sure. We are going for snorkelling.'

'We will leave at eight,' added Pieter.

'Then we will miss her. She won't be up so early. Perhaps you will see her?'

Lee fidgeted with his empty glass. 'I'm not sure. I mean . . . I could . . . I can look for her but . . .'

It would be easy enough to do, of course.

'I know,' said Els. 'Do you have some paper? We will write her a note and put it under her door when we go back.'

When Lee returned, clutching a pad of paper and a pen, Els was clearing the table. 'Okay,' she said. 'What do we put? What about seven o'clock. Is it good?'

Lee thought for a moment. 'You go at seven, I will follow as soon as I can. Don't wait for me. I will tell Joseph – '

Els had started to write, but now she stopped. 'Joseph?'

'My friend – Joseph. His place is Coconut Café – just after MK Seafood. You know MK Seafood don't you?'

'Yes, we do,' replied Els. 'That's your friend too, isn't it?' She laughed. 'You have a lot of friends here.'

'Small-small place,' replied Lee.

∞

Isabel was sitting on her verandah, wondering what creature was making such a racket in the forest behind her. It was angry, she thought at first. But a moment later and the sounds had become intensely mournful; she could only wonder what was making it so sad.

Last night she had stood in the garden with Lee, and listened to the very same sounds. But that was yesterday. Today everything was different. She was sure that Lee had been avoiding her.

She turned back to the book that was resting on her lap.

He had become wary of affections that seemed always to end in tragedy.

It must have been the fourth or fifth time she had read that same sentence; she couldn't concentrate. She read the sentence once more.

'Huh,' she snorted, 'you can say that again.' And although she knew that the author was referring to the tragedy of death, she couldn't help reflecting that her own affections usually ended up in the wrong places too, and any relationships she embarked upon seemed, also, to end in tragedy. She folded the corner of the page, to keep her place, and closed the book.

'I've had enough of today,' she told herself. 'I may as well go to bed.'

She had just stood up when she heard the crunch of gravel on the path. She froze. The footsteps got closer. He had come to find her after all. She sat down again and opened the book, quickly smoothing out the corner she had turned down.

He had become wary of affections that seemed always to end in tragedy.

The footsteps stopped.

'Hiya.'

She hesitated for a moment before she looked up, already knowing who it was.

Phil was standing on the bottom step, one foot resting on the next, poised to come up. She noticed that he'd had a haircut since the last time she saw him; she could see the reddish skin of his scalp through the closely cut curls. There was something about the way his head stuck out at an angle from the neck of his shirt that made her think of a bird of prey.

'What you doing?'

What does it bloody well look like? she thought. 'Just reading,' she said. 'I was about to go in. The light isn't very good.'

'Wanna go for a drink?'

She made an effort to sound polite. 'No thanks, it's a bit late and . . .'

'Come on – I'm goin' to the village,' he interrupted. 'You don't wanna stay here on your own all night it's early.'

'I'm a bit tired actually.'

'What you reading?'

She held up her book, so that he could see the title, then –

That was stupid, she realized.

Seeing it as an invitation, he took the few remaining steps up to her verandah then leant his back against the rail and pulled a packet of cigarettes from his pocket. He took one out and held it out to her.

She shook her head.

'Got any matches?'

Isabel thought of the small red box on the table inside, next to the mosquito coil. 'No, sorry,' she replied. 'I don't smoke.'

He slipped the cigarette back into the packet and put it in his pocket. 'So – what you up to tomorrow?'

'Don't know yet. Stay here I think.'

He scuffed at the wooden floor with the toe of his boot. 'Yeah. Me too.'

Isabel's heart sank. The prospect of a day spent avoiding Phil.

'Thought I might walk to that waterfall,' he went on.

Recalling her own walk to the waterfall, she suppressed a smile.

'Wanna come?'

'No – no thanks. I went up there a couple of days ago.'

He scratched at the skin on the back of his hand then inspected his fingernails. 'Huh. Well, if you change your mind . . .' He started off down the steps, but when he got halfway he turned and shouted up to her. 'See you tomorrow then.'

Not if I can help it, she thought.

She watched him slouch off in the direction of the village. Was it possible that he could be so thick skinned, or was she giving out the wrong signals?

She picked up her book and went inside, shutting the door firmly and leaning on it until she had turned the key and heard the lock click into place. She pulled on the handle just to make sure.

Isabel hadn't been asleep for long when Els crept up the steps to her chalet.

The folded sheet of white paper made a faint swishing sound as it slid under the door. It lay there, still and silent, for the remainder of the night.

PART SEVEN

London
March 1996

∞

6.40 pm

J ust as Emma had turned the corner into Romily Street, it had started to rain. But she had already seen the restaurant's white neon light at the far end of the street; it was only a few blocks, she told herself, it wasn't worth the bother of getting out the umbrella for such a short distance. But now, standing in the restaurant foyer, trying to catch her breath, she wished she had bothered. Her hair was ruined; all she wanted to do was to dive into the cloakroom and sort it out; but there was this absolutely gorgeous man walking straight towards her, and he had the most alarmingly beautiful smile, which, at this precise moment in time, was directed straight at her. She could feel her cheeks beginning to burn as she let her eyes take in his delicately tanned skin, the blonde hair teasing around his ears and neck, the pristine white shirt skimming his muscular torso.

'Good evening Madam.'

It was the 'Madam' that caught her off guard. For a split second she thought he must be addressing someone standing behind her. But there was no-one else there.

'Hello,' she said, trying what she thought was her most alluring smile. 'We have a table booked for eight – eight people I mean, not eight o' clock.' She was dismayed to hear herself giggle. 'It's seven – seven o'clock – the booking. I. . .' She forced herself to stop. She wished she could go out, come in, and start all over again.

'And the name?'

He had deep blue eyes, almost turquoise. She wondered if they were contacts.

'Stevens – no – Raines, I mean. I think it was booked under the name Raines – my friend.'

He glanced down at the open book on the desk. 'Yes, one of your party is already here. May I take your coat?'

Emma could sense his eyes on her as she slipped her arms from the sleeves of her coat, relieved not to get herself tangled up in the process. As she handed it to him, her fingers brushed against the inside of his wrist. A moment later and she had worked out that she was probably old enough to be his mother. Almost. Life was so unfair.

He led her down a corridor and into a room. There was a single round table, laid to perfection with starchy napkins, ranks of tall-stemmed glasses and a vase of flame-red flowers.

Lynn was already seated at the table, her hair and the flowers matching beacons in a sea of silver and white; a pearly balloon bobbed on a string tied to the empty chair beside her.

Emma had wanted to be the first to arrive, and was slightly put out that Lynn had got there before her; but it was the sight of the balloon that made her grimace.

'Okay, okay, it's only a balloon,' Lynn responded. 'Give me a break.'

Emma knew that the young man was still hovering behind her, waiting, she suspected, to hold out one of the chairs for her. 'It's fine,' she said to him, 'I'm going to sort out the seating arrangements first.' She watched him glide out of the room and then turned back to Lynn. 'I thought we had agreed . . .'

'I know,' Lynn interrupted, 'no hen party stuff. But I had to do something.'

'Not here.'

Lynn scoffed. 'Well, it's too stuffy for its own good.'

'Well, I think it's very tasteful. And Isabel will like it. That's the main thing.' She rested her hands on the back of the nearest chair. 'How are we going to do the seating?'

'Why don't we let everyone sit where they want?' Lynn said. 'Who's coming anyway?'

'Well, there's us – and Isabel – and Simon, of course.'

'Simon? You can't have a bloke at a hen do.'

'Well, you can if it's Simon. Anyway he's Isabel's best friend.'

Lynn pulled a face.

Emma knew that Lynn liked to think of herself as Isabel's best friend. 'I know you don't like him,' she went on, 'but . . .'

'That's not true.'

'Well he's coming, anyway. Then there are four people from her work – or they used to work there, I'm not sure. I'm glad we've got a round table. It makes life easier. Ah, look – here's Simon now.'

Simon and the gorgeous young man were standing in the doorway, chatting away to each other as if they were the best of friends.

'Oh God, I hope they're not swapping telephone numbers,' Lynn said. 'He's such an old tart.'

'Shush,' whispered Emma, 'he might hear you.'

Simon strode towards them.

'Hello possums.' He reached Emma first and planted a melodic *mwoa- mwoa* on both of her cheeks.

He then cavorted round the table and bent towards Lynn. 'How are we all? Oooh – excellent – a round table. Where are you putting me then?'

Emma giggled. 'Well we can't do boy-girl-boy-girl, so you'll just have to choose which girl you want to sit next to.'

He pulled out the chair next to Lynn. 'Well, this'll do me for now. I'll sit here.' He folded his arms and beamed round at them. 'Champagne's on its way – I told Roberto to keep it flowing.'

Emma snorted. 'Roberto! He's no Roberto. I had him down more as a . . . Well, I don't know what. But he's not a Roberto. He's gorgeous, but there's not an inch of Italian in him.'

'Oooh, I bet there's more than an inch, sweetie,' replied Simon. 'So,' he continued, ignoring the squeals of laughter, 'are we all set to send our girl down the happy road to matrimony?'

'Road to ruin you mean,' said Lynn.

'Who's jealous then?'

'I'm not jealous. Just concerned, that's all. As her friend.'

Simon stopped smiling and turned to face her. 'Concerned?'

'Yes. That she's doing the right thing.'

Emma glanced towards the door, worried that Isabel might arrive at any moment. 'For heaven's sake, you two. Shut up. This is her hen night if you haven't forgotten.'

'I wouldn't say it to her. Of course I wouldn't.'

'Good,' said Emma, in a way she hoped would signal the end of the conversation.

'But does anyone know what's the big rush?' Lynn went on. 'I thought they weren't getting married until summer at least. She's not . . .? You know . . .?'

Emma shrugged. She didn't know the answer to any of that. The truth was, she also had been worried about Isabel; not so as she could pin it down, but there had been something different about her in the past few months, a sort of graceful withdrawal, as if she had become tired of living her life. But when she tried to pursue it, Isabel had insisted that she was perfectly happy.

Emma returned her attention to the conversation bubbling on without her – Simon was describing a club that had recently opened on Shaftesbury Avenue. She was glad that he had managed to change the subject away from Isabel. She knew, too, that he wasn't keen on David, so she was doubly pleased that he hadn't reacted to Lynn's remark; although she had spotted the expression on his face.

'Here she is.' Simon had leapt to his feet.

Emma looked up and saw Isabel standing at the entrance to the room, along with four women she didn't recognize. Isabel had her head bent towards one of them; they were laughing.

Simon was making his way towards the group. 'Sweetie, you look fabulous. Divine.'

Emma stood up too. She could see Roberto standing by with a huge, silver ice bucket, and two bottles of champagne; another waiter held a tray of glasses. Emma wished she had a glass in her hand right now, so she had something to do, just until everyone settled down.

But Isabel had spotted her; she made her way over to the table and gave her a hug. 'Emma, it's great to see you. How are you?'

'I'm fine. Yes, really good. You look fantastic – elegant – as always.'

Isabel looked down at the dark red dress she was wearing. 'Do you like it? I wasn't sure. It was ever so expensive.' She giggled. 'But what the hell – it's a special occasion isn't it?'

'Suits you.' said Emma. 'And your hair – it's lovely. You should wear it like that more often.'

Isabel tossed her head, so that the soft dark curls skimmed her shoulders. 'Emma, Lynn – meet Adele and Louise. Emma, Lynn and I were at university together,' she explained. 'In fact Lynn and I went to the same school as well. And this is Yvonne and Kate. I think you met once, ages ago – Yvonne and Kate used to work at Fromer.'

Kate laughed. 'Yeah, about four years ago. Seems like ten.' She looked at Emma for a second or two. 'I remember you. We went to a club once – in Camden – then back to Isabel's flat, on a night bus.'

'Shall we sit down,' Isabel was saying.

'Yes, come on, come on. Drinky time.' Simon steered Roberto through the group, and while Roberto opened the champagne, the others arranged themselves around the table.

'Well, cheers to everyone and especially the blushing bride,' said Simon, as soon as they all had a glass in their hand. 'Although, I have to say I've never seen Isabel blush at anything.'

'Oh thanks for that,' said Isabel, laughing. 'My reputation in tatters.'

'My pleasure,' replied Simon, waving his glass at her. 'Come on Roberto, fill 'em up.'

As her glass was filled, Emma felt the tingling of the bubbles as they skittered over the rim and onto her fingers. She looked up and caught Roberto's eye. Out of my league, she thought, and almost certainly gay. Far too pretty not to be.

Emma leant back in her chair with a sigh. She had eaten too much and was wondering whether she was going to have to undo the top button of her trousers. She wanted to reach over to the middle of the table for the water jug, but Louise was leaning across her, talking to Kate.

'I sometimes wear a ring when I go out,' Louise was saying. 'When men think you're single, you're fair game. In their eyes.'

'I know,' Kate said. 'It's like that at work. The guys never took me seriously – until I got married. You know, stopped telling me all their dirty jokes and whatnot.'

'Yeah, you're respectable now, you see. You're not supposed to like dirty jokes any more.'

'That's the trouble with working in a male dominated environment.'

'Where do you work now, Kate?' Emma asked, taking the opportunity to lean forward and grab the water jug.

'In the city. A far cry from publishing, I know. But it pays more. What about you? Didn't you used to work at the British Museum or something?'

'Still do.'

'Oh, just round the corner from us then,' Louise said. 'We're on Montague Street.'

'Yes, I know, I've been to your offices to meet Isabel.'

Emma saw Louise glance at her hand.

'Are you married Emma?'

'No, I'm absolutely single. No boyfriend. Nothing.'

'Oh God, I hate being single,' Louise said. 'It's like, everyone else in the whole world has someone. Except me.'

'Weekends and bank holidays.'

'Yes, aren't they just the worst? I can just about cope with Saturdays, but Sundays . . . They're the pits. All those bloody magazines full of smug couples walking their dogs, lounging about on cruises, buying sofas. It makes you want to throw up.'

'But don't you think it's pathetic?' Kate said. 'Even in this day and age, we are still supposed to need a man in tow?'

'It does make life that little bit easier though, doesn't it?' Louise replied. 'I mean, who do you get to do your odd jobs around the house?'

'No man I've ever met,' Lynn rejoined.

Simon banged on the table and waved a menu in the air. 'Who's for pudding?'

'I'll have a look at the menu,' Adele said.

'Me too,' said Lynn, 'though I'm not sure I could eat another thing.'

'Did you ever finish that novel you were writing?' Yvonne asked Isabel.

Isabel shook her head. 'No. Still working on it.'

'Isn't it hard to find the time, when you're at work all day?'

'A bit. But I work in the evenings – or try to. Problem is, I can always find something else that needs doing instead. You know, scrub the kitchen floor, polish the furniture, reorganize my wardrobe.' She laughed. 'Tell you what – my house is never cleaner than when I am supposed to be writing. I bet Virginia Woolf never had such a clean house.'

'Well she would have had servants, wouldn't she?' added Lynn.

'And how are you managing now?' Emma called across to Simon. 'Now that you are on your own.' She had just remembered that Simon had recently left Fromer Press to set up his own agency.

He looked up from his menu. 'Not bad – not bad. I'm just waiting for Isabel to finish that novel of hers. Make me a rich man.'

'You'll have a long wait then,' cut in Isabel. 'In any case, I might not want to share all my profits with you. What if I don't want an agent?'

Simon shook his head in mock despair.

'Won't the place where you work publish your book?' asked Lynn.

'What Fromer? No, they only publish academic stuff. It's far too lightweight for them.'

'What's it about then?' Louise asked.

Isabel thought for a moment. 'Oh, you know – life, love, the usual things.'

Emma smiled to herself, pleased to hear that Isabel was working on her novel again. She knew how much it meant to her, and how she had thought she'd lost the ability to write.

The conversation had moved on now. They were talking about America. Isabel had recently come back from Chicago – one of David's business trips.

'Does he get sent overseas a lot?' Adele asked.

'Yes, a fair bit, but I don't always go with him.'

'Oh, I would,' said Louise. 'I wish I got sent abroad on business. All those five-star hotels. What bliss.'

'Ha! You should be so lucky,' exclaimed Lynn. 'When I get sent anywhere I'm in the Dogsville Motel. My bosses have got penny-pinching down to a fine art. Only other people get sent to Hiltons and Hyatts and what-have-you.'

'That's because you are public sector,' said Simon 'and we, the public, are paying for your trips.'

'No, it's actually the students' fees that pay for my trips.' Lynn turned back to Louise. 'I work in education, by the way.'

'But don't you think,' asked Isabel, 'that the Dogsville Motel is often more interesting than a boring old Hilton?'

'Oh, who wants character when you can have luxury?' replied Lynn.

Isabel reached for the bottle of champagne and filled Lynn's glass, then her own. 'But those chains,' she said, holding the bottle aloft, 'they're all replicas of each other. It doesn't matter where you are in the world – you could be anywhere. And anyway,' she went on, passing the bottle to Yvonne, 'business trips aren't all they're cracked up to be. More often than not, you don't get to see anything of the country – just the inside of hotel rooms.'

'That's true,' joined in Simon, holding out his empty glass to be filled. 'Once you've seen one you've seen them all – like most things in this world. So tedious.'

'And lonely,' added Kate.

'Well I wouldn't mind a bit of that sort of tedium,' Adele said. 'Doesn't Fromer *ever* send anyone overseas?'

'Isabel went once, didn't you?' Kate said.

'Oh? Where?' Adele asked.

'She got sent to Kuala Lumpur.'

'Wow! Malaysia? How wonderful.'

'Twice, actually,' Kate continued.

'Twice?'

The bottle of champagne had just reached Emma; she up-ended it over her glass. 'That one's dead.'

'Yeah, that's right,' Yvonne said. 'From what I remember, you saw a bit more than the inside of a hotel room – or maybe not,' she added. 'Didn't you meet some guy out there?'

Isabel had been concentrating on her napkin, painstakingly folding it, over and over again, until it resembled a fan. She let it drop back down on the table and looked up, smiling.

'Yes I remember now,' Yvonne went on. 'You went to some really amazing island.'

Emma saw Simon shoot Yvonne a look, but Yvonne didn't seem

to notice; she carried on talking, oblivious. 'Did you ever go back? You know, when you went out there the second time?'

'Yes, I did actually.'

'You've never told me that,' said Kate. 'You went back? To that island?'

'Didn't I? Well, there was nothing to tell, I suppose.'

Emma glanced at Isabel, trying to read her expression. Her lips were set in a smile, and her cheeks were flushed – perhaps from the effect of the champagne. But she remembered it all very well. She remembered the night Isabel had appeared on her doorstep. The moment she had laid eyes on her, she knew that something was terribly wrong. Once Isabel had stopped crying – at least, enough to tell her the story – and before she had managed to cry herself to sleep – Emma had heard all about the guy in Malaysia. It appeared that Isabel had fallen head over heels – not for the first time, but this time it was serious – and she had been sure that he felt the same way about her. When he failed to get in touch, Isabel couldn't understand why. But as far as Emma knew, he never did contact her. And when Isabel went back to where she had met him, he had gone. In fact the whole place had gone, if she remembered correctly.

'There was nothing in it,' she heard Isabel saying. 'Just a holiday romance. Not even that, really. I thought there might have been something – but there obviously wasn't. And it wasn't the first time I'd got that wrong, was it?' She flicked her long hair back over her shoulders. 'Anyway. Who's for more champagne?' She turned to Simon. 'I'm absolutely sure you would love to go and find Roberto, and get us another bottle.'

∞

1.30 pm

L ee pushed open the heavy door and stepped outside. It wasn't raining but the sky was swollen with cloud. These days he didn't mind the cold too much, but today it was the dampness pressing down on him that made him turn up the collar of his too-thin jacket, and walk away from the building with his shoulders hunched and his head bowed low.

When he had first come to London, he had feared he would never be able to tolerate the weather – the dullness, the heavy skies, the biting winds, the perpetual drizzle – but he had become accustomed to its eccentric moods; he marvelled at how the sky could change colour so many times in one day, and that you could look out of your window one morning to find that everything outside had turned white overnight. He had even enjoyed the eerie vagueness of a foggy day, when the buildings seemed to come adrift from their ancient foundations and hover, disconcertingly, above the street. At least he now knew why the British people talked so much about the weather – just like the Chinese and their obsession with food. He had once explained this to Isabel: that when Chinese people greeted each other, they would sometimes say '*chī fàn ma*?' And she had been greatly amused to think that an entire nation went around asking each other 'have you eaten rice?'

But that was not what he was thinking about now, as he walked through the car park and out towards Russell Square. It was not that he had stopped thinking about Isabel – that would never happen, as long as he lived – but when he found his mind wandering, when her face, or the sound of her voice, would glide into his consciousness, he tried to focus on something else.

Without much success, it had to be said. Time and time again, he would catch a glimpse of someone in the street – someone with dark, wavy hair and beautiful eyes – and he would feel a tightness across his chest, just for those few seconds it took to realize that it wasn't her.

He had planned to cross the road, to take his usual route across the square: not because it was a short cut back to his room, but it was a way to leave behind, just for a moment or two, all those imposing blocks of stone, and concrete, and brick, and escape to an island of green, one of the many hidden in the midst of the city. But while he stood waiting for a gap in the traffic, he changed his mind, turned, and started walking in a different direction. He needed to clear his head. He was feeling restless and frustrated; he had wasted the entire morning at the library in Senate House, trying to figure out their filing systems, and there was work due in on Monday. Perhaps he should walk to the library at LSE, where he knew his way round. He stopped in his tracks and leant against the black iron railings that kept the street from the tall, elegant buildings behind. Or should he give himself the rest of the day off? It was Saturday after all. And the essay only needed another hour or so before it was finished. He could soon polish it off tomorrow.

He pushed himself from the railing and started to walk, his eyes fixed on the gum-blotted pavement sliding beneath his feet, his mind concentrating on each separate movement required of his body to push one foot in front of the other. And soon, his mind had swivelled back to what had been worrying him for weeks now. Was he doing the right thing? Or should he give up and go back to Malaysia? There was a time when he had truly believed that getting this qualification would set him on an even footing with his competitors, would open the doors he had always imagined were closed to him. But was it just too much to pay? Simply to gain a bit of respect? And he had started to wonder if he hadn't been fooling himself all along: however many degrees he had, if he didn't know the right people then he may as well give up now. And although he tried to be careful with money, he was racing through what he had earned in KL and close to drawing on his savings again. That was not good. He mustn't touch that money.

It had to remain intact. If he didn't have enough to start up his business when he finally got home, then everything he was doing now really was a complete waste of time.

Preoccupied with his thoughts, his pace had quickened, but now something was forcing him to stop; he could hear a voice, it was saying something that seemed to be meant for him. He looked up. There was a man, standing in his path, looking at him.

'You know tooting-hammer-street where is it?'

Lee shook his head. 'Sorry. I am a stranger here too. I think you have to ask someone else.'

Quickly, he turned his attention back to his own problems. If he gave up now, he thought, then all the money he had spent so far would have been wasted. So that meant he must carry on and see it through to the bitter end.

It was true that none of it was anything like he had imagined. Then there were the other students. No wonder they sat in lectures looking pallid, and vacant, like wretched cows in a field with no grass. It seemed to him that their lives revolved around the bar, and pubs, and clubs, and he tried to remember what he had been like at their age. But it had been different for him: he had just turned eighteen when his father had died, and he had started work at Buah Lodge; by the time he was twenty-seven, half of the business had belonged to him.

As he continued to walk, it struck him that the man who had stopped him for directions was probably looking for Tottenham Court Road, and he felt bad about dismissing him so quickly. He should have tried harder to help. He had once been new to this city, and he knew what it was like to be lost. He looked round, wondering whether he could run and catch up with him, but the man had already disappeared into Russell Square.

Lee had reached the end of the street he was on; he glanced up at the wall, to see what this one was called. The sign said Montague Street. He recognized the name; he had been this way before, and he knew that if he turned right, he would walk past the British Museum and eventually find his way to Oxford Street. He hadn't made a conscious decision to go there, but the idea now appealed to him. When he had first come to London, he used to walk up and down Oxford Street on a Saturday afternoon, making out he had somewhere to go, even if he hadn't. Somehow, being in the midst of all those people, even strangers, made him feel less alone, less disconnected.

Now he had decided where he was going, he felt happier. Perhaps he would walk down as far as Selfridges, he thought, and go into the food hall. And with any luck, they would be handing out free samples of things to eat and drink – which meant he wouldn't need to buy himself any lunch.

On his right were the tall railings of the British Museum. As he drew level with the open gates, he stopped.

Or should he go in here instead?

He had walked past the place often enough, but had never been inside. He wondered how much it would cost. At least it would be warm, he thought. Better than trudging down Oxford Street. And it had just started to rain.

A bearded man, with skin the colour of strong white coffee, was seated half-on, half-off a wooden stool, in front of a small kiosk. He wore a blue uniform and a matching blue turban. Lee couldn't decide whether or not he was selling tickets, but when a group of Japanese tourists wandered through, and the man in the turban just stared at them, unmoved, Lee joined the tail end of the group and followed them into the wide, open courtyard. When the group stopped, to take photos of each other, Lee left them to it and made for the steps leading up to the huge, stone columns at the front of the building. A notice outside informed him that entrance was free of charge. That was good, he thought. He might be able to afford a dish of something in Chinatown later on.

He had been wandering aimlessly for almost two hours, but now his head was aching and he was feeling hungry; he had seen enough relics for one day. He hadn't known how much stuff there was in here. He looked around for an exit sign, and when he couldn't immediately see one he had visions of getting lost and locked in. If he had to spend the night here, he thought, he'd stay well away from those Egyptian mummies, that's for sure.

He walked through an archway into another room, then stopped to consult a floor plan. When he looked up again, he noticed a large piece of fabric hanging on the wall by the door.

There was something familiar about it: the colours, the shapes in the pattern that was woven through it; and its familiarity was strangely comforting. Then he realized what it was. When he was very young, his mother used to have something similar, draped over her bed. He was always drawn to that bedcover: he liked its colour, of warm red brick, and the golden threads which he once thought were real gold; he could remember how he used to pull it from the bed and wrap it round himself, and be a prince, or an emperor. That was when they had lived in the big wooden house in Malacca: before his father had died. That house wasn't there any more, either

After a moment, he moved closer, to study the caption beneath it. The neat lines of typed print told him that the rug was from Borneo, and he mused on how this solitary piece of fabric – something that conjured up so many memories – had found its way here. A dull ache infused his body: the ache of nostalgia. It surprised him. The idea of being homesick had never occurred to him before. After all, where did he have now, that he could truly call home?

He knew, then, that he must carry on with his studies and pursue his dream. He would build the new resort, whatever the cost. He had managed to let too many other things slip from his grasp; that dream was now the one constant thing remaining in his life.

Underneath the rug, in a glass display case, were some coins. He had to bend his head to the glass to read the card propped up beside them.

'Portuguese coins produced for their settlers and traders in Malacca'.

His father had told him that their ancestors came from Portugal. That was the reason, he had explained, why Lee was taller than many of his friends. And he remembered how it had bothered him so much, how he had hated to be different. Whether or not the story was true, he never knew.

He straightened himself and looked around the room. There was nothing else that caught his eye, and he really should get going; he had been here long enough. He took one more look at the rug then turned and walked away.

*

By the time Lee left the museum it was almost dark. But it had stopped raining, and the sky had cleared itself of the heaviest layers of cloud that had been a permanent feature for the past few days. He looked at his watch; it wasn't even five o'clock, but he was very hungry now. He disentangled himself from a group of school children who were jostling their way out of the museum entrance, and stopped in front of one of the wide, stone pillars. He was considering whether to go back to hall first, to see if he could find Julie. He knew he would have to offer to pay for her if she came with him, but at least the meal would be jollier if he didn't have to eat alone. It would also fill up more of the evening.

He had never thought of Julie as his girlfriend, although he suspected that many of their classmates did. They had been drawn together merely by the fact that they were both from Malaysia, and he had invited her out a few times – he enjoyed her company. But recently he had started to worry that she might think they were 'dating', as she would have put it. Or was that exactly what they were doing?

As he walked back towards Endsleigh Place, where they both had their rooms in the students' residence, he wondered whether he should think more seriously about Julie. She was intelligent, kind, and at one time he would have found her very attractive. So why not now? Wasn't it about time he moved on? He grinned to himself. That was exactly what his friend Chi Wan had said to him last week. Those very words. He had made an impromptu visit to Lee's room, and had found Lee in low spirits. 'You should get out more,' he had nagged, 'start enjoying yourself.' And perhaps he was right, Lee thought. But it was what Chi Wan had said later that evening that had really stuck in his mind. 'Memories are good,' he had told him, 'and you should hold onto them. But you've got to live your life as well, so you can keep making new ones. Or you'll look back one day, when you are an old man, and realize you have wasted all that time.' Quite the philosopher was Chi Wan when he'd had a few drinks.

By the time Lee reached the building where he lived, he was feeling quite cheerful. He would find Julie, ask her out for a meal, and maybe they could see a film as well. It was a while since he had been to the cinema. He couldn't afford it, but if Chi Wan was right, he couldn't afford not to either.

He ran up the two flights of stairs and through the double doors to Julie's corridor. But when he got to her door he found a note attached to her pin-board. Neat, square letters informed him that: 'U can find Julie Wong in the D 'n D'. Underneath the note was a blue pig hanging from a ribbon; the pig stared back at Lee with dull, plastic eyes. He read the note again then turned and retraced his steps down the corridor. The Duck and Dive. Did he really want to spend the evening in the packed, smoke-filled bar at the students' union? No, he couldn't face it. He didn't know that Julie went there either; he supposed he had never thought about it before, but it surprised him. He wondered who she was with.

He took the two further flights of stairs to his floor and walked the length of the corridor, past eight identical doors, until he reached his own. As he walked, his eyes scanned the notes and messages and the now familiar scraps and snippets pinned to each door, all giving clues – often intended, sometimes not – to the personality of the room's occupant. His own pin-board was empty, apart from his name, 'LEE KIM CHENG', written out in bold, black type.

As soon as he got inside he turned on his cassette player. He grabbed the remote control and lay down on the narrow bed. The track that started up was fast, noisy, intrusive. Instinctively, Lee hit the volume control; but then reckoned that everyone would be out, so what did it matter? In any case, he had to put up with their noise often enough.

The song finished abruptly, as if someone had cut off the end by mistake. And he couldn't help smiling. Must be one of Chi Wan's cassettes, he thought.

He heard the machine hiss for a second or two before the next track began. It was very different to the first. Lee closed his eyes and let the melody flow over him. As soon as he started to listen to the lyrics, he realized they were unfolding a story, and one that was all too familiar. There was something about the song that dug straight into the core of him, something that made him want to play it again, and again, and again. He pressed the re-wind button and found the beginning of the track; the plaintive notes of the electric guitar cut across a gently rhythmic drumbeat. Lee felt his eyes fill with tears.

It's just the song, he told himself, rubbing briskly at his face. Can't you listen to something more cheerful? He reached out for the empty cassette box and squinted at Chi Wan's scratchy handwriting.

'Shit.' He threw the box onto the bed and cradled his head in his hands. He couldn't believe that the pain was still so raw. Especially after all this time. And he hadn't even been thinking about her. These days he tried not to let himself think about her.

He wound the track to the beginning once more, turned up the volume and walked over to the window. For once, the sash slid open without complaint and the cold air charged through, mingling with the current of warmth coming from the ancient, iron radiator. Lee gazed into the darkness of the square, listening to the words filling the room behind him.

Here come the late night blues again,
Here comes a face
From long, long ago.
So many years since you lay in my arms
But there's still a place
In my heart for you.
You and the late night blues.

A row of dark, skeletal trees reached up to the sky with their gnarled winter branches, and high above them was the moon, partly obscured by the swathes of cloud creeping across its face. There was a star too, a tiny pinprick of yellow piercing the blackness, and as his eyes started to focus on the void, he could see others, fainter, barely there, flickering in and out of existence.

He pressed his hands on the sill and leant out. The cold air hit the wetness on his cheeks, stinging his face, tightening the skin around his eyes. Was she out there somewhere, he wondered, somewhere in this vast, sprawling city? Was it possible that she might, at this very moment, be looking at the same moon, the same stars? He was shaking now and the tears were flowing freely. He reached behind him and pulled a sweater from under a pile of books, using it to wipe his eyes before pulling it over his head.

With his arms folded tight across his body, for extra warmth, he turned back to the window and stared out at the London sky.

Where is she? he thought. Where the hell is she?

PART EIGHT

Malaysia
July 1991

∞

26 July 1991
Kampung Teluk

I sabel checked herself in the mirror one last time. Now it was the necklace that was wrong. She fumbled underneath her hair, trying to unhook the end of the chain; but her fingers had decided not to co-operate, and the tiny lever would keep springing from her grasp. The fan was on at full blast but her skin was already moist with sweat.

'Bloody hell!' She dropped down onto the bed and thumped the pillow in frustration. Despite the fact that she had started getting ready over an hour ago, she was going to be late. It was five minutes to seven. She took a deep breath, stood up, and went back to the mirror to have another go at the clasp. This time it responded, and the necklace swung off. She stared back at her reflection for a moment then pulled a face. Something still wasn't quite right. She pulled off her earrings, picked up her jewellery bag and tipped the contents onto the bed. But nothing would do.

She wondered if she should visit the bathroom once more before she left.

'For goodness sake, Isabel. Just go.'

She grabbed her bag and headed for the door. As she passed the table she paused. On it was the note she had found under her door that morning. She picked it up and re-read it, just one last time, just to be sure.

> *Dear Isobelle*
> *How about coming out with us tomorrow night. We are going*
> *to the village – Lee too!*
> *See you in the Gula House at 7pm.*
> *Elsxx*

She had read the thing so many times, she already knew it by heart; but it was those two, simple words that sent her into a state of trepidation and elation – in equal measures. 'Lee too'. The words appeared to have been added as an afterthought; and each time she had read the note, she had searched for clues that might be hidden in the childlike writing on the paper. Was Lee really coming out with them? Why the exclamation mark? Had they asked him or might it have been his idea? Did it mean Lee on his own, or Lee and whatever-her-name-was? And when had they planned all this? It must have been last night, after she had left them. And she cursed herself, as she had done many times that day, for having left so early.

She folded the note and put it into her bag. And then made one final visit to the bathroom.

Once the door was closed behind her, and she was on the path to the Gula House, she felt much better. A slight breeze was playing with the hem of her skirt and stirring the wisps of hair she had left free of her ponytail; the graceful stems of bougainvillea tumbling over the boundary wall nodded their approval as she passed. But the spring disappeared from her step as she climbed the familiar wooden steps to the reception: Els and Pieter were there, but they were alone.

Of course they were, she told herself; it had been foolish to imagine that Lee would be going out with them. They might have asked him, and he would have been too embarrassed to refuse the invitation, but he would have found a way to get out of it, one way or another.

'Hey!' Els jumped up as soon as she saw Isabel. 'You look great.'

'Thanks.' Isabel forced a smile. 'So do you.'

Els twirled round. 'Shall we go? We are going to Coconut Café.' She took Isabel's arm. 'And Lee will join us, a little bit later.'

'Lee? Lee is joining us?'

'Yes, didn't you know?' She beamed at Isabel. 'I said it in my note, I think. He will come as soon as he has finished here.'

Isabel hadn't been to Kampung Teluk since the day she got lost, trying to find the waterfall. She remembered it being empty; all shuttered and sleepy. But this evening the village had the air of a street party about it. It was wide-awake and, like her, didn't seem able to contain its own excitement. Shutters and doors had been thrown wide open, lights blazed out, and the dainty verandahs looked in danger of collapse under the weight of people, animals and furniture. As Isabel, Els and Pieter made their way down the street, they were greeted with broad smiles and giggled attempts at 'hello' from the children. From behind the scenes came the convivial clatter of pots and pans, and the breezy rise and fall of women's voices; dogs barked intermittently from the scrappy patches of land at the back of the houses. And the heavy evening air was filled with alluring but unfamiliar scents, which mingled with the burning incense and the occasional wafts of smoke from nearby wood-fires.

Isabel recognised the path through the village – the simple row of concrete slabs laid unevenly onto the sand – but this time she saw something she hadn't noticed before. Halfway along, standing almost upright on two shiny metal poles, was a wooden sign. As soon as she read it, she started to laugh.

'Look,' she said, pointing, 'this is Main Street.'

But before anyone had chance to respond to her comment, a small boy emboldened by a frantic game of chase had come crashing into Pieter's legs and was now attempting to recover himself, with a helping hand from Pieter. As soon as he was upright, the boy stood in their path, staring up at them with wide, innocent eyes: eyes like deep, dark pools.

He was soon joined by his two companions.

After a few moments, one of them tried a cautious 'where you from?'

The little girl who was with them looked at her friend in amazement, then immediately mimicked the sounds she had just heard. 'Wah you fom? Wah you fom?' She covered her mouth with a tiny brown hand and, giggling, ran off into a nearby house. Isabel glanced in through the open shutters. The single room was small; a huge table dominated the space and a large family had, somehow, managed to cram themselves around it. Isabel thought she could count nine or ten heads and guessed there were three if not four generations of people living together in that tiny house.

The table was the centre of activity: elbows jostled, forks moved to mouths, spoons to bowls; a cup was raised to be filled from a jug, a young boy reached to help himself from a plate in the centre. But all eyes were focussed upwards, to a television set perched on top of a dark and solemn armoire. The picture was faint and unsteady, but the sound seemed to be in perfect working order as the stream of incomprehensible chatter could be clearly heard from outside.

Coconut Café was the very last building before Main Street petered out and submitted to the encroaching sand from the beach. Like some of the buildings in the village, it was made from wood and had a corrugated-iron roof. There were tables and chairs arranged under a canopy of palm-thatch, and still more spilling out onto the beach. As they approached, Isabel scanned the faces of the people already seated, hoping to see Lee. But he wasn't there.

Els had marched ahead and had claimed a large, circular table close to the sea. It was adorned with a blue batik cloth; in its centre, a night-light flickered inside a lantern. She stood by it, beaming. 'This is the best table,' she whispered to Isabel when she had finally caught up.

Isabel slung her bag over the back of a chair. 'It's lovely,' she whispered back; then laughed. 'Why are we whispering?'

She spent some time taking in her surroundings. Whoever owned the place had certainly made the most of their little patch. Beneath the canopy roof, multi-coloured lights swayed and twinkled in response to the slightest hint of a breeze coming in from the sea. Old metal tea chests, and oil drums cut down and painted red, gold or blue, served as a boundary wall and it took Isabel a few moments to realize why the plants inside them looked so familiar: they were larger versions of the ones growing in pots on her mother's windowsill.

Els and Pieter had taken their places at the table; they were now both looking at Isabel, waiting for her to do the same. Reluctantly, she lowered herself into a chair, aware that, in no time, she would be back to her usual, dishevelled self, conscious of the time she had wasted pressing her clothes with the tiny travel-iron.

'Whoops!' The chair had tipped sideways into a patch of softer sand; Isabel jumped up, glad of an excuse to be on her feet again. She slipped off her shoes and danced towards the sea. 'Just getting a pebble,' she shouted over her shoulder, 'to prop up the chair.' And if she took long enough, she thought, when she turned around, he might be there. They would walk towards each other across the sand; he would sweep her into his arms and . . .

'God, you're pathetic,' she muttered to herself.

Even so, she held onto the scene for a moment, fixing it in her mind, so she could come back to it later; then she grabbed the nearest pebble and walked up the slope towards her friends.

There was someone standing at their table, talking to Els and Pieter, and for a split second she thought it was Lee.

'This is Joseph,' Els said, 'the owner of Coconut Café. Lee's friend.'

Joseph grinned and held out his hand to her. 'Hi, Isabel, I am pleased to meet you.'

He looked older than Lee, and smaller, but had the same finely sculptured face, the same boyish appearance, and the same dark, almond-shaped eyes – eyes that were now looking directly at her, as if they were puzzling over something.

She dropped the pebble she was holding and shook Joseph's hand.

'*Baik-lah* – okay. What is everyone going to drink? Beer? Cocktails? I can make a very good cocktail for you – coconut, rum, pineapple juice.' While Joseph was speaking he moved round behind Isabel's chair. 'This one is wobbly,' he said. He pressed down on the back, pushing the legs into the sand.

'A cocktail for me,' said Els. 'How about you Isabel?'

Isabel nodded.

'I will have beer,' said Pieter.

'Pieter thinks that cocktails are for girls,' Els explained.

'It isn't true, Pieter,' said Joseph, shaking his head. 'You don't know what you are missing.'

'I will risk it.'

Els laughed. 'One day he will try something new, for a change.'

Pieter sighed and shook his head, then took off his glasses and started to polish them with the handkerchief he always seemed to have with him.

'He is not so adventurous,' Els went on. 'You know, he has the same lunch, every day, in the hospital.'

Pieter stopped what he was doing and held up the glasses to inspect his work. 'And so? What if I like it? What is the problem? And when you have finished taking to pieces my character, I would like to say that it was my idea to come here to Malaysia. So how unadventurous is that, if you don't mind me asking. What do you think Isabel?'

'I'm not taking sides,' she replied. In fact, she hadn't taken in much of the conversation at all. Her seat faced out towards the path and each time someone approached the entrance to the restaurant, her heart would leap; by the time Joseph had arrived back with the drinks, her insides were turning somersaults.

Joseph pointed to a board. It was the day's menu, chalked up in large white letters. 'This is what we have to eat tonight,' he said. 'Lee told me you would all be hungry, so I have plenty of food ready for you.'

'Shall we wait for Lee? Yes I think so.' Els answered her own question. 'He won't be long now.'

Unless he has changed his mind, Isabel thought. She tried to sneak a look at Pieter's watch.

'Ah – and here he is now.' Els was pushing back her chair.

Isabel was afraid to look up, afraid of what she might see. But there was too much activity going on around her now, so she took a deep breath to steady her nerves and forced herself to raise her head. Lee was approaching their table, he was walking quickly, he had almost reached them and, most importantly, he was alone.

Joseph clapped him on the back. 'Welcome my friend. Good to see that you could get away. How are things?'

Lee grimaced.

'Beer?'

'Thanks. I need one. Or two.'

'See,' Pieter said pointedly, to no-one in particular. 'Men prefer beer.'

'I will find you a good cold one,' said Joseph.

Isabel moved her bag from the back of the chair beside her and put it on the table.

Lee sat down with a sigh of relief.

'So, how was it today?' asked Pieter.

'Not too bad – not too bad. Better than yesterday.'

Isabel's eyes were fixed on her drink. She sensed him turn in his seat.

'So, Isabel –'

At the sound of her name she looked up and found herself staring straight into his eyes.

'What did you do today?'

'Oh, you know – the usual. I went to my beach – well it's not mine really.' She laughed, then wished she hadn't when she heard the sound of it echo back inside her head. 'But that's what I call it.'

Although she could hear herself speaking, she didn't recognize her voice: it was thin, high, and it was too loud. She wished, too, that she hadn't put on so much perfume.

'And then I swam to the little island and sat there for a while,' she continued. 'Just thinking really. And looking for shells. There are some lovely shells –' She tried not to look at Els, afraid to catch her eye.

'That's a very interesting drink.' Lee was inspecting her glass. It had arrived complete with red paper umbrella and a generous amount of fresh fruit. He seemed amused. 'I didn't know you liked those things. I would have made one for you. Mine are just as good as Joseph's. No – that's not true. Mine are better than his.'

'I heard that,' said Joseph, who had returned with Lee's beer, and a plate of snacks.

'How's the girl today, Lee?' Els asked. 'Still having trouble?'

Lee turned to Isabel. 'I have taken on a new staff, he explained, 'just while Set Yen is away. Her mother is ill and she has gone home for a day or two.'

Isabel looked away, trying to keep her expression in check. So she had been wrong about the girl; but it still didn't mean she was wrong about Set Yen. She twirled the little umbrella between her fingers and listened while he told them about Set Yen's replacement.

Her name was Su Pei.

'She is like a nightmare,' he said. 'She thinks she is better than anyone else, just because she has worked at the Mayang Palace. *Hai!* That's a joke. In just one day, she has managed to upset more or less everybody.' He stopped talking and took a long drink from his glass, then he grinned round at them. 'I am very happy to have got away from there tonight.'

By the time they had got round to choosing their food, they were also ordering their next round of drinks.

'You should watch out,' Lee said, 'his cocktails are very strong. I will drink beer only. Someone must help you to find the way back to Buah Lodge.'

Joseph laughed. 'I wouldn't trust him, either,' he said. 'I've had to carry him home many times.'

'Ha-ha. Well, maybe once. But that was a long time ago. When I was a young man.'

'You're still a young man,' said Joseph, laughing. 'You'll never catch up with me!'

'Yes, that's true,' said Lee. 'That's very true.'

Joseph pulled a chair from a nearby table and sat down, between Els and Peiter. They were soon discussing local diving sites. Isabel sipped her drink and tried to follow the conversation. But she had never been diving and couldn't get very excited about it. She drained her glass and leant forward to put it back on the table. Her bag was still there, in the spot where she had left it. She noticed that Lee had the strap in his hands and was twirling it between his fingers. He was clearly not listening to the conversation either. She watched his hands move over the velvet, and thought how easy it would be to reach out, to touch him. How would he react, she wondered? She imagined what it would be like to lace her fingers through his, to touch the smooth, dark skin –

He must have sensed her watching him; he smiled shyly and let go of the strap. 'Sorry!'

'That's okay,' she replied.

∞

'So what were you saying about Penang?' Els passed her empty plate to Joseph who had got up from his seat and was now busy clearing the table.

'It's simple,' said Lee. 'They built too many resorts. Packed them all together, one on top of the other. Then the sea got polluted, the coral died, and the beach washed away. No-one wants to go where there is no beach. A simple example. How tourism can destroy tourism.'

Joseph pulled a face. 'He's off again. Don't encourage him. Now you know what his favourite subject of conversation is.' He grinned at Lee. 'But, sadly, what he says is true. What they did in Penang is a good example of what you should not do.' He walked round to Isabel; she handed him her plate and he piled it on top of the others. 'And people like you won't visit, if there is no diving – nothing to see.'

'I suppose that's true,' said Pieter.

'It's like I said before,' continued Lee, 'many people see things in the short term only. Get rich quick.' He stood up and gathered together the rest of the empty dishes and passed them to Joseph. 'But our resources need to be looked after, very carefully.'

'The problem is,' said Joseph, 'you need the government to understand these things.'

'And they will never regulate development – not if it stops the flow of investment from overseas,' added Lee.'

'Yes, I can see that you would have a problem – if you need support from the government,' said Pieter. 'They will only look at the economic benefits.'

Joseph balanced the two piles of plates and dishes on top of each other and turned away, picking his way through the tables and chairs on his way towards the kitchen. 'Taman Negara. That's another example,' he shouted over his shoulder.

'Hmm. Taman Negara. That's one of our national parks,' Lee explained, wafting at a mosquito. 'Do you have any insect coils?' he shouted in the direction of Joseph's back.

'I have heard of Taman Negara,' Els said. 'I think it is the first national park in Malaysia – no?'

'Correct.'

'National parks are a good thing for your country I think?'

'They are,' Lee replied, 'or they should be. But it depends how well they are managed. In this case, not so well.'

'What do you mean?' Isabel asked.

'Well . . .' He paused for a moment, and moved his finger round the top of an empty bottle. 'There is a very big difference between protecting something and exploiting it. You know, inside Taman Negara there is one of the few big areas of rainforest left. And last year we had more than fourteen thousand visitors there. You can imagine the effect of that.' He stopped toying with the bottle and looked at each of them in turn as he continued. 'At least, once, there were some rules. But now, everyone stamps around wherever they like, damaging plants, bothering the wildlife. People feed the animals, they leave garbage lying around, the whole balance is upset. And it is not only the tourists who do this.'

'Don't the local people worry about protecting it?' Els asked.

'I'm not sure if enough people really care. It is a shame they don't value what they have. If they did, they might want to save it.'

Isabel would have been happy to sit and listen to Lee all night. The sound of his voice was intensely soothing; there was a confidence too, that she had noticed before when he talked about the things that were important to him. She watched his lips as he spoke, and was disconcerted to find herself imagining them pressed against her own. Embarrassed, she tried to focus her mind on something else. She reached inside her bag and took out a tube of mosquito repellent.

'You know, our government could step in and do more, if they wanted to,' Lee was saying. 'They could control the size of new developments for a start. And, instead of giving cheap loans and tax breaks to the big boys, they should encourage smaller projects – like ours, I suppose – those which put less strain on the environment.' He sighed and tugged at his ear. 'But they won't. They are short-sighted, and their advisors are economists – not interested in the environment. That's for sure.'

'Instead of tax breaks, they should make them pay more tax – those big resorts that pollute evrything,' said Isabel, squirting a large dollop of the insect repellent onto her palm. She started to rub the cream on her bare arms; it was cold and it made her flinch. 'Then give loans to small businesses, to set up . . .' Set up what? she thought. She had no idea what she was talking about. 'Solar power units,' she said, suddenly.

Lee laughed. 'Exactly right.'

Cautiously, she dotted a tiny amount of the cream onto her face.

'And stop building the disgusting concrete blocks,' Els added.

'And encourage the use of local labour,' Isabel said, warming to the subject. 'And use local building materials.' She had remembered Lee saying that once before.

'And no more golf courses.' Els banged her hand hard onto the table.

'And stop chopping down the rain forests,' Isabel banged the table in response.

'Show people how to re-cycle their garbage.'

'Stop dropping litter.'

'Get rid of nasty souvenirs '

'That are made from bits of animal.'

'And ban all Dutch tourists,' Pieter joined in at last, banging down both his fists, making their glasses bounce up in the air. 'Ban *all* tourists – they mess up the country.'

At this, they all collapsed into giggles.

'You should be the politicians,' said Lee. 'I would vote for all of you. By the way,' he turned to Isabel, 'you have some of that stuff, still on your face. May I?'

She had no time to respond. He had reached out a hand and smoothed his thumb across her cheek.

Her own hand went to the spot he had touched. 'Thanks,' she

said. She glanced up and saw that Els was grinning at her.

'More drinks?' Joseph was back, this time with a tray of drinks – cocktails all round by the look of it – and more snacks. 'On the house.'

They had already eaten so much; Isabel wasn't sure how she would be able to force down another thing.

'And the same is going to happen all over again.' Joseph went on, rescuing one of the little paper umbrellas which had fallen from a glass. 'Pulau Langkawi.'

Isabel smiled to herself. It was as if he had been carrying on the conversation with himself, all the time he had been away in the kitchen. She liked Joseph. He was serious, like Lee, and had a quiet sense of humour. She was not surprised that they were good friends. 'What's happening in Langkawi?' she asked.

'A few years ago our government decided that we needed another high profile – their words – tourist destination,' Joseph said, as he handed out the drinks.

Isabel was sure they were even larger than the last ones.

'And chose Pulau Langkawi,' Lee said.

'Where is that?' Pieter asked.

'Another island, north of Pulau Penang,' Joseph replied.

'Not far from the border with Thailand,' added Lee. He thrust his hand into a bowl of corn snacks. He brought out a handful then held them in his open palm, studying them for a moment before he continued speaking. 'The scheme wasn't so good for those who lost agricultural land, and their way of making a living.'

'The government is too powerful,' Joseph said. He sat down in the seat he had vacated earlier. 'And it *is* run by economists.'

'Anyway,' Lee went on, 'some people protested, but nothing could be done. Now the cost of land is so high that no local can afford to buy there. So they leave.'

'Doesn't anyone think that the new developments are good?' Els asked.

'Most of the money – from the government – went to those big overseas companies,' Joseph said, spreading out his arms to illustrate his point. 'So it is their shareholders only who see the profits. Never the local people.'

'The whole area was a mess,' Lee continued. 'No-one had

thought about the details. Waste removal. Water supply. Didn't they know how much water they would need? It is difficult to believe. They must have been stupid.'

'Corrupt,' Joseph muttered.

'There was a mountain river – Telaga Tujuh – the main water supply to the area. They drained it dry. Then they cleared loads of jungle, they ripped up the mangroves, they took away the beach, used the sand for building.'

'And so the water silted up.' Joseph continued the story. 'Then all the fish died. And the fishermen lost their income as well as the farmers.'

'They just left it like that, for a long time,' went on Lee. 'It looked as though all the money had dried up. Just like the water supply.'

'And now?' Pieter asked.

'Things are moving again,' Joseph replied. 'More resorts are being built and all the small-small places – places like Teluk – are being eaten up.' He delved into his pocket. 'Sorry, I forgot,' He brought out a mosquito coil and a box of matches, then proceeded to light the coil as he carried on talking. 'But the water is still polluted, and the fish still die. That is because of the chemicals they use on the gardens, and on the golf-courses. So that you can all have nice green grass to look at.'

Isabel knew that Joseph was teasing them, but she felt guilty all the same. 'What can you do?' she asked. 'Can't anybody do anything to stop it happening?' She felt ashamed that she knew so little about it.

Lee shook his head. 'According to the government, it is good for the economy. Maybe it is. But nobody is looking at the real costs. These big schemes are not good for any of us.' He sighed. 'It's a shame the government doesn't consult the local people, and listen to them. They could learn a lot.'

'You mean listen to you,' said Joseph, laughing.

Lee shrugged. 'Okay, I mean me.'

'God, I hope nothing like that happens here,' Isabel said.

'No,' agreed Els, 'that would be terrible.'

'Who knows?' Lee said.

Isabel saw Joseph glance at Lee, and wondered if he had heard any more from the people at the Mayang. Could it really happen here? It didn't bear thinking about. But how could people like Joseph and Lee fight the 'big boys' as they called them? And yet, they both seemed so committed to what they believed in.

'I told you, it's his favourite topic,' said Joseph.

It was as if he had read her mind. She looked up, surprised.

'Or one of them,' he went on. 'Destruction of the rain forests, pollution, over-development . . . Have I left anything out?'

'No, I don't think so.' Lee reddened.

Isabel smiled at him. He grinned back.

'I can see that you know a lot about it,' Els remarked.

'That's because he spends all his spare time reading books,' Joseph said. 'Figuring out what could be done better. Instead of enjoying himself.' He turned to Lee. 'Still planning to become a famous ecologist or something?'

'No. Not really. I thought about it. Once, I thought about a lot of things. Like playing the saxophone, joining a band. Going to the moon.'

'Shame you didn't. The ecologist thing, I mean, not the moon.'

'I chose not to.' Lee seemed to be getting more and more embarrassed.' And I wasn't very good at the saxophone either.'

'Hmm,' Joseph grunted. 'It's still a shame.'

'Why? What happened?' Isabel asked, then recalled the story Els had told her. 'I mean . . .' she stumbled. 'Sorry, I didn't mean to pry.'

'Waste of a good brain, and . . .' Joseph stopped.

'But I couldn't help it,' said Lee. 'That's how it was – my choice. So I came to Buah Lodge, to work, instead.'

'And we are all very glad that you did,' Els said, raising her glass. 'Here's to Lee, and the best resort in Malaysia.'

'And to Joseph, and the best eating and drinking place on this island,' Lee added.

The other tables in the restaurant had long been empty by the time Els decided that they should go. 'We need to be awake very early. And we haven't finished packing our bags.'

'Oh God! You're leaving tomorrow aren't you?' Isabel said. 'What a shame.'

'And what about you?' Joseph asked Isabel. 'When must you leave us?'

'Never – I wish.'

She saw Lee glance up; their eyes met, then he looked away.

'Well,' she continued, 'I mean in an ideal world, of course, but in the real one – in four days.'

'Lucky you,' Els said. 'Four more days. But you'd better watch out – when we are gone, Phil will have you all to himself.'

She ignored the comment. 'I won't enjoy any of it,' she said, hastening the conversation on, 'because I'll be worrying about going home.' She didn't add that there was no home to go back to.

Pieter laughed. 'That's silly.'

'I know, but I can't help it. Those four days will just fly by.' She wondered if her landlord had managed to re-let her room.

'Well, Pieter and I will come back next year,' Els said. 'We have decided. So why don't you come too?'

'I would love to come back,' she replied. 'Yes, of course, I would –'

Lee was studying his empty glass.

'So, that's good,' Els said. She stood up. 'We will all meet again next year for sure.' She pulled a scrap of paper from the pocket of her jeans then she said something in Dutch to Pieter, who produced a pen. 'I will write our address in Amsterdam.' She scribbled onto the paper and handed it to Isabel. 'And come and visit us if you would like to.'

Then they were all on their feet. Els hugged Joseph, and Pieter shook his hand. And then Joseph turned to Isabel. 'I hope to see you again before you leave.' He looked at Lee. 'Lee, you will bring Isabel here again soon, won't you?'

Lee grinned back at him. 'Okay *tuan*.'

As they walked through the village, Els and Pieter continued to talk about their plans for the following year. Els had a friend who lived in Brisbane; she was getting married this time next year, and they were going to the wedding.

'It is perfect,' Els told Lee. 'We didn't know where we should make our stop-over. Now we know. It will be here.' She turned to

Isabel. 'So everything fits together. Perfectly.'

Isabel nodded, chilled by the thought of the twelve, long months stretched ahead of her, already cut into neat little chunks by projects, deadlines, commitments – things which, at this very moment, seemed terribly remote and alien. Here was all that mattered. She couldn't imagine being anywhere else but here.

As soon as they veered off the main street, Lee produced a torch. The path was narrow and they were forced to walk in pairs; Isabel found herself walking alongside Pieter. As if it were already on his mind, he proceeded to tell her about the cat which he had left with a friend in Amsterdam.

'Willem is definitely my cat, not Els's cat,' he explained. 'He arrived with me, and I am the one who feeds him. I am not sure that Els was so fond of cats before she met Willem. But she treats him well.'

While Pieter seemed content to chat away about Willem, Isabel concentrated on her feet, and the latticework of roots pushing up through the path. It was only when Lee dodged ahead, to catch hold of a low branch, that she looked up.

He held it as they each ducked underneath. Isabel was last to pass through.

'Are you okay?' He lowered the branch, carefully, and fell into step alongside her. She nodded.

Els and Pieter were ahead of them now; she could hear them chattering away in Dutch and she knew they were talking about the cat because she kept hearing its name – Willem – the one word she recognized.

Isabel and Lee walked in silence, a silence broken into from time to time by some strange and beautiful sound emanating from the forest. Every now and then she felt his sleeve brush against her bare arm. His closeness was almost too much to bear; and if she could have, she would have stopped time dead in its tracks, and allowed her entire life to implode into this one, exquisite, moment.

They stopped, and Lee produced a set of keys from his pocket. 'Staff entrance,' he explained, as he unlocked a gate. 'Now we don't have to walk all the way round.' Then they were in the grounds of Buah Lodge. Soft, white lights glowed from the chalets scattered amongst the trees, rich fragrances floated out from the night-scented plants, an owl hooted from a place within the mass of dark foliage above their heads.

It was not long before they arrived at Els and Pieter's chalet. There were more 'goodbyes', hugs and handshakes; then the pair skipped up the steps and disappeared inside. Isabel heard their door click shut behind them and the sound of a key being turned in the lock. She stood for a moment, not daring to shift her attention from the closed door.

'I will walk back with you,' Lee said.

'It's fine. I can manage.' She cursed herself the moment the words left her lips. Why? Why had she said that?

But he insisted. 'No, it is late. I should make sure you get back.'

'Is it not safe?'

He looked at her, quizzically. 'Of course it is safe, but . . .' He looked down at the ground.

This wasn't going at all well, Isabel thought. If she wasn't careful, she was going to ruin everything –

'Thanks,' she said. 'That's kind of you.'

He turned, and they continued along the path, their feet pounding out a brisk rhythm on the gravel. This was the only sound she could hear now; the forest was unusually quiet. But she knew that out there, somewhere, millions of creatures – tiny insects, nocturnal animals, birds, reptiles – were busy foraging away in the pitch blackness; and as if to prove a point, a high-pitched shriek cut through the darkness. Then it was silent again.

Isabel was fearing the moment her own chalet would come into view. What would happen then? Would he simply say goodnight and walk away? And she wasn't sure what else she expected him to do. Yet she was gripped with a sense that something had changed, something inchoate, something that had to be dealt with; she could feel it stretched between them, like an electrically charged thread.

They stopped at the foot of the steps and Lee rested his arm on the wooden rail. She needed to think of something – to keep him there a bit longer. And she wished now that she hadn't had so much to drink; her brain wasn't up to this.

She pushed a hand into her bag and made a pretence of rummaging around for her key. Twice she let her fingers slide over the length of smooth, cool metal. Just as she was wondering whether to extend the search to her pockets, a couple of fireflies flickered past her head. 'Look!' she exclaimed, following the sparks with her finger, genuinely thrilled by the sight but glad of an opportunity to fill the silence.

The fireflies settled on a nearby bush where they rested for a while, glowing companionably in the darkness.

'Yes, but look over there.'

Isabel looked over to where he was pointing.

'And there.' He put his hand on her arm and turned her to face a row of shrubs. Each one contained hundreds of the insects, woven through the dark outlines of the branches like strings of tiny Christmas lights.

They both stood still for a moment, watching as the pinpricks of light flashed on and off in unison. The stem of a low-lying plant scratched at her leg, but she was determined not to move. She wondered if he would kiss her. If it had ever been his intention to do so, now would be the perfect time. Perhaps if she turned round to face him –

But at that very moment he started to speak. 'The flashing lights . . . they are signalling out for a mate,' he said, letting go of her arm. 'And I'd better get going. Another busy day tomorrow.' He rubbed at his temple for a moment. A half-smile flit across his face, then died away in an instant. 'So, er – goodnight then.'

The disappointment pushed through her. 'Goodnight,' she replied.

He still hadn't moved but she knew that, at any moment, he would turn, he would walk away. She could almost hear the seconds slipping away, one by one, ticking down, like the detonator of a bomb.

'Goodnight,' he said once more.

Isabel stood on the lowest step and watched him set off down the path. There was a hollowness inside her, as if someone had pierced her skin with a knife and released all the air. She stretched out a hand and curled her fingers around the section of rail where he had leant; she would wait until he had disappeared from view –

But he had stopped. He wasn't going after all. He was walking back to her. She held her breath; she brushed away a flower head that had fallen onto the step. It was the same colour as the skirt she was wearing, she noticed.

He had reached her now. He was standing in front of her again, his hands rammed into his pockets. 'I wondered . . .' He took a sharp intake of breath then started again. 'I wondered – if you are not busy – the day after tomorrow – my friend is getting married and . . . Would you like to come, with me? Joseph will be there too,' he added quickly. 'Or maybe you are busy. Or . . .'

She interrupted him. 'No, of course I'm not busy. I would love to go.'

'Ah. Good.' Now he had her reply, he seemed unsure what to do with it.

But her mind had already raced ahead and was busy sorting through the motley collection of items in her suitcase. Did she have anything suitable for a wedding?

'I don't have the right clothes – for a wedding, I mean. Is it formal? Are weddings here formal? I don't know anything about weddings in Malaysia.' She realized she should probably stop talking.

He was smiling now. 'You can wear anything you like. It's just a party – in the afternoon. Just a big lunch.'

'Does your friend live on the island?'

'Benny? Not yet. He comes from Malacca – like me and Joseph. But his girlfriend lives here – in Kampung Bakau. And he will live here too, after they get married.'

'But what about Set Yen?' The words had found their way out before she could stop them. 'Shouldn't you take Set Yen?'

She saw his smile fade, turn to a frown.

'Set Yen? Why would I . . .? I don't think . . .'

'Sorry,' she rushed in, 'I . . .' God! Why couldn't she keep her mouth shut? But she had got this far –

'I thought that you and Set Yen . . .' She started again. 'I thought that Set Yen was your . . . girlfriend.' There, she had said it.

'My girlfriend.' He looked away; he had developed a sudden interest in a leaf lying on the ground, next to his foot. 'You thought that,' he said.

'Yes,' she replied, in a small voice.

'Ah.'

She wondered if that was all he was going to say.

He shuffled some bits of gravel.

'No,' he said at last. 'She is not my girlfriend. I don't think that it is a good idea for me to choose girlfriends from my staff.'

'No, I suppose not,' Isabel said. Nor from your guests either, she thought.

'So you see,' he laughed nervously, 'I don't have any girlfriend. I am a free man.'

He had gone.

Isabel sat down on the steps and put her head in her hands, frozen to the spot with embarrassment. She stared at the space where he had been, just moments before, wishing she had the power to rewind the last half-hour, to start it all over again. It was hard to tell whether she had offended him; she just wished that, for once, she had used her brain before opening her mouth. The problem was, Lee wasn't at all like the sort of man she was used to dealing with. He was thoughtful, unassuming, careful. And although he could be painfully shy at times, there was also a strength and assuredness about him that was immensely appealing.

She sat where she was for a while, willing him to come back but knowing full well that he wouldn't. The forest behind her was a fantasia of squawks and clacks, booms and whines, and it made her think of something he had said, earlier that evening. The forest was never at rest, he had told her, it was alive with things going on every second of the day and night. But deep within its heart, there was a world you would never see. For the more you ventured in, the more everything would retreat – further and further away – until all that was left were just traces of what had been there before you. That was the wonderful mystery of it all. And he had become more and more animated as he had explained how man was encroaching upon these wonderful places, cutting down and clearing away, until the forests were becoming smaller and smaller, and all the living things inside them found they had nowhere else to go.

She would have gone on picking over the evening's events, but something had started up in the jungle behind her: a great commotion; a crashing of branches; a roar – like a lion. But she knew what it was. Lee had told her about the howler monkeys – the ones that thundered around the trees, making as much noise as they could. And this one was no exception. It roared and bellowed at the world in general until, with a superb and clamorous crescendo, it got whatever it was out of its system, and the noise stopped, as abruptly as it had begun.

And for a moment the forest was still.

PART NINE

London
December 1997

∞

3.45 pm

From where he was lying, Lee could see the sky: no roofs, no chimneypots, no trees or telegraph wires, just sky. And what had, minutes before, been a simple billow of silvery cloud was now an arrangement of swirls, all tinged with coral, which, even as he watched, were lengthening themselves out into streaks of deepening red.

The doorbell rang. For a moment, Lee was confused by the metallic noise taking up space inside his head. Then it was quiet again. Too quiet. Because hadn't he been listening to music? From across the room he saw the tiny, red light blinking at him from the machine. The cassette had ended. He rolled himself to the edge of the bed and sat there for a moment, staring at the floor. He noticed a hole in one of his socks.

The bell rang again: an irksome drill of a noise. He ran a hand through his hair and got to his feet.

'Why you sitting in the dark?' Chi Wan dodged past him and made for the kitchen. Lee followed.

'Didn't know I was.' He flicked on the light-switch. 'It wasn't dark last time I looked.'

Chi Wan shook his head. 'Well it is now. Merry Christmas by the way. Saving electricity are you?'

Lee laughed. 'No, of course not. And merry Christmas to you too.'

Chi Wan held up a plastic bag. 'I've brought a chicken.' He dropped the bag onto the worktop. 'They were getting rid of them at Sainsbury's. I think it's good. But you'd better get the oven on. If we cook it now we can eat it in a couple of hours. What have

253

you got? Electric?'

'Gas.' Lee glanced at his watch. It was nearly four o'clock. He cursed under his breath. How had it got to be so late? He had exams in a couple of weeks; he should have been studying this afternoon.

His whole day had, somehow, slipped off its axis. He had managed to sleep through his alarm clock, and by the time he had finished his breakfast it was almost lunchtime. He had intended to work. He had sat down at his desk, set out some books, sharpened his pencils, had even written the first paragraph of a paper on budgeting systems within organizations. That was when he had developed a sudden urge for chocolate. He had tried to ignore it, but minutes later he was putting on his coat, ramming a woollen hat over his ears, and stepping out into the honeyed winter sunshine in search of a shop that might be open.

He had found one eventually: one solitary going-concern in a miserable parade of vacant premises. He had discovered a park as well, tucked between a couple of rambling brick terraces. And he had munched his chocolate, and half a packet of biscuits, perched on the trunk of a fallen tree, with only a scattering of inquisitive pigeons for company.

He crumbled one of his biscuits and threw it down on the ground. 'Here you are, Christmas dinner.'

One of the birds stopped in its tracks and surveyed him with a bright, beady eye, its head cocked to one side.

'Do you know it's Christmas?' Lee asked it. 'Do you know what the hell I'm talking about?'

The pigeon shuffled aside, to join its companions.

'No, I didn't think so.' Lee laughed and stood up, sending the birds flurrying off in a variety of directions.

He had meandered back to his flat, choosing one street rather than another as the impulse took him. This was all new territory. Although he had been living in the area for the past five months he'd done little else but study. He had been cooped up for too long; it felt good to be outside for a change.

He liked the houses in this neighbourhood – solid, squat terraces, with narrow strips of garden that pushed them back from the street: gardens that now lurked, dead and colourless, behind scrappy walls of brick or stone. The occasional house was screened from view by a neatly clipped hedge; some of the houses had no garden at all, just a patch of concrete – a place to keep a car, and a couple of bins. And as he had passed by, he couldn't help peering into the windows – or at least those that hadn't been sheathed with a greying net curtain.

'Funny lot these Brits,' he said now, tugging a length of tinfoil from a roll.

'You could say that,' Chi Wan replied. He had opened the oven door and was crouched down, peering inside. 'How does this thing work?'

'You need a thing – to light it with – it's in that drawer.' He pointed with his elbow. 'You get it – I've got chicken on me.' He stopped what he was doing and watched his friend rummage around in the drawer. 'I could see them all inside their houses,' he went on, 'sitting round, in their paper hats.'

'Yeah? All miserable? Not talking to each other?'

'Something like that.'

'They're probably all knackered. I saw them all in Sainsbury's yesterday – it was mad in there, just mad – and I looked at all those trolleys piled up with stuff.' He puffed out his cheeks. 'They'll burst, man, I'm telling you. They'll burst if they eat all that.' He fished out the gas lighter and held it up, dubiously. Lee nodded.

'Remember that English girl I went out with?'

'Ginny?'

'Yeah, Ginny. One Christmas we went to her parents – they lived in some village near Birmingham. It was so fucking boring 'cos we didn't do anything but eat, and sit around, and watch crappy television. You know I like to eat but . . .' He sighed and shook his head. 'All this food kept coming out, and I couldn't eat it.'

Lee laughed. 'I can't imagine you turning down food.'

'I tried, man – tried my best.' He went over to where he had flung his coat and reached into one of the pockets. He pulled out something that could only be a bottle, wrapped in a brown paper bag. 'And they had all these cousins and aunties and uncles and grandparents there, and none of them talked to each other. It was really strange.'

'Right,' said Lee, 'it's in.' He straightened up and walked to the sink to wash his hands. 'Hey! What are we having with it?' he asked.

'Dunno, what you got?'

Lee opened a cupboard and looked inside. 'Not much. How about rice? I can make fried rice.'

'Sounds good.'

Chi Wan pulled out a half-bottle of whisky from the paper bag. 'Got some glasses?'

Lee squinted at his watch. 'Better go and look at the chicken,' he said.

'Fill you up?' His friend reached out for the bottle and started to unscrew the top.

'Later, later.' Lee covered his glass with his hand, so that Chi Wan couldn't pour in any more whisky. 'I'll be too pissed to make the rice.' He stood up – a little too quickly it seemed, as he had to clutch the back of the chair to balance himself – and carried his glass into the kitchen. The room had filled with the smell of roasted chicken.

'Smells good,' said Chi Wan, who had followed him in.

Lee brought down a wok from the top of a cupboard and poured in a measure of oil. He was glad to have something to do: Chi Wan might be able to sink endless amounts of whisky without any ill effect, but he wasn't. And he had work to do tomorrow.

He glanced over at his friend, who was trying to force the top from a bottle of chilli sauce. He was wearing his trademark jeans, the sort with wide, fraying slashes cut at the knees. His bright orange hair stuck up at all angles, making him look as though he had just got out of bed, although Lee knew that he never went anywhere without a tube of gel in his pocket, and spent ages pulling and poking at it until he was happy with the result. 'Have you decided what you're going to do when you finish?' he asked. 'What's left now? PhD?'

Chi Wan laughed. 'You must be joking. Get the hell out of here, that's what. I've been in this dump for too long. Time to go home.'

Lee wondered what Chi Wan would make of home or, more to

the point, what home would make of Chi Wan. True, nowadays, he might blend in amongst the crowds of KL, but it was hard to imagine him settling back into sleepy Kuching.

Chi Wan had changed a great deal since the day he had introduced himself to Lee. It had been their first day at college in London, both new to England, both from Malaysia. Despite the difference in their ages, they had struck up a friendship that had helped them, each in different ways, over the last four and a half years. Even when Lee had gone back to KL for a year, working at any job he could find, to boost his savings, they had kept in touch; and Chi Wan had surprised him by turning up at the airport to meet him when he returned.

'Couldn't have picked a worse time though,' went on Chi Wan. 'There won't be many jobs around with this mess going on.'

Lee knew that he was talking about the economic crisis that was crippling their country. He had already seen the value of his savings slashed by almost fifty per cent by the sudden devaluation of the *ringgit*. He just hoped that it wouldn't fall any further. At least this was his final year, and he had already paid his tuition fees; now he just had to worry about getting through the next six months. If the worst came to the worst, he could get a job in Chinatown. 'You're right,' he replied. If it gets any worse, a lot more businesses will close down. People are already losing their jobs.'

Chi Wan had lifted the chicken from of the oven, and was now busy carving off huge hunks of meat. 'How will it affect your plans?' he asked.

Lee thought for a moment. 'Dunno. But one thing's for sure. People won't be investing. There'll be no chance of any loans.'

'Yeah, but think about it this way – you've still got money put away, haven't you? Some other poor sod who's gone under will have to sell up, and you'll be in a position to buy – cash – and prices will be at their lowest.'

The thought sent a cold shiver through him. Thank the gods they had sold Buah Lodge before all this had started, before its value had plummeted as well.

'And just think,' went on Chi Wan, 'if foreign investors are pulling out now, there'll be no competition. The path will be nice and clear for you to set up. Isn't that what you wanted?'

Lee grinned at his friend. It was typical of Chi Wan to jump in and make the most of an opportunity. He, on the other hand, was far too cautious for his own good. 'I'm just not sure it's the best time to start up a new business,' he said. He brought the wok of freshly made rice to the table and started spooning it onto the two plates of chicken.

'It's the best time,' Chi Wan replied. 'Couldn't be better for what you're planning. Everyone got fed up with all those big, shiny, new places springing up all over the place – half of them never even finished. Too much hot money coming into the country, if you ask me. When prices get too high – where else can they go? Basic theory.' He sat down and sucked on the chicken bone he had brought with him from the chopping board. 'Anyway, with any luck, it might be all over by June. And I tell you what – if my dad would fork out some of that money my gran left, I'd go in with you. What you've got in mind is a bloody great idea. It'll go down well. And we'll be rich.'

'Hmm . . . but I still think the timing is a disaster. In any case, don't forget, it isn't all about making money.'

'Yeah, yeah, I know. It's all about the environment, giving back, sustainability, blah-di-blah.'

Lee punched him on the shoulder. 'Okay. Ha-ha. But do you really think it could work?'

Chi Wan pulled a serious face. 'Yes, I really do think it will work. One day I'll be very proud to say that I once shared a chicken with the famous billionaire, Lee Kim Cheng. Now shall we eat? I'm starving.'

Lee was still busy breaking up the chicken carcass and cramming the pieces into a plastic container.

'What are you doing anyway?'

'Be there in a second.'

'Are you ever going to sit down?' groaned Chi Wan.

'Can't afford to waste any.' He put a lid on the dish and took it to the fridge. 'I'll make some soup tomorrow.'

Chi Wan poured out the rest of the whisky. 'I'll get some beers later if I can find a shop open.' He raised his glass. 'To the future – wherever we end up. And merry Christmas.'

'Merry Christmas,' replied Lee.

PART TEN

Malaysia
July 1991

∞

28 July 1991
Kampung Teluk

It had just gone twelve-thirty. The silent heat of a tropical afternoon was starting to weigh upon the forest, wrapping itself round the resort like a shroud, forcing everything, and everyone, into a sleepy sluggishness. Even the cicadas were quiet.

Inside her air-conditioned room, Isabel was getting ready. Her clothes had been spread out on the bed since breakfast time – not that she'd had the appetite for much, and she regretted this now because her stomach was making strange, rumbling noises. In less than fifteen minutes Lee would be here.

Despite her fears that she had upset him, by saying the wrong thing about Set Yen, he had sought her out the day before, to confirm the arrangements. She had been having breakfast in the Gula House when she had seen him approach, scanning the tables. She thought he looked anxious; but the moment he had spotted her, his face relaxed. He smiled, shyly, and crossed towards her. As he pulled back the empty chair next to her, Isabel saw Sandra watching them from a table in the opposite corner. Isabel raised a hand in greeting, but Sandra had already lowered her head, seeming to find more of interest in the coffee cup that she was nursing against the string of pearls hanging from her neck.

Their conversation had been somewhat formal, she thought; and she had rather hoped he might stay and chat over a coffee. But he had come, he said, to tell her about the plans for the following day. He would call for her at quarter to one and they would walk to the jetty to catch the boat. Then he had stood up and apologized for having to rush; he had somewhere to go, he said, but hadn't mentioned where. And there was no reason at all, she told herself, why he should. Even so, she had spent the entire day wondering where he was, and what he was doing. She had walked to her usual beach, and was relieved to find it deserted; she had read a little, although she had found it impossible to concentrate; and searched for shells, walking up and down the shoreline, foraging in the pale, powdery sand with her toes.

She glanced at her watch. He could be here at any minute. She checked herself in the mirror one last time, and decided that the coral-coloured top went well with her newly-tanned skin; then she stepped outside and locked the door behind her. She dropped the key into her bag and stood where she could see the path.

Glad to have something to occupy her mind, she watched a pair of butterflies take to the air and flutter about, like two coloured petals being pitched about by a breeze. But after a moment or two she heard footsteps. Even before he came into view she knew it was going to be him and then, suddenly, he was there, smiling up at her, no longer the subject of her day-dreams but the real thing. Real flesh and blood. And looking incredibly attractive.

'Are you ready?'

She nodded and picked her way down the steps, careful not to stumble, or get a heel caught in the hem of her sarong. When she arrived at the last one he moved towards her, but stopped just before he reached her.

'You look . . .' He paused and took a breath. 'Beautiful.'

'Thank you.'

The sun seared into her bare shoulders.

He remained where he was, his hands in his pockets.

There was definitely something different about him today; whatever it was, it was unsettling. She wanted to say something else – anything – to cut through the silence, but her mind had emptied itself. However much she tried, it gave her nothing.

It was only a second or two but it seemed like an eternity.

He ran a hand quickly through his hair, pushing it back from his eyes. It was a gesture she had come to recognize: it was what he did when he was nervous.

'Shall we go?'

They walked along the path leading out of the grounds and then onto the walkway spanning the mangrove swamp. Masses of tiny crabs scuttled to and fro on the mud beneath them. This was now a familiar route: the shady web of palms and rattans; the lianas, with their rope-like stems hanging like festoons; the resident monitor lizard spread across a fallen branch, idling away the afternoon. It was barely a week ago when he had first brought her along this very same path from the jetty; yet it had become as commonplace as her daily walk to Manor House station. She lowered her head and looked at the ground, conscious of a smile beginning to play around her lips. It was the thought of Lee, that day, striding ahead with her enormous suitcase, and all the while she had been thinking that he was a member of staff, come to collect her from the airport. She couldn't prevent the smile from getting wider. And now, there was the prospect of a whole afternoon with him by her side. The hours dangled enticingly ahead of her, like a string of precious stones in a jeweller's window: there for the taking, to be possessed and cherished, maybe for a lifetime.

Joseph was waiting at the jetty. As soon as he saw them he waved.

When they had drawn up beside him, he reached out a hand to Isabel. 'Hello again. Good to see you.'

Someone had cut his hair, leaving nothing but short, black tufts that sprung from his head like a covering of velvet.

'How are you both today?' He clapped Lee on the back. 'The boat is coming,' he said, before either of them could reply.

Along with everyone else, they watched the boat manoeuvre round and sidle up to the jetty to be tethered to one of the ancient, weather-beaten posts. Behind all this activity, four painted fishing boats rested on the sand, their nets spread out to dry.

Isabel reached for her camera. 'I'll be back in a second.' She kicked off her sandals and stepped down onto the beach to get closer to the boats. Her feet sank into the sand and it felt warm and silky against her bare feet. With one hand clutching the hem of her sarong, the other holding the camera to her eye, she picked her way towards the boats, not stopping until she had found the picture she wanted.

When she got back to the jetty Lee and Joseph were deep in conversation, gabbling away in one or other of the Chinese dialects – she hadn't a clue which. They stopped as soon as she approached, and switched to English.

'So it's the bank tomorrow,' Joseph was saying.

'Yep,' Lee replied.

'Good luck.' Joseph turned to Isabel. 'Here,' he said, holding out his hand for the camera, 'let me take one of you both.'

Isabel hesitated.

But Lee had already jumped to her side. 'Where do you want me?'

'That's fine as you are,' Joseph replied, taking the camera from her. 'Hold on.' He pulled a pair of glasses from his shirt pocket. 'I need to figure out how this thing works. It looks complicated.'

She could feel the fabric of Lee's shirt brush against her bare arm.

'It's not,' she shouted, determined to stay glued to her spot. 'It's the button in the top right hand corner.'

Then it was done. Joseph was walking back towards them, holding out the camera.

They moved apart.

They were on the fast service. Not that the boat itself was particularly fast, but it didn't stop at each and every village along the way. They had been unable to find three seats together, so they stood at the front of the upper deck and, as they chugged steadily round the coast, Isabel was glad of the breeze that cooled her face and roused the folds of her sarong.

They were talking about the wedding.

'Benny was in the same class with us at school,' Joseph explained. 'And Natalie owns a restaurant here.'

Isabel changed position, to rest her back against the deck rail, sneaking a glance at Lee as she turned. He was standing next to her, one arm on the rail, squinting into the sun. His shirt was open at the neck, the gold chain glimmering against the brown of his skin. She imagined what it might be like, to undo the next button and slip her fingers under the crisp white cotton, then up towards his shoulders, drawing him to her. But instead she asked: 'So how did they meet? Benny and Natalie?'

'Benny came here. To visit me,' said Lee. 'We went to Natalie's restaurant. And that's how it happened.' He clapped his hands together. 'Just like that. Simple.'

'So it's all your fault,' Joseph said.

Lee laughed. 'I guess so.'

'But she lives here. And he lives in Malacca – you said he came from Malacca?'

'Correct.'

'Long-distance relationship,' added Joseph.

'That must have been difficult,' Isabel said, not daring to catch Lee's eye.

Lee shrugged. 'Not really, they were happy. It was fine for them.'

'So are they going to stay here now, or move to Malacca?'

'Stay here, I think,' Lee replied. 'The good life.'

'His job – he's an accountant – he can do it anywhere,' Joseph said. 'He will have lots of work when the big resorts come to the island.'

Isabel looked at Lee. She knew that Joseph was joking but, still, it was a sore point. Lee's expression gave nothing away. His attention was on other things. The boat was slowing down; she could see a wharf ahead. It looked as if this was where they were getting off.

The crew had positioned a makeshift gangplank between the boat and the landing pier; it didn't look very steady. She watched as Joseph negotiated it without a hitch; then Lee stepped aside to allow her to go next. She hesitated, cursing the fact that she was wearing high heels, praying she wouldn't stumble. She tested the board with her foot, then stepped back, unsure. But Lee had jumped ahead, and was standing in front of her, holding out his hand. Grateful for the support, she stepped onto the moving board and crossed to the other side.

'Where's he got to?' Lee said, looking around.

'Over there,' she replied. She had spotted Joseph waving to them.

Their hands dropped apart; Lee glanced at her and smiled. She smiled back.

Joseph was sheltering under a tree with a cluster of people so neat and polished that there was little doubt that they, too, were headed for the wedding. As Isabel approached, five eager faces turned towards her; then she was in the midst of the group, being introduced to them one by one.

'Ping Li.'

'Kin Mun.'

'Kui Hing.'

Cheery faces; shiny, black hair; nodding heads. But those names! She would never remember them all.

'Eileen.'

That's better, she thought.

'Heng Meng.'

And that was easy enough.

'You can call me Albert,' he added, helpfully.

Isabel smiled back at him, struggling to fit the old-fashioned name to the bright young face in front of her.

They joined the procession snaking away from the jetty and around the edge of the village; a shingle path conducted them up a steep slope until it stopped at a low, stone-built house with a large, walled courtyard to one side. Behind it was just the great dome of forest, dominating the village, seeming to shut it off from the rest of the island.

Lee pointed to the gateposts, where lengths of sugarcane had been tied with long red ribbons. 'To show that a wedding has taken place,' he said.

Isabel glanced through, into the courtyard. It was lined on three sides with long trestle tables; some of the guests were already sitting shoulder to shoulder along narrow benches. Garlands of orchids and red frangipani hung from almost every available surface, and elegant heliconia stems, with their waxy red bracts, adorned the centre of each table.

They had come to a standstill outside the open gates and Isabel wondered why they weren't going in. A small boy in front of her was swinging on his mother's arm, straining to see inside. As soon as he caught sight of Isabel, he stopped what he was doing and stood still, eyes wide, staring at her. But when Isabel smiled at him, he turned away, hiding in the folds of his mother's printed cotton skirt.

The mother peered up at Isabel, her face precisely framed by the lime-green scarf covering her head. 'Sorry-*lah*. So shy all of a sudden.'

With nimble, childlike hands she plucked at the squirming boy and turned him around to face Isabel. 'Can say hello – to the lady.'

The young woman was slender and delicate; she fitted neatly, elegantly, into her colourful costume. In comparison, Isabel felt like a great, pink mountain towering above her; and she wondered why she had ever considered wearing a sarong.

Having done with the 'hellos', the mother and her son merged back into their own party. Isabel scratched absently at her arm. The itch transferred to her shoulder and she scratched there too, wishing now that she had taken the trouble to light a mosquito coil the night before. She had stayed out on her verandah well into the evening, trying to read, and all the time hoping that Lee might pass by on his way back from wherever he had been. But he hadn't. Only Phil had appeared, making out that he had just come from the village. Which was a lie because she had spotted him earlier, loitering around the Gula House.

She glanced at Lee who was happily chatting away to Kin Mun – or was it Kui Hing? – then they were moving again, and she realized that they were lining up to meet the bride and groom. She pondered over the fact that she was at the wedding of two people she had never met. *Benny and Natalie*. She recited the names to herself, so she wouldn't forget.

The family in front had gone through the gates and it was her turn to move, but she held back, to let the others go ahead – after all, they had more right to be there than she did. She was beginning to feel like an impostor.

But Lee had caught hold of her hand. 'Shall we go?'

They took a few steps forward then stopped again. But now Isabel could see the bride and groom standing on a low platform just inside the courtyard. Benny was speaking to the little boy; he was crouched down low so that their faces were level. And next to him, stunning in a long red *cheongsam*, stood Natalie.

Isabel had never considered that Natalie would be anything other than Chinese, but she couldn't have been more mistaken: Natalie was tall, slim and very fair.

She wondered if she was British.

Last night's insect bite was stabbing away at the skin on her shoulder, but Lee was still holding onto her hand; if she scratched it, she would have to let go. Joseph and Albert had reached the platform now; someone had evidently made an amusing remark, because they were all laughing. A slight, almost imperceptible, movement of Lee's thumb sent a tingling sensation across her palm. Eileen, Ping Li and the other two were talking to Benny; it would be their turn next.

Lee gave her fingers a gentle squeeze before stepping forward to shake Benny's hand.

'Ha,' said Benny, slapping Lee on the back, 'here he is. My oldest friend.'

Lee gave Natalie a hug. 'Congratulations to you both. And I'm not sure I like that oldest friend stuff. I'm the same age as you.'

Isabel felt his hand press against her back.

'This is my friend, Isabel.'

She stepped forward, on legs that didn't seem to be hers.

My friend Isabel.

With Lee's words echoing inside her head, she shook Natalie's hand.

'I am very pleased to meet you,' Natalie said, 'very pleased.' Her pale, champagne-coloured hair was arranged in an elegant chignon with a red flower tucked into one side. She leant forward, kissing the air to each side of Isabel's face. Her skin felt smooth and powdery when it brushed against Isabel's cheek.

Isabel was trying to place Natalie's accent, but Benny had stepped towards her; he placed his hands lightly on her shoulders and planted a kiss on each cheek.

'The French way,' he said.

Then it dawned on her, and before she could stop herself she had turned back to Natalie. 'You are French!'

Natalie laughed. 'Yes, that is true. I am from France – originally.' She beamed towards Benny, who was now deep in conversation with Lee, then turned back to Isabel and whispered: 'But my heart it is here.' She placed a hand on Isabel's arm. 'I will see you later, I hope?'

Isabel nodded. Then they were moving on again, and someone

was ushering them towards a table where drinks were being served.

'What would you like to drink?' Lee asked her. 'Ice-tea? Mango juice? Champagne?' Not waiting for an answer, he took up two glasses of champagne and held one out to her.

'Thank you.' Their fingers collided as she took the glass. She looked away, quickly, but she could sense that his eyes were still on her.

'Cheers,' he said.

When she raised her head, she saw that he was holding out his glass. She looked back into his eyes – eyes that were almost black: deep, unfathomable. His gaze didn't falter for an instant.

'*Gān bēi*,' she replied, tapping her glass against his.

∞

It was clear that most people knew Lee and Joseph, and their corner of the courtyard was soon buzzing with activity.

'It's a small island,' Lee said, apologetically, as a tall, dark-skinned man in a white pyjama suit headed towards them, his hand raised in greeting; a wide, white smile cutting across his face. When he arrived, he grasped Lee's hand in between his own and pumped it up and down, rattling off a string of words that seemed to lack either beginning or end.

As soon as the man paused for breath, Lee took his opportunity. 'Hashim,' he said in English, 'this is my friend, Isabel. From UK. Isabel, this is Hashim. Hashim used to work for my uncle.'

'Yes, is true – I did – long time ago.' He straightened the gold-embroidered *songkok* on his head. 'I am pleased.' He bowed and took her hand. 'And . . . hmm, I sorry . . . for my English. Is not good. I try.'

'It's fine,' she said. 'And you two carry on, in Malay. I don't mind.'

Nevertheless, she knew that Hashim would try to struggle through in English – everyone did, when she was there. But she meant what she had said: she was more than happy to stand by and watch as Lee chatted away to Hashim, or any of them; just to be there, with him, was enough. Yet here he was, sharing his friends with her as if it were the most natural thing in the world. Not once had he left her side, nor made her feel awkward in any way; and her mind flicked back to the last party she had been to, when she had been left standing alone, at a bar, while Ian flirted his way round the room. 'It's all part of the job,' he had snapped at her later that night, when they were lying side-by-side in bed:

limbs drawn in, stiff, intransigent; as far from each other as was possible. But by that time she had already realized what he was up to; she knew which one of the girls it was. It was fairly obvious. Ian simply wasn't that clever.

Now it didn't matter any more; that episode in her life was well and truly over, and good riddance to it. But was there something else about to begin? Unless she was very badly mistaken –

She glanced at Lee. One of his hands was resting on a table, close enough for her to touch. She studied the long, slim fingers; watched them curl and uncurl as he spoke. Less than half an hour ago, those fingers had been wrapped tightly, protectively, around her own –

Oh God!

She gave a sharp cough, to disguise what she feared might have come out as a whimper. Quickly, she tuned in to the conversation. They were talking about food, and who made the best *laksa udang* – she recognized the words for the spicy prawn and coconut stew which she had eaten several times at Buah Lodge. It became clear that Lee's *laksa* was famous.

Someone was asking her a question.

'Have you tried it yet?'

'Yes, I have.' She nodded, smiling.

'Blow your head off?'

She laughed, possibly a little louder than was necessary, relieved to have an outlet for the euphoria bubbling up inside her.

'No, not at all,' her voice sang out, 'Lee's *laksa* is perfect. Just right.'

At last, everyone sat down, and the next few hours sped by in a riot of eating and drinking. A stream of men and women in immaculate white uniforms carried plates and bowls of food from inside the house, setting them down on the tables until there was simply no room for anything else.

Lee made sure she tried each of the dishes that appeared. '*Sate udang*,' he announced, offering a plate of skewered prawns. 'And *acar awak*.' Plates were shifted about to make room for the mixed vegetables.

'And here is *sambal ayam*,' joined in Hashim, pointing over

Lee's shoulder. 'You try this, Eezabel – is very good.'

Each time she managed to clear her plate, one of her neighbours would push something else at her.

'Isabel, you tried this yet?'

'You take spicy?'

'Hey, Joseph, pass rice for Isabel.'

'See, your plate is empty. You have not had enough.'

She had eaten so much that she felt she was going to burst. Finally, she managed to prevent anyone from putting more food onto her plate by covering it with her napkin. She leant back in her chair.

Eileen was leaning back next to her. 'Eaten so much-*lah.*'

'So have I,' replied Isabel. 'I think I may need to loosen this.' She tugged at her sarong.

'It's nice. Where you get it?'

'From a shop in the town.'

'Here? In Teluk?' Eileen sounded surprised.

'Yes.'

'Not long back, you wouldn't find any good shop here. Now is changing.'

'Do you live on the island?' asked Isabel

'No, I am from Malacca.'

'Like Lee?'

'Yes. And also Ping Li and Kin Mun?' she waved a hand in the direction of the other two. 'We attend school together. When we were juniors. With Lee and Benny.'

On hearing her name, Ping Li turned to join in the conversation. 'Lee was good student,' she said. 'Work very hard.'

'Not true. Not true.' Lee was in the process of balancing a tray of cakes someone had handed to him. 'Here, try one of these.' He offered the tray to Isabel.

The cakes were bright green – the colour of pea pods. She took one and put it on her plate.

Lee passed the tray to Joseph. 'I didn't work hard,' he said. 'I was always dreaming.'

Eileen leant towards Isabel's ear, one hand over her mouth in a stage whisper. 'He was top of the class.'

'That is not true.' She could feel his breath stirring her hair as he whispered in her other ear. 'Don't believe what they say.'

The round bone of his shoulder was pressing against the top of her arm; she could feel the warmth of his skin through his shirt. Very, very, slightly, she leant her body into his.

∞

Lee was vaguely aware that the others were still talking about their schooldays. He recognized all the words, but his brain didn't seem able to organize them into anything coherent. He could focus on one thing only: her closeness. He was almost close enough to . . .

He tried to push away the thought.

A few more centimetres . . .

He reached out for his glass and took a gulp of champagne; the bubbles hit a place between his eyes.

But he *had* held her hand. Not that he could quite believe it now, and he tried to fix in his mind the sensation of their fingers linked together. There would be a time, he supposed, when such memories were all he had left.

And she hadn't run away.

Ah, but she couldn't have got very far.

He felt a smile begin to work its way across his lips, at the thought of her running away from him.

Anyway, he reasoned, you can't just kiss someone at the table, in front of everyone; it would be a very odd thing to do. And the very idea of it made him want to laugh out loud, so he clenched his fist, making his nails dig into his palm, and tried to think of something unpleasant.

Ping Li's shrill voice broke into his thoughts.

'Remember Chan *taitai*?'

He realized that she was waiting for an answer. He forced himself to focus. Mrs Chan had been their science teacher.

'Yes?' he said warily, hoping he hadn't missed something important. His throat felt tight. He coughed and said it again, this time, he hoped, in a more normal voice. 'Yes.'

It seemed to be a satisfactory response.

From further down the table Kin Mun's voice boomed out. 'Chan *taitai* – small-small lady with big, big voice.'

Everyone laughed.

Lee wanted to look at Isabel, to check that his thoughts hadn't somehow jumped out of his head and danced over to her. He moved slightly, so he could see her from the corner of his eye. She was studying her plate, looking at the cake she had taken.

Had he embarrassed her?

No, that was stupid. Because she couldn't possibly have known what was going through his mind. And perhaps that's where such thoughts should stay – securely locked inside his head. He had to be sensible about this after all; she would be leaving in – he did a quick calculation – the day after tomorrow. But what was the alternative? Simply let her go? Never see her again? He couldn't bear to think of that. And would she come back, he wondered, if he asked her to?

Hell! This woman is turning my brain inside out.

He made himself turn his head, to look at her. She had taken a tiny bite from the cake, and was now pushing it about on her plate. He could tell that she didn't like it. He wasn't surprised. A lot of westerners found the Malay sweets not quite to their taste.

He risked his voice. 'Don't you like it?'

She smiled – her big, beautiful smile. He couldn't believe it was just for him.

'It's a bit sweet,' she replied.

'Yes, we have sweet tooth.'

She was still looking at him, as if she were waiting for him to say something else. But he couldn't think of anything, except that he wanted to kiss her.

A strand of her hair had fallen out of place; it skimmed her cheek as she moved. He loved the colour of her hair, the way it glinted red in the sun, the way it never seemed to stay put when she tried to wear it knotted at the back of her head as it was now; and although he had never seen her do it, he could visualize her working with it – as he had seen other girls do – pulling it into a bunch, winding it round, taking the metal clasps from her mouth, one-by-one.

'Isabel, where's your name from? Is it from France?'

The sound of Eileen's voice made him jump. He hoped no-one had noticed. Isabel had to turn away from him now, to answer Eileen's question. He saw that she had a red bump on her shoulder, an insect bite probably, just at the point where her skin disappeared beneath the silk of her blouse. He liked the colours she had chosen to wear today, colours of the earth, and of fire; they suited her. He cast his mind back to the day she arrived, how pale she had been then; and how he had noticed the colour of her skin becoming deeper and deeper as each day passed.

She was still talking to Eileen. The plate with the half-eaten cake had been pushed to one side. He wondered whether he should offer to finish it for her.

'– but it might be of French origin,' he heard her say. 'There was a Queen Isabella of France – I think. No – it was Spain – I'm not quite sure.'

Her hand went to her shoulder. He watched her press her fingers hard against the bite. He knew she was trying not to scratch it; but then she gave in, and scraped at it with her nails.

∞

The insect bite was driving her mad. She knew that she shouldn't scratch, but she couldn't help it. And she hated having to turn away from Lee, but Eileen had wanted to talk. She couldn't just ignore her.

'So how do you choose your names?' she asked. 'I mean, your non-Chinese ones.'

'Different ways. I think that some people like to choose the name from a book they read at school, or the name of their favourite film star. Mine was easy. I chose Eileen because my Chinese name is Ai Lee – you see – sounds the same – Ai Lee – Eileen. Usually, it is the ones who have been overseas for education who want to choose a western name.'

From the corner of her eye, Isabel could see that Lee was now talking to Hashim. His arm brushed against hers whenever he moved.

'Did you go overseas?'

'Yes. From our senior class, two of us went overseas. I went to UK.'

'Where to?'

'I went to Leeds University. Benny went to Melbourne. Australia is closer, and it is less expensive. But I wanted to go to England.'

'Why did you choose to go abroad, rather than go to a university here?'

'No choice,' Eileen replied. 'It is more difficult for Chinese to go to university in Malaysia now. There is a quota, set by the government. There are only enough places for the top students. So we go overseas.'

'Did you like England?'

'Yes I liked it very much. But I didn't like the food.'

Isabel looked at the wedge of cake on the plate in front of her. She picked it up and turned it round in her fingers. It was the colour that put her off. She took another bite. She didn't like it, but she couldn't just leave it like that, half-eaten. She popped the last bit into her mouth.

'Have you put anything on those bites?'

She spun her head round. Lee was turned towards her, one elbow propped on the table, his chin resting on the palm of his hand.

She swallowed the piece of cake quickly, without chewing. 'No I haven't.'

He stood up and extricated himself from the bench. 'I know something you can use. It will help.' He touched her shoulder. 'Don't go away. I'll be back.'

Then he was gone.

∞

Hashim was trying his best to hold a conversation with her. But his English was poor and he was struggling to make himself understood. She knew he meant well, and she was truly grateful that he was making such an effort, but she was having difficulty focussing her mind on what he was saying. Every so often, she sneaked a glance around the courtyard, hoping that she might spot Lee. He had been gone for some time now and the gap he had left on the bench was becoming smaller and smaller, as Hashim edged closer and closer; soon there wouldn't be any space at all for him to come back to.

'He has left you alone?'

She turned round. Natalie was standing behind her, a bottle of champagne in one hand and a glass in the other.

'Here, sit down.' Eileen jumped up to offer Natalie her seat. 'You must be tired.'

'Thank you. But no, I am not tired, not at all. I am just . . .' She paused to beam round at everyone. 'I am just happy. But I will sit for a while.'

She put the glass and the bottle on the table and sat down next to Isabel.

'Lee does not look after you?'

'Oh, he is doing – really,' Isabel replied. 'He's just gone to get something for me. I don't even know what. And he's probably got talking to someone. You know what he's like.'

Natalie looked amused. 'I am sure he will come back.'

Isabel forced a smile in return. But why should he come back, she thought. Why would he want to spend the afternoon sitting with her, when there were so many other people to talk to?

She tried to push Lee from her mind for a moment and turned her attention back to Natalie, who was tipping the champagne bottle towards her empty glass. Isabel watched the creamy bubbles surge up until they stopped just short of the rim.

'Thanks.'

She waited for Natalie to fill her own glass.

'And congratulations again. Lots of luck and happiness.'

'Thank you.' Natalie raised her glass to Isabel before taking a sip.

'So how did you come to be here? On this island?' It was a question Isabel had wanted to ask since the moment she had seen Natalie.

'I came here for holiday. Like you, I think?' Natalie was looking at her, her head to one side; something was making her smile. But she seemed happy not to have an answer to her question. 'And I fell in love with it,' she went on. 'So I decided to stay for longer. But it is very funny – you see, all that time I was here, Benny was in Australia, and still we hadn't met. The life plays funny games sometimes, doesn't it?'

Isabel nodded and was about to reply, but one of the waiters had stepped up behind them.

'*Puan – maafkan saya.*' He leant forward to speak to Natalie.

She giggled, and then said something back to him in what sounded like fluent Malay. She was still laughing when she turned back to Isabel. 'He called me Madame – Mrs. It sounds . . .' She thought for a moment. 'It sounds very funny to me but . . . Yes, I think I like it. And he wanted to tell me – soon is the time for some music and dancing.'

'You can speak Malay?' Isabel said.

'Yes, I can. It is necessary – in my restaurant. And Benny is teaching me Mandarin too. But that is very difficult.'

'So you must have been here for a long time?'

'I came here when I was twenty-three. So that is . . . Yes, a long time. Eight years.'

Isabel did a quick calculation; they were about the same age.

'Yes,' Natalie laughed, 'I can see you are adding. I am thirty-one. And Benny – ah, he is here – Benny is my toy-boy.'

As if on cue, Benny arrived at the table. He stood behind Natalie and put his hands on her shoulders.

'No I'm not,' he argued, kissing the top of her head, 'I am only one and a half years younger than you.'

'You are still my toy-boy. Anyway, I am telling Isabel how it was fate that brought us together.'

'No it wasn't,' Benny said. 'It was Lee.'

Natalie laughed. 'Yes, you are right. It is because of Lee.' She turned to Isabel to explain. 'Lee and Benny came one day to my restaurant and . . . Well, you know the rest.'

Isabel heard herself join in the laughter.

It wasn't difficult to imagine: two young men walking into Natalie's restaurant; and there was Natalie waiting to greet them, her blonde hair swaying and shining in the sunlight. What if Lee had fallen for Natalie instead? How easy it would have been for things to have turned out differently.

She laughed again, laughing out the relief she suddenly felt at the outcome of that chance visit to Natalie's restaurant. And how very strange it was that all this had been taking place in one small corner of the world, while, thousands of miles away, she had been getting on with her own life, unaware of a chain of events that one day might stretch out to encompass her.

Fragments of conversation sliced through her thoughts: Natalie was telling someone about her dress; Benny and Joseph were discussing flight times; and all of them speaking in a language that was not their own, just for her sake. She wished that Lee would come back; she felt strangely bereft now, without him by her side. She put her hand to her shoulder, and rubbed at it gently, the warmth of her own touch reminding her of his.

Then she saw him. He was working his way through the crowd and in no time he was there, at her side, squeezing himself back into the space between her and Hashim.

'Move up Hash.'

'Sorry, sorry Mr Lee.' Hashim shuffled back to his original position, flashing them his wide, white grin.

'Aha,' Benny said, once Lee was settled back on the bench. 'You are back. We have been looking after Isabel for you.'

Isabel pretended not to have heard; she took a long draught of champagne, almost draining her glass. She felt their eyes on her but couldn't think of anything to say, so she just smiled – at no-one in particular. Then the moment passed; Benny told Natalie that they should move on, and talk to some more of their guests. Natalie slid from the bench and moved to where Benny was standing. She put her arms around his waist.

'It is lovely to meet you Isabel, she said. 'I will see you again. And I hope that you will enjoy the dancing.'

As soon as Natalie and Benny had gone, Lee put his hand into his pocket and pulled out a tiny bottle. He put it on the table in front of her. 'Put some on your bites.'

She picked up the bottle and squinted at the label, but all she could see were Chinese characters. 'What is it?' she asked.

'White flower oil.' He took the bottle from her and unscrewed the cap before handing it back to her. 'Try it. You need just a little bit.'

She dabbed her finger at the open bottle, as if it were perfume, and then she rubbed some of the oily liquid onto the bites on her arm. The smell of it reminded her of Vicks ointment. She transferred more oil to her finger and bent under the table, to put some on her ankle. Then she reached up to her shoulder, feeling around for the bite she knew was there.

'Need help?' He held out his hand for the bottle.

Without stopping to think what she was doing, she passed the bottle to him; then she watched, mesmerized, as he took it from her, tipped it, and dabbed some of the oil onto his fingers. From another part of the courtyard came the frenzied rise and fall of Chinese being spoken into a microphone. She saw Lee's hand move towards her and then disappear out of sight behind her shoulder. Then she felt his finger press gently onto her skin.

'There's another one here – and another. One – two – three –' he counted, as he touched each bite in turn.

'Thank you,' she said, managing no more than a whisper. 'That feels better.'

It was true that the oil had started to produce a pleasant burning sensation on her skin.

Lee turned away and busied himself putting the cap back onto the bottle of oil, twisting and untwisting it, checking and double checking that it was secure. He appeared to be very engrossed in what he was doing.

Isabel could hear music, someone was singing; it surprised her, because she hadn't noticed it before.

∞

At the far end of the courtyard people were dancing. Isabel found herself swaying to the music; she longed to be on the dance floor, but everyone was busy chatting, still catching up with each other's news. She forced her body to be still and tried to concentrate on the conversations that were going on around her. Her skin was still tingling from the effects of the white flower oil and she realized that she hadn't once scratched her bites since she had applied it. She wondered if Lee might ask her to dance. Of course she hoped that he would, but the thought still unsettled her. How long was it since she had danced with anyone? She might make a fool of herself? And what about Lee? Maybe he didn't dance. Maybe he couldn't. She tried to push the thoughts from her mind. After all, it probably wasn't going to happen anyway, so there was no point in worrying. She tried to see the hands on Eileen's watch but the neat little watch face nestled in the child-sized silver bracelet was too small to read. The party couldn't last for ever, she thought. Natalie and Benny had a plane to catch – the seven-o'clock to the mainland – the same one she would be taking the day after tomorrow.

Despite the heat in the courtyard, this thought sent a chill coursing through her; then came the wave of nausea. Soon she would be leaving. To go back to what? The mess she had made of her life? And everything good was slipping away, out of her reach. She closed her eyes for a second, but that made it worse: the downward dip of a roller coaster ride. She opened them again, but she couldn't still her mind. England – London – Manor House – Ian – her impending homelessness. She put out a hand and grasped the edge of the table, to steady herself, almost knocking over a glass. She looked up and saw that Lee was watching her. His face was lit by a smile, but his eyes were enquiring.

'It is lucky – I had almost finished that,' he said, reaching to pick it up. He put the glass to his lips. 'Is it how you tell me that I have had enough?'

She grinned back at him, wishing she could think of a witty response. But none was needed: Natalie and Benny were walking towards them.

Natalie put a hand on Lee's shoulder. Isabel noticed that her nails were painted bright crimson – the exact same shade as the dress she was wearing.

'I have come for my friend,' Natalie said, 'to take him to dance with me.'

Lee stood up. 'It is my pleasure.'

Isabel looked away, she concentrated on the table, she stared at Lee's empty glass; her head felt as though it had been filled with cotton wool.

'And Isabel – I have brought Benny – for you to dance with.'

She knew she had to look up at them; she forced her face into a smile and focussed her eyes on Benny.

He held out his hand. 'May I ask you for this dance?'

She let Benny lead her across the courtyard, her eyes fixed on Lee and Natalie. She watched them as they pressed their way through the other dancers, until they disappeared from sight. Benny took hold of her and she tried to relax, to think about the music.

Her hand was resting lightly in the curve of his waist; the fabric of his shirt alien to her fingers. It had been a long time since she had been held like this, and somehow it seemed wrong to have the unfamiliar contours of another body drawn up against hers in this strangely intimate way. But Benny was a natural dancer and they soon fell into an easy routine. Out of the corner of her eye she caught a glimpse of red: Natalie's dress.

She didn't want to look at them now. Instead, she fixed her eyes on Benny's shirt collar, following the neat line of stitching down one edge, then to the corner, where it made a sharp turn and continued up the other side: tiny, intricate stitches, stitches that someone, somewhere, had sewn, bent over a machine, feeding the material down and round, surrendering their fingers to the jumping point of the needle –

There was a slight pressure on her arm and she realized that the music had stopped. Benny was looking over her shoulder; he was speaking to someone.

What was she supposed to do now? Stay where she was? Walk back to the table?

'I have brought him back to you in one piece.'

Isabel recognized Natalie's voice. She turned round.

They were both there: Natalie and Lee.

'He's all yours now,' Natalie whispered. She sashayed past Isabel and put her arms around Benny, pulling him close. 'And I have come to reclaim my husband for the next dance.' Her eyes were sparkling. She looked radiant.

Everything started to unravel. Natalie had done this deliberately – to get them both on the dance floor. And she felt such an enormous wave of gratitude towards her new friend that she might have reached out and hugged her, had she not already moved away.

Lee stepped forward. 'Are you sure you want to dance with me? I am not very good.'

'That is nonsense,' said Natalie, over her shoulder. She and Benny had started to dance; her arms were resting against his chest, her fingers linked behind his neck. 'He is a very good dancer.'

Lee was holding out his hand. 'Shall we?'

She was aware that all around them people were swaying to the gentle pulse of the music, bodies pressed close; but her feet had chosen this moment to root themselves to the floor.

She couldn't help thinking that they probably looked rather odd standing there, in the middle of the dance floor, staring at each other.

∞

Lee was well aware that they had been set up by Benny and Natalie. And if he hadn't felt so nervous about what might happen in the next few seconds, he would have found it extremely amusing.

Ever since the music had started up he had wanted to ask her to dance, and now, here was his chance, and he was acting like an idiot. What was he waiting for? All he had to do was step forward and take hold of her – before she could come up with an excuse and walk away.

'Okay.' Her voice was barely audible over the music.

It wasn't quite the response he had hoped for, but it would do for now. He took her hand and pressed his fingers around it – firmly – in case she changed her mind. But she didn't. She took a step towards him. He could feel her body brush against his as she began to move to the rhythm of the music. He put his hand on her waist and pulled her closer to him. Her hair grazed against the side of his face; he could smell her perfume – it was the same one she had worn the night they had gone to Coconut Café.

There was no awkwardness in the way their bodies moved together, in fact, holding her like this seemed the most natural thing in the world; and perhaps that was not surprising: it was a scene he had played and re-played over and over in his mind for days. But there was one thing he had never imagined, and that was the intensity of what he felt for her: he had the suspicion that something had sneaked into his body when he wasn't looking, and was now scrabbling away in his nervous system, tugging and squeezing and generally tying it in knots; it was almost too much to bear. All he wanted to do was enfold her in his arms and draw out every last bit of pleasure from the moment, while it lasted. And then shout out, to anyone who cared to listen, that he, Lee Kim Cheng, was absolutely, unbelievably, head over heels in love.

She had slipped her arm around his waist and one hand was pressed flat against his back; her other hand was resting on his shoulder. He felt her fingers reach over and pull at the gold chain he had round his neck.

'What's this?'

'It is for good luck,' he told her. 'The Chinese character means good fortune.' He waited for a moment before adding: 'I think it works.'

She turned her head away, but not before he had seen the hint of a smile cross her face.

He moved his hand and placed it over hers, letting his thumb trace across her skin, round each of her knuckles, until he felt her fingers curl over his, and squeeze very, very slightly. Without daring to think about what he was doing, he lifted her hand to his lips and kissed it, before placing it back onto his shoulder, folded tight into his own.

∞

If anyone had asked how long they had been there, she wouldn't have been able to say. For as long as the music had played, they had danced. But then, mid-song, it had stopped; a voice hissed and crackled through the loudspeakers, someone was speaking into a microphone.

Like many of the other couples on the dance floor, they had stopped moving but had remained locked together, in readiness for the music to start up again. But it soon became clear that there would be no more dancing for now; people were starting to drift apart, milling around, trying to get closer to whatever was happening on the platform nearby.

She felt him start to pull away. She, too, took a step backwards, registering how it felt to be standing alone, to be just Isabel once more, without Lee's arms wrapped around her; and almost immediately she ached to be held by him again. But the dancing was over. The gap between them could only get wider and wider now as they were swept up, once more, into the party going on around them. She wanted to look at him, to study his face for clues to what might happen next, but her eyes remained fixed to the floor, focussing on some tiny grains of sand that had found their way into the courtyard.

Why couldn't she look at him? What was she afraid of?

Someone else had the microphone now. The voice coming through was louder, clearer. She guessed it must be one of Benny's friends from Melbourne.

Out of the corner of her eye she could see Lee's shoes. They were brown, and suede. She tried to calculate the distance between their feet, trying to visualize the inches as she counted them off: one – two – three – four. The Australian had made a joke; there was a ripple of laughter; she saw Lee's feet move. Then she felt a light touch on her arm.

'Isabel?'

She looked up.

There was a waiter standing in front of her. He was carrying a tray of glasses, each one full of tiny, tiny bubbles, rising up and bursting into the space just above.

Lee reached out and selected two, bringing them round, carefully, to avoid spilling the contents.

'For the toasts,' he said, holding one out to her.

She had to look at him then. His eyes gazed steadily back at her: they moved over her face, seeming to drink in every last detail; the warmth that was in them acted upon her like a restorative burst of sunshine on a winter's day. She knew then that things were different now. Whatever happened next, nothing would be quite the same again.

PART ELEVEN

London
December 1999

∞

10.45 am

It was a day most people had chosen to spend at home: a shadowy, no-man's-land of a day marooned between Christmas and New Year's Eve.

The centre of London resembled a city after war: its roads desolate, its people missing. Just their debris remained, strewn over those very same pavements on which, not so very long ago, they had marched to work, or play, or tramped from shop to shop in search of gifts. The few who had dared brave the elements now struggled down ravaged streets, heads bowed low against pebbles of hail being fired from above.

Nor had the fallout spared the stunted city trees: for while their concrete-covered roots remained oblivious to season and the passage of time, their sickly branches had to host the grubby odds and ends launched by each successive gust of wind. In a nearby alleyway, a couple of empty cans had been brought to life and now they jangled in unison over the historic cobbles. A stray piece of tinsel, the aftermath of earlier revelries, shimmied around a urine-splattered lamppost; a silver trophy for its fortitude.

Through the window of a bookshop on Charing Cross Road, Isabel watched the needles of rain lash against the glass. She stared out at the greyness of the street, seeing it momentarily transformed when a red double-decker slid past, spraying the pavement with arcs of muddy water. A damp, yellowish light seeped through its misted windows revealing the occasional hunched form of a passenger, and other mysterious shapes, like markings found in some primitive cave, left by the hands or sleeves of people long since gone.

She reached out and touched one of the books on the table in front of her, running her finger over the letters that spelt out her name. Then she looked back to the window and attempted to read the back-to-front writing on the poster that faced towards the street. Slowly, methodically, like a child faltering over words seen for the very first time: 'Thursday – the 30th – of December – eleven am – to – one pm – Isabel Adamson – will sign copies – of her latest book – *Passing Ships.*'

'Isabel Adamson,' she repeated. Then she tried something else: 'Isabel Raines will sign copies of her latest book.'

She splayed out the fingers of her left hand and examined her ring. There was a patch of dry skin where it had rubbed against her little finger.

Now something made her look towards the door, and there was Simon, struggling to close an enormous, yellow umbrella. The words 'CHELSEA SPORTS' were emblazoned in large, red letters across the outstretched fabric, and she wondered how it had come into his possession. The thought of Simon being linked in any way to sport was highly unlikely.

Both Simon and the troublesome umbrella were wedged in the doorway. Streams of rainwater were making their way down the folds of his mac and a small puddle was forming near his feet. Isabel couldn't imagine how he had managed to get quite so wet, having had the ample protection of *Chelsea Sports.*

'I see they've set you up then,' he shouted, shaking drips from his wavy blonde hair, just like a dog that had come back from a swim. And suddenly she was thinking about Henry, the new puppy she had found in the kitchen on her eighth birthday. The last time she had seen Henry, he was being bundled into the back of their blue and white Triumph; he was going to see the vet, they had said. But he never came home. It was the only time she ever saw her father cry.

At last, Simon was inside. With some disdain, he dumped the umbrella by the staircase. He had still not managed to close it.

'Sorry I'm late. Couldn't get a cab. Any business yet?' Before Isabel could reply, he continued. 'Where's Nigel? Need to have a word.'

'He's in the back making me a coffee.'

It was normal for Simon to be late, he was always late – for everything – and he always blamed the transport – whatever form of it he had opted to take.

'Not sure this was a wise choice of date – for this, I mean,' she called after him. 'Just after Christmas. Everyone's still off.'

'Don't worry, hon,' he shouted over his shoulder. 'It'll be fine.' He clapped his hands. 'Right – where's that coffee?'

Isabel toyed with her pen, trying to recall what she had been thinking about before Simon had come in. The stockroom door was ajar and she could hear him gossiping with Nigel, the bookshop manager. She wondered if they would remember her coffee.

Not long after Simon's dramatic entrance, the door opened once more to reveal a woman with a small child in tow. But with eyes fixed on her destination, she manoeuvred the child straight past where Isabel was sitting, and on into the section where the children's books were kept. A few moments passed; the door opened again. An elderly woman walked in. With her neat bun and no-nonsense, dark-green suit she looked more promising, Isabel thought. But the woman peered over the top of her spectacles then wandered past, as if she were looking for something in particular; her sensible, brown lace-ups made a gentle thudding sound on the carpeted floor. It was not long, though, before she had sauntered back. She picked up one of the books from the pile and began to leaf through the pages, holding it at arm's length. Isabel smiled, and was about to speak, but the woman shut the book, dropped it down onto the table and scuttled away, like a mouse caught with its nose in a few spilt crumbs.

It was at this moment that Isabel wished for nothing more than to be tucked away in her study, in front of her computer. She wasn't cut out for this, it was clear. It was unlikely anyway, she concluded, that the woman was the sort who would read her book. And she tried to picture her, sitting at home, with a cat (there had to be a cat) and blushing when she reached the bedroom scenes – not that there were many of those, it wasn't that sort of novel. It was 'a contemporary romance in an historical setting', according to the blurb on the back cover. But some of the characters did have sex; contemporary people had sex; perhaps even the old lady had sex – possibly more often than she did. She tried to remember the last time she and David had made love. She couldn't.

She turned her attention back to the stockroom and the rise and fall of voices in animated conversation. She supposed that sitting here in an almost empty bookshop was marginally better than being at home with David, who would be at a loose end, and bored, because he wasn't at work, and almost certainly grumpy because he was having to look after Tom.

She looked at the clock. It was eleven thirty. David had agreed to pick her up at quarter past one but would very likely be somewhere in town even now, wandering the streets with Tom in his pushchair, because he would have given himself far too much time to get there, and to find a parking space. Nevertheless, she knew that he would stay away from the bookshop until the very last moment, to avoid running into Simon, 'your gay friend' as he called him.

She was sorry that they didn't get on, but it couldn't have been otherwise: from the very start, Simon had posed a threat to David's conventional and efficiently-structured lifestyle and her reluctance for them to meet had been well founded. But David had insisted she bring him to dinner, at his flat. So she did. David had prepared a faultless meal, in fact he had gone to rather a lot of trouble; but Simon drank too much and was sick on a new carpet. It was a long time ago, but David had never forgiven him. In fact, he avoided having anything to do with him at all, if he could help it. According to David, Simon was coarse, morally degenerate, anti-Establishment, over-emotional and too flamboyant for his liking. And if only they could have managed a sensible conversation, without it turning into an argument, she might have conceded (suppressing a smile) that he had a point – at least on a couple of those observations. As for Simon, when he had heard that she and David were getting married, he had made it very clear what he thought. In his usual, forthright manner he had told her not to do it. 'David's a lovely man and all that,' he had said, 'but he just isn't right for you sweetie. It'll end in tears – and I should know – I know you better than anyone.'

Isabel picked up one of the books from the pile in front of her. The brand new cover creaked as she opened it. She turned a page and felt its starchiness as she caressed it between her finger and thumb. She buried her nose into the middle of the book and breathed deeply, luxuriating in the fresh, sweet smell of the new paper. Then she turned it over to inspect the back cover, and found her own face smiling back at her – a bright and happy face, but somewhat unfamiliar. Like someone she used to know.

The picture they had chosen was a few years out of date and she was grateful for that: her skin looked clear and radiant, there were no shady circles under her eyes, and her shoulder-length hair was dark and shiny, and showing no evidence of the grey that was beginning to appear. Had she aged so much in just two or three years, she wondered.

A noise behind her made her jump. Someone was attempting a wolf-whistle. Rather unsuccessfully. She turned to find Simon looking over her shoulder. He was holding a mug of coffee.

'And who is *that* gorgeous young woman?' he intoned. 'Even I could fancy that.' He handed her the mug. 'Are we ready for the press?'

'Would that be the royal we?' she asked.

He pulled a face. 'My God! What a thought. Don't be disgusting.'

'Yes, I'm ready.' She sat up straight in her chair, tilted her head to one side and gave him a mock grin. 'As ready as this old lump will ever be.'

He made a loud tutting sound. 'We'll have none of that – none of that – do you hear? You can bloody well stop putting yourself down for once and enjoy – okay? Right . . .' He put his hands on his hips and frowned as he looked around the shop. 'I hope we get a few more than this. I want to see you thronged – oooh, thronged darling. Mmm, yes please.'

Isabel laughed as she watched him sashay back to the stockroom. Simon always managed to cheer her up; and while it was true that he *could* be extremely outrageous at times, and was generally 'as camp as Christmas' – as he liked to put it – he had always been there for her when she needed a friend. One time, he had left his guests at the dinner table so he could rescue her from a date that was rapidly turning into a disaster. 'The company was as interesting as a nun's knickers anyway,' he had informed her later. 'Bet they never even noticed I was gone.'

She thought about those days now, glad they were over. Blind dates, gay clubs with Simon, solitary rides back on the night bus to North London: it wasn't a happy time, although there were moments –

Isabel picked up the mug of coffee and hugged it to her chest, taking comfort in the familiar aroma and the warmth of the steam on her face.

But that period of her life was over – gone – and, good or bad, it was time that could never be got back.

Then, her friends – the ones that had left school, married, started a family, and lived a pram's push from where they had started – thought her brave, foolhardy, carefree, exotic. Living in London? How exciting! Was it exciting? They feasted on her stories, and went away confident that it wasn't for them. Yet all along she had been yearning for what they had – the stable relationship, the house, the garden, children. And she never told them about the loneliness, or the sense of life passing her by; or about the times she would miss her bus, and wait the hour or so until the next one, talking to strangers at the bus-stop, just to avoid going back to an empty flat.

It was strange, she thought now, how things were never quite how they appeared, once you had scratched the surface and had a good look inside. It was strange, too, that you could live with someone by day, share a bed with them at night, and find a different sort of loneliness. And that was the worst kind of all.

As the morning went on, a few more people trickled into the bookshop. One or two made their way to Isabel's table, some ignored her and strode by to other sections, others browsed amongst the shelves, possibly taking refuge from the cold.

From where Isabel was sitting, she could sense that the sky outside had turned brighter and that the rain had eased off. A few glimmers of weak sunshine had made their way into the shop and were lighting up dingy corners, revealing fine specks of dust on the shelf edges.

The arrival of the photographer at twelve o'clock coincided with a surge of customers. It was clear that a few of them were only there to see what was going on; others, maybe, killing time in their lunch break. But to Isabel's amazement, there were some who had genuinely come for the book signing. It seemed they had simply been waiting for the weather to improve, before venturing out.

It was a fairly restrained crowd. People formed a queue in front of her and, while the photographer set up his equipment, Isabel signed copies of her book. A few of the customers asked intelligent questions; some just thanked her and hurried away. If anyone crowded around her, or dared to pick up a book from the table, Simon would be there, shooing them away: 'Over here, please. That's right, form a queue. Yes, queue here. Thank you.'

Amused, Isabel watched him strut up and down the line; she knew that he was loving every minute of it.

She turned to greet the next person in the queue. As she did, she noticed someone peering in through the bookshop window. And she felt something cartwheel inside her stomach.

'Can you put – to mum, happy birthday?'

Isabel tried to focus on the person standing in front of her. A large woman, of indeterminate age. She was wearing a long, red mac. Seconds passed. She realized that she was staring abstractedly at the woman's sleeve. There was a white stain: maybe chalk, or paint, or toothpaste.

'Ah, sorry. Yes, of course. From who – whom? Who from?'

She looked to the window again, to get a second glance.

He was still there, still looking in; his hand was raised, shielding his eyes as he tried to see inside. The stirring in her stomach was making her nauseous. She wished that he would move his hand away from his face. Then she could be sure.

The big red mac moved, cutting off her view of the window.

'From Penny, please.'

'Penny? Right. Okay. Penny.' She signed the message as quickly as she could, hoping that Penny wouldn't ask any questions.

But Penny wanted to talk.

'Thank you so much. And I really loved the book. That's why I'm getting it for my mother, I'm sure she'll love it too –'

Isabel smiled up at her, and at the same time tried to get another view of the window. But Penny was still in the way, and still talking.

'– and it will be just right for the beach. She's going to Barbados next week.'

'Ah. Good. Well – thanks very much.' Isabel stood up. She knew that what she was doing was incredibly rude, but all she could think about was getting to that window.

And yet Penny remained rooted to the spot.

'Please . . . you'll have to excuse me for a moment.' Isabel raised a hand to her forehead, wiped away the sweat that was turning cold on the surface of her skin. At least she could see the window again.

But there was no-one there. He had gone.

Perhaps she had been mistaken. Her mind playing tricks again. There was a time, once, when she would see his face in every crowd, in every street: but surely now, after all these years –

What if it *was* him this time?

She had to know.

Oblivious to what was going on around her, she pushed the chair aside and, still scanning the window, moved to the front of the table. She could see that there were a few people standing outside the shop, looking in, and for a moment she was distracted by a couple of boys who were leaning against the glass, eating chips from crumpled white paper packets. Then she saw a figure, hunched against the cold, a gloved hand clutching the upturned collar of an overcoat: a figure moving slowly away. Further and further away.

'I'm sorry. Please excuse me – sorry . . .'

She had started to push her way through the crowd.

'I have to pop out for a second.'

'Isabel?' Simon was moving towards her.

She had almost reached the door.

It *was* him, she was sure. But what on earth was he doing here? Hadn't he recognized her? Why had he walked away?

She had to catch up with him.

'Isabel? What's happening? Where are you going?' Simon was behind her, bobbing his way through a clutch of bewildered customers.

'Hang on, I won't be a second. Just have to go somewhere.'

He had disappeared from view. She couldn't lose him now. She mustn't – not again.

'Isabel, you can't go now, the photographer is just about to . . .'

'Simon, I'm sorry. He'll have to wait for a minute.'

She had managed to reach the door.

At last. She was outside.

∞

S ince Isabel had been inside the bookshop, the street had become
a seething mass of people: shoppers and office workers, family
groups, tourists, pushchairs and shopping bags, backpacks, maps,
all coming at her from every angle as she stood on the pavement
and peered in the direction she thought he had gone. And he *had*
gone; there was no sign of him anywhere. But his image remained,
like a shadow-play unfolding in her mind: a figure standing by
the window, looking, hesitating, thinking, moving away. That was
him, she thought: careful, circumspect.

A lone ray of sunlight glinted through the racing clouds and her
eyes, unaccustomed to the brightness, started to water.

'Isabel, what on earth are you doing?' Simon had finally caught
up with her. 'We need to get some shots while there are still plenty
of people around . . .'

She had turned to face him.

'God! What's wrong? What's happened?'

'Sorry about that. Tell you later. Come on. Let's get those
photos done.'

They went back inside.

'Sorry everyone. False alarm. I thought . . .' She stopped in her
tracks. She had caught sight of David. He was at the far end of the
shop; he had his back towards her and appeared to be engrossed
in a book.

How long had he been there?

She started to walk towards him but changed her mind: her
knees were still shaking. Then she noticed that he didn't have Tom
with him, and she tried to ignore the mounting wave of irritation;
she would have to come back to that later, she had enough to think

302

about at the moment. But they'd made a deal. He had promised. Who on earth had he left Tom with this time?

David looked up from the book he was reading and raised a hand in a half-hearted wave. She waved back.

Isabel returned to her table. Now she was worrying about Tom, as well as wishing she hadn't made an exhibition of herself. As she sat down, Simon put his hand on her shoulder and gave it a squeeze.

'Are you okay?' he whispered.

'Yes, fine thanks.' But the voice she heard was unfamiliar. 'Better get on,' she added.

She offered up her face to a woman yielding a loaded powder puff. She felt silly now for making a scene. It was, most likely, all a figment of her imagination anyway.

'This way please.' The photographer was adjusting the lens on his camera.

So why was she still doing this to herself? she wondered. After all these years? Was she really so disappointed with her life, that her mind had started to compensate – with fantasy?

She forced her mouth into a smile.

Click.

'And again.'

Click.

The flash of the camera brought more tears to her eyes and she had to dab at them with a tissue, trying not to spoil her makeup.

∞

Lambolle Road, NW3

1.45 pm

While David was parking the car, Isabel let herself into the house and headed for the kitchen. She opened the fridge and peered at the neat stack of plastic containers, and the two dishes with upturned saucers for lids, trying to remember what they contained. She lifted the foil cover from a plate to see what was underneath: there was enough turkey left for some sandwiches. Or she could make a decent soup with the leftover vegetables.

As soon as she heard David's key in the latch she walked into the hall, still clutching the plate of turkey.

'Do you want some lunch?'

Without looking up, he took off his coat and threw it over the banister. 'I need to work this afternoon.'

'Yes, but, you'll want lunch won't you? I was thinking about some sandwiches – turkey I'm afraid – or a soup? I just wanted to know if I should make something, before I go and get Tom.'

Now he looked at her, or at least at a point just behind her left shoulder. 'I said I was working. If I want anything I'll get it myself.'

He had already reached the first landing, where the stairs made a forty-five degree turn, but now he came back down and removed his coat from where he had left it. 'And I wish you'd stop trying to plan out my life for me. I can't keep having you control what I do all the time.'

She felt tears pricking behind her eyes. 'I'm not, I just wanted to know if . . .'

'I don't want any lunch. Okay?'

Isabel turned away and made her way back to the kitchen. The bewilderment at his outburst was beginning to give way to anger.

Why had she thought it might be pleasant for them to have lunch together for once? Well fine, if that's what he wanted, she would let him stew; there was nothing else she could do when he was in one of his moods. She just hoped it wouldn't last too long and that they could get back to normal again – whatever normal was. At least not arguing all the time.

Isabel had just finished clearing away the remains of her lunch. She had loaded her plate and fork into the dishwasher and was about to switch it on. She had heard him come down the stairs and sensed that he was now there, behind her, probably standing in the kitchen doorway, watching her. She continued with what she was doing. She heard him open the fridge door and start to forage around inside.

She couldn't stop herself; she knew she should keep quiet, but the words were suddenly there and jumping out of her mouth.

'I thought you didn't want any lunch.'

'I didn't. But I do now.'

'I would have waited if I'd known.'

'I told you – I didn't want any then. At that exact moment, I didn't know when I would want lunch. You can't plan everything out to the last detail, Isabel. Just go with the flow for once, why don't you.'

Isabel didn't have the will to carry on the conversation. Suddenly it felt as though she were sharing her home with someone who didn't like her very much – let alone love her. She looked down at the floor, willing herself not to cry it only made things worse. She wondered when he had stopped loving her. Had there been a specific event? A date? Or had love just been pushed aside by their busy lives; by habit or familiarity? Sometimes she wondered if he had ever loved her – really loved her. Or had she simply been part of a plan, a box he had to tick before he could move on to the next stage. University, career, marriage, family.

And what about her? Did she love him? She thought she had, once. And if the capacity to be hurt by someone was a measure of how much you loved them, then she still did.

But she wasn't sure of anything any more.

∞

3.25 pm

L ee stood by the window of his hotel room, listening to the sounds coming from the street, three floors below. London sounds. The constant, dull hum of traffic, then a car door being slammed shut – once, twice – then voices, and an engine starting up; while somewhere further off sirens undulated their way down a distant street. He wandered back to the bed and slumped down. The book was there, beside him, but he turned away, avoiding the eyes of the woman who gazed out at him from the back cover. He put his head in his hands and closed his eyes, squeezing his eyelids tight behind the cover of his fingers. That face – how often had he tried to conjure it up? – the features becoming more and more indistinct with the passing of every year, until he could barely pull them together to form a likeness. And now, just an arm's length away, there she was, in full and perfect detail, and all he had to do was open his eyes and look at her.

He did open his eyes but continued to stare down at the floor, at his feet, neatly aligned on the dark grey carpet. He was wearing what he called his graduation shoes: good, solid brogues, over five years old and still going strong. 'You get what you pay for,' he said out loud, and then laughed, surprised by the sound of his voice.

Even now, he could remember buying them. It was his first year in London, and the day of the final exam at that place on Essex Road. He knew that he had passed those exams; he knew he could have passed them without attending a dodgy college that existed merely to line the pockets of its owners. And he knew that he would return to continue his studies, as soon as he had replenished the money he had spent. But the wasted year, he could never get back.

And that was why he had bought the shoes. As soon as he saw them he had vowed that those would be the shoes he had on when he shook hands with Princess Anne, and accepted his degree.

He could remember the shop too – a small, cramped affair, somewhere off the Strand – and how he had saved for those shoes, coin by coin, in a large, pink pig (he had no idea what became of the pig) and how often he had forfeited lunch; and how disappointed he had been when the stiff, new leather had caused blisters to appear on his heel and toes. By the time he did meet Princess Anne the shoes had stopped hurting his feet. And they still looked like new.

He doubted that the shop was there now. It had always seemed out of place, quaintly squeezed between its more modern neighbours; and when he was here last year, he had noticed that the whole site was earmarked for redevelopment. It was more than likely that the shop, along with the rest of the parade, had been sacrificed to some glitzy new office block.

Lee sat up straight and glanced at his watch. He had booked his taxi for four o'clock and it was now three-thirty; half an hour left, then he would be on his way.

Half an hour. Thirty minutes. Then that was that. He'd had his chance, and he had let it go. He glanced towards the door where his suitcase, locked and secured with a bright green strap, was waiting, ready for him to take downstairs; and he was overwhelmed by a wave of despair. It was the sight of the packed suitcase, the finality it represented. He knew, of course, that he would come to London again, but from now on it would be very different. A door that had been open, in his imagination at least, had just clicked tightly shut.

He stood up, with the intention of getting the rest of his things together, but he stayed glued to the spot, still staring at his suitcase. What else could he have done? he asked himself. There was nothing he could have said to her. He knew now, for sure, that there would have been no point.

He crossed to the wardrobe and took out his coat, checking that his wallet was in the inside pocket. From another pocket he pulled out a *Hotel 2000* flyer and looked at it briefly before screwing it up and throwing it in the bin. He had enough of those in his briefcase; it was straining at the seams with all the papers and brochures he had accumulated during the week. He put on the coat, walked back to the bed and picked up the book. He opened it and turned, once more, to the page where the publishers had provided some information about the author.

> *Isabel Adamson was born in Edinburgh in 1958. After graduating from Warwick University in 1980 she . . .*

Yes, he knew all that. His eyes skipped to the end of the paragraph.

> *She worked in publishing for several years before embarking upon her first novel, Darkness and Light, which was a major international bestseller. She lives in London with her husband and son.*

Husband and son – husband and son. The words beat out a rhythm in his head. He closed the book and turned it over to look at the photograph. Isabel smiled back at him.

So, she had written her novels, just like she'd said she would. Good for her. And she had a husband and son. What had he expected? That in eight years nothing would have changed?

In the hotel foyer, Lee stood by the revolving glass door until he saw his taxi draw up – spot on four o'clock. It had started raining again: long slanting arrows of it, turning to silver as they hit the shafts of light from slowly moving headlamps. He turned up the collar of his coat and dashed down the steps of the hotel, almost colliding with the driver who had run round to open the cab door for him.

'Where to mate?' the driver asked, once he was back in his seat and shaking drops of water from his cap.

'Heathrow. Terminal three,' replied Lee.

PART TWELVE

Malaysia
July 1991

∞

The sun – now a huge, amber ellipse – had completed its swift descent towards the horizon leaving in its wake a sky streaked with red-tinged clouds; a few silvery stars were making their first, tentative, appearance.

It had taken some time for everyone to be hugged and kissed, and for the bride and groom to be congratulated again, but eventually Natalie and Benny had been whisked off to the airport and the remaining guests began to filter away in various directions. The group from Teluk, along with Ping Lee and Kin Mun who were to stay the night with Joseph, followed the trickle of people making their way to the jetty.

It was still hot and the air seemed unusually heavy for the time of the day. Isabel guessed it must be close to seven o'clock. In less than an hour – much less than an hour, because they had been offered a lift back in a motorboat that had come from a neighbouring village – they would be back in Teluk.

And then what?

She tried to push the thought from her mind and focus on something else: on a long-tailed bird that was perched on a wire above her head, on the familiar-looking trees which Lee had told her were common on the island; but what were they called?

Cas-something? Cas-u-a . . . ?

So what would happen when they reached Buah Lodge? Would they just skate around everything that had happened this afternoon? And something had happened, hadn't it? Or was she making too much of it –

'What are you thinking?'

The last time she had looked, Lee had been saying goodbye to some friends who were boarding the ferry. Now he was standing next to her.

'You were far away,' he remarked.

'Oh, er . . . No, not really,' she stuttered.

He was still looking at her. She watched him blink: once, twice.

'I was just trying to think of the name of that tree,' she said.

It had been an opportunity and she had squandered it. She cursed herself.

But if he had been hoping for a different response to his question, he didn't show it. 'Which one?' he asked.

She pointed at one that looked like a huge Christmas tree.

'The Casuarina?'

'Yes that's it. Cas-u-ar-ina. I couldn't think of the name. I, er . . .' She trawled her mind for something else to say. He had his head to one side; he was waiting for her to finish her sentence.

She picked at a thread hanging loose from the hem of her top.

Then a signal from someone indicated that the boat had been brought round; and she was spared. For now. Bundles of rope had to be moved, so that they could all fit in; cushions had to be arranged; and soon she was making her way down the ramp and stepping into the rocking hull of the boat. One by one they squeezed themselves along the narrow benches, and she found herself sandwiched between Joseph and Lee.

In an attempt to make more room for them, Lee put his arm round the back of her, resting it along the metal rail behind them. He was talking to the man who owned the boat; they were speaking Chinese. As she listened to the choppy, unfamiliar, words seesaw between them, she let her body lean gently against his; and felt the vibrations inside his chest as he shouted over the sound of the engine. This was one journey she most definitely did not want to end.

∞

They had been dropped off at the jetty and they were now making their way over the sand towards the path. Isabel was walking ahead of him, with Ping Lee; she was barefoot, holding her sandals in one hand and the hem of her sarong clutched in the other. Her hair had come down and was tumbling over her shoulders in long, dark twists.

Lee smiled to himself. She was beginning to look as though she had lived here all her life, and he wondered how she would react if he told her that. He suspected that she might be pleased.

They had come to the fork in the path. One way led to Buah Lodge, the other to the village. This was where they would separate from Joseph and the others – unless, of course, they decided to come to Buah Lodge. And as soon as the thought crossed his mind he felt guilty for wishing his friends away. But Joseph had already stepped forward and was saying goodbye to Isabel. Lee inwardly hugged him. Had Joseph read his mind? It wouldn't surprise him. They had known each other for a very long time.

Joseph held out his hand to Lee. 'See you soon. And good luck for tomorrow.'

Lee grimaced. 'Thanks, I think I'll need it.'

He watched the small group disappear round the bend in the road and then, at last, they were alone. He glanced at Isabel. She was inspecting the bites on her arm, rubbing her finger across each one, tentatively scratching at them with her nail. He could still hear the others talking: just a murmur of voices receding further and further into the distance.

They started to walk.

Reach over, take her hand, he told himself. That should be easy enough. But instead, he reached out and picked a leaf from a nearby bush.

What was the matter with him? Less than an hour ago they had been dancing together; he had held her close; he even –

Oh God!

It must have been the champagne that had made him so unusually confident; now they were alone together, he was acting like an idiot all of a sudden. He puzzled over this for a while, absently tuning in to the sound of the branches thrashing about above their heads. He hadn't noticed it before, but it was clear that the wind was getting stronger – a good sign that rain was on the way. He would be glad of a bit of rain – it saved him from having to use the sprinklers on the garden – although it didn't please the guests, who would mope and drift around like lost souls –

Come on Lee! Stop wasting time.

He had realized that he was in danger of dodging his way out of the situation. And if he kept delaying –

They had already crossed the mangrove swamp, and the dark, irregular shapes looming up ahead of them were the shrubs and palms that marked out the perimeter of Buah Lodge.

He needed to slow down.

He glanced at Isabel. She had switched her attention to another bite now, a new one by the look of it, and was clawing at her elbow. 'Don't scratch,' he said, 'you'll make it worse.'

'I can't help it,' she replied, continuing to scratch. 'But that oil did help before.'

'I've still got it.' He stopped walking and dug in his pocket. He produced the bottle and held it on the palm of his hand. 'It's for you.'

She reached out to take the bottle from him. The tips of her nails tapped against the centre of his hand and he curled his fingers towards hers –

'Good evening.' It was a man's voice.

Their hands jerked apart.

Lee looked up and saw two people approaching from the opposite direction. How come he hadn't heard their footsteps on the gravel? They looked familiar, but it took him a moment or two to register who it was; it was the dress he recognized first. The lady with all those flowery dresses – the English couple – what were they called? – Wilkes, that was it. Mr and Mrs Wilkes.

'Good evening,' replied Lee.

Mr Wilkes nodded his head at them. 'Pleasant evening again. We're off for a stroll.'

Lee realized that he still had the bottle of white flower oil in his hand. She hadn't taken it. He twisted it around in his fingers and moved his thumb over the bumpy lettering embossed on the side of the bottle. From the corner of his eye he could see Mrs Wilkes watching, as if fascinated by the movement of his hand.

And then, suddenly, she turned to Isabel. 'We'll see you later dear, shall we?'

Lee saw Isabel shift her weight from one foot to the other.

'Yes, I . . . I'm not sure.' She scratched violently at her arm. 'Probably.'

Mrs Wilkes studied her for a moment then turned her attention back to him. The skin of her neck had flushed a deep pink; he watched as the colour rose up to meet the blaze of her already sun-reddened face.

'Well, bye for now.' She plucked at her husband's sleeve and they set off in the direction of the jetty.

'Bye then,' called out Mr Wilkes from over his shoulder.

'Bye,' muttered Isabel.

She had started to walk on and Lee had to take a couple of long strides in order to catch up with her.

He had to act soon. Before he lost the best chance he would ever have. They had already reached the main gate and he pulled on the latch to open it. The path ahead of them was lit with tiny, silver lamps – one of Gilbert's ideas. They looked pretty, and he was glad that Gilbert had won that argument. He turned his attention back to more pressing concerns. He calculated that he had about three minutes – unless someone else came along, and whisked her away from him. It was now or never. And he had decided what to do. So why was it proving to be so difficult – to get out the few, simple words necessary?

He took a deep breath. Right. Here goes. He leant on the gate and clicked it shut, then he turned to Isabel.

She was standing beside him, waiting.

He pushed back a wedge of hair that had started to irritate him. 'Thanks for coming with me this afternoon,' he said.

'Thank you for asking me. I really enjoyed it.'

He began the sentence he had already practised: 'I wondered . . .' then lost his nerve. 'I was thinking . . . Would you like to come back – for a drink – to my house?'

There. It was done.

He raised his hand to his forehead and pushed at his hair again, wondering if he would have time to get it cut when he was in KL tomorrow.

∞

I sabel followed Lee down a small path tucked away beside one of the chalets. Then they came to a gate marked private and she could see the house towering over a row of trees.

She wondered if Gilbert lived there too, and how he would react to Lee bringing her here. He probably wouldn't approve. Nor would Sandra, she thought, recalling the expression on her face. Poor Sandra: if only she could see them now; she certainly wouldn't know what to make of it.

She followed him up the steps to the front door, feeling the soles of her bare feet connect with each of the smooth wooden slats: one – two – three – four – five. Then she was there, beside him, on the porch – his porch – standing outside his door. Her heart was beating so hard now that she could feel it thumping inside her chest, behind her ears. She stood, transfixed, watching his hands as he searched inside one pocket – then another.

At last, he pulled out a bunch of keys, selected one, and lifted it to the lock. She heard the rasp of metal against metal as it slid inside. But then he stopped what he was doing and turned to face her, leaving the keys still protruding from the door.

He was having second thoughts.

Act as if it doesn't matter, she told herself. And she needed to rescue her sandals; they were still at the bottom of the steps where she had dropped them.

But he was moving towards her; he was standing very, very close.

'Welcome to my house, Isabel.'

Before she could say anything in reply, he had reached out a hand and was touching the back of her neck, drawing her close.

She felt him lift a section of her hair and wind it through his fingers; he was bending his head towards her, brushing his lips against her ear, her cheek. Their lips met.

At first, his kisses were soft, questioning –

But then she felt him pull away.

'I'm sorry,' he said, 'I shouldn't have . . .'

She reached out and put her finger to his lips. 'Don't apologize,' she whispered. 'It's the nicest kiss I've ever had.'

She put her arms around him, moving her hands over the soft cotton of his shirt, down the length of his spine, feeling the tightness of the muscles in his back. She rested her cheek against his body and nestled into the hollow between his neck and his shoulder, breathing in the scent of him, every last atom of it: something to hold within her and treasure, for ever.

She heard him sigh.

When a flock of birds exploded from the forest behind the house, they jumped apart, startled.

He laughed. 'I think we are nervous.'

She pulled him towards her again and he kissed her, his hands clasped behind her head, his fingers tangled in her hair.

'Isabel,' he whispered. 'My Isabel.' He was looking at her now; his dark eyes staring straight into hers, as if he were trying to see into her soul. She raised her hand to touch his face, then his hair, recalling how often she had longed to do that, imagining how it might feel; it slipped through her fingers like silk.

He caught hold of her hand, linking each of his fingers through hers, and kissed the inside of her wrist. 'I think we should go inside and have that drink,' he said.

She nodded.

Still holding onto her hand, he turned back to the door, opened it, and led her into the house.

PART THIRTEEN

London
December 1999 -
January 2000

5.25 pm

The lantern in the porch cast an amber glow over the hallway; the ceiling and walls were smudged with the colours thrown out by the lights on the tree. The poor thing was past its best but still decked out in its baubles and bows, still making an effort to look cheerful; its branches, though, were dry and spindly, and a scattering of pine needles lay on the floor.

Isabel bent down and started to pick them up, one by one, her mind wandering to the Christmases of her childhood, when she used to go with her father to the farm, to collect a tree. They would wrap themselves against the cold (gloves and scarves and woolly hats – just like the people in the American films) and they would always return with one far bigger than they needed. Her mother pretended to be annoyed. 'Och now, Andrew,' she would chide. 'And where do you think we are going to put that?' As the only child, it had been Isabel's task to decorate those trees. Each ornament would be lifted from its nest of tissue, pondered over, looped with care onto the selected branch (there would be carols on the radio, too – or was that just a trick of her imagination?). The years passed by, but the ritual never changed. Even on those reluctant visits home from university, a large glossy tree would be there, waiting for her (the same old tub – red, imitation wood – in the same corner of the living room), so full of promise – just like the start of the holidays. Then the cherished baubles would come down from the attic, be assigned to the branches in the usual way, and there the tree would stand for the duration, like a guest at a party that never quite came off, ill-at-ease in its finery, obliged to witness the tears and the squabbles; until it was finally relegated to the bottom of the garden, a stray piece of festive tinsel clinging resolutely to its bare, brown branches.

'Right then. Thanks anyway.' David replaced the receiver – *click* – then there was silence.

She could sense him gathering his thoughts; then she heard him pad into the hall and towards the kitchen, where she was sitting. As he approached, she slid from her stool, opened a nearby cupboard and, for no real reason, pulled out a heavy glass bowl and lifted it onto the empty worktop.

She opened another cupboard above her head and looked inside. She knew that he was watching her.

'Well? Any luck?'

'Nope. No cars available. That's what they all say. Everyone's booked up. Guess that's it then. I've rung five now.'

Isabel wandered to the sink, taking the bowl with her. She peered at the window. It was only half past five, but it had been dark for hours. She couldn't see it but she knew that the sky was laden with cloud, that a wind would be shaking the pear tree at the end of the garden. All she could see was herself; and the image that glared back at her from the glass caught her by surprise. It was an expression she had seen on her mother's face: tense, drawn, narrow-lipped. Was that really her? She stood for a moment and watched raindrops stream across the windowpane – across the face.

She didn't want to have an argument, not today.

'Of course they're booked up,' she said. 'What did you expect? It's New Year's Eve.' Only now did she turn round to face him.

He was standing in the open doorway looking down at his socks. Isabel looked at them too. A couple of Santa faces grinned back at her: a present from Tom.

David breathed in, blew out noisily. 'I can cook a meal, he offered. 'We can open a bottle of bubbly.' He paused, waiting for a response.

Isabel remained silent.

He rubbed at his head. 'Might as well stay in now – if we can't get a cab –' He peered at her over his glasses – round-framed, John Lennon style – which he chose to keep perched low on the bridge of his nose.

She knew this was what he had wanted all along – stay at home, watch television. No effort required, no money spent. But she wasn't going to give in, however contrite he might look. Not this time; not tonight. The start of a new millennium. Because wasn't it supposed to be something you would always remember?

Even so, she still wondered what had got into her. Up until now she hadn't much cared about the millennium, one way or another. Yet, suddenly, it was vital for her to get away from the confines of the house, from the remoteness of the street; and the thought of not being in the centre of London, right now, at this very moment, was beginning to turn into something like the cold chill of panic.

'No. No way,' she said. 'If we can't find a taxi to take us, we'll have to go by tube.' As she spoke, she returned the glass bowl to the cupboard and knocked the door shut with her knee. It was more of a slam than she had intended.

David groaned. 'God! Not the tube. You must be joking.' He leant against the doorframe and folded his arms. 'It'll be packed.'

He was no longer facing her and appeared to be talking to the wall. 'Anyway, I thought you were the one who couldn't stand all this millennium business,' he went on. 'Last week you were saying it was over-rated. You said . . .' he paused and kicked his foot at the door.

'Well it isn't. It's the mill-enn-i-um.' She emphasized each of the four syllables.

'You said . . .' he went on triumphantly, 'you said, it was only another bloody day the same as any other.'

'No, I didn't.'

But she *had* said that, she remembered. Those very words. He must have been taking notes. And so what if she had? That was before.

'You did,' he argued. 'And I agree with you. It's only another way to get us to spend more money. Didn't you know that . . .?'

'Money, money, money,' she interrupted him, 'is that all you care about? It's New Year's Eve and I'm going out. I've washed my hair.'

Without looking up to see his reaction, Isabel hopped over his extended leg and strode down the hallway, glancing into the sitting room as she passed. Tom was sitting on the floor, surrounded by bits of farmyard and an assortment of plastic animals: cows and sheep grazed contentedly alongside giraffes, lions and an elephant. He was barely awake.

'And I thought you were putting the young man to bed,' she added, over her shoulder.

When she got to the third stair she stopped and leant over the banister.

'If you're coming, we need to leave about seven-thirty. The table's booked for nine. Kathy will be here at seven. We asked her to baby-sit, don't you remember? We can't let her down now, she'll have been looking forward to it all day.'

'Why do you always want to go out?' he muttered, after a long and loud sigh.

She was meant to hear; she knew that.

'I *don't* always want to go out,' she said quietly, to herself. 'Just now and again would be nice.'

With rather less skip in her step, she went into the bedroom. The curtains were still not drawn across the bay and she saw herself reflected in the glass as she pulled them to, her fingers finding brief comfort in their soft, velvety fabric. She felt guilty now about making a stand, but it was hardly a crime to want to go out. And they had planned it, weeks ago. She even recalled the conversation they'd had about asking Kathy to baby-sit (Kathy lived two doors down; she was fifty-nine going on seventy, had never been married, but adored Tom. And he adored her). They had even joked about it, perhaps a little unfairly, saying that she'd only be at home on her own, watching the television, so she may as well watch theirs; it would all look just the same, but the picture would be bigger. She also knew that they had discussed booking a taxi, and she was certain that David had agreed to sort it out.

The dress she had chosen was hanging on a hook behind the door; she frowned at it now, as though it were to blame for everything. She had bought it from Nicole Farhi some time ago, but had never worn it; now it would have to go back in the wardrobe again. It wouldn't be suitable, not if they were going by tube.

She scanned the rail and pulled out some black trousers and a green velvet shirt. As she turned back to the bed, she noticed the small box that David had given her on Christmas morning. It was still where she had left it, on top of her bedside table. She felt sad that she didn't much like the earrings – although, of course, she hadn't said so. She knew they were expensive too – because he had told her how much they cost – but they weren't at all the kind of thing she ever wore. She would wear them tonight, though.

While her bath was running she put on her makeup – some blusher, a smear of brown shadow, a black pencil smudge under each eye, a dash of mascara; it barely took more than a minute to go through the routine – because hadn't she read somewhere that it was best to do this before a bath? Because of the steam? Or was it the other way round? Pity she couldn't remember.

She lay back in the lavender-scented water and closed her eyes, wondering why she and David always had this same argument whenever she suggested going out. And she tried to remember if it had been like this when they first met. Did they go out more then? They must have done. But she couldn't recall.

It was true that David had liked to cook at home, and had been eager to show off his repertoire. So there had been lots of dinners in – dinners and Saturday-night TV. He had lived in a flat perched at the top of a rather grand mansion block, near Hampstead Heath, and she had been happy enough to spend her weekends there (her place being too small for two, he always said). She had spent many an hour sitting by the open window, looking out over London, watching the lights come on – lights which twinkled in the sharp, winter air; or shimmered through the stillness of a summer's night – and in the background, the comforting sound of David clattering about in his kitchen, and the murmur of the tireless city below: all those people moving around, like ants in a nest – millions of people in thousands of streets, in houses and offices, in shops, theatres, parks and gardens – talking to each other, talking to themselves, laughing, crying, declaring love, breaking up. Somewhere, a dog would be barking. A cat with whimsical markings on its fur might be pawing at a door to be let in. Perhaps someone was being born, someone dying –

And there, in David's flat, she had discovered something that was missing from her own life: a sense of calm and security. And belonging.

But never excitement, she thought, as she tugged on the bath plug. Or passion. There had never been passion. She stepped out of the bath and wrapped herself in a warm towel. She had been lonely, and so had David, she supposed; that was how they had come together in the first place. She pulled at a thread on the towel and wound it round her finger. But was it the reason they had stayed together? A fear of loneliness?

'Gin and tonic, Isabel?' she asked her reflection in the mirror.
'Yes please,' she replied. 'That would be very nice, thank you.'
She felt better now that she was dressed and ready to go out –
'But first . . . A kiss goodnight for my little man.'

She tiptoed across the corridor towards his room. The door was ajar and she pushed it open. He was lying on his back in the cot with Rabbit squashed against his cheek. He was fast asleep and didn't stir when she leant to kiss the top of his head. She stood over him for a while, watching his chest rise and fall as he breathed. Every so often his fingers would make tiny movements, as if he were playing an imaginary piano. She wanted to pick him up and hug him to her, but she knew he would not take kindly to being disturbed, so she made do with another kiss before creeping out again.

On her way to the kitchen she paused to look into the sitting room. David was lying on the sofa in front of the television. She glanced at the screen. Teams of Lycra-clad men and women seemed intent upon testing their bodies to the absolute limit and were performing stunts in front of a noisy and energetic studio audience.

'Bathroom's free,' she shouted, over the racket.

He propped himself up on one elbow and peered over the back of the sofa. 'You still want to go out then?'

She waited. In a moment he would say she looked nice, maybe notice the earrings.

'So I suppose I've got to get changed,' he said.

'I'm having a G and T. Do you want one? While you get ready?'

'No thanks.' He produced a bottle and held it up. 'Got a beer on the go.'

*

The tube wasn't as crowded as she had expected; they even managed to get a couple of seats together.

'See,' muttered David, as he eased himself into the seat next to hers, 'everyone's been sensible and stayed at home.'

Isabel smiled in response. She suspected that he was wrong, but didn't want to argue with him. He seemed in a better mood now.

She had been surprised, and relieved, when he had bounced down the stairs, stood to attention by the front door and asked if he would 'do'. And it was clear that he had made an effort. He was wearing a shirt that she liked and the leather jacket he had bought in Cairo last year, when he had been lured by that irresistible combination of 'sale' and 'duty free' (but the sleeves were too long and it was probably a size too big).

As they left the train she thought about slipping her arm through his. Then they would be just like all the other couples she could see. A step closer, take his arm, give him a hug. Too late. He was already striding towards the exit and she had to speed up, to keep level with him. And so the moment passed.

They emerged from the depths of the Northern Line at Leicester Square, having decided to go the rest of the way on foot rather than trek along dingy corridors to another tube line. Isabel wasn't keen on the underground at the best of times, but the recent spate of bomb-threats was making everyone jumpy.

In the short time they had been below ground, the weather had improved and the sky was almost empty of clouds – the few that remained were being swept across the black expanse by a gusty wind. The streets, however, were swarming with people trying to get somewhere else.

'Bad move,' David shouted back at her.

Isabel watched as he very nearly ploughed into a huddle of giggling girls. They broke ranks just in time, tottering away on dangerously high heels: masses of blonde curls; a set of novelty antennae apiece. Without missing a step, David strode on. A couple, also in his path, were forced to part, mid-sentence, to let him through.

Isabel looked on, wistfully, as they re-linked arms and continued with their conversation. She envied the way they were oblivious to everything around them; so wrapped up in each other; in love. Struggling to keep pace with David, she weaved her way in and out of the oncoming procession. At times she wondered if he had forgotten she was still there. She had to strain to keep him in sight, peering over people's heads, focussing on the brown shoulder of his leather jacket. And then –

Walking towards her now, no more than six or seven feet away, was a man and a woman; they were holding hands, talking, laughing. They were getting closer; she could see the man's features more distinctly now –

But it wasn't him.

Competing emotions thrashed about inside her: fear, disappointment, relief.

What would you have done? she thought. What would you have done if it had been him?

The two were level with her now; they were both looking at her, and she realized she was still staring at him. She looked away. She wasn't even sure what it was that had caught her eye. A gesture, perhaps? Or the way he had smiled at his partner? She turned to look again but they had disappeared into the crowd.

Confused, and realizing that she had lost sight of David, she stopped in her tracks. A couple of men wearing *Pierrot*-style hats lumbered towards her.

One of them attempted to grab her. 'Happy New Year, darling,' he yelled into her ear. 'I'm Brian, and this is . . .'

While Brian was trying to remember his friend's name, Isabel tried to disentangle herself. She was relieved to see David had turned back.

Brian caught her again and planted a beery kiss on her eyebrow; his still nameless friend was more successful in his aim, catching her on the side of her mouth.

'Happy New Year, mate.' Brian was attempting to put his arm round David, but David managed to extricate himself; he pulled Isabel away.

'Do you always let strange men kiss you in the street?'

'Yes of course,' she replied. She managed a smile, but there wasn't a trace of amusement on David's face.

'God, it's a nightmare' he said. 'Where have they all come

from?' He headed towards a dingy alleyway. 'We'll cut through Soho. It'll be quieter off the main road.'

But the number of people milling around the narrow backstreets made them seem even more crowded, and progress was slow; pavements were cluttered with debris from the day's trading: soggy cardboard, unsold vegetables, discarded meals congealing in their foil trays. David tripped over a bottle, sending it clattering to the other side of the street. He swore under his breath.

Because of the heaps of rubbish, and the relentless streams of people piling into and out of the restaurants and bars, it was almost impossible to walk on the pavement, so most people had strayed onto the road. Undeterred, cars and taxis continued to edge their way through, their drivers cheerily pounding the rhythm of 'Happy New Year' on their horns.

Another street had become a festive night market: candles and incense sticks, trinkets and scarves, roasted chestnuts, hot-dogs, noodles and rice; the cold night air was filled with an eclectic but familiar mix of smells. Coloured lanterns swayed and twinkled, buffeted by the wind, and the coarse, wooden structures, no doubt scruffy and mundane by day, took on a magical air as their welcoming lights shone out and sparkled back from the dark, wet pavements.

They were passing the doorway of a Chinese restaurant; three young men stumbled into David's path, chattering noisily to each other, laughing, oblivious to David's undisguised annoyance. One of them caught Isabel's eye and gave her a smile. He was taller than the others, with glossy, black hair that fell down over his eyes. As he walked by he pushed it back with his hand.

Isabel felt the familiar lurching motion in her stomach. She wished they had not come this way.

∞

9.15 pm

B y the time they reached *La Toison d'Or* they were fifteen
minutes late. It had taken them well over an hour to make a
journey that should have taken no more than forty-five minutes.

Isabel followed David up the sweeping stairway to the first-floor
restaurant. She was feeling hot and dishevelled, and a blister had
formed where the back of her shoe had rubbed against her heel.
At the top they were greeted by a young man in a tuxedo. He was
holding a large clipboard and this, evidently, was making him feel
important. Isabel doubted that he was old enough to drink alcohol,
legally. Once the lad had established who they were, he showed
them to a small table for two – in a corner, near the toilets.

'What can I get you to drink?' he asked.

They were still struggling to fit their coats over the tiny chair-
backs.

'List? Menu?' David snapped back at him.

They read their menus while a man sang into a microphone.

Isabel sat back in her chair to get a better view of the room, and
as she did, her coat slipped off and onto the floor. She scooped it
up, pretending not to notice David's reaction.

Now she could see that there was a small dance floor in the
centre, and a lone couple engaged in a tentative foxtrot. She
turned back to look at David, who was still reading his menu. It
was pointless even to hope that he might agree to dance.

'What are you having?' she asked.

'Not much to choose from is there?' he muttered, without
looking up.

'Oh, I think it's a good menu. Look! They've got *cassoulet*, with *marron* – that's chestnuts. That sounds good. I . . .' She realized that she was talking to the back of his menu.

I may as well have a conversation with the table, she decided: *And what are you having Isabel? – Well, I think I'll have the chicken – Oh, how lovely. Shall I order something different so we can share? – Yes, let's – Isn't this fun, Iz –?* Now who used to call her that? She hunted around for a name. Paul – Paul Shepherd. That was it.

But she preferred Isabel.

Eez-a-bel.

'For goodness sake!' David's voice sliced into the as yet unformed memory.

'Where has he got to now?' David turned in his seat, knocking against the table; the empty glasses quivered on their elegant stems; the legs of his chair scraped the tiled floor. 'We haven't even ordered our drinks yet.' He waved his menu at no-one in particular.

'Have you chosen?' she asked. 'Are we having some wine?'

'This service is abysmal, you know.'

'I bet they had trouble getting people to work tonight.'

'You must be kidding. They'll be on double pay at least. Triple more likely.'

'Well, it makes a change – not to be rushed. It's nice just sitting here, soaking up the atmosphere and . . .'

'Can't you see anyone?' he interrupted. 'You're facing the right way.' He turned his attention back to the menu.

'I expect they haven't come over because you are still reading. It looks as though you haven't decided what you want.'

With a sigh, David put down his menu then picked up one of the empty glasses and started to twirl it round by the stem.

'Can I get you any drinks?' A waiter had appeared at David's shoulder.

'Right – yes – I'll have a Budweiser.'

'Aren't we having wine?'

'Not for me. I fancy a beer.'

'But with your meal – don't you want wine with your meal?'

'Not really.'

She could sense the waiter shifting from one foot to the other.

'Right. So . . . I'll have a . . .' She scanned the list. 'I'll have a glass of *Côtes du Rhône-Villages* please.'

'I'm sorry madam, that particular wine isn't available by the glass. Our house wine is served by the glass.'

House wine. She thought about the stuff they served up at the local pub: dry, soulless, poured from a bottle that had been standing open for days, bits of cork floating around on the surface; she could already feel its sharpness biting into her tongue. She thought she heard the waiter tap on his note-pad.

On the other hand, this was a French restaurant, the house wine ought to be okay. It was just not what she'd had in mind.

She looked across at David, hoping for help – inspiration – input – she wasn't quite sure what. But he was engrossed in his menu once more.

To hell with it, she thought. I'm celebrating the new millennium, even if he isn't. She knew it was slightly decadent, but she would rather have a whole bottle of something good, than several glasses of something mediocre. She turned to the waiter.

'I'll have a bottle of *Côtes du Rhône-Village* please.'

David had wolfed down his starter. Now he was staring at his plate.

Isabel broke the silence. 'You must have enjoyed that.'

He shrugged. 'It was okay – what there was of it.'

'Well, we've got another three courses to come, so . . .'

'That's French cuisine for you,' he interrupted. 'Big plates and little food.' He seemed amused by his own joke and sniggered to himself as he buttered a bread roll.

He laughed so rarely these days. And that was a shame: laughing suited him. Her eyes scanned his face. He always said that his nose was too big, too long, too thin. She thought it elegant. His eyes were a bluish grey, like the sea on a cloudy day, with lashes long enough to make any girl envious.

'Well I enjoyed my soup,' she said. 'Sweet red onion.' She took a sip of wine, then another. 'It was delicious.'

'I can do a good soup,' he retorted. 'I'll do one tomorrow.' He turned to peer over his shoulder. 'A big pot, lots of veg . . . It'll be much better than what you've just had.' He turned back to face her. 'Can you see the waiter?'

'Not at the moment, what did you want?'

'Well another beer for a start. And the next course. I bet it's hanging around in the kitchen getting cold.'

Isabel didn't want her next course straight away. At this rate they would have finished their entire meal within the hour.

The place was bustling with activity. It was clear that the waiters were rushed off their feet, but the other diners didn't seem to care if they had empty plates in front of them; most of them were too busy talking, laughing, being happy, having fun. Perhaps no-one would notice that she and David were not.

She smiled feebly at the wine bottle in front of her, as if she were admiring the picture on the label.

She wondered when they had stopped talking to each other – really talking. They used to talk for hours, and share jokes, opinions, enjoy each other's company. Or was that just her mind filling in the blanks?

She felt something brush her shoulder. The waiter was taking away her plate.

'Thank you.'

'You're welcome.' He smiled back at her as he moved round to the other side of the table.

'And another one of these.' David waved his empty beer bottle at the waiter.

'Certainly sir,' he replied.

As Isabel watched David drain his glass, she tried to picture them on their first date. It was something she found herself doing often now: re-running their early days together, trying to re-kindle some of the feelings she must have once had.

They had met at some dreadful place in Islington. Even then she had been surprised at his choice of restaurant, now she knew exactly how out of character it had been. She had picked the venue for their second date – an Italian restaurant at the top of Heath Street – Giovanni's? Giuseppe's? It was a Sunday lunchtime. She had forgotten what they ate, and had no recollection of what they had talked about, but the time had flown by and it was dark when they left. Anyway – whatever it had been called – it wasn't there any more; the building had been taken by one of those chains: burgers and chips and beer served in bottles.

From the corner of her eye she could see their waiter approaching with the next course. A huge bowl of *cassoulet* was put down in front of her. She wafted away the steam.

She remembered it had been a cold day. He had lent her his scarf. 'Are you sure?' she had asked him. 'You can let me have it back next time,' he had replied. And she had been pleased that there was going to be a next time. She had worn the scarf to work every day the following week, breathing in the smell of him, feeling a tingle of contentment as she snuggled into it: her boyfriend's scarf.

Many of the diners had finished their meals and were drifting onto the dance floor. It was a shame, Isabel thought, that David disliked dancing so much. Still, she might be able to persuade him, after a few more drinks. Or maybe not. It could go either way. It was a long time since she had danced. She used to. A lot. The best form of exercise, she used to tell herself. Better than the gym. In those days she went to clubs with Simon, and they would dance together until he had spotted someone he fancied; then he'd be off, leaving her to dance on her own, fuelled by a few drinks but safe in the knowledge that no-one would bother her. But afterwards, sitting alone on the bus, as it trundled its way through the empty London streets, she had come to the conclusion that she might be missing out on something.

And so she had turned to the pages of *Lonely Hearts*.

She topped up the wine in her glass and took a quick swig. 'Fancy a dance?'

'Not right now,' David replied. He stood up. 'Just off to the gents.'

Isabel moved round in her chair so she could watch the dancers. There was a couple at the edge of the floor; the girl was tall, elegant, with a boyish haircut and a close-fitting black dress; she clung to her partner in a swaying embrace – there wasn't space enough for them to do much else. And as the pair continued to move in front of her eyes, a different scene – hazy, half-forgotten – occupied her mind. Another couple, another dance floor; it was all starting to unravel, and she closed her eyes, straining to catch it before it flitted away. If she tried hard enough, she could feel the pressure of his hand on her shoulder as they drew closer and closer together –

'For your desert madam?' The waiter's voice jolted her back into the present.

And now David was walking back to the table. The waiter had also spotted him, and was waiting to help him into his chair.

Isabel knew how much David hated that.

'One – two – three –' David was counting the strawberries in the bowl in front of him. 'Four – five –'

'What are you doing?' asked Isabel.

'Do you know how much profit this place is making? It's outrageous. These actually cost . . .'

'I wish you'd keep your voice down. And we're not just paying for the food anyway. It's the atmosphere, the . . .' She waved her arms about helplessly. 'It's New Year's Eve. It's . . .'

There was no point. It was an argument they'd had before. But she was damned if she was going to have it tonight – not at this price. She concentrated on the berry-red wine in her glass, swirling it around for a second before putting it to her lips. She closed her eyes for a moment while she savoured its deep spiciness.

When she had managed to attract the attention of the waiter she ordered another bottle of the same.

'Another?' This was David.

'Yes, another,' replied Isabel. 'I'm going to enjoy myself even if you've decided not to.'

He picked up the empty bottle and squinted at the label. 'You know you can get this in Sainsbury's for a quarter of the price.'

'Oh, for God's sake.'

She tilted her head and looked at the ceiling: an attempt to keep back the tears welling behind her eyes. It seemed to work.

She took a breath. 'It doesn't matter how much it is in Sainsbury's.' But her voice had become unsteady. 'We're here now. We're supposed to be enjoying a meal out and each other's company –'

He was looking at her. He thinks you are going to cry, she told herself. He's waiting. Don't cry. Don't cry.

'– is that too much to ask?' She played with her napkin for a moment, brushed invisible crumbs from her blouse. 'I'm going to the toilet.'

She managed to get to a cubicle just in time: before the tears spilt out and rolled down her cheeks. She put her hand over her mouth to stifle the sobs.

What was happening to her? Why, honestly, was she crying? Was it for David? Was it for herself? Or was it simply that she'd had too much to drink? Or was it something to do with the huge, aching space inside her? The one that, at this precise moment, was turning itself inside out, threatening to suffocate her?

As she walked back to the table she saw that David was settling the bill. He looked at her, bemused. 'It was only a bottle of wine,' he said. 'Bit of an over-reaction?'

She felt a stab of guilt. It was stupid to have got so rattled, and over something so trivial. She had spoiled his evening out too. After all, he didn't know what was going on inside her head. Any more than she did.

The second bottle of wine she had ordered was on the table. She noticed that it was not full; David had drunk at least a glass of it, although he had not poured out any for her.

As she made to sit down, he stood up.

'I thought we should make a move. Before everyone else starts trying to get home.'

Isabel looked at his watch. It was just ten minutes to twelve.

'Jesus! I don't believe you sometimes.'

'Why? What's wrong now? I thought you wanted to go. You don't seem very happy.'

'We can't leave before midnight – that's the whole point of tonight. So at twelve o'clock, when everyone else is celebrating, we'll be walking down the stairs of a restaurant, or in a tube station, or . . .' She could hear her voice start to wobble. 'And we haven't had coffee yet.' She grabbed the menu and stabbed at it with her finger. 'Look! It says coffee and *petit-fours*. It's included.'

She really, really didn't want to cry again.

She cast about for something else, anything, to sidetrack those tears; she spotted a waiter carrying a tray of glasses.

'See, they're bringing round champagne. Hey! And it's free of charge. You'll enjoy that.' She swiped a glass from the passing tray, spilling some of its contents onto the floor.

'Nothing's free,' replied David, taking a glass for himself. 'We've already paid for it, you can be sure of that.'

Someone had switched on a radio and the obligatory countdown was blaring out at them. *Ten – nine – eight – seven –* the diners joined in *– six – five – four –* everyone was on their feet – Big Ben chimed twelve.

'Happy New Year!'

A cloud of silver balloons floated down from a net that had been looped across the ceiling. Few made it to the ground intact. To add to the din, people were letting off party poppers; a stream of the gungy ribbon landed on Isabel's shoulder. They had all squeezed themselves onto the tiny dance floor. Isabel had been hugged and kissed by half a dozen strangers before she'd had the chance to wonder whether David was going to acknowledge her.

He was standing next to her and she took a step towards him.

He brushed her cheek with his lips. 'Happy New Year.'

∞

7.00 pm

Tom had been to a birthday party and had clearly tired himself out; he had fallen fast asleep almost as soon as his head hit the pillow. Isabel had been looking forward to the bedtime story, but it remained unread. She sat by his cot with the book in her hand, and stared vacantly at its cover. A chubby-cheeked sun beamed back at her from a patchwork-quilt land of rolling meadows and winding, blue rivers. The picture made her feel safe and she wished she could step into it and be a child again: carefree, happy; when the most pressing concern in life was 'what's for tea?'

Her thoughts were interrupted by the sound of a key in the lock downstairs. She put the book back onto the shelf, bent over her sleeping son and kissed him gently. She reached the stairs just in time to see David come through the front door, carrying their dinner in two white plastic bags.

In the kitchen, she took the lids from the foil trays and spooned the contents onto two plates. She picked out a large piece of ginger and bit into it; it was still crisp, and the heat in it made her breathe out quickly. She moved it around her mouth, as if she were sucking a boiled sweet, relishing the fire on her tongue and lips. She walked to the fridge and opened the door. There was an open bottle of white wine, but she had a sudden urge for beer.

'Fancy a beer?' she shouted.

'What?'

David appeared in the doorway, but there was no need to repeat the question; she could see from the glass in his hand that he had already poured himself a large measure of whisky.

It wasn't long before David was asleep, the empty glass on the table beside him. It was inevitable, she supposed. He had spent the day working on a paper he was due to present at a conference; then he had been expecting an important email – which hadn't arrived. Her remark that most people would be away – given all the bank holidays and so on – and wouldn't be around to send emails, probably hadn't helped. Yet she would have been happy to share his anxieties – if she knew what the paper was about, or what the problem was. She had tried to talk to him while they were eating their meal. 'It's just politics – office politics,' he had told her. 'You wouldn't understand.'

For once, she was glad of the solitude. There was something she had been meaning to do for a couple of days – ever since the day at the bookshop.

Leaving David stretched out on the sofa and oblivious to the heated discussion taking place on the television in front of him, Isabel walked up the stairs and into the spare bedroom. She closed the door behind her.

The bottom shelf of the pine tallboy was crammed with old shoeboxes. She knelt on the floor and cast her eyes over the script marked along the spine of each box in black, felt-tipped pen: 'ITALY/TURKEY '86', 'EGYPT '98', 'NEW YORK '88', 'THAILAND '96'. She had to pull out five or six boxes before she could get to the ones at the back, and she chided herself, as she always did, on the state of the cupboard. One day she would go through this lot and . . .

'Bugger!'

She had dropped one of the boxes, spilling its contents over the floor. A photograph had landed by her knee; two faces smiled up at her – a couple of young monks in saffron-coloured robes. The rest had fallen face down and she started to turn them over, one at a time. A beach: pale sand, a palm tree leaning towards a shimmering sea. A giant Buddha, perched on the top of a rock. Street scenes, teeming with people – in Tuk-Tuks, on bicycles, packed onto buses, grinning at the camera through the open windows; and everywhere, the monks – splashes of orange – going about their daily business with all the rest.

'Honeymoon,' she remarked to herself, cramming the pictures back into the box.

There was one left: a picture of herself and David, standing in front of the Grand Palace in Bangkok. She wondered who had taken it. They weren't holding hands, he didn't have his arm around her, but they were both smiling towards the photographer. They appeared happy enough. She was sure they had been happy, once. And what did happy look like, anyway?

She dropped the photo back into its box. This was not what she was looking for.

She scanned the remaining boxes in the cupboard, then lifted one out and removed the lid. It wasn't as full as the other. She hadn't taken so many pictures in those days.

Lying on top of the photos were pieces of tissue paper. She peeled away the top layer, wondering what was underneath.

A dried flower: its petals brown and brittle; if she tried to pick it up, it would surely fall apart. She stared at it, sifting through her cache of memories for clues to its significance.

How many other things had she forgotten?

Carefully, she lifted the sheet of tissue, without disturbing the flower, and placed it on the bed. She would think about that in a minute. She went back to the box and pulled out two photographs at random. Another beach – more blue sky, white sand, and a sapphire sea – but this was a different kind of beach; there were no sun-loungers, no umbrellas, just a row of blue fishing boats pulled up onto the sand, their nets bundled inside or strewn around their hulls. The second picture showed a cluster of houses perched on wooden stilts. There were strings of washing, too – gaudy-coloured shirts, lengths of batik, white sheets – making the dwellings look more like market stalls – all caught mid-flutter, all moved by the same warm breeze which stirred the lush, green leaves of the banana plants nearby.

She put these photos aside and thumbed through the rest in the box, pausing to glance at the odd one. She knew what she was looking for, and she knew there was only one.

When she found it, for a moment she couldn't bear to look at it. Instead, she tried to re-capture the warmth of the sun on her skin, the silky, soft sand between her toes, the sound of the waves lapping around the jetty. They were about to get onto a boat, she recalled. It was the day of the wedding party.

'Isabel? Are you in there?'

The door handle turned and she threw the pictures back into the box. She found the lid and had just managed to jam it on when the door opened and David walked in.

'Ah! Photos.' He had spotted the box of honeymoon pictures, which was still open at her side. 'You're looking at photos. Right. Well . . . I'm going to bed.'

'Okay. Won't be long.'

'Goodnight then.'

'Goodnight.'

Still kneeling in front of the cupboard, Isabel listened to the sound of David moving around in their bedroom: the wardrobe door being opened, and then closed, a pillow thumped, the click of the light being switched off.

Once all was still and quiet again she took up the box marked 'MALAYSIA '91' and lifted the lid. The photo was still on top of the pile. She picked it up and studied it.

Her hair had been longer then, and she was definitely a few pounds too heavy – although she had always thought herself overweight in those days – but the brightly-coloured sarong and coral top complimented her nut-brown skin. They were standing side-by-side, as close as two people could be, without actually touching.

The surprising thing of all was how radiant she looked. She hadn't often seen herself smiling like that.

'That's happy,' she said out loud, without meaning to.

Her eyes now focussed on the figure standing next to her. She studied the face, let her fingers trace the outline of the head, then the shoulders. Could it really have been him, the other day? Or had it been a figment of her imagination?

She felt her throat constrict; tears pressed against the back of her eyes.

What if it had been Lee she had seen, looking in through the bookshop window? Even if it had, there was nothing she could do about it now?

PART FOURTEEN

Malaysia
July 1991

∞

I t was not yet ten, but already the air was dense and sluggish, all freshness sucked from it by the heat. Around the compound, the palms, normally ruffled by the slightest sea breeze, had an unusual passivity about them. The intense sunlight had burned away any trace of colour from the sky: it forced people to screw up their eyes, or raise a hand to protect themselves from the glare; it glinted down on every available surface, creating intricate patterns of light and shadow, silvering leaves, turning a lizard's greenish skin to burnished bronze; and in the garden, and along the walkways, everything remained silent and eerily still. Only behind the lowered rattan blinds of the Gula House was there any respite from the searing rays: here the sunlight, where it struck the dark wooden floor, became nothing more than a scattering of crystals; and here the air was stirred a little by the blades of a fan. Seemingly indifferent to the heat, Set Yen weaved her way between tables clearing the remains of breakfast, disappearing every so often with a tower of crockery, letting the kitchen door flap listlessly behind her, coming back with an empty tray tucked under her arm. From time to time her eyes settled on the only other occupant of the room.

Phil was sitting at the far side of the dining area. He had positioned his chair so he was facing out towards the centre of the room. He had dragged over a second chair and had his feet up on its seat; his elbow rested on the table, his chin pressed against the clenched fingers of his hand. The skin at the base of his neck, where he had undone the first few buttons of his shirt, was a lobster red, and there was a clamminess about his hair, as if he had just taken a shower.

*

Set Yen put down the plates she was holding and batted at a fly that was circling the air in front of her. It swerved to one side and drifted off in another direction. She wondered where Miss Isabel had got to this morning; it wasn't like her to skip breakfast. She glanced over at the American man. She hadn't meant to look at him, but she had sensed him watching her. She thought he looked like a vulture: it was the way he was sitting, his shoulders hunched around his ears, and his long, red, miserable face. About ten minutes ago he had waved her over to get another cup of coffee. How many had he had now? This must be his fourth at least. It was hard to believe someone could drink as much coffee as he did. She wouldn't mind if he had been more polite, but he was always wanting this and wanting that. And he never smiled. She wished he would hurry up and go, so she could clear his table; she had a thousand things to do and was here on her own until Amir came in at lunch-time. She also wished he wouldn't put his feet on the chairs like that. It just wasn't a nice thing to do in her opinion. People had to sit on those.

She moved to pick up the plates, but then spotted some crumbs camouflaged amongst the swirls and zigzags of the batik cloth. She brushed them away with the palm of her hand. Ah well, she thought, at least it would be quiet until dinner time. They were expecting some new guests later and she hoped that Mr Yeow would remember to go and pick them up, as Mr Lee wasn't here today to take care of things.

∞

Phil picked up his napkin and used it to mop the sweat from his forehead, before wiping it round the back of his neck. It was far too hot in here. It was crazy that they didn't have air-con, instead of those old wooden fans. And that was another thing he was going to complain about when he got back.

He stuffed the crumpled napkin into his cup and watched the dark liquid travel up through the cotton, turning it brown, the colour of muddy water.

He couldn't work out how he had missed her. He had been

sitting here for over an hour. He looked at his watch, then shifted in his seat, pulling at his shorts where they were sticking to his skin. She was always at breakfast before him. Except today.

The waitress was getting on his nerves. She kept looking over at him – when she wasn't shooting around trying to look busy – and it was clear that she wanted him to leave so that she could clean the table. Hell, he would leave when he was good and ready.

He supposed he could try the beach. She might have gone straight there. And if that was the case, he knew exactly where to find her. She always sat in the same spot.

He slid his feet off the chair and stretched his arms above his head, then opened his mouth wide to let out a yawn.

Busy day ahead, better get moving. And sometime soon, he thought, he should tell them he was quitting two days ahead of schedule, or he might end up having to pay for them. He felt his lips twitch into a smile. He was looking forward to a couple of extra nights in KL, and he'd found a place at ten dollars less than what he was paying here. Now he just had to find out which flight Isabel was taking and with any luck he might be booked on the same one. He levered himself from the chair and hoisted his bag onto his shoulder. She had told him once, but he'd forgotten. It hadn't been relevant then.

He started to walk away from the table but then stopped in his tracks. Which path would she take? He scratched at a mosquito bite on his knee while he thought about it. Too many decisions. He was feeling dog-tired, because he had got up too early; and now he couldn't make his mind up which way to go.

He moved into the lounge and flopped onto the nearest armchair. If it wasn't so God-dam hot in here, he thought, he could sit in this chair until lunchtime. On second thoughts, he needed to catch her before anyone else did, before Sandra and Rob got their noses in and spoilt his plans. But he didn't have the energy to go anywhere right now.

Half-heartedly, he looked around for something to read.

Nothing doing.

If the batteries in his Walkman were still good, at least he could listen to some music. If not, he was stuck. Until he got to KL. Civilization.

He decided to check out the batteries.

He pulled over his bag and dug around inside. He had already figured out what he was going to say. He rehearsed it again, now, in his mind. It was his last night here – they should have a beer together – and he had found a good place to eat in the village.

His hand found the Walkman, but . . .

'What the heck?'

There was something sticky, and greasy about it. He lifted it to his face, and sniffed.

Medicated. Like the inside of a hospital.

He reached back into the bag and brought out a crushed tube of antiseptic cream, without a lid.

'Fuck!'

Even if she said no to the drink, he would get her address. Rob and Sandra had already invited him to stay –any time he was over they'd said – but he figured it was better to go to London. He had no clue where Devizes was anyway – and he was pretty sure it was less exciting, even, than Brockport.

And thinking about Rob and Sandra now, brought to his mind something Rob had told him last night. They had been out for a stroll, Rob had said, and had seen Isabel, walking back from the jetty with that guy who worked here, the gloomy-looking one.

He frowned. Bet he was trying it on – wasn't that what all these local guys did?

He scraped some of the cream from the Walkman and rubbed it into the bite on his knee. He wiped the rest on his shorts – they were well past needing a wash anyway – but then he remembered he'd have to wear them in KL. Now he was going to smell like a drugstore for the next few days. He rubbed his palm down his arm, to get rid of the remaining cream. The drag of his fingers against the bare skin made him think about Isabel again, and what it would be like to move his hands across her skin; how it would feel to have her warm mouth over his, and her breasts crushed against his chest. He snickered to himself. Yeah, tonight would be his best chance. So long as he could get rid of the other deadbeats sniffing around.

∞

Isabel brought her feet up to the edge of the chair and hugged her knees close to her chest; she let her fingers trace over the contours of her arm. Fragments of yesterday floated behind her closed eyelids. Unable to force back the smile pulling at the corners of her mouth, she shook her head, and pressed her lips hard against her leg, breathing in the clean, soapy smell of her skin, conscious of the sensation that raced through her body whenever her mind flitted back to last night.

With a sigh that came from nowhere, she unlocked her arms, dropped her feet to the floor and reached for the book that was lying, unopened, on the table beside her. She would read for a while. Or should she go for a walk in the garden? Or walk to the village? She opened the book. One of its pages had come adrift and she concentrated on pressing it back into the glue on the spine, glad of something useful to do. Once it was fixed, she turned back to the page she had been reading.

She had read an entire paragraph before she realized that she had failed to take in a single word. She read it again, this time trying to concentrate. But while her eyes were scanning the lines of print, her mind was busy elsewhere: scenes, words, sensations were still drifting in – even things she had previously forgotten; and all had to be paused, re-run, savoured – in every last detail. She closed the book and used it to fan at the air in front of her face. She got to her feet, then immediately flopped back down into the chair. It was so hot this morning. Too hot to read. She reached out to touch the paper-like petals of a bougainvillea growing from a pot near her feet, then she stood up once more and set off to walk the length of the verandah, stopping for a moment to stare down at the fresh, green shoots of fern sprouting from the sand underneath her chalet, marvelling at how something could manage to survive in such a hostile medium.

Without any purpose, or even any real consciousness of what she was doing, she wandered back towards the open door and stood on the threshold, looking in, at nothing in particular. It was hopeless. She was never going to be able to settle. Whatever she did today would simply be filling in time, until she could see him again.

Part of her longed for the day to be over, so that she could go to sleep, knowing that when she woke up it would be tomorrow, and Lee would be back from KL. But tomorrow was also her last day at Buah. And the thought of being parted from him so soon tainted the happy prospect of seeing him again. It was more than ironic, she thought, that all this should have happened now, just as she was about to leave.

She went inside, closed the door behind her, switched on the overhead fan and sat down on the bed. Her notebook and pencil lay nestled in the folds of the single white sheet, crumpled from where she had been sitting not more than ten minutes before. She picked up the notebook and stared at the writing. She could barely decipher it; there had been such an urgency to get the words out and onto the page before any detail could be forgotten. Now she felt shy of reading it back, in case it all sounded rather foolish. She cast her eyes over the very last section she had written.

> *I have tried to remember the first time I saw him – when he met me from the airport. I think I'd spotted him, before he saw me, and I said, 'I think you are looking for me' – !!!! He hardly spoke on the journey back here. Later, he told me that he thought I looked sad. (I was!). I know I was tired, and miserable. I must have looked awful! I thought he had a nice smile – or was that another time? I don't think I thought about him much at all on that day.*

When was it that she had started to think differently about him? Was it when he had taken her shopping? Or before that? She closed her eyes and tried to squeeze out even the smallest fragment – anything – a scene, a snippet of conversation – but nothing would come. Yet she knew it was important not to let a single one of those precious moments disappear, for ever, just because she hadn't thought them significant at the time. And that was why she needed to write it all down.

She turned her attention back to the notebook.

> *I have to come back here – soon – but can't take more time off work until the New Year. Shit! Anyway I can't just*

invite myself. And I think he might be too shy to ask me. But we can't simply leave it like this. And if neither of us does anything . . .

Isabel let out a small groan. It was getting too complicated – all this waiting and wondering, guessing and scheming. Last night, everything had seemed so very simple. 'And maybe he won't want you to come back,' she said out loud, looking down at the notebook and finding that was exactly what she had written.

And maybe he won't want you to come back – and maybe you are reading far too much into this. But last night, on his balcony, when you were looking at the stars – all the things he said – about how it must be fate that had brought us together, and how, at last, he felt complete, as if he had come to the end of a long journey – one which had never had a clear destination – until now.

And when he put his arms around me, it was as if that was where I had always belonged (yes, I know it's a cliché – but it's true).

And he said I was beautiful. No-one has ever said I was beautiful.

I can't have got it all wrong. Can I?

'You usually do,' she said out loud.

She flicked back a couple of pages and carried on reading.

I had wondered – well, you do hear about these things – maybe I was not the first – but he introduced me to his friends, he never tried to hide me away, he made me feel special. Or is he just clever?

No. That was a terrible thing to say. How could she think that about Lee? On the other hand, was she the best judge when it came to men?

She picked up the pencil and turned to a fresh page of the notebook.

For the briefest of moments it was my turn to be happy.

She paused and chewed at the end of her pencil then started writing again.

He is a good person, I am sure of that. I am sure I will never find anyone like Lee, however much I search.

She stopped, and re-read what she had just written; then wrote:

And maybe I will never see him again after tomorrow, but I will never, ever forget him. And at least I will always have beautiful, beautiful memories.

She drew a couple of lines under the final sentence then threw down the pencil and the notebook and cradled her head in her hands. Less than half an hour ago she had been feeling on top of the world, and now . . .

She stood up and straightened the sheet on the bed. There was nothing she could do about any of it now. She would have to wait and see how tomorrow turned out.

∞

Kuala Lumpur

After the sedate and cavern-like interior of the bank, the noise and bustle of Jalan Tun HS Lee was comfortingly loud and brash. Lee stood outside the building, his hand raised to shield his eyes from the glare of the sun, his back against the plate-glass window that had divided the two worlds as effectively as if it had been made of solid stone. He stayed where he was for a moment, re-acquainting himself with the smells, the sights, the general hubbub of the street, before it sucked him back in and claimed him as its own.

Cutting through the stench of rancid oil, rotting vegetables, and the sweet and acrid tang of drying fish, was the unmistakable aroma of smoke and spice coming from a nearby food stall. Lee realized that he was hungry. He looked at his watch. His meeting had lasted for exactly fifteen minutes.

Had it gone well? He wasn't even sure of that. All he wanted was a simple loan, so why couldn't they give him a straightforward yes? Or no? And in the meantime he was losing almost two whole days – precious time he could be spending with Isabel. His stomach tightened. How could he concentrate on business when all he wanted to do was think about last night? But somewhere, at the edge of his dazed, Isabel-charged, mind, he knew that it was now more important than ever for him to keep hold of Buah. How could he ask her to come back, if there was nowhere for her to come back to?

He moved off up the street, sidestepping a dog that had chosen to stretch itself out on the pavement outside the Hindu temple.

And was that what he was going to do? Ask her to come back? He hadn't been aware of any process that had led him to that conclusion; but he knew that was what he wanted to do. If only he had the courage.

He crossed the road and turned down a narrow alleyway leading to Jalan Petaling. Much later in the afternoon many of these streets would be closed off, transformed into a traffic-free *pasar malam*, a bustling night market. But now pedestrians had to vie with the chaos of lorries and cars, motorbikes and cycle-rickshaws, all snaking their way through. This was the heart of Chinatown, dense with crumbling shophouses, and the occasional modern boutique squeezed in between moneychangers and coffee shops, food stalls, medicine shops, Chinese temples; and the all-pervading scent of burning incense.

Staying in the shade offered by the colonnaded shop-fronts, Lee made his way round baskets of fruit, sacks of rice, buckets, brooms, and the omnipresent plastic chairs and stools – for this, not the dim and dusty areas to the rear, was where the storekeepers passed their time, gossiping, working, eating. Many of them were now dozing off their lunch, or still chowing their way through bowls of noodle soup or chicken rice.

But Lee was far too lost in his own thoughts to notice any of this. What if he didn't get the loan? What then? He could never afford to buy Gilbert's share without it. Nor could he stay and watch Buah Lodge being sold to the Mayang people. He had to get it – he *had* to.

Someone stepped out from the doorway of a shop, and would have collided with Lee if he hadn't looked up at that exact moment and dodged out of the way. The shop was a *kopitiam*, and Lee remembered why he had come this way in the first place. He looked at his watch again. He hadn't had anything to eat since the cake he had bought at the airport. That was over five hours ago. But he also knew that his mother would have been in the kitchen all morning, preparing his favourite dishes. He should wait, he decided.

He turned round and headed north towards the bus station.

∞

Pau Ling was on the phone, talking to her friend Suzi, when she heard the five short raps on the door. Suzi was in the middle of a long story about her boss and someone else that Pau Ling didn't know. She wasn't sorry to have to interrupt.

'Suzi – sorry – sorry – got to go. My brother's here – call you tomorrow?'

She put down the phone and ran to the door.

'Who is it?' she called out, smiling. She knew full well who it was – only Kim Cheng knocked like that.

'It's me,' came the reply. 'Kim Cheng.'

As soon as she had undone the catch and opened the door wide enough to let him in, she found herself being swept off her feet, squashed in between his chest and the bunch of flowers he was carrying. She noticed that his shirt smelled faintly of washing powder. Or was it his aftershave? Whatever it was, it was vaguely familiar.

'How's little sister?'

She pulled away from him so that she could breathe, and speak.

'I'm fine. Why don't you use your key?'

He grinned and shrugged.

She hadn't expected an answer: she knew he didn't like using the key they had given him when they had moved to this flat.

Lee picked up the bag he had dropped on the floor and walked through to the living room. 'Where's mom?'

'Gone to the shop. She only just left. I'm surprised you didn't see her on your way up. She said she'd forgotten something, but I can't imagine what – she has already got enough food for twenty people.'

'I wish she wouldn't.'

'You know she loves to do it for you. She's been at it since eight this morning.'

'It's getting too much for her.'

'No it isn't – she's fine. She wouldn't let me lift a finger to help.'

Pau Ling perched on the arm of a nearby chair and watched her brother wander round her living room, as if he were reacquainting himself with everything in it. He looked tired she thought. 'How was your meeting?'

He shrugged. 'Good, I think. Who can tell? They'll let me know.'

'It's getting you down, isn't it?'

'No.' He looked up and met her eye. 'Yes. I suppose so.'

'Want a drink?'

He nodded.

'Tea? Or beer?'

She waited just long enough to see a grin spread across his face.

While she was in the kitchen she could hear the rustle of paper coming from the room next door. Mom had bought a newspaper this morning – her brother always complained he never had time to read the papers. She opened the fridge and took out a couple of beers. 'So what have you been up to?' she shouted.

The rustling stopped, but there was no reply. She wondered if he had heard her. 'Kim, what . . .'

He was standing in the kitchen doorway. 'I've met someone,' he said.

She turned away for a moment while she rummaged in a drawer for the bottle opener, trying to hide a smile. She was tempted to shout 'and about time too'; but she had noticed something in his expression. It would probably be better if she kept quiet for now. She handed him one of the bottles, and the opener. 'It's serious?'

He nodded.

'Want to talk about it?'

He gave her a sheepish-looking smile. 'I don't know.'

She picked up her own bottle and a couple of glasses, and ushered him back into the living room. She wanted to talk about it, even if he didn't.

'Go on then,' she said.

He was fiddling with the cap of his bottle. 'You didn't need an opener,' he said, twisting it off in one sharp movement. 'It's a screw-off one.' He held out his hand for her bottle. She waited while he opened it.

She glanced towards the door. Their mother would be back soon; but she mustn't rush him, she had to let him do this in his own time.

At last, he had finished with all the opening, and pouring, and getting rid of the bottle-tops, and then the bottles. He took a sip, sat back in his chair, and stared at the glass in his hand.

'I don't know what to do,' he said. 'I mean, it's been a bit sudden – sort of – but the main thing . . . Well, one of the things . . . She's going home tomorrow. And if I don't . . .'

'Going home?' she interrupted. 'What do you mean?' Then it dawned on her. 'One of your guests?'

'Yes.'

'A foreigner?' As soon as she had said the word, she wished she hadn't. She put down her glass. She needed a moment for this to sink in. Kim Cheng was looking at her, chewing on his lip. He appeared to be waiting for her to say something else. More than anything she wanted to see her brother happy. But she couldn't sit by and watch him get hurt. It wasn't that she had anything against mixed relationships – she was sure that some of them worked well enough – but it was always going to be an extra complication, a potential stumbling block. Was he walking into this with his eyes open, or closed?

'You don't make life easy for yourself do you?' she said at last, trying to look pleased. 'And does this girl . . .'

'She's called Isabel.'

'And does – Isabel – know how you feel?'

He nodded.

'And does she feel the same about you?'

'I think so. Yes,' he paused. 'I think.' He added, as if for good measure.

'But she's going back to . . .?'

'To the UK. She has to go. She has a job.'

'Then what can you do?'

'I want to ask her to come back.'

'You mean for a holiday or something?'

He looked away for a moment. She saw that he had closed his eyes; it was as if he were still striving to reach some sort of decision. But her brother didn't usually do things on impulse; she was confident that whatever he decided would have been carefully weighed and thought through.

When he looked up again he said. 'No. Not for a holiday. I mean, to be with me.'

'What? To stay? Live together? Get married?'

He shrugged.

'Isn't that all a bit soon? I mean . . . How long have you known her?'

'Do you think it will scare her if I . . .'

'No, I meant . . .'

'But I have to do something now. If I don't, it will be too late.' He moved his thumb up and down the side of his glass. 'It doesn't matter how long I've known her,' he went on. 'Because . . . Well, it feels as if I have known her all my life.' He turned the glass in his hand and continued rubbing away the condensation.

'I feel . . . I just feel close to her. And today, now that we are not together . . .' He sighed. 'I can't explain it.'

Pau Ling had never heard her brother talk like this before; he was someone who normally kept things very much to himself. It was clear that he had been badly affected by this girl.

'What do you think I should do?' he asked.

'I don't know Kim – I really don't. I haven't met her. So it's hard to say. But you know that you will be asking her to choose, between you and all she has back home – her family, her friends, her work. Is it fair to ask her to do that?'

He shook his head. 'No, it doesn't have to be like that. I wouldn't ask her to give up anything for me.'

Her heart went out to him. She knew that he was wrong. There would be such a choice – for one or the other of them. Suddenly she was afraid of hearing him say that he would leave Malaysia, and go to England – if she wouldn't come here.

'Kim Cheng, you won't do anything rash will you?' she asked.

He looked at her. 'What do you mean?'

'Well, what with all this uncertainty about Buah Lodge and everything. You've worked so hard. Don't throw it all away now.'

He reached out and gave her hand a squeeze. 'Don't worry. I don't intend to.'

They both jumped when they heard the key in the door. Lee shot her a look. She knew it meant that it was the end of their conversation – for now, anyway. Reluctantly she stood up and made her way to the front door to relieve their mother of her shopping.

∞

Kampung Teluk

Isabel woke to find that the sun had disappeared behind a flat, pewter-grey sky. Her right arm was numb, lifeless, as if it didn't belong to her any more. She shook it and felt the blood pricking its way back through her veins. Shivering, she reached for her sarong and draped it around her shoulders.

It took her a moment or two to realize that things were not quite as they had been when she had settled herself down to read her book. The sea was no longer smooth and clear and blue; now it was stacked with muddy waves edged with white, each one gathering strength as it pressed towards the shore. Dark, foreboding clouds were heaped against the horizon.

She had no idea what time it was. There wasn't another soul on the beach – in fact it all seemed strangely quiet: as if the world had stopped turning, and no-one had bothered to tell her.

Her mind still fuggy with the remnants of sleep, she stumbled to her feet and started to gather up her belongings. She pulled the sarong from her shoulders and wrapped it around her waist, knotting the ends together twice. She had been using her T-shirt as a pillow; now she picked it up and shook out the sand before easing it over her damp swimsuit. If it was going to rain, she thought, she should get going. She had a long walk back to Buah Lodge.

∞

Phil was sitting at a table facing onto the street. He had just been handed what he hoped was going to be a toasted cheese sandwich. He lifted a slice of barely cooked bread and found three slices of

359

tomato. He pulled them out and pushed them to the side of the plate, along with the bits of cucumber that had been added as a garnish. When he raised his head, he noticed a solitary figure walking in his direction. It was a woman. Her features were still blurred, amorphous, but even from a distance he knew that it was Isabel. She was dressed as if she had just come from the beach. And yet he had looked for her there –

He watched as the familiar outline got closer and closer, crystallizing into the very person he had been seeking out all day; in a few moments she would be right there in front of him. As she walked, he could see a section of bronzed flesh each time her leg pushed through the split in her sarong. She hadn't spotted him yet, but she would.

A sudden gust of wind picked up the square of paper napkin from beside his plate, sending it drifting to the floor. He pushed out his foot with a vague intention of stopping it, but the napkin had scuttered out of reach. When he looked up again, Isabel was almost level with him. All that separated them now were the raggedy stems of a shrub that had sprouted from the sand. Was she going to walk straight past? Surely she had seen him. He stood up, knocking his thigh hard against the corner of the table.

'Isabel.'

For a moment she appeared not to know where the voice was coming from, then her head shot round. 'Oh! Hi. Phil.'

He saw her hesitate, as if unsure what to do. He sensed she was about to walk away. 'Where've you been?' he asked.

She stopped, and turned to face him; she seemed to be gathering her thoughts. 'The beach,' she replied.

He was puzzled. She had come from the wrong direction. 'Yeah? I've been down there all afternoon too,' he lied.

She was staring at him, as if she were waiting for him to say something else. Her dark hair curled loose over her shoulders, he could see the flat brown orb of the mole just beneath her eye. 'Didn't see you,' he added.

His eyes moved over her face. He saw the slightest movement of her lips as they started to form a reply.

'No, I wasn't at the beach near Buah Lodge. I mean . . . Is that where you were?' She didn't wait for him to answer. 'I went to another one,' she waved her hand behind her, 'round the headland.'

'How so?'

Her eyebrows dipped together into a frown. 'How . . .?' She paused. 'Ah. For a change, I suppose. Change of scene.'

'You found a new beach?' he asked.

She seemed to have to think about this for a moment. Behind her head, across the narrow strip of street, he could see assorted items of linen – white sheets, pale blue pillowcases – flapping about on a line strung between two of the wooden houses.

'Someone told me,' she replied eventually. 'What's the time?'

Phil flicked over his wrist. 'Just gone half four.'

She glanced away. 'I should . . .'

'Wind's getting up,' he cut in. 'Looks like there's a storm on its way. Still, I'm outa here tomorrow so I don't care. Long as it keeps off till then. Reckon it could be a rough ride in those old planes they use.'

He saw her glance at the sky. Whatever it was she was thinking made her bite down on her bottom lip. Now was his chance. 'Hey – aren't you leaving tomorrow too? What time's your flight?'

'Er, I don't . . .' she faltered. 'The late one.'

'The seven-o'clock.' he provided.

Isabel shrugged her shoulders. 'Something like that.' She made an *mmm* sound, her lips pressed together. But then her head shot round and she was looking straight at him, her eyes wide with interest. They were a shade of grey, he noticed, not brown as he had imagined: a surprisingly seductive, deep, dark grey.

'What about you?' she was asking. 'When are you leaving?'

He realized that he didn't yet know which flight he was on.

'Good question,' he replied. 'They're supposed to be booking it for me. If they can get their act together. I don't get why it should take so long to . . .'

'Who's booking it?' she cut in.

'Oh, I dunno – that guy – you know – the manager.'

'Lee?' Her eyes were still fixed on him; her lips had curved, for an instant, into a smile, then dropped down again.

Why was she so curious about his flight all of a sudden? he wondered. And wasn't Lee that guy who'd been with her yesterday? He screwed up his face, pretending to think. 'Who?' he said. 'Don't know his name. The old guy. The one who picks you up from the airport.'

'Ah,' she said, rolling a pebble under her foot. 'Gilbert.'

'Yeah. Maybe.'

Phil pushed at the other chair with his foot. 'Why don't you sit down, get a beer?'

Isabel looked at the chair, then at him, then away again. Somewhere further down the street an empty bottle was being moved by the wind; a wind-chime jangled; a dog barked – once, twice. He watched her take a deep breath, saw the fabric of her T-shirt tighten over the rise and fall of her breasts.

'No, it's okay,' she said. 'I should get back.'

'Aw, come on. Just one beer.'

'No. Really. I've still got packing to do.'

Fuck. Why was this woman so fucking difficult.

'Actually,' she went on, 'I'm not feeling too well. I . . .' She hesitated, and then added, 'it's probably something I ate.' She took a step backwards and drew her arm across her chest, to hitch up the straps of her bag.

He knew he wasn't going to get anywhere. He felt himself shrug his shoulders. Suit yourself, he wanted to say, but didn't. Instead he said: 'Hey, that's too bad.' Then, as an afterthought: 'Is there something I can get for you?'

She turned towards him again, a puzzled look on her face. 'Er, no. No, thank you. I'll be fine. Enjoy your beer, or whatever.' And before he had the chance to say anything else, she had moved away and he had to shift round in his seat to watch her tall, almost stately, figure retreating down the street.

'See ya,' he said.

∞

When Isabel arrived back at Buah Lodge she went directly to the Gula House. First she saw the pile of luggage on the floor in front of the reception desk and then the people: new arrivals, fresh from the airport. There was a woman – possibly in her early forties – a blonde – but her hair was too yellow to be natural; she was slumped in an easy chair. A man was perched on the chair arm, leafing through the pages of a magazine. He wore a pair of wide, flapping shorts, which only accentuated the pinkness and skinniness of his legs. Two others were moving aimlessly about the room. A woman in tight red jeans had picked up a carved figure from a shelf near the bar. Isabel saw her run a finger down its length before turning it over to examine the underside. The second man had wandered back to the reception desk and was looking at the various leaflets provided for guests. Every so often he reached out to take one, which he would scan without much interest before putting it back into the display stand. She wondered why they had been left alone, why there was no-one here to give them a welcome drink, or to show them to their rooms.

She stood still, not sure what to do. She could cross to the other exit, which would mean walking past them – and she had no desire to get into conversation with anyone at the moment – or she could turn round and go back the way she had come. And why had she come up here in the first place, instead of going straight to her room?

She ignored the question, even though she knew the answer. All the way back from the village, she had toyed with the idea that Lee might have returned from his trip to KL sooner than planned. But it seemed that he hadn't, and now there were these people, whose very presence was a reminder that her own time here was almost at an end.

She leant on the balustrade at the top of the steps, looking out over the garden, and thought back to the day when she herself had arrived on the island, conscious of the glowing faces and bronzed limbs of the people waiting in the airport terminal. Which of them had seen her? she wondered. Who had noticed the paleness of her skin, the shadow of apprehension on her face? Maybe someone had felt the same stab of envy towards her that she was feeling now. And had any of them witnessed the moment she had met Lee? Had they understood the significance of what was taking place in front of their eyes?

She was distracted by the sound of a blind flapping against the wall. A strong wind was pushing at the fronds of the coconut palms, making them chatter and sigh like things possessed. But the forest behind the compound was abnormally quiet.

She turned back into the room and crossed to the other side, conscious of the sound her flip-flops were making on the wooden floor. Four faces turned towards her, looking her up and down for clues as to who she might be, but evidently losing interest when they realized that she was simply another guest, and of no particular use to them.

As she walked back, past the various chalets, she could see that many of them had been vacated. Their wooden shutters were closed, their verandahs empty of evidence that they had ever been occupied: no books, no shoes, no towels draped over chairs to dry. Here was the one where Els and Peiter had stayed; next would be the one still occupied by the Japanese couple; and when she turned the corner, she would be able to see the red-tiled roof of Lee's house, partially hidden behind a line of slanting palms. She stopped for a moment, trying to fill her mind with everything she could see, and hear, and smell, wondering how long it would be before she could no longer conjure up a clear and perfect image of it. The few photos she had taken would always be there for her to look at, but would she be able to re-capture the heady scent of the creeper that had attached itself to the wall outside her bedroom, the symphony of sounds that came each night from the depths of the forest, or the feel of Lee's hair brushing against her skin as he had kissed her?

When she arrived at her own chalet, she searched her bag for the key. Once it was found, she pushed it into the lock but then had second thoughts and, leaving the key where it was, threw her bag onto the floor and slumped into the wicker chair. How on earth was she going to fill the hours before she could go to bed?

She reached for her bag and pulled out her book. Its pages were crimped and brittle now; a few grains of sand fell onto her lap as she searched for her place. She stared at the print, but the words swung in and out of focus. Eventually her mind latched on to what had been niggling her. It was something that Phil had said – about the weather.

What if flights to and from the island were disrupted? Lee was due back tomorrow – on the afternoon flight. Just three hours together before she had to catch her own flight to Kuala Lumpur.

They had so little time left. Was there a chance of even that being snatched away from them?

A creature moved around, unseen, in the vegetation below; she could hear the snap and rustle of twigs and leaves. Then there was a different noise. She sat still in her chair, listening. She couldn't make out whether it was the roll of distant thunder. Or was it just a plane flying overhead? There it was again; it was a long way away. But it was the unmistakable rumble of thunder.

∞

The Gula House appeared to be empty when Phil walked in, but then he noticed two people sitting in armchairs on the verandah. Although they had their backs to him, Phil knew that one of them was Gilbert Yeow – just the person he had been looking for.

Phil made his way across the room and through the open doors. He edged round the chairs, so that he was facing the two men. On a table in front of them was a tray of used coffee cups and a glass ashtray filled with the debris of what looked to be an entire afternoon's worth of smoking.

As soon as he spotted him, Gilbert raised his hand in greeting. 'Ah. Mr Morten. Yes, I jus' comin' to find you.'

Phil reckoned that was unlikely. 'So, did you get me on a flight for tomorrow?' he asked.

'Yes – yes. All book for you. Ten o'clock, morning. We take you to airport eight o' clock. It's good?'

He'd been hoping for the evening flight – the same one that Isabel was on. And he didn't much like the thought of eight o'clock in the morning.

He was about to ask if it was necessary to get to the airport quite so early, when a sudden flash of lightning ripped into the sky. For a fraction of a second, night turned to day; patches of garden were bathed in a bright, white light; leaves, trunks, branches, petals, all caught unawares – as if by some phantom photographer – revealed in perfect detail against an angry sky. Then all was dark again. The thunder boomed out moments later.

Phil guessed that the storm was directly overhead. He turned back to Gilbert. 'Hey, what happens with flights if the weather is bad? Will they operate?'

Gilbert took a long last drag on the butt of his cigarette before pressing it into the overflowing ashtray. When he was satisfied that it had been extinguished, he eased himself round in his chair and looked at the sky. Then he settled himself back and reached for another cigarette. 'Depend what happen tomorrow,' he said, eventually. 'Better you take early flight. If flight cancel, will be second one.' He held up his hand, palm down, the unlit cigarette lodged between his first two fingers, and made a gliding movement towards the table. 'If storm bad, no aeroplane come from mainland.'

'Could be bad,' said the other man. He too raised his arm, but pointed towards the black void surrounding the garden. 'It comin' from that way.'

Gilbert shrugged. 'May be – if it come over. If it pass round – will be nothing.'

Phil was about to leave when another thought crossed his mind. 'One of your other guests – she's booked on the evening flight. Shouldn't she try to change it – to the earlier one? She needs to get to KL to make a connection.'

Gilbert was trying to light his cigarette. His lighter had the word 'Malaysia' written on it in spidery, green lettering. He lowered it and took the cigarette from his mouth. He gazed at Phil for a moment or two, his eyes narrowing to a mere slit in the leathery face, his mouth looking as if it might be about to break into a smile at any moment. He made a shrugging movement with his shoulders.

'May be,' he said. 'See if it get worse tomorrow.'

∞

She had been dreaming; she knew that. Fragments of it still clung to her conscious state: scenes, faces, all still clearly visible. But something had woken her. There had been a sound: harsh, regular. Or had that been part of the dream too? She lifted her head from the pillow. Everything was quiet. The shutters were closed and the room was dark; there was no sunlight penetrating the slats. She reached for the light switch. Then she heard the sound again. This time she knew it was real. Someone was knocking at her door.

Still dazed by sleep she shouted out: 'Okay. I'm coming.'

It was quarter to eight, according to her watch. So why wasn't it light outside? And why was someone knocking on her door? For a split second she thought it might be Lee, arrived back early from his trip.

The knocking continued.

'Okay – okay.'

She had pulled the cover from her bed and had wrapped it around herself; even so, as soon as she opened the door she was aware that the temperature had dropped, sharply.

Gilbert Yeow, was standing on her verandah. When he heard the door being opened, he turned round. In the brief moment before he spoke, she had time to take in the dark sky, the wind buffeting the side of her chalet.

Now she was there, standing in front of him, he seemed to have forgotten what he wanted to say. A few moments passed. Then he spoke.

'Miss Isabel? Yes?

She nodded.

A silence, then he coughed, quietly and: 'Er, I . . . I think . . . You . . .'

Although it was clear that he struggled with his English, there was something about the way he spoke – soft, hesitant – that reminded her of Lee.

Anxious now, she interrupted him. 'Is everything all right?' Something had happened to Lee, she thought. That was what all this was about. 'What's the matter?'

'Nothing the matter. You leaving today? Yes?'

'I'm leaving this afternoon, but . . .'

'We worry for you – weather no good – goin' get worse. Better you catch flight now. No evening flight – evening flight cancel.'

Her sleep-fuddled mind was trying hard to process the information she was being given. 'What do you mean? I mean, I can't go now. I'm booked on the seven-o'clock flight. I don't leave until later. I'm leaving this afternoon.'

He waited for her to finish and then gave a small sigh before he continued to speak: gently, as if he were talking to a child.

'Yes-yes. I know. Miss Isabel, we change for you. Can give me ticket. I do it for you.' She saw him glance behind her, through the open door of her room.

'Have you pack?'

Her suitcase was lying open on the floor; small piles of clothes lay, in a circle, around it.

'No, not yet,' she replied.

The implications of what he was saying were beginning to filter through. She couldn't leave now: if she left now she wouldn't be here when Lee got back.

'But Lee – Lee is taking me to the airport,' she blurted out.

'Lee not here.'

'Yes, I know but . . .' She hesitated. How could she explain this? 'Lee is coming back,' she went on. 'So he can take me to the airport.'

'I take you. No problem. But you pack up quickly. Better we leave soon – half-hour.'

Up until that moment she had been confident of her grasp on the situation: she could leave when she chose, she didn't have to do what they said. But her resolve was ebbing away, and what was bubbling up in its place was nascent panic. It was unthinkable to leave without seeing Lee, without saying goodbye, without saying anything. But she couldn't afford to miss her flight to London either. She didn't have enough money to buy another ticket, and she had to be back at work in a couple of days.

But she had to see Lee.

'No, honestly,' she said. 'It's fine. I'll keep the flight I have. But thank you for thinking about me.'

Gilbert Yeow hesitated, then turned and made towards the steps leading down to the path.

Isabel moved onto the verandah to watch him go, wondering whether this really was the end of the matter. She walked from one end to the other, and back again, with growing apprehension. The sky was a mass of bloated, blue-black cloud, sunk low against the earth. There was a strange disorder about everything around her: branches, leaves, flowers were all embarked upon some wild and frenzied dance; the large trees swayed from side to side, the smaller ones in such agitation that it looked as if they might rip out their own roots from the soil. Twigs, leaves, odd bits of vegetation, took to the air, gliding about like the winged creatures of a bygone era. And from somewhere not very far away came what might have been a rumble of thunder.

Soon, all doubt was cast aside when a flash of lightning split the sky, followed, a second later, by the unmistakable sound of thunder cracking overhead. Within moments, huge drops of rain were striking the ground, leaving pea-sized craters in the sand around the chalet.

She found herself running to the top of the steps, shouting towards Gilbert's retreating form.

'Wait.'

He had heard her; he was turning round. He had his hands held above his head, as if they might protect him from the rain.

'Wait – I'll come over – bring my ticket. I'll be five minutes.'

She had given herself time to think.

The rain was coming down in sheets, the wind lashing at everything in its reach. Things that had been perfect, unblemished, even a day ago, were now dishevelled, broken: plants were flattened, their flowers lost forever; the sandy paths had been turned to mud. By the time Isabel reached the Gula House she was soaked. Her clothes stuck tight to her skin; water was running down into her eyes.

There was one person there: Phil. Dry as a bone, hunched over a cup and an empty plate, a large rucksack by the side of his chair. By the look of him, it was possible that he hadn't been to bed at all. She thought he might be asleep. Why was he there? she wondered.

But he looked up when he heard her approach. 'They found you.'

She stared at him, puzzled.

'So you coming with us?' His pale, lizard eyes darted over her. 'We've been waiting for you.'

She remembered then, that he was due to leave that morning, on the early flight.

Finally, she spoke: 'Waiting? Why are you waiting? I'm not leaving yet. I've just come to find out if . . .' She stopped. She didn't have to explain herself to Phil.

She could hear the sound of water pouring from overloaded gutters, swirling down drains, hammering onto a zinc roof. A door slammed.

'Yeah, but I don't reckon you've got a choice. Look at it,' he flapped his hand in the direction of the garden. 'They'll cancel flights. You could be stuck here for days.'

She looked outside. 'I thought tropical storms passed over quickly.'

He pulled a packet of cigarettes and a lighter from an outside pocket of his rucksack. As soon as he had one lit, he turned back to her. 'Not this one. This one's a biggie.'

She wondered how he knew, whether she could trust his information. His face told her that he was enjoying this: enjoying, at last, a sense of his own superiority, his confidence boosted by the power he knew he had over her. She promised herself that it would be the last time he ever would. Nevertheless, between them, he and Gilbert had succeeded in sowing a seed of doubt in her mind. What if they were right?

If Lee were here, she thought, he would know exactly what she should do.

But any time for considered thought had run out. The kitchen door swung open and Gilbert emerged, rubbing at his head with a small yellow towel. He paused to scan the room and seemed relieved to see her there. 'You got ticket?'

Out of the corner of her eye she saw Phil lean back in his chair and fold his arms. 'Yes,' she replied.

The ticket was safely in her pocket. She wasn't going to give it up yet. Her mouth felt dry, she was conscious that she hadn't cleaned her teeth. She thought about the glass of water standing on her bedside table; she imagined reaching out, bringing it to her lips, taking a long, satisfying drink. 'Are you sure they are going to cancel my flight? Has anyone told you that for sure? Have you rung the airport?'

He put up a hand to silence her. 'No. Not rung yet. Waiting for you come with ticket. Sure they will cancel. This storm, bad one. Look – Miss – outside – can see – you lucky they fly now.'

She made her decision.

'I need to finish packing. Can you wait for me?'

'Can-can. I do ticket now.' He pulled a large umbrella from a bucket standing near the reception desk, and held it out to her.

Reluctantly she reached inside her pocket, pulled out the dog-eared flight voucher, and handed it to him.

PART FIFTEEN

London and Edinburgh
June 2001

∞

3.15pm

I sabel watches the plane glide soundlessly from one side of the window to the other, daubing a ragged white line, left to right, across the rectangle of cornflower-blue sky. Some of the line is breaking up; bits of it are already indistinguishable from other wisps of cloud patterning the sky.

When the plane has disappeared from view she turns back to the game of solitaire on her computer screen. She deals herself another round; the cards flutter into place. But then she repents, and stabs at the mouse until the game is replaced by a page of writing. She glances at the clock in the corner of her screen, and makes a tutting noise with her tongue: she has been playing solitaire for almost an hour.

'For God's sake, pull yourself together,' she tells herself. But it is her mother's voice she hears, not her own. 'Get a grip,' she adds, for good measure.

She searches around for her glasses and finds them on top of a pile of books; she puts them on and scans a page of notes lying next to the computer.

She has no idea why this one section is causing so much trouble. But she has been stuck on it for days, and it is getting her down. Maybe, she thinks, the time has come to give up altogether and do something else with her life. She pushes at her glasses, letting them rest on the top of her head, and levers herself from the chair. She has decided to look in on Tom, who is having his afternoon nap in the bedroom next to her study.

From her position in the doorway, she can just make out the shape of his body underneath the covers. He is lying on his back, his feet making two small peaks in the white cotton blanket. She

375

steps away and crosses the corridor to her own bedroom.

As she makes her way round the end of the bed, her slippers tap out a gentle rhythm on the wooden boards. She holds back the curtain and pushes open the window, feeling the rush of cooler air sweep past the bare skin of her arms, momentarily dazzled by the sun shining hard on the milky-coloured render of the houses across the street. Isabel enjoys the symmetry of these houses, the way their fronts remind her of faces: the curtained windows, eyes – sometimes open, sometimes closed – and the door in the middle like a mouth in a permanent state of surprise.

She leans against the sill to look down at the garden. She has never had a front garden before, and it still gives her a thrill to think that this little bit of the planet actually belongs to her. From this angle, the flowers and shrubs are nothing more than abstract blobs of colour, like the ones used by architects to signify their artfully arranged flowerbeds – not that there is anything artful about this particular garden: David says it is untidy, but to her it is a place where things are allowed to happen, by chance, organically –

Organic? Organically? She ponders over the words for a while, debating their correct usage. And she's supposed to be a writer! Even that, she thinks, is starting to look questionable.

She straightens up and turns away from the window. It's just writer's block, she tells herself as she pads back to her study. It's happened before. She just hopes it won't last much longer.

Back at her desk, her computer has reverted to screen-saver. It is a standard scene offered by her version of Windows (she isn't up to installing her own) and she finds herself gazing at a clutch of palm trees on a patch of flawless, white sand: nowhere in particular, just a stock image, a deserted island in the middle of a turquoise-blue sea. She reaches out to touch the mouse and the picture is gone, quick as a flash. She scrolls down the lines of text to the piece that has been causing the problems:

> *Man at a party – sitting at bar – alone. About same age, maybe bit older, not particularly good looking, slightly balding. Something about him – warmth in his eyes, maybe. Gentleness in his face. She might imagine what it would be*

like to be in his arms – dancing – rest her head against his
shoulder, feel his lips brush against her hair. These thoughts
shocked her. Why? Hungry for small expressions of affection
- absent from her life.

Artless, inelegant sentences; strings of words bereft of verbs: all
missing the punctuation that might, at least, make them whole and
meaningful. She peers at the screen, hoping for inspiration, but it
simply glowers back at her. And in no time at all, what started as
a mere flicker of subconscious thought is already prickling with
discomfort. It is something that happened a couple of weeks ago.
They had been at a party – a fiftieth birthday – someone that
David had known at university. They had both been puzzled by
the invitation. David hadn't had much contact with the person
over the years, and they had never been what you would call
bosom buddies – they had simply found themselves circling the
same pubs and bars during a post-university stint in London. But,
impelled by curiosity, David had reluctantly agreed to go. And so
they had found themselves in this rather down-at-heel venue – a
vast, cavernous place underneath a railway line, in some far-flung
outpost of south London, surrounded by people they didn't know.
However, the music was good and Isabel, enlivened by the novelty
of a night out, and a few drinks, had started to enjoy herself. As
David flatly refused to dance 'to this rubbish', she had resorted
to dancing on her own, and was happily ensconced on the dance
floor when he announced that it was time they were leaving. She
wanted to stay and dance. They had argued. He told her to act her
age, behave like a married woman: she told him to stop behaving
like a pompous, middle-aged bore. For the next two days, the
argument had hunkered between them like some wizened old
Harijan. Bouts of snapping were followed by caustic silences
until, eventually, the two of them had settled into a routine of
mutual avoidance; and, by a kind of unspoken agreement, they
had not pursued the matter further – possibly for fear of what
might be dredged up in the process. Now the whole episode has
come racing back, and with it arrives the feeling that all vitality
has seeped away, leaving nothing but a great, yawning void.

So, this is it then; this is her life. And she, alone, is responsible:

she made all the choices.

She realizes that she is still staring at the screen even though her eyes have long ceased to focus on any of the words. Her neck is aching and she brings up a hand to rub the spot that is troubling her. Small bones glide about under her fingers making soft snapping noises as they move. With her other hand, she nudges the mouse and clicks on an icon at the top of the screen, then studies the list of options presented to her. Another click; and she is invited to adjust the way her words appear on the page. She plays around for a while, increasing and decreasing the margins, trying out different fonts; next, she turns her attention to the paperclip-man, moving him from the top of the page to the bottom, from the right-hand side to the left, and finally putting him back where he was at the start. At last, she takes her hand away from the mouse and leans back in her chair. Seconds later, unaware of having made the decision to do so, she is on her feet and heading for the stairs.

The kitchen is bathed in late afternoon sunlight, giving the propensity of whites and creams a soft, apricot hue. She fills the kettle from the tap, pulls a mug from the drainer, opens a box of teabags, and looks out of the window while she waits for the water to boil. Her eyes fix on a row of geraniums in terracotta pots: a flamboyant, red barrier separating the yellowing lawn from the dun-coloured blocks of patio stone. One of the pots is empty. Did the plant die? Did she remove it? She isn't sure. But now, and with a glimmer of satisfaction, she is instantly acquitted of all other obligations: she has found a job to be done, has to be done. And done today. That means a drive to the garden centre and maybe even . . .

Whatever bit of prevarication she is about to come up with next is lost, unceremoniously pushed out of her mind by the sound of the telephone. She abandons the kettle, which is now bubbling furiously, and strides to the hall. The ringing gets louder, more aggressive, as she approaches. She picks up the receiver, relieved to put a stop to the noise, but now there is a loud hissing noise in her ear, and then . . .

'Hello?'

The voice sounds as though it is coming from the far end of a long tunnel, but she knows it is David, calling from Vancouver.

'Hello,' she shouts into the receiver. 'David?'

'Can you hear me?'

'Yes.'

'You're a bit faint.'

'Is that better?' she tries. But the effort makes her voice higher rather than louder.

'No. Never mind. It's okay –' a pause, while the line crackles ominously, then: 'How are you?'

'I'm fine,' she replies. 'What time is it there?' She peers towards the kitchen, checking that she can see the clock on the oven, preparing herself to make the necessary calculation.

'Er . . .'

She imagines him looking at his watch – or maybe he isn't wearing his glasses – so he'll be patting down his pockets, trying to locate them. She waits.

'It's . . . Er, it's just gone eight o'clock,' he says.

'Morning?'

He makes an *mmm* sound.

'So you are eight hours behind?'

'Something like that.'

'Have you just arrived?'

The line fizzed back at her.

'What?'

She repeated her question.

'I'm in the hotel. Lobby. Can't get into my room just yet.'

'Is it nice?'

'Is what nice?'

'The hotel.'

'Seems okay. Dunno.'

There is a pause. She waits for him to say something else, but he doesn't.

'When's your first meeting?' she asks.

'When what?'

'Your meeting – do you have any meetings today?' She annunciates each word, carefully, as she would if she were talking to someone who didn't understand English.

'Yeah – later – after lunch. Hoped to get a bit of sleep first.'

'Didn't you sleep on the plane?'

'Not a chance.'

In the pause that follows she thinks she hears other voices – or one voice – a woman's.

'But anyway,' he continues, 'I flew out with Bob Shand. He reckons they're going to want me out here for more than a week.' He stops. He is waiting for her to respond to this piece of information.

She doesn't. Not yet.

'Hello?'

'I'm still here.'

'So what do you think?'

She finds that she doesn't think anything at all.

'Isabel?'

She breathes in, parts her lips, slips her tongue between her teeth; she effects the very precise sequence of movements required of her to make the next word. At the same time, a different part of her brain is already flicking up reasons why she won't mind at all if he has to stay a week longer. She will be able to write, without feeling guilty, watch the films she has saved on video, play music and dance (even though people her age don't dance around the sitting room – that is, according to David – listening to Craig David or George Benson, or any other of the long list of musicians that he finds unpalatable – in fact, come to think of it, that would be her entire CD collection). And how ironic, she thinks (in that very same fraction of a second): that having spent so long searching for someone to share her life with, it appears she is more than happy to spend it on her own.

'That's fine,' she says. And she means it. She hasn't thought of any reason why it isn't.

They don't talk for much longer; David has to run through some papers with Bob and then he is meeting people for lunch.

Isabel replaces the phone onto its stand and returns to the kitchen.

The mug and teabags are still where she left them, next to the kettle. She concentrates on these three objects in turn: the pattern of daisies round the rim of the mug, the acid-green letters spelling out *'Thé Vert'* on the box of teabags, the sleek, silver curves of the kettle. All this extraneous information circling around, while another part of her mind is following its own agenda, raking up a slurry of other, less congenial observations. When – and why – did she stop going with David on his business trips? Did she never miss him when he went away? Not even at first? There is no such memory, just the contentment she is experiencing now: the prospect of having the house – and the bed – to herself for a little bit longer.

The other day, she bumped into one of their neighbours while she was putting out the rubbish for the weekly collection. Pam and Harry are the sort of neighbours anyone would wish for. They must be well into their eighties, but have more energy between them than the average forty-year-old. They had moved to this street when they first got married, over sixty years ago. They never had children of their own, but they both take a keen interest in Tom and, whenever Isabel takes him to visit, they always find some small gift for him. Pam will look at Harry – a gentle, knowing smile that lights up her face and turns her back into the happy bride of the photograph on their mantelpiece – and then, bending down to one of her cupboards, she will pull out something from behind a pile of folded napkins, or a rose-patterned tea service. Often it is a book, sometimes a toy; and Isabel wonders when Pam and Harry buy these gifts – as they rarely go out – and how they manage to choose something that is always so perfectly right for Tom.

Pam seemed quite concerned when she heard that David was going away again. 'He does go away a lot,' she remarked. 'Won't you get lonely on your own?' Isabel had assured her that she would not, because she had mountains of work to keep her occupied, although she knows that this was only half the truth. In fact she has never felt quite as lonely as she does now – but this has nothing to do with David being away – the truth is, there is no lonelier place in the world than a bed shared by two people who are no longer in love.

At some point, she must have switched on the kettle; its noise rouses her from her thoughts and she turns her attention back to the kitchen worktop. There is the mug, with a teabag and spoon in it, but the box of teabags has gone, and a container of milk has been taken out of the fridge. She doesn't recall doing any of these things and marvels at how her body is able to execute the necessary manoeuvres without her being the slightest bit aware of what is going on.

Conscious, now, of her actions, she fills the mug with boiling water and watches the steam rise into a perfect curl. She is angry with herself: she was supposed to be working today. She picks up the tea and carries it to her study.

Back at the desk, she opens her briefcase and pulls out the manuscript she has been editing – if she isn't going to do any writing of her own, she may as well concentrate on fine-tuning the product of someone else's hard labour. She has selected a red pen from a pot on the windowsill and now she pulls off the top, fixing it to the opposite end with a satisfying click. What she loves about editing is the attention to detail it requires, and the way she can become absorbed in what she is doing – which is a welcome respite from the sometimes tortuous, and emotionally draining, process of writing. And she wonders, for the second time that day, if she shouldn't give it up altogether. Maybe, in the end, two novels are all she is going to manage.

From the room next door she hears a sound – one that is both beautiful and mildly awe-inspiring. It is the sound of her son, gradually casting off sleep and laying claim to his day. For a moment or two, she is delivered from her anxieties into a state of calm and contentment. The surge of love for the tiny human being she can hear chattering away to himself, fills her with joy; but at the same time is almost too painful to bear: such profound love is inevitably loaded with fear – fear for his innocence and vulnerability, fear of her own responsibility, fear of the unknown.

She rests her pen on top of the papers she hasn't yet started to read. She will get him up, maybe take him downstairs, let him play in the garden for a while. And what does it matter if she has lost her inspiration to write? She has a truer, purer purpose to her life. She has Tom.

She leans over his bed and scoops him up. 'Gosh, what a weight,' she tells him. 'What a heavy sack of potatoes.' And he giggles at her, and shakes his curls. She can't get over the rate at which he grows: looking at him now, it is hard to see him as the baby she used to carry around in her arms.

As her mind skips comfortably through memories of Tom as a baby, something else passes like a shadow across her thoughts, indistinct, as yet, but enough to cause unease, a heaviness around the heart. She knows what it is – because, these days, it is always there lurking around in the recesses of her mind.

Six months ago: the worst argument that she and David had ever had; it was an argument that sliced so keenly through the very essence of their relationship that, at the time, she wasn't sure if they could ever recover from it.

She had mentioned, casually, that it might be nice if Tom had a little brother or sister. And in the time it had taken to open a bottle of wine, most of the certainties of her life, things she thought she knew and believed in, were all invalidated, in one fell swoop. Having any children at all, David had told her, had never been on his agenda, never part of his plan.

She can still picture the scene quite clearly. They were in the kitchen, David had just picked up the bottle of wine – it was their second – and he was cutting away the foil top – something he managed to do with one deft movement of the knife. He didn't look at her as he was speaking; his words were directed at the bottle he was working on. The fact was, he had gone on to say – this was as he was twisting in the corkscrew, pushing it further and further down into the cork – they should never have started a family in the first place, and he certainly didn't see himself with any more. There was a promotion in the offing at work – it might mean more travel – and a brood of children was certainly not going to improve his chances. This last statement was punctuated by the sound of the cork leaving the bottle.

In one dull pop she had been left with a completely altered perspective on their marriage.

The subject hasn't been mentioned since. At times, she wonders if the whole episode hadn't simply been the effect of the drink – he had downed several whiskies before they had even started on the wine. But things had been said that cannot be unsaid, and some of those things she is unable to put out of her mind.

Tom has wriggled free of her arms and is pulling on the hem of her skirt, entreating her to join him on the carpet and share in the pleasures of running a dumper truck up and down the ramp of his model garage. She notices that he has emptied the contents of his toy box onto the floor; she has just bent down to pick up Rabbit, when the phone rings again.

This time it is her mother, asking if she would like to take Tom up to see them.

'Maybe you could leave him with us for a few days,' she says. 'Give yourself a bit of a break, since you are on your own. We'd love to have him.'

It was a good idea, she thought. It would give her the chance to get on with her writing. She holds the receiver to her ear, lulled by the familiar voice, as her mother talks on: about the weather in Edinburgh, and how early the lilac was this year – it is over now, so she will miss it – but the roses are really coming on; and what she said to Mrs Kaplan who used to have the shop on the corner, 'you remember her don't you love, the one who married a Pole, then found out he was already married to someone else.'

By the time she has agreed to go, and they have resolved whether she will fly or take the train, Tom is yowling like a caged monkey.

'Better go,' she tells her mother.

'I can hear. So we'll see you then? On Sunday?'

'If I can get a ticket. Bye then.'

'Take care.'

Isabel hears the click of the receiver being put down on its stand.

∞

7.00 pm

Most of the visitors have left the exhibition hall. A few weary people still wander the aisles, clutching their complimentary bags stuffed with the bits and pieces they have accumulated during their visit: brochures, flyers, badges, promotional pens, the odd key-ring; items that have been transported halfway round the globe, many of which will end up in a waste bin.

Some of the exhibitors are dismantling their stands. Across from Lee, the girls from Tour Borneo are struggling to collapse the metal frame that has held their publicity material. For the past two days Lee has been charmed by the baby orang-utans featured in those giant display panels; he has snatched the odd, quiet moment or two to stare into the dark, imploring eyes looking back at him. Now the same pictures are in pieces. Bits of animal are scattered over the floor in front of him: patches of orange fur; huge, disembodied limbs; those liquid eyes; a hand with creased, leathery fingers.

The girls appear to need some help, and he is about to go over and offer his services, but then he sees an elderly gentleman making a beeline for his stand.

Five minutes later, and they are still deep in conversation. The man, Lee learns, is a retired chemistry teacher. He had visited Malaysia – or Malaya as it was then – in the 1950s, but hasn't been back since. Not that he hadn't wanted to, he assures Lee, but, what with one thing and another, he never had the opportunity.

'I wasn't married back then, you see. But once you start raising a family . . .' He tails off and looks at Lee for assurance.

Lee nods.

Satisfied, the man continues. 'I'm on my own now.' He fidgets with one of Lee's brochures. 'The thing is, I've got all the time in the world, and I've enough money to do a little travelling, but sadly I don't seem to have the stamina any more. And it isn't the same when you are on your own is it?'

The man is keen to talk, and they discuss the many changes that have taken place in the region: what happened after the '69 riots, and whether the measures taken caused even more resentment amongst the people; how the economy seems to have stabilized since the '97 crisis; the increasing pace of rainforest clearance and whether it is too late to reverse the effects of logging.

The longer he talks to the man, the more Lee is filled with admiration, and some surprise: he has never met anyone quite so knowledgeable about his country. But the hall is emptying, and it turns out that the man is in danger of missing his train. So, with what appears to be a tinge of regret, he picks up a couple of Lee's brochures, stows them away in his bag, then holds out his hand to Lee.

'Alexander Wallace is the name,' he says. 'It was a pleasure to meet you.' He takes a step away, then stops and makes a quarter turn back towards Lee. 'I have so enjoyed having this chat with you.'

Lee leans against the trestle table, and smooths down the corners of a hand-drawn plan of Kubah National Park. He is surprised by the sense of loss he is feeling now that Alexander Wallace has gone. He glances across to the stand opposite, but the girls from Tour Borneo have left.

He reaches under the table and pulls out an empty box, he tears off the old address label then starts to re-pack it with the material he has left on his display. When the box is full he folds down the flaps, tapes it closed, then starts on a second box.

It hasn't been a bad couple of days, he thinks. He has got rid of more brochures here than at the last venue, but now he is exhausted, and hungry. He works out that he has been standing in the same spot for almost ten hours, telling people why they should visit Muara Reserve, explaining why a small-scale resort like his is less intrusive, and less of a drain on the environment, and how the money paid by visitors will help support local businesses and local facilities, and not leak out of the country into the pockets of foreign share-holders. But it isn't the standing around that tires him, nor the lugging of heavy boxes from place to place, nor having to set up and pack away his stand each time the exhibition changes venues: it's the non-stop talking, and smiling, and having to be friendly and polite to an endless stream of people. That seems to sap the energy out of him. He pushes down hard onto the lid of what he hopes will be his last box; he has tried to squeeze in more than will comfortably fit. And if it hadn't been for Chi Wan tripping up and breaking his ankle, he muses, he wouldn't have been here at all. But at least he will be home soon, doing what he does best: managing his resort. He just hopes that Chi Wan has remembered to water his palm seedlings.

He has been packing, taping and labelling boxes for several minutes now, and he stops for a moment to catch his breath and consider what he has left to do. The boxes he has already packed are piled up in the corner, all clearly marked with the address of the London venue. Soon they will be spirited away by the couriers and, for thirty-six hours, out of his hands. However pleased he is to see them go, he is always glad to see them turn up at the other end. There are numerous tales in circulation of boxes going missing and exhibitors having to make do with bare stands, and a few photocopied leaflets – if they were lucky enough to have the master copy, or the initiative to get something faxed over from base. Now, all that remains for him to do is to take down the photo panels and stash them away in their special container. Then he will be able to go and get something to eat. He wishes now that he had spoken to the Tour Borneo girls, they might have been at a loose end too. The two things he hates most about all this travelling around are: never having the time to get to know the city you are in, and having to eat alone.

He has been sitting on a wall, not far from the famous castle. He has seen it from below – a constant backcloth to the city, perched high on its own piece of rock with the strange, vertical sides – but it is far less imposing now. And from this position, he has watched the dusk sneak in, and the lights come on, one by one; and now the streets and buildings glint and sparkle as if they housed a million glow-worms. It reminds him of London: just another city, crammed with people moving about from place to place; and the way a person can simply disappear from sight in its midst.

As he sets off down the hill, he is conscious of the weight of his briefcase (it is full of brochures and leaflets, in case his boxes go astray); the leather strap is biting into his shoulder. And he is disappointed. He had come this way, to the top of the hill, hoping to find a decent restaurant – one that would give him a feel for where he is, one that wasn't a fast-food-chain. Last night, when he had been flicking through one of the magazines in his room, he read about the famous Scottish haggis – something he has been looking forward to trying. But it turns out that haggis is not easy to find. He decides that he must be in the wrong part of town. It is odd, though, he thinks, that on a street so clearly aimed at tourists, there should be so few places to eat. But at least he can say he has been to the castle.

He is walking faster now, as if he has a purpose: down the hill; past grand-looking buildings; past rows of tiny shops, cramped and crowded like rows of crooked teeth. They are packed from floor to ceiling with racks and shelves of tartan – tartan skirts, tartan scarves, tartan bags, boxes, and tins. In fact they are so full inside, that more of the stuff has been put out on the pavement, flung into plastic tubs or loaded onto rails. He stops walking and peers into the nearest tub. He pulls out a crude, tin model of Edinburgh Castle – or so it says on the base in wobbly, indistinct lettering. He turns it upside down. 'Made in Slovakia'. He places the object back on top of the pile and moves on to look at a display of whisky in the shop next door; there are bottles and bottles of the stuff, in all shapes and sizes.

At least the local whisky industry is still a booming one, he thinks. And he is reminded that he wants to buy something to take back to Chi Wan. No doubt he will see much of the same stuff at the airport, tomorrow, but he has spotted the perfect thing: a miniature bottle in the shape of a cow, complete with horns, a coat of fake fur and a screw cap for a nose where the whisky pours out. It is the most tasteless thing in the shop: and he knows that Chi Wan will love it.

The man behind the counter wraps the cow in layer upon layer of tissue paper, carefully taping each side of the package, before placing it in a neat cardboard carrier with the name of the shop embossed across each side. Lee stands and watches the procedure, embarrassed at the attention being lavished on such a modest purchase. He wishes that he had chosen something more expensive.

The parcel packed, he leaves the shop and stands outside, wondering what to do next. He is glad that he has bought the gift, but now faces the prospect of having to carry it with him all evening. He considers going back to his room, but he is still determined to find haggis, so he continues on down the hill, in the opposite direction to his hotel. In another street, someone is playing the bagpipes – one monotonous drone, followed by another, and another, until the sound begins to resemble something approaching a tune. He thinks he recognizes it; he has heard something like it often enough in the last few days, and he wonders if it might be some sort of national anthem.

Waiting to cross the road, his mind still busy with the tune, he notices a heap of grubby blankets that have been left on the pavement and next to the blankets, a couple of beer cans and an abandoned slice of what may have been pizza. Then he sees a grimy face, and a head with a sparse covering of white hair, just visible over the top of the heap. There is an old man sheltering underneath. Lee takes a sharp breath; the flow of air makes a hissing sound between his teeth. He reaches into his pocket and scoops out all the coins he has, and drops them into the man's upturned cap. He has never got used to this, even after the years he spent living in London. Where he comes from, elderly people are taken care of by their family, whatever their circumstances. Or at least that used to be the case; but, like everywhere else, the counry is in a state of change: modern ways and ideas will continue to sweep in from the West – good and bad indiscriminately.

Now he is on the opposite side of the road he turns to get another glimpse of the castle – its floodlit form still looms large behind him – and stumbles over someone crouched on the pavement. The person swears, before asking if he has any spare change. When Lee looks down, he sees that there are three figures huddled together. The one asking for money is a girl; her outstretched hand is streaked with dirt, her long hair matted into clumps of red and purple. All three of them have bits of metal protruding aggressively from lips, noses, ears, eyebrows. The abundance of piercings makes Lee's stomach flip over, but it is the large stud attached to the girl's lower lip that bothers him the most. On the ground in front of them is a dog. Its mouth is open in a wide, goofy grin, its tongue lolling out over a row of sharp white teeth.

At least the dog seems happy, and healthy, he tells himself.

He walks on, and can hear words being muttered behind him, but he doesn't understand what is being said. He has less sympathy for these young people than he does for the old man: they could probably earn some sort of a living, he supposes, if they really wanted to.

The street is lively with people animated by drink, or maybe just youth, all making the pavement difficult to negotiate. Lee is glad that he isn't wearing his suit. For the past week he has submitted to the trend for blatant power-dressing, but when he got dressed this morning he decided to break with convention and wear something a little more cheerful. As a result, he has spent the entire day feeling out of place, his batik shirt shining out like a beacon amongst a sea of grey, black and dark blue. But now, at least, he can slip, unnoticed, between the skeins of sightseers and the young people setting out for a night on the town.

He decides to turn into one of the smaller streets that lead into the dip between the two parts of the city. Immediately, he recognizes it: he was here, in this very same street, a couple of days ago, trying to buy a notebook. He had spent precious time searching for a shop that sold ordinary, every-day items, as opposed to the rubbish being passed off as souvenirs. He should have remembered that this part of the city was strictly tourist territory; there was nothing practical or useful to be found here: a cow-shaped whisky bottle maybe, but not a notebook, or a plate of food. Even so, stumbling across somewhere familiar boosts his mood and gives him an unexpected sense of belonging. At least he knows where he is.

The street is steep and is lined on both sides with tall, multi-storied terraces with identical stone facades; the buildings appear to lean inwards, like conspirators, making the street feel narrower than it is. The stone is grey, but has a mellowness about it, something he hadn't noticed the other day when the buildings had seemed stark and imposing, turned the colour of steel by the heavy rain.

Did Isabel ever walk down this street?

The question pops up from nowhere; but he already knows it is impossible to avoid the subject. This is the city where she once lived and, for the last three days, that fact has been hanging there, like a lead weight in the back of his mind. It has been there each morning and evening when he has stared out from the vantage point of his hotel window, over the jumble of towers and spires of the city and the distant hills beyond; it was there yesterday when he sat for an hour on a bench, in a neat garden square in the centre of town, scrutinizing a terrace of elegant, white houses, trying to draw out some essence of her. His eyes have rested on innumerable rooftops, scanned untold streets and crescents, searched as far as the boundaries of the city and beyond where, in his imagination, lie suburbs with orderly rows of solemn, stone housing.

He knows she doesn't live there now; she lives in London: he read that once, on the cover of a book. But has he, without even knowing, laid eyes on the house that was once her home? Could he be walking past it even now?

He has found it difficult to imagine Isabel amongst these extraordinary buildings: their bleakness and soaring oppressiveness in stark contrast to her warmth, her gentle manner. Or could it be that his memory is flawed, skewed by time, like a beam of light through a prism? It was a long time ago. Though now he thinks about it, he does recall a certain elegance, a dignity, rather like the buildings themselves. But it seems that the image has faded over time, and her precise features elude him.

It is ironic, he thinks. He didn't want to make this trip in the first place, and coming here, to Edinburgh, has stirred up memories he thought were neatly settled into a place where they could no longer cause him too much pain. Or is it that she is always there, in the inner recesses, having taken possession of his mind in the same way she once took possession of his heart?

He finds that he has reached the end of the street and is faced with a choice of direction – should he go further down the hill, into the glitz and glare of the city centre, or left, into a sparsely-lit alleyway, where he thinks he can see the illuminated façade of a pub.

A pint or two will take the edge off his appetite, he decides, and no doubt he will be able to get haggis at the airport tomorrow.

∞

3.40 pm

I sabel pulls a blade of grass from Tom's hair. 'Have you been helping grandpa with the gardening?'

He is carrying a silver plastic dagger.

'Nope.' He presses his fingers to the top of his head, feeling for more grass. When his hand comes back down he stares into the empty palm, disappointed.

'I think you have.' She ruffles his curls and, as he makes to run away, she catches him up in her arms and gives him a hug. 'Are you going to be a good boy for grandma and grandpa?'

'Nope.'

She holds him tight for a few seconds more, pressing her cheek hard against his ear, taking in the scent of his skin; but he is wriggling too much and she is afraid she will drop him.

As soon as she puts him down he prods cautiously at her leg with the dagger. 'You're dead now,' he tells her, 'and I'm going to eat you all up.' With that, he catches hold of her hand and pretends to gnaw at her fingers.

The animal-like sounds he is making in his throat to accompany this action are quite unpleasant, and Isabel wonders, not for the first time today, how such a small boy can produce so much noise.

Her mother is obviously thinking the same. 'Goodness me,' she says, setting down a vase of ivory-coloured stocks on the sideboard. 'I don't know where he gets all this energy from.' She stands back to survey the flowers from a different angle, makes a soft clicking noise with her tongue, and then steps forward again to poke at a couple of stems, making, what seems to Isabel, an almost imperceptible and unnecessary adjustment to the arrangement.

Annette Raines is in her late sixties, but has retained a youthfulness conferred upon her by the scarcity of lines in her olive-toned skin, the still clearly defined cheekbones and the dark, almost black, eyes that shine bright and alert, and seem never to miss a thing. Her hair, once raven-coloured, is now the colour of dry slate, and is worn tightly coiled at the back of her head; this, along with her above-average height, adds a measure of stateliness to her appearance: something which is not belied by her personality.

'Are you sure you will be able to cope with him for the week?' Isabel asks her.

'Of course we will,' Annette replies. 'He's no bother at all, and your father and I will enjoy having him – after all, we don't get to see him that often.'

Isabel ignores the remark, refusing to be drawn into an argument. She would like to say, 'there's nothing to stop you both from coming to stay with us,' but she doesn't. She knows it will elicit an arched eyebrow, pursed lips, possibly a bout of hymn singing (*All People That On Earth Do Dwell* being the current favourite) – a couple of lines sung in a thin and wavering soprano – this, as Isabel well knows, indicates that her mother is not prepared to discuss the matter further, she has said her piece and the subject is now closed.

She tries to think of something else to say, something to divert her mother's attention. 'Those flowers are lovely, are they from the garden?'

Annette nods and catches hold of Tom who has been chasing around her legs.

Isabel looks at her, trying to make eye contact, but her mother is determined to brush more grass from Tom's shorts.

There's no point in discussing it anyway, Isabel reflects. Her mother's views on David are as fixed now as the day she first aired them. As far as Annette is concerned, David is arrogant, selfish and lacking in manners, and whilst he might have used his undoubted charms on her daughter, and possibly the rest of the world, he wasn't going to be able to charm his way round her.

For as long as she can remember, Isabel has been frustrated by her mother's knack of seeing through people and homing in on the very core of what they are about. It was wrong, Isabel would argue, to make up your mind about a person, without even bothering to get to know them first. But any attempt by her to defend someone's case was always taken personally, as if she were questioning her mother's judgement. The annoying thing was, that her mother's judgement was often spot on. Not that Isabel would ever have admitted it. And she wasn't about to admit it now: admit that her mother might have been right about David all along. Anyway, she muses, she no longer has the energy to defend him; she has spent most of the seven or eight years they have been together doing that, and to no avail.

For some reason, Annette has pulled up Tom's T-shirt and is now examining his back. Isabel can see the outline of his ribs pushing through the gossamer-fine skin that covers his body. He is trying to wriggle himself free of her grasp; he is still clutching onto his dagger.

'He's been eaten alive by those midges,' says Annette, touching the tips of her fingers against a series of red bumps on his skin.

Tom has stopped squirming; he is trying to look at his own back. 'What's smidges?'

'They are nasty insects that bite little boys.' She turns to Isabel. 'Didn't you put any spray on him before he went out?'

Tom takes advantage of the lapse in her attention and breaks free. He wanders over to Isabel, holding up his T-shirt so she can inspect the bites.

'Do they itch?' she asks him.

He shakes his head.

Her travel bag is on the floor, packed ready for her departure. She digs into one of its side pockets and pulls out a tiny bottle of white flower oil. She kneels down next to Tom, dabs her finger to the bottle and starts to rub drops of oil onto the bites.

'What a peculiar smell.' Annette has moved closer; she has her head bent to one side, as if she is trying to read the writing on the bottle. 'I've got some Savlon in the bathroom cupboard, she says. 'Let me go and get it. I won't be a second.'

Isabel continues to apply the oil. The window is open and she can hear the sweet trill of a blackbird's song.

When she has finished, she pulls down Tom's T-shirt and pats the top of his head, feeling her palm bounce against the soft springs of hair.

'I would be careful what I put on that wee lad's skin.' Her mother hands her a tube of Savlon. 'It's more sensitive than yours.' She moves to the sideboard and picks up the vase of flowers, holding it at arm's length. 'Now where am I going to put this?'

'It's fine mum. It's the best thing for bites.'

'Well I don't think you should use that foreign stuff on him. Not if you don't know what's in it.'

'I do know. And it isn't foreign.'

'Well where did you get it from? China or somewhere.'

'I've never been to China.'

'Well, you know what I mean.'

Isabel doesn't want this, not now, not just as she is about to leave. They have already argued once this morning, a trivial thing to start with, about what time she should leave to get to the airport. But by the time it had been tossed backwards and forwards between them, it had taken on an importance out of all proportion to its original size; and even now, three hours later, its bulky form still inhabits the space between them. But her faith in the white flower oil is strong; and so is the need to assert herself as a fully-functioning adult, as opposed to the perpetual fourteen-year-old she becomes whenever she is in her mother's company. So they will argue again, she has no doubt; and she will be left with the emptiness, and the guilt, which she will carry around for the remainder of the day, and all the way back to London, until she is settled into her own home and her own routines once more.

She puts the cap back onto the bottle and gets to her feet. 'I don't remember where I got it from – an airport probably.' There is a tightness in her throat; she longs to do just one thing that would gain her mother's approval. 'I always use it – it really does work,' she adds weakly, smiling up at her mother. But Annette has turned away again and is busy rearranging the photos on the mantelpiece.

Through the window, Isabel can see Tom and her father; they are both kneeling on the grass, they have their heads together, they are looking at something on the ground. The sun has just slipped behind the house at the end of the garden, casting a wedge of shadow across the lawn. Isabel guesses that it must be about four o'clock: it is time she was thinking about setting off for the airport.

∞

Edinburgh Airport

L ee scans the departures board. There are two flights to London before his – one of them is about to depart – and he can't understand why his travel agent hadn't booked him onto either one of those. In fact, he is sure he had asked for an earlier one. At this rate he won't get to his hotel until after nine: too late to have dinner; too early to go to bed.

Most times he enjoys mooching around airports, particularly once his baggage has been offloaded and abandoned to fate, when he can finally enter the inner sanctum sheltered behind those sliding doors marked 'Passengers Only', where the shops and cafés bask in the prospect of frivolous, pre-holiday consumption, and are always newer and shinier than the drab, utilitarian ones on the outside. But for the time being he is on the wrong side of the doors, and he needs to find something to do, to fill the time until the check-in desk opens.

He is relieved that, for today at least, he is not obliged to talk to anyone. He is tired; all energy has leaked from his bones; he is sure he could sleep for a week. And he might do just that, he promises himself, as soon as he gets home. But then he remembers Chi Wan's broken ankle and the reason he is here in the first place.

He knows, as well, that his weariness is more than just physical. And while these exhibitions can take their toll – the travelling, the constant packing and un-packing, waking up in different hotel rooms, losing any awareness of where you are – it's nothing he hasn't done before, on many occasions.

This is something more than that.

Ever since he arrived in Edinburgh he has had a sense of being disconnected; it is as if he is looking through a long, narrow tube, as if everything he does is being done by someone else.

It was bound to happen.

So he had resolved to spend as much time as possible in his hotel room: he would catch up with paperwork, read a book – anything; watch movies on the television if it came to it. Yet the evenings had invariably found him walking the streets and alleyways, looking for clues to her in the very fabric of the city where she had spent the first twelve years of her life. Had she walked on this pavement? Had she touched that part of the castle wall? – and he had imagined her fingers playing over the same rough, sun-warmed stone. Her likeness would glance back at him from darkened shop windows, and from oily puddles of still, black water. But it was never the face of Isabel, the child, he saw: it was the Isabel he had known, one summer, exactly ten years ago.

So long ago.

The airport is starting to fill up with people. A dozen or so children in smart, navy-blue uniforms file past where he is standing. A school trip? Probably. They are excited, noisy. And he realizes that he has been standing in this same spot for some time. People seem to think he is the start of a queue for a check-in desk that is yet to be opened. He moves. Perhaps he can find a corner out of the way, where he can sit down and do some work. He is behind with his accounts. He needs to get them done.

He doesn't mind doing the accounts, in fact he enjoys the time he spends hidden away in his study with just the spreadsheets for company. He enjoys it more than the marketing side of the business and he usually leaves this to Chi Wan, who has the necessary gift of the gab and a particular ability to charm his way around the most awkward of customers. He, on the other hand, would rather spend the day tinkering with the water-filtration system, or helping to feed the orang-utans at the nearby rehabilitation centre. And in five days' time, he thinks, he will be back home, doing all those things he likes most.

He is still wandering around, still looking for somewhere to sit, but all the seats appear to be taken. He stands his suitcase against a wall and squats down on it, gingerly, remembering Chi Wan's bottle of whisky tucked in amongst the sweaters he brought but never needed. A girl in a faded denim jacket catches his eye and grins at him. She, too, has devised a makeshift seat and is perched on the edge of a luggage trolley with her back against a stack of bags. She has short, dark hair and a pretty face. French, he thinks, or Italian. He smiles back at her then opens his briefcase and pulls out a stack of papers. On the top is the sketch he made last night. It is a design for a tree house he is going to build.

Each month he and Chi Wan visit the local school and talk to the children about the environment they live in, hoping to persuade them that it is precious, something that needs help. He needs them to understand why people should stop chopping down trees in the forests, why it is important for them not to drop litter on the beaches, why they should respect and protect the living things around them. And the other day, Chi Wan had an idea: if they held events at the reserve, then children from further afield – from Kuching, or even other parts of Malaysia – could also experience forest life at close quarters. They could see for themselves the complex ecosystems that exist in the matting of plants on the rainforest floor, and in the miniature world of the mangrove swamps. Perhaps then, they might understand how everything fits together; and maybe they will be less inclined to do the things that will ultimately destroy it. They could come in small groups, in their school holidays, if there was somewhere to accommodate them. Tree houses would be perfect.

There is another project too, that he is eager to start on, as soon as he gets home. In a village close by is a community of weavers. Their form of weaving unique to the area, and it is their main source of income, but their products lack market exposure. He would like to employ them to weave wall hangings and bedcovers for the rooms at Muara; perhaps he could also sell their work to the guests. Then the villagers could make a living, and he could help save a traditional craft. He had been looking at the figures last night, but at some point he had stretched out on his bed, closed his eyes, and fallen asleep. He had woken up in the early hours of the morning, still dressed, with the papers scattered around him. And he had woken in the shadow of a bad dream.

The dream has continued to taint his day. The details of it are brittle, elusive. He only knows it was about her.

What he needs most, he thinks, is a good night's sleep.

He spots a chair that has become empty. He hopes he can get to it before someone else does.

∞

Isabel checks her watch. It has just gone five. She can't quite believe that she got here so quickly. The taxi driver evidently had some sort of death wish; she feels relieved to have made it in one piece.

Her father had wanted to drive her here, they had almost argued about it, but in the end she had convinced him that a taxi would be a more sensible option. She knows she made him feel redundant, expendable – she feels guilty about that – but she worries about him driving so far on his own. And she wishes that he would carry the mobile phone she bought him a few Christmases ago. But when she had raised the subject he told her that, at eighty, he had no intention of looking like one of those 'Jack the Lads' who strut around with phones permanently pressed against their ears. The thought of this makes her smile. She would have enjoyed his company; it was the only time they got the chance to talk, when it was just the two of them.

She wanders to the check-in desk. Although it is not due to open until half past five, people have already started to form a queue. But she is feeling restless, on edge; she doesn't want to stand there. Not just yet. She remembers that she needs a new toothbrush, and she isn't sure if there is a Boots on the other side. It is quite likely there is, she thinks, but she is pleased to have found something to do.

As she heads to the shop, she is conscious that the airport is unusually busy. She wonders whether it is the school holidays but, no, she is sure that it isn't; and she has just spotted a group of school-children in charge of a mountain of luggage. She thinks how smart they look in their uniforms, and how well behaved they seem to be.

In Boots she chooses her toothbrush, and a box of Paracetamol. Only one till is open and the queue stretches back into the interior of the shop. While she waits, she looks at vitamins and massage oils, pills to help you sleep, creams to remove corns, plasters to relieve corns, stuff to stop you snoring. A girl in a pale denim jacket asks if she has the time. When Isabel tells her it is nearly quarter past five, the girl swears, in French, and tells the queue she should be boarding now. Isabel lets her go ahead.

∞

From where Lee is sitting he can see that people are lining up to check-in for the London flight. He decides to wander over. He puts away his papers and finds his ticket and passport.

There are two desks about to open, and two queues have formed. He hesitates, while he decides which one to join. As he steps forward, he collides with a loaded trolley being manoeuvred towards the queue he has chosen. It catches the back of his leg; it is painful and he wants to rub it, but he tries not to. The woman behind the trolley is large – very large – certainly too large for the clothes she is wearing. Her scanty top is stretched to its limits over a bulging stomach; the narrow straps push out mounds of moist, pink flesh. She grimaces at him, a half-grin, which he takes to be apologetic. She must be wearing the entire contents of her jewellery box, he thinks, judging by the cascade of gold chains around her neck, the massive, hoop-shaped earrings and the ill-matching bracelets on both of her arms.

He steps back, to let her go ahead, but she waves him on with a freckled hand, and an arsenal of rings.

'No love, you're alright,' she says. 'You'll be best off ahead of me with this lot.'

So he slips into the queue in front of her, surreptitiously rubbing the spot on his leg where the trolley had hit it.

∞

At five thirty-five, Isabel returns to the check-in area and joins the end of the nearest queue. After some time, she realizes that her line hasn't moved, while the other one does seem to be inching forwards, slowly. She switches across.

As she waits, she glances through the magazine she has just

bought at WH Smith. There is an article about two people she has never heard of – although there is clearly an assumption that she has – whose marriage lasted for just forty-eight hours. There is a photograph of the ecstatic couple in some tropical location, posing with an elaborate, multi-tiered cake. A wedding cake that outlasted the marriage, she thinks, and grins to herself, amused by her own joke. She turns the page and scans a list of 'Your Top Ten Secret Holiday Destinations'. There is nowhere that she wants to go, but she can't help thinking how senseless it is to call them 'secret', when they are splashed all over the pages of a popular magazine.

She closes the magazine and stuffs it into her bag. It will soon be her turn to check in. She glances across to the other queue and notices that it has, in the end, moved faster than her own. Never mind, she thinks, no-one is going to arrive in London any faster.

There is a woman towards the front of the queue, who has a disproportionate amount of luggage although, considering her size, it is not surprising that her clothes take up more space than anyone else's.

Isabel tells herself not to be so cruel; but even so, she is glad that she isn't stuck behind her. She will certainly have to pay extra for that lot. Or perhaps the suitcases aren't all hers, after all. Maybe she's with someone else. That guy, for example, standing in front of her; they could be together. On second thoughts, probably not. And although she can't see his face – he has his back to her – she knows that he is Chinese, or Asian. It might be the hair, or the build, but she can always tell; is always drawn by it. In any case, the guy has moved forward now, and he is alone. He is standing at the desk, checking-in. She sees him raise his hand to push away a lock of hair. It is a gesture she has seen a thousand times: a gesture which never fails to jolt her heart. He has turned now; she can see his profile quite clearly.

He looks like Lee, she thinks. And she is annoyed that her mind still plays these tricks on her.

But she can't take her eyes off him.

Now he is moving away from the desk, away, into the crowd; soon she will lose sight of him.

Aware only of the blood rushing inside her head, she has picked up her bag and is pushing her way through. She can hear people sighing, tut-tutting. She responds to them: 'Sorry – not pushing in. I just need . . . there's someone I . . .'

She can see him. She has almost caught up with him. She reaches him.

She puts out her hand, touches his arm. 'Lee?'

He turns.

'Isabel?'

∞

They stand, looking at each other, neither of them believing what they are seeing. Then, regardless of the people around them (some watching to see what is going to happen next, some studiously looking away) they are in each other's arms.

Isabel is the first to speak.

'I can't believe it,' she whispers. 'It's you.'

He pushes her away, gently, as if he, too, is doubting what he has seen.

She looks back into his eyes. They are just as she remembers, she thinks: perhaps a little sadder. 'How come . . .? Why . . .?' But she finds she is unable to speak. All she knows is that the very person who has occupied a place in her mind, conscious and unconscious, for the past ten years, and whom she thought she would never see again, is now there, holding onto her, in the middle of Edinburgh Airport.

'Isabel . . .' He wraps his arms around her again, and she thinks she won't be able to breathe, but she doesn't care.

When he pulls back once more, she notices that his eyes are moist.

'Where did you go?' he asks.

∞

This is the question he has been waiting to ask ever since she disappeared from his life. And now he has asked it, he doesn't want her to answer; he wants to keep her in his arms for as long as possible. And he wants to kiss her. But he doesn't. Because now he has started to think about what he is doing; he feels self-conscious, and even a little surprised at his impulsiveness.

And now she is crying: gently, but he can feel the sobs lurching through her body. He is aware that people are looking at them.

He picks up the red bag that she has dropped on the floor and takes her hand. 'Let's go somewhere else,' he says.

He leads her out into the warmth of the late-afternoon sunshine. He has seen a low wall just outside the doors; they can sit there for a while, away from the crowds and the noise of the departures hall.

Once she has sat down, she uses her free hand to search her pocket. She pulls out a paper handkerchief and dabs at her eyes.

As he watches her, he knows, without any shadow of a doubt, that he still loves her more than anything in the world. It is a love so potent that it physically hurts. And what has just happened is something he has wished for since the day she vanished, all those years ago; for the rest of his life, he will thank the gods that he had the opportunity to hold her in his arms, one more time. But he knows that this is a temporary gift. She belongs to somebody else. He glances down at her left hand; the simple gold band glints amber in the reflected light of the sun. It confirms what he already knows.

He wonders where she is going, whether she has checked in. But these questions will have to wait. For now he simply needs some time to be with her. He feels as if he is drowning in his love for her, and he needs to breathe her in, feel the closeness of her, just for a few minutes, before they have to part and go their separate ways, back into the real world. If it comes to it, he will miss his own flight. He doesn't care.

∞

Isabel has found a piece of old tissue in her pocket and is using it to wipe her eyes, well aware that she is also wiping away the makeup she had put on in a spur-of-the-moment gesture, just before she left the house.

'I'm sorry. I'm making a fool of myself.'

He shakes his head, and smiles at her; it is a smile filled with so much warmth and tenderness, she can hardly bear it.

Utterly confused now, her lips begin to form a question.

'Why . . .?'

She stops. No, it's too soon. That question will have to wait. Instead she says: 'This is crazy. I mean, what on earth are you doing here? Here in Edinburgh?'

He is still smiling at her. The familiar, lopsided smile. He looks older, she thinks, but then he would. It was ten years ago –

She notices, for the first time, that he is wearing a suit, a smart one too, and there is a leather briefcase on the ground at his feet. He looks well-groomed, important and, still, incredibly handsome. Suddenly she feels shy. But he is still holding her hand.

'I'm representing my business at a travel fair,' he replies, at last. 'We've been in Scotland for the last week, now we're moving on to London.'

She wonders who he means by 'we'. 'Your business?' she asks.

'Yes, my resort.' He looks away for a moment. 'Another one, I mean.'

'Ah.'

He looks back at her, his face bright and eager now, his eyes sparkling. Just as they used to do. 'Resort – maybe it isn't the right word, it's . . . Do you remember? It's what I told you I wanted to do.'

She nods. Of course she does. Hadn't she wanted to be a part of it too? Hadn't she told him as much in her note? The one he never replied to.

'It's called Muara Reserve,' he continues. '*Muara* means river mouth. You would . . .' He breaks off and stares down at his feet.

He is speaking so quietly that she hasn't caught what he said. She asks him to repeat it.

'I was going to say, I think you would like it there. So what about you?' he asks quickly. 'Are you still writing?'

The question unsettles her. How does he know that?

'Yes. On and off,' she replies. 'I do a bit of part-time work too – editing other people's books –'

It isn't what she wants to talk about. 'So you left Teluk?' she asks.

'Yes.'

She knows that already, but she is not going to tell him that she went back, that she had seen the construction site that had once been his precious garden.

'I lost it,' he says. 'I lost the fight. I couldn't compete with them, so I sold my share. I had no choice.'

She recalls the trip he had made to KL, the day before she left. The meeting at the bank. So they hadn't loaned him the money after all.

'I waited for a while though,' she hears him say.

'Waited?'

'Yes, I waited. In case you came back.'

She doesn't understand what he means. In case she came back? All he had to do was to ask. This isn't making much sense.

She is going to have to do it – to say the words that have been pestering to get out, ever since she saw him. Go on, she tells herself. Say it – now – before it is too late.

'But you never replied to my letter.'

That stupid note. The one she had so often wished unwritten. And the rejection that followed – its backwash eroding her confidence, lap by lap.

'What letter?' He looked startled. 'You wrote a letter?'

'Yes – well, a note – I left you a note – when I had to leave Buah – on the last day. Don't you remember. I left you my address – and my telephone number. I said I would like to stay in touch – I said that I would . . .' She pauses, to choose her words. 'I said I might come back to Malaysia –' She is going to add, 'if you wanted me to', but he has turned away from her; he is leaning forward and has covered his face with his hands.

She doesn't know what to do. She reaches out to touch his arm. 'What? What's wrong?'

He looks up. 'I don't understand it.' He shakes his head. 'I didn't get that. I didn't get any note.'

PART SIXTEEN

Malaysia
July 1991

∞

I sabel loaded the last of her things into the suitcase and closed the lid. She glanced at her watch. She had five minutes to write the letter. She sat down and leafed through her notebook until she found a blank page. Through the closed shutters came sounds of the encroaching storm: the wind gathering strength for its next attack – a primeval howl, a cry to arms – the palms, menacing, rattling their fronds as if in response. When a violent gust bounced against the side of her chalet she could feel the raw power of it: power enough to lift the tightly thatched roof and toss it aside like an abandoned carcass; it shook her door, as if someone were desperate to get inside. She picked up her pen and started to write:

> *Dear Lee*
> *I hope you read this before you start wondering why I have left, without saying goodbye. I can't believe our bad luck. Because of the storms, I have been told I need to leave now, otherwise I will miss my flight to London. Gilbert is taking me to the airport to catch what might be the last flight off the island (so everyone is saying). I hate leaving without seeing you – but it won't be for long, because I am definitely coming back (and I've got lots more ideas for the new Buah Lodge!) –*

She put down her pen, not sure how to go on. Did that sound too presumptuous? On the other hand, if she didn't tell him what she had decided, he might assume that she didn't want to see him again. She rested her elbows on the desk and cradled her head in her hands. She had to get this right, and she needed more time to think. But time was one thing she didn't have –

She looked at her watch again. They would be waiting for her. She didn't have time to start all over again. She picked up the pen and added:

– if you want me to!

The main thing was to let Lee have her address.

Let me know what you think. You can write to me at –

It was then that she realized: she didn't have an address to give. In just under three weeks' time she would be moving from the flat in Green Lanes; and she didn't have a clue where she would be going.

She decided that she had no option but to give her current address, and hope that Susan would forward her mail. Some hope! But three weeks should be long enough. And he could always phone.

She printed out each letter and number of the address, making sure that everything was legible, unambiguous. She also wrote down her telephone number, adding that she wouldn't be there after August 21st. As she didn't have an envelope to put it in, she folded the note in half, and half again, and wrote his name in large letters on the front.

The gravel paths were now waterlogged, making it impossible to wheel her suitcase; she had to stop every so often to swap the case from one hand to the other. Long tails of wet hair clung to her face; she could feel water dripping down the back of her neck, and from the end of her nose.

Phil and Gilbert were waiting for her at the top of the steps. She noticed that they were both holding umbrellas and she remembered that she had left one on her verandah.

As soon as Gilbert spotted her, he hurried down and took charge of her case, handing her his umbrella at the same time. 'We go now,' he said. 'We got forty-five minute. We just make it.'

'Hang on a second, I need to . . .'

Without finishing her sentence, Isabel ran up to the reception area and looked around for somewhere to leave her note.

The desk where guests were greeted on arrival was always kept neat and tidy, but today it was littered with items, as if someone had started to clear out a cupboard and then left, suddenly, before the job was finished. There were loose sheets of paper, a collection of dog-eared novels in various European languages, a couple of old ledgers with tired, water-stained covers, and a giant ring-binder with its metal clasp gaping open, waiting to be filled. It would be a mistake to leave her note amongst that lot.

Then she noticed the wooden hornbill perched on a shelf behind the desk. It was a model of Malaysia's national bird, once painted in primary colours, now faded and dull. She knew that it belonged to Lee; it had been a present from his sister, he had told her, when he had first come to Buah Lodge. He would be bound to see the note if she left it there. She dodged behind the desk, took the note from her pocket and propped it against the hornbill, making sure that Lee's name was clearly visible.

Phil was stubbing out the cigarette he had been smoking. 'You're lucky,' he drawled. 'They said it was fully booked, but Gilbert got you a seat. Dunno how.'

He heaved his rucksack onto one shoulder. 'And it was a close thing they didn't cancel this one as well. Seems they want their planes in the right place for the next day, or something. Otherwise they would have.'

Isabel set off down the steps, struggling to put up the umbrella Gilbert had given her. One of its spokes was broken and as she tried to pick her way through the puddles she soon realized that, instead of offering protection from the rain, it was allowing the water to cascade down onto her arm. But it hardly mattered any more. She was already soaked to the skin.

Phil had caught up and was trying to walk alongside her. But the path was too narrow for them both; with every step, his umbrella pushed insistently against her own.

'Fancy spending a day in KL?' he shouted, trying to make himself heard over the noise of the rain. 'You have time. Your flight doesn't leave till nearly midnight, right?'

She stepped aside, giving him no option but to pass in front of her. She had forgotten that he was staying in the capital for a few days. The last thing she wanted was to be stuck with him today.

'Think about it,' he shouted back over his shoulder.

Behind them, the rain continued to lash against the Gula House; it drummed down onto the corrugated-tin roof above the kitchen, and made makeshift rivers of the gullies that ran beside the paths; it flooded the tiny concrete yard outside the kitchen door, where Patrick the kitchen-boy, liked to sit when he was peeling the potatoes; and it flattened the patch of Chinese cabbage that Set Yen had been growing in a rusty oil drum.

Sharp gusts of wind pulled and pushed at the long rattan blinds that had been lowered over the open sides of the dining area; the edges of tablecloths rose and fell, flapping around like happy ghosts; a vase toppled, and shattered to pieces as it hit the ground.

The folded rectangle of paper propped up against the wooden hornbill was swept into the air and sent gliding to the floor; and there it lay, jerking and quivering like a dying moth, amongst the stray leaves and the jewel-coloured petals that had been blown in by the wind.

∞

It seemed to Isabel that matters may, after all, have been taken out of her hands. As they crossed the hall she could see that the check-in desks were deserted: they were too late. If only Phil hadn't insisted on running back to the Gula House, to retrieve his packet of cigarettes, they might have made it in time.

Now what? She wasn't sure whether to be relieved or upset about missing the flight. One thing she was sure about, though: her life was just about to get very complicated, one way or the other.

But when she looked round again, she saw that Gilbert had managed to find someone in charge. He was half-walking, half-running, towards them, and with him was a young woman wearing a smart, turquoise uniform. It looked as if they might be getting on the flight after all.

Before Isabel had time to register this latest turn of events, she and Phil were being whisked through the check-in formalities, and out to the narrow strip of tarmac, where the miniature blue and white plane was waiting, its propellers already turning, as if it were anxious to get on its way.

Following behind Phil, Isabel climbed the few steps to the door of the aircraft. When she reached the top she took a deep breath, one last lungful of the place she was about to leave behind.

But not for ever, she told herself: she would be coming back as soon as she could, she was certain. Almost certain.

Just before she ducked into the cabin, she looked back to see if Gilbert was still standing at the departure gate where they had said their hurried goodbyes. Gilbert: her last link to Lee.

But he had already gone.

Her vision blurred and she rubbed at her eyes, willing herself not to cry.

Once the plane had taxied to the end of the short runway, it seemed just seconds before it had lurched into the air and was soaring over the thatched roof of the airport building, over bright, white walls with their vivid patches of bougainvillea, over the palms, then the canopy trees; and then, in an instant, everything disappeared, lost to the storm-filled cloud that shrouded the island.

Isabel held on to the edge of her seat and craned to catch any glimpse she could of the land below, wondering whether they had flown over Teluk, desperate for a gap in the cloud, for any clue as to where, exactly, they were. After a while, she gave up. The sudden dips and rises, as the plane was tossed around by the turbulent air, were making her feel queasy. And there was nothing to see any more: just thick, grey cloud.

'What time's your flight out?'

She had been given a seat next to Phil, and he was still trying to persuade her to spend the day with him in KL. 'I just need to find my hotel and drop my bag,' he went on, 'then we can . . .'

'I'm only in transit. Don't I have to stay in the airport?'

'Nah, it's easy. Just walk out. It's a different terminal. Jeez, there's no way I'd spend twelve hours hanging about there. It's a dump.'

She was going to have to think of a way to shake him off. She knew she was grabbing at straws, but wasn't there a chance, even a tiny one, that Lee might be at the airport too?

'I'm staying some place near the bus station.' Phil was flicking through the pages of his guidebook. It was grubby, and had lost its cover. 'I think it's Pudu-something. I'll find it in a sec.'

Isabel stared out of the window, and focussed her eyes on what looked like heaps and heaps of dirty grey cotton wool; she tried to imagine what it would be like to step onto it and lie, cushioned and enveloped, in its bulk, wondering if the plane was ever going to break through and into to the piercing blue she imagined would be there, somewhere, above them. She knew that Lee was booked on the twelve-thirty flight from KL. Would he know that flights back to the island had been cancelled?

'Pudu Raya – that's the one – it's right there.' Phil was nudging her arm with his book, jabbing his finger at a map she was supposed to look at. 'Right next to Chinatown.'

She took the book from him and let her eyes rest on the map. If he didn't know his flight had been cancelled, she thought, he would still go to the airport. Her flight was due to land at about half past eleven. That meant that if she could get to the departures area before he tried to check in, then she would see him –

She made a point of turning the pages of Phil's guidebook, as if she were looking for something.

 – and when he discovered his flight was cancelled, wouldn't he call Buah Lodge? And they would tell him she had left. And he would be there, waiting for her.

She closed the book and handed it back to Phil. 'It looks good,' she said, trying to sound as pleasant as she could. 'Your hotel, I mean. Very central. And very convenient.'

'Yeah, not bad. It'll be good to be back in the city. Need to see some TV. So, what d'you reckon? Lunch in Chinatown? Stroll round the market? Back in time for your flight.'

'It sounds great. Honestly. But I can't. I've got to make some calls when I get to the airport. I need get some work done I'm afraid. I keep forgetting that I'm supposed to be on a business trip.'

And it was true, she had almost forgotten. Sitting here in this tiny plane cocooned by a churning mass of cloud, her skin browned by the sun, her hair still dry and sticky with sand and salt, it seemed a very long time ago since she had waved goodbye to the uniformed doorman of the Istana Hotel, and set out on her adventure to an island she had never previously heard of.

Yet it had been just nine days.

∞

Subang Airport, Kuala Lumpur

L ee stared at the departures board in dismay, reading and re-
reading it, as if the action itself might, in some perverse way,
force the display to change in front of his eyes. But no, there it
was, alongside his flight number. 'CANCELLED'. The letters
were bold and red, as if they were taunting him, as if they were
happy to shout out the message he did not want to hear. An icy
chill made its way up his spine and hit the centre of his cranium,
contracting the spot just behind his eyes. He looked again, in case
he had made a mistake.

But he was familiar with the timetable. It couldn't be simpler.
There were just two flights a day back to the island; the other one
had been at half past seven that morning. There were no more
flights until tomorrow.

Another glance at the board. Still cancelled.

His day, the day he had planned so carefully, was beginning to
unravel around him.

It was his own fault. He should have been on that earlier flight
– would have been, had he not left it too late to book his ticket.
Why had he left it to the last minute? Because some junior clerk
at the bank had forgotten to confirm his meeting. And why was
he here in the first place? Because of some futile attempt to keep
hold of the business he loved, and believed in.

Who was he kidding? Anyone would tell him he had no chance
against a slickly-run outfit like the Mayang. Even if he did get
the loan he wanted, it would never be enough to fend them off
forever – the multi-national corporations, the government-backed
developers, the big guys who always won out in the end. He was
just a minnow in their eyes. How could he have thought that he

would be able to compete against them?

He looked up at the board once more, cursing his own inadequacy, cursing the bank, the Mayang, and all the people who had managed to get a seat on the seven-thirty flight.

The word 'CANCELLED' was still there; it was like an accusation, a metaphor for his plans, and his life: the life he seemed to be spectacularly messing up, by the minute.

He needed to think. He might still be able to salvage something from the day, set it back on track; but his mind seemed incapable of any clear thought. He knew he should go to the desk, find out what was going on, and then phone Buah Lodge. He had to let Isabel know why he wasn't going to be there as arranged. But even as he was thinking this, he still didn't move from the board. It had developed a strange hold on him; he was convinced that the moment he turned away it would change.

All around him it was business as usual: people saying goodbyes; mountains of luggage being pushed to and fro on trolleys that had seen better days; obsessive checking and re-checking of tickets, the patting of pockets for the reassuring bulk of passport or wallet; over-excited children; and parents with studiously-glazed faces, avoiding eye-contact with the outside world. And finally, Lee tore his eyes from the board and with a glance at his watch – it was now twenty-five past eleven – he gently slipped back into the undulant mass of humanity.

The Pelangi Air desk was tucked away in a dim corner of the departures hall. He could see that there was already a long line of people waiting, and just one person there to deal with them. He walked over and joined the queue, hoping that this wasn't going to take too long.

The girl behind the desk was unruffled by the battalion of frustrated travellers; she treated each person that landed up in front of her with exactly the same measure of politeness, and firmness. When it was his turn at last, she confirmed what he already knew.

'Sorry sir, your flight has been cancelled.'

'Yes, I saw that, but do you know why? You see, I need to get back today. Is there any chance of a flight out today?'

Of course, she had heard the same story over and over again. He knew that. But he couldn't stop himself from adding: 'It's urgent.' He imagined Isabel, sitting on her verandah, in the wickerwork chair he had recently noticed was in need of some repair (it was a job he could do himself, when he had a moment to spare); she was waiting. Waiting for him.

But as the minutes ticked on, he started to realize that he wasn't going to get there in time; and he imagined her face, her beautiful, grey eyes, sad but resigned, as if she had been through it all before.

He couldn't let her down. He wasn't going to let her down.

'We apologize, sir, but weather conditions are not allowing any more flights to or from the east coast today.'

Weather conditions. He might have known. It wasn't unusual; it was something that happened frequently during the monsoon time. But that wasn't now. And when he glanced up at the narrow windows fringing the roof of the building, he could see a perfect, picture-postcard sky outside.

'Then what about tomorrow?' he asked. 'Will there be flights tomorrow? What about the seven-thirty?'

For the first time, she looked at him, really looked at him. She was, Lee noted, very pretty. She was wearing the *tudung*, the traditional head covering worn by some Malay girls; its frame-like presence set off to perfection the flawlessly made-up face within its confines.

She smiled, sympathetically, or perhaps in the way someone might humour a child. 'I am sorry,' she said. 'Unfortunately, I can't tell you what the weather is going to do.' She looked back at her computer screen. 'I am afraid that both our flights are full tomorrow. But I can put you on standby.' She tapped away at her keyboard. 'Yes, you are now on standby.'

Lee knew that there would be no point in arguing with her, no point in shouting out that standby was of no use to him. It wasn't her fault. She was just doing her job.

She scribbled a number on a slip of paper and pushed it towards him. 'I suggest that you phone later for an update on the weather conditions.' She was already looking towards the next person in the queue.

Reluctantly, Lee moved away from the desk. If only he could

get to Mersing, he thought, then he could get a boat – the express service would take an hour and a half. But how would he get to Mersing? That in itself could take a day.

Suddenly, he remembered something the girl at the desk had said. 'All flights to and from the east coast had been cancelled'. To *and* from. Of course! That meant Isabel's flight would be cancelled too. Why was he being so dense? He knew the workings of Pelangi Air well enough. There were only a couple of planes that shuttled backwards and forwards to the mainland; the plane he should be on – now cancelled – was the same plane that she would have taken later that day. Isabel wouldn't be able to go anywhere either.

The surge of relief that hit him was, however, soon tempered by guilt: it meant that she would almost certainly miss her flight back to the UK. He knew that he was being selfish, but all he could think about was the need to see her again before she left. And now he had gained some more time; if only he could get to where he wanted to be.

At least the fog had cleared from his head, and he knew that he needed to contact her – urgently. As things stood, she would have no idea that he was stuck in KL, and although he hoped that she wouldn't think him so shallow, she could be forgiven for thinking that he had deliberately failed to turn up as arranged. And until he could speak to her, she wasn't going to know otherwise.

He dug into his pocket and pulled out a couple of ten-*sen* coins. He was surprised to find them, but thankful for whatever occurrence had led him to put them there. The coins were small, light, but he held them tight, digging his nails hard into his palm, as if they might escape. As he scoured the area for a phone, he longed to be outside, in the fresh air, away from the oppressive heat of the airport.

The first telephone booth was out of order. The next one didn't take coins. Had he got a *kadfon*? He looked in his wallet just in case, hoping that the same bit of good fortune that had kindly deposited the coins in his pocket, had mysteriously produced a phonecard that he had never bought. But the wallet was empty of cards, of any sort. For a second he hesitated, unsure what to do. Should he try to find another coin-operated phone? He took a few steps away from the phone booth, stopped for a moment, then turned round and walked in the opposite direction. He was wasting precious time. He needed to find a kiosk where he could buy a *kadfon*.

With the receiver pressed against his ear, all he could hear was the sound of static coming though the line. What the hell was the matter with it? He pulled out the card, re-inserted it and dialled the number again. A long pause, some promising clicks, then that noise again. He tried the operator next; this time he got through. The operator asked him to hold on while she tried the line. In his mind he could see the desk at reception; the old, grey telephone sitting next to the telex machine; the giant, leather-bound book where guests signed in –

Who would be there to pick it up, he wondered. He wasn't sure if Set Yen would be back, but Gilbert should be around. And Amir had been told he should answer the phone if no-one else was available. But the phone wasn't ringing: it was hissing and crackling at him from a distance.

The operator came back on. 'I'm sorry sir but there is a fault. It seems that some lines may be down due to the weather conditions.'

Lee thanked the operator and carefully replaced the receiver.

'Hell!' He slammed his fist hard against the wall, causing several people to turn and stare at him. He had no idea what he was going to do next. All he knew was that he mustn't, not for one single minute, let her believe that he had abandoned her.

He decided then, that his best option was to go back to his sister's flat and keep trying to phone from there, in the hope that they sorted out the lines quicker than they usually did when they went down. If he got a taxi straight away he would be back at the flat in just under an hour. He took one last look at the departures board and, reluctantly, walked out of the airport building. He didn't think that he had ever felt more miserable.

∞

Isabel unbuckled her seat-belt and attempted to stand up without banging her head on the overhead lockers, wishing that Phil would stop faffing about with his bag and at least look as if he were trying to get off the plane. From her half-standing, half-kneeling position, she craned round to see what was going on behind her. Why hadn't they opened the doors? They had been on the ground for at least five minutes. And it was already ten to twelve.

'Come on – come on,' she muttered under her breath. Her heart was beating double-time; her skin was beginning to feel clammy. She rubbed at her face with the back of her hand wishing, at the same time, that she had a mirror handy, so that she could check what had happened to her hair after its earlier soaking. Just in case.

Inches from her left ear the Tannoy system pinged into life, making her jump. An announcement was being made and her heart sank. It could only mean one thing – that there was a problem. The voice coming over the system was speaking Malay; all Isabel recognized was the now familiar *terima kasih* – thank you very much. But as soon as the announcement had finished, it was repeated, in perfect English.

> *'Ladies and gentleman – we apologize for the delay. The captain has informed us that there is a mechanical fault with one of the doors. An engineer is on his way and we would now ask you to sit back in your seats and make yourselves comfortable until we are able to finally open the door. Thank you very much.'*

By the time they did leave the aircraft, and had been ushered into the terminal building, it was almost quarter past twelve. Now, all that stood between her and the arrivals hall – and Lee – was luggage collection and, of course, Phil.

But he was easier to shake off than she had imagined. His enormous rucksack was the first piece of baggage to appear on the miniature carousel. He heaved it off, slung it onto the floor, and then turned to her.

'Right, I'm off then,' he said. 'Sure you're not gonna come along for the ride?'

She repeated what she had told him earlier – that she had some business to attend to.

'Aw well. See you around.' He took a step towards her, kissed the side of her face then picked up his bag and, before she had time to say anything in response, he was walking away towards the double doors marked '*KETIBAAN* '– arrivals.

At last, she was alone.

As soon as she had collected her suitcase, she too, with racing pulse, stepped through the doors and emerged into the arrivals hall.

She was initially taken aback when she saw the mass of bobbing dark heads (and the occasional fair one, looming above the crush with an almost comic contrariety); and once again, she had become a giant, cast up in a land of dainty, perfectly formed, if somewhat excitable, beings. She had assumed, she supposed, that the whole of the country had been affected by the weather, and that the airport would have been deserted, but she couldn't have been more wrong. Not only was the arrivals hall packed with people, but her plane had landed in almost perfect conditions. Over Kuala Lumpur, there wasn't a cloud in the sky.

She scanned the crowd, with a mixture of hope and apprehension, willing him to be there, desperate to see his face: the cautious smile, the bright, inquisitive eyes. But he wasn't there. At least not in the meet and greet area. He might have wandered off somewhere, she reasoned. After all, her plane had come in late. So she waited, repeatedly shifting from spot to spot to avoid being in anyone's way, careful not to intrude upon the fond reunions of strangers.

Eventually she found herself a place by the wall and squatted down next to her suitcase to wait a little bit longer. When she had been there for almost forty minutes she realized that he wasn't coming.

Feeling drained and weary – but why had she raised her expectations so? – she got to her feet and started to walk.

The domestic terminal was small, with little to interest anyone not taking a flight in or out. There was the odd souvenir shop, and some kiosks selling snacks, cigarettes, magazines. Without any awareness of what she was looking at, she stared at the items on display, occasionally stopping to pick something up, to touch, to feel, working her way from shop to shop as if in a trance. Every so often, she glanced up, willing him to be there, knowing that he wouldn't be.

She was beginning to feel claustrophobic; she longed to go outside, into the sunshine and fresh air, but she was reluctant to leave. Just in case. And, as usual, her mind was busy filling in the gaps to a story she didn't yet know. It was odd that Lee hadn't telephoned Buah Lodge when he found out about his flight – for if he had, then they would have told him she had left, and he would have been there to meet her. Wouldn't he? So did that mean he didn't know? Either that or he'd had second thoughts.

Was she being foolish to think that she had meant anything at all to him?

So what now? She couldn't stay where she was. Nor could she simply give up and walk away – there was too much unresolved. And if he hadn't got on a plane, it meant that he was still somewhere in the city –

In the seconds that followed, it became imperative for her to be there too – it was as if some invisible magnet were pulling at her. He was out there, somewhere; and if she stayed where she was, she would never find him. All rationality abandoned, she searched around for a sign telling her where she could find a taxi.

But even as she walked towards the exit, some other thought was pulling hard at the back of her mind, slowing her down; and in the end it became a burden she wasn't able to throw off.

Maybe he didn't want to be found.

∞

Phil stared out at the sprawl of modern condominiums, some completed, others half-built, that were edging their way towards the jungle-clad hills. He was glad to be back in the city at last, eager to rid his boots and clothes of the irritating sand they had acquired, and for the feel of concrete under his feet; you knew what was what in the city, even a foreign one. Every so often the bus rattled into action and progressed another few feet before jolting to a standstill; the notorious road from Subang Airport was living up to its reputation.

He still didn't understand why Isabel had turned down the offer of an afternoon in KL. It was annoying too. If he'd had her to himself for once, he might have made a little more progress. Ah well, her loss. At least he now had her address in London. And if he could get a trip to England sorted out, then who knew?

He reached into his pocket and fingered the folded sheet of paper; all the time he'd been sitting next to her, he'd worried that it might fall out. No doubt he should have copied the details, then left it where it was, instead of taking the darned thing. But there hadn't been time. And he didn't have a pen. He couldn't imagine what she saw in that jerk anyway. He'd probably done her a favour.

∞

It was time to move. Dusk had been replaced by night: the plate glass window ceased to offer a link to the world outside, and was now merely a reflection of the shabby interior. There was no point staying there any longer. It had been the one place she could find that had had a view over the main entrance, and the road outside. If he had come to look for her, she would have seen him arrive. There was no other way into the building.

From the corner of her eye, Isabel saw herself stand and gather up her bag, and the can of drink she had long since tired of. She had been sitting in the same position for too long and her body was stiff; her blood, when it started to flow unimpeded once more, sent pins and needles to her feet. Catching one last glance of herself, she turned her back on the window and walked towards the stairs leading down to the main hall of the international terminal.

There was a harsh finality about going through the doors marked 'Passengers Only', but she had put it off for as long as she could.

On the plane, she stowed her hand luggage in the overhead locker and took her seat. Moments later she was up again, retrieving her camera from the bag. She sat down once more and fastened her seatbelt, holding the camera close, running her fingers over its contours, gently, as if it were a living thing. What was inside that rigid body was something of great value, that had to be protected at all cost. She slid the camera from its case and switched it on, checking to see how many frames she had left before the roll of film was finished. Ideally, she would have wound it to the end, taken it out, and stored it safely inside its plastic container; but she had lost more than one set of photos trying to do just that. She prayed, too, that the film hadn't been affected by the security x-ray. What it contained was all she had of Lee. She could picture his face for now, but the image would certainly fade with the passing of time, and all she would have was the photograph.

She could sense that the man seated next to her was watching what she was doing and that, given a chance, he might attempt to engage her in conversation. She had glanced at him, briefly, when he had seemed to fold himself into his seat and apologized for knocking against her arm; and they had exchanged cautious pleasantries. She felt sorry for him. So many hours confined to such an inadequate space. He had a kind face: intelligent, thoughtful. But she hoped he wouldn't talk to her. She didn't feel like talking to anyone at the moment.

She looked out of the window, but all that was visible to her was a vast stretch of pale metal. Then the aircraft banked, and for a precious few moments she could see the glittering lights of the city below: lights from homes, from mosques, from the cars still snaking round the highways, even at this late hour. Lee was down there, too; he was in one of those streets, in one of those buildings. She was sure of that. Her throat tightened and there was a pricking sensation behind her eyes. Then the plane tipped back again, and there was nothing more to see.

At last, the tears came. They spilt onto her cheeks, down over her jaw, to her neck, and formed dark, damp patches on the fabric of her blouse; they obscured the view of the grey metal wing. But still she kept her face turned to the window, lest her kindly neighbour should see that she was crying.

PART SEVENTEEN

Edinburgh and London
June 2001

∞

6.15 pm

For a second, Isabel thinks she has misheard what he said, but his words are still there, hanging between them: *I didn't get any note.*

'You didn't get . . .? I don't understand. I left . . .'

No, she thinks, this is all wrong. Memories: just fragments now – things that once needed to be said, things she once needed to know; all this is spinning around in her head. She is finding it difficult to think. And still, she clings to the one thing that is going to make everything all right: he is mistaken; she did leave a note. But he is looking at her now. And his face tells her everything she needs to know.

'You didn't get my note.' No longer a question. 'You thought . . .' It is beginning to make sense. 'You thought I'd left. Without saying goodbye, or anything?'

Lee nods. 'Yes . . . no . . . not exactly like that. I didn't know –' And softer, so she could barely hear him: 'I didn't know what to think. I tried to find you.'

∞

He had carried her address around with him, in his wallet. For weeks it had stayed there, a crumpled piece of paper, the only bit of her he had. Even afterwards, he had kept it, as if letting it go would be a betrayal; he couldn't bring himself to throw it away, even when he knew it was worthless.

He had been in London for three weeks before he had summoned up the courage to go there, not sure of the welcome he would receive. When he had found out what had happened that day, he knew, deep down, that she had done the right thing; in fact he would have told her to do the same, had he been there. And Gilbert wasn't to know what devastating consequences his actions were to have. But all the same, he had been disappointed that she hadn't left a message for him. No note. Nothing. And he was puzzled. He asked everyone – were they sure there was no message? He became angry, convinced that someone must have been given a note, forgotten about it, lost it. He simply couldn't believe that she hadn't tried to contact him. But as the days went by, weeks, months, and the one friendly postcard he had sent went unacknowledged, he came to the conclusion that she must have changed her mind about everything. He couldn't blame her for that.

By the time he found himself in London, the intervening couple of years had helped to blunt the pain of rejection. So he decided to challenge fate and take control of his own destiny, or at least put an end to the doubts and uncertainties that had been clawing at him ever since she had left. And why shouldn't one old friend look up another? he had asked himself. It was nothing more than that.

He remembers the journey: it was supposed to be easy; just one line – the dark blue one – Piccadilly – and no changing. And he couldn't believe that for the past three weeks he had been living just a few tube stops away from her. He had studied an *A-Z* – get on at Holloway Road – get off at Manor House – names now as familiar to him as the street names of Kuala Lumpur; but then they might just as well have been places on the moon. The train had clattered through the grimy black tunnels, accelerating towards each station, pulling up with a force that flung stranger against stranger; it wasn't until he reached Kings Cross that he realized he had been travelling in the wrong direction.

When he finally reached Manor House, he was confused by the number of exits to the streets above. How was he to know which one to take? He took one at random, and when he emerged he was faced with a busy intersection. Four wide roads. Four streams of traffic. Four different ways to choose from. But he was relieved to discover that he had, at least, found the street he was looking for, then was soon perplexed to find that it extended in opposite directions; and the numbering system made no sense to him. In the end, he turned and walked in the direction that appealed to him most: the road that contained the most trees, and the fewest dilapidated buildings.

The number he had on his piece of paper corresponded to a three-storey house, set back from the road. A narrow strip of yard contained some wilting shrubs that had outgrown their pots, a couple of motorbikes, and four plastic dustbins. There were three doorbells: 'Flat One', 'Flat Two', Flat Three'. The first two bells produced no response, but in answer to the third, he was surprised when a tall, bearded guy had opened the door.

The man was bare-chested, bare-footed and wearing a pair of faded, blue jeans. 'Yeah? What's up?'

Lee almost lost his nerve and was ready to pretend that he had made a mistake, come to the wrong house. If this was her boyfriend, his turning up out of the blue like this might cause problems. But having got this far – further than the guy at the door could ever have imagined – he resolved to carry it through.

But the guy had never heard of anyone called Isabel. 'Tried one of the other flats?' he had asked. Then, before Lee could do more than shake his head: 'Sorry – can't help you.'

Lee had stood beside the closed door for several minutes, studying his piece of paper, not knowing what to do next. There was no mention of a flat, just one number, the number of the house. He could come back later, he thought, and try one of the other bells again. But there had been nothing of Isabel in the grubby net curtains that shielded the windows, nor in the parched looking plants, or the flaking paint on the door: nothing to give him any glimmer of hope that she might, somehow, be connected to this building. He never did go back.

When he looks at her again, her head is bowed, her hands busy with the piece of tissue she is still holding. She has folded it carefully into a neat square, now she is unfolding it, twisting it, untwisting it; finally she balls it up into her fist.

All the time he is thinking: she did leave me a note after all; and she thought I never replied.

Now she has looked up at him. 'You tried to find me?'

Her face is pale, her eyes wide, fearful, like an animal frozen in the headlights of an approaching car.

'When did you . . .? How did you try to find me?'

'I had your address,' he tells her. 'You know, the one you put in our guest book, when you arrived at Buah Lodge.'

He can see her struggling to make sense of what he is telling her; her mouth moves, makes shapes, as if she is rehearsing the words before allowing them to come out.

'My address?' she says, almost to herself. 'Oh God.' And then to him: 'I'd forgotten about the book. Which address? – no, you'll have forgotten it now – but I moved. You wrote to me?'

'It was in north London – N4.'

'You still remember.'

He thinks: how could I forget? 'Not far from Manor House tube station,' he adds.

'How do you know Manor House?' she asks.

The bewildered look on her face makes him want to smile. He wishes now that he hadn't let go of her hand. It would be easy, he sees, to take it up again; it is lying just inches from his own. But he is not sure, not sure of anything at the moment. Some things had changed; some things were still the same.

'Yes, I went to find you,' he says. 'But you weren't there.'

'What? In London? You came all the way to London to find me?'

Not exactly, he thinks, although he would like to tell her otherwise; he would like to tell her that he had jumped on a plane and followed her to England.

And yet, why did he go to London? Why there? Hadn't that decision been all about her – a consequence of the distorting fog he had found himself in after she had left – and nothing to do with the lure of the British education system? It is true that he had justified his actions, time and time again (yes, the course was available in Malaysia; yes, he was aware of the costs; but think about the value of a British qualification) to friends, to his family, all concerned about what he was doing. Who had he been deceiving? Them or himself? And yet, he would never have been able to achieve what he had without it.

'Partly,' he replies. 'But I also came to the UK to study. I went to LSE. Got a degree. Business and Economics.'

He can see she is surprised.

'You came to London, to study?' she asks him. 'When?'

He thinks for a moment, then says: 'Long time ago. But I was there for five years.'

Five tough years, he thinks, but it was worth it. For along with the bits of paper, and the seals and the crests, had come the confidence; and then followed a sort of grudging respect, something he would never, otherwise, have been given. He found, at last, that he could take on the government, and the developers, talk to them in the only language they understood. Because what he had gained, in the end, were the very tools he needed – the tools to give economic value to his beloved environment and its conservation.

'You were in London? For five years?' she asks.

'More or less. I had to go back to Malaysia for a year, to earn some more money.' He laughs, thinking about his time in the kitchens of the Regent and the Pan Pacific, and suddenly he is back there, re-living the heat, and the noise, the clash of steel against steel, the clamour of tongues of at least ten different nations, the sweat dripping from his pores, the smells of the day's cooking always in his nostrils, clinging to his hair, his skin, accompanying him home each night. Until then, he had never experienced the sort of extreme exhaustion that turned his limbs to lead weights, and his mind into a vacuum that continued to resound with shouted orders and instructions long after he had laid his head on his pillow. But those jobs had provided him with a lifeline: they had given him the means to continue with his studies. 'Living in London was more expensive than I had ever imagined,' he says.

There is so much more he could tell her: about his time in London, about his life as it is now, back in Malaysia; but he is aware of the minutes ticking by. Soon, he suspects, she will tell him that she has to go, to catch her flight. And there are other things he would like to tell her too; but he knows he won't. He knows it wouldn't be right –

'I can't believe you were in London all that time,' she is saying, 'and . . . It's just not fair, it's just . . .'

Something in her voice makes him turn to look at her. She is staring down at the ground; he reaches out a hand and lifts her face towards him. There are tears falling onto her cheeks. As he draws her into his arms he can feel her body start to shake.

She tries to talk through her sobs. 'All – those years – wasted – we could have – and you tried to find me.'

'I didn't give up you know,' he says, letting his lips brush against her hair as he speaks. 'I didn't stop looking. Even when I couldn't find you at that address. I thought you must be staying somewhere else, so I looked for your name in the telephone books. I never found it though.'

'No,' she mumbles into his shirt. 'I was ex-directory.'

'But I was always looking for Isabel Raines. I don't think you are Isabel Raines any more. Isn't it Adamson now?'

As soon as the words are out he wishes them unsaid, and he curses himself for being so stupid. He can't see her face but he senses that she has become very still. Perhaps she didn't hear. He prays that she didn't hear.

But she has lifted her head and is staring at him, rubbing at her cheek with the palm of her hand.

'How do you know that?'

∞

They had made it to the departure gate with just minutes to spare. And now, obliged to separate once more, they are sitting in their allocated seats, at opposite ends of the plane, waiting for the seat belt signs to go off, the cue for Lee to switch to the empty seat next to Isabel.

Lee had been astounded to discover that they were both on the same flight, relieved that they were to be allowed more time together. But he knows that this is just a short reprieve, a delaying of the inevitable. And what will happen, he wonders, when they get to Heathrow? Who will be there to meet her? He doesn't know how he will find the strength to walk by, a stranger, while she is reunited with her family. It is a scene he has already played over and over in his mind.

At last, he hears the sound he has been waiting for. While the stewardess is advising passengers to keep their seatbelts fastened when in their seats, he swiftly unbuckles his and stands up, at the same time craning round to locate Isabel. She raises a hand in acknowledgement, then smiles. As he walks down the aisle towards her he keeps his eyes locked on hers, oblivious to anything else around him. He is recalling the first time he saw her, how then, as now, her smile was like a precious gift: not recklessly given away, but bestowed with care; and how it lit up her face, turning mere beauty to radiance; and how it always made his legs turn to jelly.

∞

Isabel is struggling to adjust to everything that has happened. The situation is impossible, she knows that, but the evident strength of feeling she still has for Lee has left her stunned. She watches him approach, her mind in turmoil, her heart full. She can't help noticing how several of the women glance up at him, let their eyes linger on him as he passes: expectant, hopeful. But his eyes are for her alone, and for a moment she enjoys the inner glow that comes with that awareness; she allows herself the flutter of pride that, by rights, should not be hers. She has no claim on him. Yet she now knows what she must have known all along: that she has never stopped loving him.

She is still trying to make sense of what he told her just before they boarded the plane – that he had seen her once in London; he had seen her and walked away. So she hadn't imagined it after all. It *was* Lee she had spotted through the window of a bookshop.

He had seen her face on a poster, he had said, and had come along that day to the book-signing event, hoping to meet her. He was early, and so he had gone into the shop to browse around. That was when he picked up a copy of her book for the first time. He had already noticed that she was using a different name, but had tried to convince himself that it was simply a name she used for writing. But when he read what was written on the cover – about her having a husband and a son – when he saw the stark facts there in black and white, he had decided that turning up like that would be wrong. And so he had left. He hadn't got far when he changed his mind and decided to go back. But when he looked in through the window, saw her surrounded by all those people, he lost his nerve. It wasn't until that moment, he told her, that he had finally understood: she could never be a part of his future; and he needed to get on with his life. Without her.

If only he had come into the shop, she thinks, if only he had spoken to her. But would it have changed anything? Wasn't it already too late?

That, she realizes, is one question she will never be able to answer.

She has so many other questions to ask him too, so many things she wants to know, but he is not with her yet; he is still standing in the aisle, opening and closing luggage lockers, looking for somewhere to put his bag. Another passenger has stood up; he is going to move his luggage to make more room, they exchange pleasantries. Then, at last, Lee eases himself into the seat next to her.

He glances at her and then looks away. 'This feels strange,' he says. 'Now I'm here, I don't know what to say.'

'Same here,' she replies. She manages a smile, although she is not sure now that she feels like smiling. 'If I wrote all this in a novel, people would say it was far-fetched.'

'I read your novel,' he says, quickly. 'The one set in . . . Vietnam, wasn't it? I hope it wasn't based on real life. It was sad.'

She pauses to think for a moment, using the time to pull down her tray-table, hoping he won't notice that her hands are shaking. 'I expect most novels have something of the writer's life in them,' she replies.

He nods.

She wonders if he is waiting for her to say more. But there is nothing more she can say.

At last, he speaks: 'Were you disappointed when I didn't reply to your letter? Or angry? Or . . .' He tails off.

'No I wasn't angry,' she says. 'I was disappointed, and a bit confused. Yes, confused more than anything. It didn't feel right, especially after everything . . .'

She glances up at him but he is fiddling with a button on his shirt. 'I just couldn't believe you had changed your mind so suddenly, that's all.'

'I hadn't,' he says, quietly. 'I never changed my mind.'

He looks at her now, his eyes betraying the carefully arranged features posing as a smile. 'So tell me,' he continues, 'what did it say in your note?'

She hesitates, taken aback by the question; she isn't sure she even remembers exactly what she put. What she does recall, though, is how foolish she had felt, telling him she wanted to go back when, as far as he was concerned, she had been just another holiday romance. And when she heard nothing from him, she wished that she had never left the note at all. 'Oh, I don't remember, exactly,' she says. 'Just that I had to leave. Because of the storm. But I wanted . . .'

No, she thinks, she mustn't tell him that. Not yet anyway.

She had never been the sort of person to take risks, and she had surprised even herself when she had come to that decision. But she had made up her mind and, the day she wrote that note, it couldn't have been clearer what she wanted to do: give up her job, travel back to Malaysia, maybe help with his plans for the new Buah Lodge, and do some writing too, as he had once suggested. She'd had some doubts, of course: she knew that it wouldn't be one long holiday, that the allure of the Bohemian lifestyle she envisioned would not last for long; and that she would have no job nor friends to turn to if it didn't work out. But for once in her life, she was going to follow her heart, instead of her head. If she didn't, such an opportunity might never come her way again.

'I wanted to give you my address and my phone number,' she continues, 'In case you wanted to get in touch with me again.'

'Of course I did,' he says.

'When I didn't hear from you, I thought, at first, that they hadn't forwarded my mail. So I went round to my old flat. But my flatmate swore there had been nothing for me. Anyway, I got myself into such a state that I plucked up courage and phoned Buah Lodge –' She shook her head. 'I've often thought how different things would have been if we'd had email in those days. And it was barely a year before I . . .'

'Hang on,' he interrupted. 'You phoned? I didn't . . .'

'No, I never got through. I think there was something wrong with the lines. In a way I was relieved. I would have been too embarrassed to speak to anyone else, or leave another message. I could visualize you all having a good laugh. After a while I decided that you didn't want to be contacted and so I didn't try again.'

He is staring at her now; he looks shocked.

'I don't believe you thought . . . that I would laugh at you. I would never have done that. How could you think it?'

She shrugs. She doesn't know the answer to that either. Fortunately she doesn't need to think of one: the stewardess has arrived with the refreshment trolley and is leaning across to ask what they would like to drink.

'So what happened with Buah Lodge?' Isabel asks, as soon as the drinks have been served and the stewardess has moved on.

'Well, I think I said before, I never got the loan I needed to buy out Gilbert's share. The Mayang people were offering too much anyway. So there was nothing I could do but let them buy me out too. Of course, they offered me a job. They even said I could continue living there. But I couldn't accept that. However much they offered, I could never have stayed. How could I? To watch it all being destroyed and turned into something alien, against everything I believed in? I am afraid that I haven't been back there since. I don't want to see what they have done with it.'

'I did. I went there.'

He looks at her, astonished. 'What do you mean? You went back to Teluk?'

'Yes. I had to go to KL again on business. So I thought I would give it one more try – to contact you. I was scared – I didn't know what sort of reception I would get. But of course you were long gone by then.'

'When was this?'

'Oh, back in . . .' she has to think, to work out the dates. 'Ninety-three, I think. Summer – no, wait – it was September. It . . .'

'Ninety-three?' he interrupted, 'that was when I went to London for the first time. In August.'

Just one month, she thinks. One month too late. What twisted bit of fate had made her go in September? Why couldn't she have gone before? 'It was awful,' she says. 'Your part of the beach was fenced off, marked private, no-one could go there. It was a mess, a building site . . .' She stops speaking for a moment so she can bring it to mind, like a photograph, but one she has never taken

'You know what I remember most?' she continues. 'The poor birds – those lovely green ones that used to make such a noise in the evening – they were confused; they had nowhere to perch – just cranes and metal girders all over the place. All their trees had gone.'

She remembers too, how she had walked on to the village. It was still there, but when she drew close she could see that the buildings were just empty shells. She had gone as far as Coconut Café, wondering if she might find Joseph. But the door was padlocked and the windows tightly shuttered. There was a gaping hole in the corrugated-iron roof.

'I'm sorry,' she says suddenly. 'I don't suppose you want to hear about that.'

He reaches across to touch her arm. 'It's fine,' he says. 'It sounds just as I have always imagined it. And I have moved on now. I have my new project.'

Isabel is glad of the opportunity to change the subject away from Buah Lodge. 'So tell me about it,' she says. 'Start from the beginning, I want to know everything.'

He laughs. 'I'm not sure we have long enough for that. We will be landing in less than twenty minutes.'

∞

As soon as the words are out, Lee understands what it means: in less than half an hour they will have landed at Heathrow and will be going their separate ways. Nothing has been said about what happens next.

He suddenly realizes that he might never see her again and the thought hits him like a bullet to the chest. He has to do something, whatever the consequences: if he doesn't, he will never forgive himself. He has just found out that his entire life has been screwed up by a series of stupid misfortunes. Yet, although he can't quite believe it, he has been given another chance. One last chance. He has got to take it.

He takes a deep breath in, rehearses the words he is going to say, then turns to her and speaks. 'I am in London for a few days – until the eighteenth of June – that's next Monday. I don't suppose . . . perhaps we could meet – or would it be too difficult – for lunch, or dinner, or something. For old times?' He stops and looks down at the empty plastic tumbler that had contained his drink; he wants to pick it up, crush it in his fist. *For old times*. What the hell did that mean? Everything has come out wrong, too casual, as if he doesn't care less either way. And he does care: he cares very much.

He sneaks a glance at her and sees that she is about to speak. He prepares his face, in readiness for the reply that he knows is going to break his heart.

'What are you doing tonight?' she says.

At first he doesn't understand what she means. He tries to think of the name of the hotel he is booked into, but he can't bring it to mind. He must have been gawping at her, foolishly, because she has taken hold of his hand and is squeezing it gently.

'Dinner. We could have dinner tonight. If you are free.'

'What? When we get off the plane?'

'Well, not immediately. But in town. Where are you staying?'

'Aren't you being met?'

'No, I'm not being met.'

He wants to feel happier. She has agreed to have dinner with him. But this is overshadowed by things that have yet to be mentioned. He is going to have to ask.

'Your husband?' The word feels vile in his mouth; he has never hated anyone before in his life but now he finds himself hating and despising someone he has never even met. And he hates himself for becoming such a person.

'No. David – that's my husband – he's away.' Her mouth dips into a frown. 'He wouldn't have met me in any case.'

He wants to ask 'why not?' He wants to ask what sort of idiot would neglect her like that, to leave her to get home by herself. But he doesn't want to talk about her husband; he doesn't want to acknowledge that he exists.

'Where did you say you were staying?' she asks him.

'Islington.'

'Well – we can have dinner in Islington. There's bound to be somewhere open – even if it's late. And I can easily get home from there.'

She seems in good spirits now, excited almost. She still has hold of his hand and she squeezes it as she speaks. 'Go on then,' she says. 'Now that's settled you can tell me about what you're doing now. Where is it? No, tell me about London first. Tell me everything you have done since you left Buah Lodge.'

He laughs, affected by her change of mood. 'We only have fifteen minutes before we land. Where do you want me to start?'

'Don't be silly,' she replies. 'We've got all evening.'

There is so much he could tell her; but how much of it does he want to remember himself? His time in London, on the whole, had been the most miserable time in his life: he had been always cold, always short of money, always hungry. Maybe he can tell her about it another time; maybe they can laugh about it together. But not now. Now isn't the time for being sad. So he tells her how he had found himself with a sum of money from the sale of his share in Buah Lodge, and how he was determined to use it to fulfil his dream of owning his own, small resort.

'It wasn't easy,' he says. 'We had a financial crisis in Malaysia, and the *ringgit* was devalued, along with my savings. But, in a way, it helped me out as well. Property was cheap to buy and there was lots of it around. Companies were reluctant to invest in South East Asia. All of a sudden there was very little competition.'

'But what made you study economics?' she asks. 'Why not conservation or environmental studies, or something like that? That was what you always wanted to do wasn't it?'

'Ah, but you see, they are so absolutely linked together – or at least the way I see it – have always seen it really. Those two things – the environment and economics – need not be in opposition but, in fact, can exist side by side. I just needed to know the right words, so that I could explain it to other people. Now I can show people how to help the environment, instead of exploiting it. And I, too, can give something back, *really* do it, not just play – how do you say it? – play lip-service –'

'*Pay* lip-service,' she corrects him.

'Yes, pay lip-service like so many others are doing now.'

'So where are you based?'

'In East Malaysia – on a peninsula – it is beautiful. And near a national park – not far from Sarawak. Have you ever been there?'

She shakes her head.

'No, neither had I. And it was chance that took me there too. I had been lucky to make a good friend in London. Chi Wan. We were on the same course – right from the beginning. Anyway, we stayed friends, and when I finished all my studies in '98, that summer he invited me back to his home – in East Malaysia. Chi Wan's father was interested in my plans and, to my surprise, he offered to lend us – me and Chi Wan – the money to set it up.' Lee chuckles to himself when he remembers Chi Wan's reaction to the news.

'What's funny?' Isabel asks

'Oh I am just thinking about Chi Wan. I think he had been hoping to laze about for a bit after he had got his Masters, and was quite surprised to find himself suddenly going into business. But, you know, I couldn't have found a better partner. He's not lazy at all, by the way, he works very hard. At first he was going to concentrate on the business side of things, while I did all the other stuff. But it turned out he really enjoyed going out into the community, meeting people, all that sort of thing. Some of our best ideas have come from him. And he's great with the kids – well, he's just a big kid himself. We do quite a bit of work with the local schools as well.'

'Do you . . .'

He waits for her to finish her sentence, but she hesitates, and then says: 'I mean, what sort of work do you do then? It sounds a bit different to Buah.'

'Well, it's not quite a resort in the traditional sense. It's in the middle of a rainforest. It's more of a conservation project – where people can stay. It certainly isn't for those who want to experience Malaysia from the safety of a hotel complex – like the Mayang. Remember the Mayang?'

'Do you have children of your own?' she asks, suddenly.

Her question surprises him. He wonders if she is being funny. But he can't catch her eye.

'No,' he replies. 'Of course not.' He senses they are on dangerous ground. He decides to change the subject. 'You know, if it wasn't for Chi Wan, I wouldn't be here now.'

'What do you mean?'

'He does all the travel fairs and exhibitions these days. He enjoys talking to people – he's a perfect salesman. The last one I did was back in 2000. That was the last time I was in London. Anyway, Chi Wan was supposed to be doing this one but he fell over and broke his foot or something. He's hobbling about in plaster – and he hates it. I wish you could meet him. I think you would like him.'

'I wish I could meet him too,' she says quietly.

∞

9.30 pm

They have decided to go to the hotel first, to drop off Lee's luggage, before going out for dinner. Now Isabel stands idly leafing through a glossy magazine, her own bag at her feet, while Lee checks-in. From time to time she glances over to where he is; she studies the curve of his back, watches the way the muscle in his forearm tightens as he writes, sees him laugh at something the receptionist has said to him as she hands back his credit-card.

Eventually he moves away from the desk, clutching a key. He scans the lobby, his eyes darting over the sofas and chairs, the ornate rugs, the console tables with their displays of pungent-smelling flowers, until they finally rest on Isabel; he smiles, with obvious relief.

He picks up his briefcase and wheels his case to where she is standing. 'Sixth floor,' he says, as soon as he reaches her. 'Shall we go?'

She stays where she is. She realizes her legs are shaking. 'Don't you want me to wait here?' she asks.

He shakes his head. 'We need the lift.' He nods towards the far end of the lobby. 'I'm room 602.'

He lets her into the room and she makes for the window, while he follows with his luggage. The curtains have already been drawn, and she searches for a way to open them. She finds the cord and pulls on it; the curtains part, revealing a spread of multi-coloured lights, and a burnt orange sky that she knows will never darken.

'Look,' she says, without turning away from the window, 'you can see St Paul's from here – just about.'

He joins her at the window and they stand together, looking

out. Neither of them speaks. Her hand is resting on the window-ledge; he reaches out to touch it, running his fingers over her skin, tentatively, as if it is something new to him. Then he wraps it in both of his own.

She turns to face him, and he pulls her towards him, enclosing her in his arms. A moment later, their lips are pressed together; they are sipping, drinking, gulping each other in, as if their very survival depended on it.

Now he has stepped back. He is looking into her eyes; she returns his gaze. He touches her face with the palm of his hand; he moves his thumb slowly, gently, tracing over her cheek, following the line of her jaw, until it reaches her lips; she opens her mouth, just a fraction, letting the tip of her tongue reach out to meet it. Without a word, he takes her hand and leads her away from the window, towards the bed. But after two steps, he stops, to kiss her once more, softly this time – her mouth, her neck, her throat. She moves her hands from his shoulders and unfastens the buttons of his shirt, one by one, before slipping her fingers beneath the fabric, then around his waist, pulling him closer to her. In one movement he sweeps her up into his arms and carries her to the bed.

∞

It was as if they were making up for those ten lost years. For now, there would be no more searching; for the moment, all doubts and fears were cast away by their kisses, their caresses. It was as if they would never be able to quell their thirst for each other, never rest until they had taken in every last, precious drop, every touch, every word, every contour of the other's body, and commit it to memory: sensing, as they both seemed to, that, one day, this was all they would have. For the briefest of times in the span of their lives, they had been allowed to come together, to merge into one another, to become one.

Even when they finally slept, it was as if they couldn't bear to be parted, not for a single moment. It seemed they both understood that either one of them, without the other, would never be a complete person again. They lay, face to face, lip to lip, and breathed each other in, limbs entwined, as if each were afraid to let the other go.

∞

5.45 *am*

It is the sunlight, spearing through a gap in the curtains, that wakes her. But the events of yesterday have already tumbled into her consciousness, played themselves out behind her closed eyes, and now, without warning a tear slides out; she feels its warmth as it runs into her hair and wets the pillow beneath her head. She mustn't cry, she tells herself, but the immense surge of relief – and desolation – is almost unbearable. What will happen now? What can happen? However many times she goes over it in her mind, she is unable to come up with any answers.

For them to be together would mean tearing apart so many other lives –

How can she even contemplate it? She mustn't contemplate it. David, Tom, her parents . . . They don't deserve that. And yet, how can she not be with Lee? Must she forget everything that has happened? Unlearn all she knows of him? Because if she doesn't, her life will never be the same again: it is already re-shaping itself to contain him; and soon every thought, every action, every last mundane detail of it, will have him in it.

She feels him stir beside her, and within moments he is leaning over her – she can feel the touch of his hair as it brushes against her face – and he is kissing her; first her cheek, then her eyelids: kissing away her tears, one by one, with soft, gentle movements of his lips, like whispers on her skin.

She opens her eyes, and manages to smile.

He says her name: once, twice; there is something about the way he says it – like a caress – then: 'Don't cry, Isabel. Please don't cry. Ai! This is all my fault.'

'No, don't say that. It isn't. I don't know why I'm crying. I'm happy – I am – really. I just don't understand – I can't understand. How can something that feels so right, and so absolutely perfect, be so wrong? Is it wrong? And then you'll go away again, and . . .'

They have been lying under a thin, cotton sheet, and now he begins to pull it away, inch by inch, and as he does, he moves his mouth over her body as it is uncovered by the movement of the sheet. 'I'm not going anywhere,' he says.

She pulls him towards her, sliding her hands over the taut, silk-like skin, until they reach the curve in the small of his back; then she guides his body to where she wants it to be. As he presses into her, she hears him sigh, feels the warmth of his breath on her neck. She reaches out for his hand and grips onto it with such a force that she can feel the tiny bones moving beneath his flesh. Her head resounds with the words she has yearned to say, words she needs to say to him. Silently, she repeats them, over and over again, then, at last, she tells him: she puts her lips to his ear, and tells him that she loves him.

She wakes with a start, blinking her eyes against the brightness of the light, and the gritty remnants of her tears. The side of the bed where he had been is empty. For a long, heart-stopping second she thinks that he has gone, but no, she can hear the sound of running water in the bathroom, the clink of metal against glass, the sound of humming. She raises herself onto one elbow, pulling the sheet around her, and reaches over to the bedside table where he has left his watch; it tells her it is quarter past eight. She remembers that he has an exhibition to go to; and that he was supposed to have been there at eight o'clock.

He must have heard her, because now he is standing in the doorway, dressed: a pair of blue jeans and a white shirt rolled up at the sleeves and open at the neck, just enough to reveal the smooth, biscuit-coloured skin of his chest. He is holding a toothbrush in one hand.

'You were asleep,' he says. 'I didn't want to wake you.' He has stepped across to the bed and is leaning over to kiss her. 'You looked as though you needed it.'

'But you would have, wouldn't you?' she asks. 'You wouldn't have left without waking me.'

'Of course not.' He puts down the toothbrush and sits on the bed beside her. 'From now on, I'll never go anywhere without telling you first.'

She laughs and puts her arms around him, resting her head on his shoulder. His shirt smells clean, freshly laundered; she can feel the warmth of him through it. She resists the urge to undo the buttons and slide her hands inside.

'Are you late?' she asks.

'Yes.'

'And you've missed breakfast?'

'Yes. But I don't need any. You should have something. Ring for room-service. Now, listen to me –' He reaches out for her hand and squeezes it gently. 'I'll be back as soon as I can. You won't go anywhere will you?'

She shakes her head.

'I will set up my stand, and hang around for a while today. Then I'll leave some leaflets and stuff around for people tomorrow, and then . . .'

'Can you do that?' she interrupts him. 'I mean, not be there, just like that.'

'Of course. I can do what I want.'

'Okay.'

'And then,' he continues, 'we can do all those things you said.'

He takes her chin and tilts it, so she has to look into his eyes. They are so very dark, it is impossible to see the line separating the middle circle from the outer rim.

'Are you sure?' he asks her. 'Are you sure that you want to stay here with me until I go back? I don't want to cause you any problems, at home, with your husband.'

'I told you,' she replies. 'He's away.'

'Yes, but what about friends, or anyone else that might recognize you? You're a famous author, don't forget.'

'No I'm not famous.' She laughs and shakes her head away from his hand. 'And that's the thing about London isn't it? It lets you disappear. How else could we have been living here, both of us, all those years, without . . .?'

'I'll make up for it,' he says. 'We can go to all those places. A boat on the river, the zoo – You said you wanted to go there didn't you? And where else? You can make a list while I'm gone.'

She stretches out and puts her arms around him again, bringing him close, holding him as tight as she can for a moment and then: 'Go on,' she says, 'you'll be even later than you already are.' She pushes gently at his arm, but he seems reluctant to move. 'Go on, silly. I'll be here when you get back. I might go out to buy a few bits and pieces, but I won't go far.'

He kisses her – a long, tender kiss – then he jumps up, grabs his briefcase and makes for the door.

When he has gone, when she has heard the ping of the lift as it arrives on their floor, when she has listened out for the sound of the doors, whirring open, then closing with a muffled clunk, she lies back on the bed and presses her fingers to her lips, still moist from his kiss, wondering how on earth they are going to make up for all that lost time, in just three days.

At four o'clock she rings David.

He picks up the phone after just two rings. It is too soon.

'David Adamson.'

It is unsettling to hear his voice, at the same time familiar and yet strangely unfamiliar. She realizes straight away that she shouldn't have phoned from here, not from this room: still filled with them; and their love.

'Hello David.'

'Isabel?'

'How are you? Is everything okay?'

'Yeah – '

She thinks he has finished, so she starts to speak: 'I just, I . . .'

But he is saying something too; their voices have crossed, somewhere over the Atlantic.

'. . . good. I was just on my way to breakfast.'

'Oh – all right,' she jumps in before he speaks again. 'I won't keep you then. I just wanted to let you know . . .'

She pauses to gather her thoughts, to make sure she has it right.

'I'm staying up here a few days longer – just till Monday. Mum and Dad want to go to Gullane for the weekend – take Tom to the beach.' This is the lie she has prepared, in case he calls the house in Edinburgh. But at the mention of Tom's name, a tide of guilt threatens to capsize her.

She hears David's breath down the phone. He is waiting for her to continue. Does she have more? Yes. She remembers now. 'So I'll fly down early Monday morning but I'll go straight to T and S from the airport – they phoned to say there's some work in for me. Is that okay?' She acknowledges the futility of the question.

'Yeah, fine. What's the weather like there? Good?'

'Hot.' She almost adds 'and steamy', but stops herself just in time. Despite the innocent truth, it doesn't seem appropriate in the circumstances. 'You still back on . . .? What is it? Sunday?' she asks.

'Sunday,' he confirms. 'And I was planning to take Monday off. But it looks like I've got to go to a meeting, first thing – in town. Somewhere near Marble Arch as far as I know. You don't know where Bryanston Street is do you, by any chance?'

'No – well – somewhere around there, yes.'

'Won't do them much good, having me there with jet-lag,' he adds. 'But I can't get out of it. Anyway, I should be done by lunchtime, and I'll probably crash out soon as I get home. Don't suppose there's any food in is there?'

'No, I've been away for a week – remember. You could have a look in the freezer.'

She realizes he hasn't asked after Tom? 'And Mum and Dad wanted to keep Tom with them all next week – so I thought that would be nice for him . . .'

'Good. It will give you a break.'

'So I'll see you at home then. Monday evening.'

'Right. Do you want me to get a takeaway?'

'If you want. Yes, that would be nice.'

She feels calmer now, comforted by the veneer of normality, the nod to the old routines. He doesn't deserve this, she thinks. He hasn't done anything wrong. Except be himself. The fault is hers – in choosing the wrong man. And whatever happens, he mustn't suffer because of it. She won't walk away from him, just because she wants to spend her life with someone else.

'See you Monday night then,' he is saying. 'Got to dash – or I'll miss breakfast. Have fun.'

'Bye,' she says. But he has already put down the phone.

∞

For two days, Isabel and Lee wrapped themselves in the semblance of a perfect existence, seemingly unaware of its ultimate fragility. By day they explored the city they both knew but, until now, had never been able to share; by night they came to rest in the increasingly familiar haven of room 602, where they acted out a near as normal life in the only place they could, jointly, call home.

They fell upon London with the exuberance of children at a birthday spread, gorging themselves on its simple pleasures, finding enjoyment in everything around them, as well as in each other. It was hot, hotter than an average June, and the nights were heavy, sultry, threatening a storm that never managed to break through. They visited the zoo; they strolled by the river, and ate ice creams on Waterloo Bridge; they sat and watched jugglers and acrobats in Covent Garden, and later ate in a restaurant where the diners were served by men wearing long, brown robes.

On Sunday morning they took a bus to Shoreditch and looked for the flower market in Columbia Road. They went to Spitalfields, where he bought her a pair of jet earrings, and they ate the best curry that either of them had ever had, in a shabby-looking place just off Brick Lane. Then, that evening, they had joined a guided walk and held hands while they listened to the tale of Jack the Ripper.

To watch them, they were like any other two people in love. No-one would have guessed at the growing weight of emotion pressing down on each of them, as the hours marched on, leading them inevitably towards the moment they had both been fearing. But on the bus back to Islington, they barely spoke: they both seemed to know that their borrowed time was coming to an end; and that the conversation they had been studiously avoiding all day, must surely now take place.

∞

10.00 pm

They walk into the lobby, hand in hand, Lee making for the lift; but Isabel holds back. Although she yearns to be in the exquisite comfort of his arms, to have him ignite, once again, those feelings she thought had long since died, she isn't ready, yet, to face the room, with its subtle reminders of tomorrow: the pile of neatly folded clothes; a half-packed bag; the Malaysia Airlines ticket-wallet sitting next to the telephone – so he won't forget to call the airline in the morning.

She feels she will break down if she has to think about tomorrow. She pulls on his arm. 'Do you want to have a drink? A nightcap?'

He looks at her, as if she has said something he doesn't quite understand. He pauses for a moment before replying: 'If you want to –'

She doesn't, but she nods and leads him away from the lift, towards the bar.

When he has ordered their drinks, he joins her at the table she has chosen – a secluded booth at the far side of the room. He sits alongside her on the leather banquette, and takes her hand. They wait, in silence, for their drinks to arrive.

He has ordered a coffee, she has a glass of brandy. Half-turned towards him, her hand resting on his knee, she watches as he picks up the sachet of sugar from the saucer, tears it open, pours it into the cup and stirs. He passes her the chocolate that has arrived with it.

Three days ago, she thinks, this man was no more than a fading memory of happier days, a love that had never been allowed to blossom: until now. Now he is there, flesh and blood, sitting next to her; if she were to lean in closer she could touch his hair,

457

trace the delicate ridge of his cheekbone with her fingers, kiss his mouth. But all she wants to do is to look at him, to memorize the shape of his lips, the angular perfection of his face, the way his eyes crinkle at the corners when he smiles, and how he tugs on the lobe of his ear when he is thinking.

He is looking down into his coffee cup; she can hear the buzz of other people's conversations coming from the room behind her. 'You know,' she says on impulse, 'there is so much I don't know about you.'

He lifts his head and looks at her, then picks up his cup and takes a sip. She can't read his expression.

'I mean,' she goes on, quickly, 'I know about what you are doing now, and what you have done in the last few years, but what about before? What about when you were a child?'

'What do you want to know?'

'Oh, I don't know. What were you like at school? Did you get into trouble?'

'Ah,' he says.

She waits.

'Sometimes.' He takes another sip of coffee. 'Sometimes I used to miss classes – when I could get away with it. But my dad was a teacher. So it was a bit difficult.'

She remembers now. He had once told her about his father; that he had died, when Lee was still at school.

'What about your mother?' she asks. 'And sister? You have a sister don't you?'

'Yes, Pau Ling.'

'And now you are living in Borneo – do you ever get to see them?'

His hand moves once more to his cup, but he doesn't pick it up. His arm rests on the table for a moment. Then he turns towards her, grasping her hands in his. 'I can't do this, Isabel. I'm sorry.'

She sees that there are tears in his eyes.

'I'm sorry,' he says again. 'I can't pretend that everything is fine, and normal. I can't talk about these things – all the things that we should be talking about – when I know that in a few hours we will have to say goodbye. When my heart is breaking.'

She puts her arms around him and rests the side of her face

against his shoulder. His body is taught: she can feel no movement in him at all. Not even his breathing. Neither of them speaks for a while, they just sit where they are, holding on to each other. He is the first to pull away; he wipes his face on his sleeve.

She knows then: it will be impossible to let him go, to let him disappear from her life again; somehow, they will have to find a way to be together.

'We don't have to say goodbye,' she says eventually. 'I'll come to Malaysia – well, not immediately. But soon. I can bring Tom – he would love it – the rainforest – all the animals . . .'

The plan is forming in her mind as she speaks; it would work out, she is certain, more certain than she has ever been about anything. They could be happy – all of them.

He is shaking his head.

'Why not? It would work. Tom is still young enough; he would soon learn the language. And there must be schools.'

Lee smiles. 'Of course there are schools. Lots of schools. But . . .'

'No, don't say but,' she interrupts him. 'It could work. It has to.'

He grips onto her shoulders and leans his head towards her so that his forehead is touching hers. 'Stop –'

She tries to pull away but he is holding her too firmly.

'You know I want to be with you. I would give anything for things to be different. And I don't know how I am going to let you go. But I must. You are not free. You have to think about your family – your husband, your son, and his future . . .'

'I am . . .'

'Shush, listen to me. Please.' He kisses her lips, softly, and she lets her body relax against his.

'It wouldn't be right to uproot your son, or to take him so far away from his father. I can't ask you to disrupt their lives like that. Not for me.'

'But what about me? It would be for me.'

'Isabel, think about it. Think carefully. Think what it would mean.'

'I have. I know what it would mean. I know it is a terrible thing to do, but I also know that it would be wrong to make us part again. We belong together, Lee, we both know that. You do know that, don't you?

'Of course I do.'

'If you go, and I have to carry on with my life as if nothing has happened, wondering all the time where you are, what you are doing, having to pretend nothing has changed . . . I don't think I could do it.'

'You have to Isabel. Please. You have to help me. I can't be strong on my own.'

'I can't. David doesn't even love me.'

'But he loves his son?'

'I don't know.'

'I'm sure he does. How could anyone not love their son?'

She knows he is right – in a way. But how could she be sure? And if she wasn't sure, then how could she take David's son away from him? Yet, would it be fair on any of them if she stayed? She would not be the same person she had been three days ago; a big part of her would be missing; and she would be little more than an empty shell.

'I can't imagine life without you, she says. 'I won't be able to bear it.'

He rests his elbows on the table and buries his head in his hands. 'I don't know if I will either.'

∞

7.30 am

He wakes to the sounds of a city starting its day and for a moment he lies still, piecing it all together, making sense of it: the whine and crunch of heavy machinery on a construction site, a police-car siren – or an ambulance – he can't tell which – the low growl of an engine revving at a bus-stop in the street below their open window. He recognizes them all; once, those sounds were as familiar to him as they are now to the hundreds of people pounding the city's pavements on their way to work, clutching their briefcases, their coffee mugs made from cardboard, their breakfast in a paper bag. And to Isabel, and her son: those will be the same sounds that provide the background to their lives, too. But it is a million miles away from the life he now leads: a life rooted deep in the raucous jungles and rainforests that he loves so much.

He had lain awake during the night, turning everything over and over in his mind, trying to find a way through it all, while he listened to her gentle breathing as she lay asleep in his arms. He knew that he couldn't simply let it go – all that they had – all that they had become. So should he ask her to come with him? And be responsible for breaking up a family, a marriage. Or was it already broken? Maybe they could be a family. The three of them.

He is no nearer to it now; no nearer to any sort of decision that he likes. All he knows for sure is that, between them, there is something more powerful than either of them knows what to do with. It is clear that they belong together, but it is too late for them. If only he had tried harder to find her all those years ago. Both of their lives would be very different now.

Ai, what have we done? he thinks. What can happen now?

461

He raises himself onto one arm and looks down at her. She stirs, and he pulls her to him and holds her close. He takes in the feel of her, the scent of her, tries to imprint every detail of her onto his mind – to have something of her when she has walked out of his life once more, as he knows she will have to.

∞

He wants to go with her to the underground station, but she tells him no: she couldn't bear to say goodbye to him there. It has to be here.

He takes her hand and they walk together, to the door. As they hold each other for one last time, she grips onto his shirt, bunching the dark blue material in her fingers, as if she is going to tear it away – something to keep – a memento – because, God, she has so little of him. But she doesn't need such things any more – bits and pieces to put away in a box – she has him inside her heart, and she always will have. She has his love; she couldn't be surer of that.

'I can't believe I'm going to walk away from you,' she says into his shoulder.

He moves his hand over her head, strokes her hair, her cheek. 'It has to be,' he says. 'For now. We have to do it this way. It's the right thing. We agreed. But one day things will be different. Your son will grow up, and he will leave you. And I will be waiting. I promise.'

She didn't know she had any more tears left in her, but she starts to cry.

'No Lee, please . . . Please don't make me go.'

His body seems to buckle under the blow her words are inflicting upon him: helpless, defeated.

'Oh God. No, my love.' He pulls away from her, gripping her arms so tightly that he is hurting her. He inclines his head so that he is looking directly into her eyes. 'Isabel, I'm not making you go. I don't want you to go. But you know you must. Listen . . .' he reaches out and tries to wipe away her tears, but they are falling too fast. 'Listen to me, my love. Don't ever – ever – think that I don't want you. You won't think that will you?'

She shakes her head, unable to speak.

'I want you more than anything in the world.' He takes her face in his hands. 'You know, don't you, that I love you.'

She begins to speak, but he puts his finger over her lips. 'No, wait. Let me say this.' His voice is fragile, unsteady. 'I love you Isabel. I love you more than life itself. I have never stopped loving you, and I will never stop loving you. And when you walk out of that door you will take with you my heart, my soul . . .'

She is sobbing now, gasping, her lungs straining for air. 'No, Lee – I can't. I can't, please . . .'

'Isabel, this isn't the end. It's only for now. One day we will be together again. And – listen – we will always be in touch, won't we? You have my number? And the address? And the email?'

She nods.

'We'll keep in touch this time. Not like before.' He tries to smile, but he is crying too.

They cling onto each other again, affirming their love with their bodies. He kisses her, then she breaks away.

She doesn't know how she does it, or where she finds the strength to do it. Her mind is an expanse of black; it has emptied, collapsed in on itself. She has reached down to pick up the red bag and has opened the door. She steps into the corridor and, without daring to turn back to look at him, closes the door behind her and walks away from him; still carrying the sensation of his lips on hers, the touch of his fingers on her cheek. Mementos as fragile as an insect's wings, and just as easily obliterated by the cruel passage of time.

∞

The door closes. His heart is ready to explode with grief. He thinks: what have I done?

He runs across the room to the window. It is open at the top, but not enough for him to lean out fully, to get a better view of the street below. He tussles with the catch but it won't give, it is fixed; it is not meant to be opened more than it is. He thumps it hard with his fist, not registering the pain.

He has to see her.

And suddenly, his eyes catch a flash of orange. He sees her dress first, then the rest of her: Isabel. He cranes to follow her progress along the street. She has already crossed the road; she is walking briskly, her head lowered. It is difficult to keep her in sight: there are too many people. For several seconds he can see her, weaving in and out of the crowds. And he stands, numb, watching her. A bus slides past, obscuring his view of her. He waits for it to move aside. When he can see the pavement again, she has gone: he has lost her.

It is only at that moment, when he can contain it no longer, that he finally breaks down. He stands at the window, his forehead pressed against the glass, huge tears of despair rolling down his face.

'Oh God . . . No . . . Isabel . . . Don't go.' At last, he can say it; he can release the words that have been hammering against the inside of his head all along. 'Please come back, Isabel. Stay with me. Please, please don't go.'

∞

For almost five more hours, Lee stayed in the room that, not so long ago, had been filled with her, with them: it was the one place he knew that encapsulated what they had become, their whole existence together, as a couple. He lay on the bed; sometimes he thought about packing, checking out, making his way to the airport; sometimes he thought about her, wondering where she was, what she was doing – until it became too painful; sometimes he thought of nothing at all, just stared at the narrow, grey curtain rail and the deep-blue piece of sky he could see through the window. Sometimes he felt as though he could sleep – maybe he did sleep, briefly – then there were voices outside, in the corridor, and he remembered where he was: and the sorrow engulfed him once more.

Unable to extend his check-out time any further, he was finally obliged to leave. The hotel manager had been sympathetic, but the hotel was fully booked and the room had to be vacated, to be made ready for the next occupants. As if in a trance, he moved around, picking up the remaining items to go in his suitcase, noticing only the lack of her things, things that had become familiar to him for too brief a time: a purple toothbrush she had put next to his in a glass by the sink; her toilet bag; her comb; the orange linen dress that she had hung in the wardrobe, so the creases would drop out; the bright red holdall. Sometimes it was as if the past few days had been a dream: almost.

At quarter past two he left the hotel and stepped into the sweltering heat of the afternoon. He started to walk, barely aware of anything around him, indiscriminately turning one way rather than another, without knowing or caring why. He drifted into shops, picking things up, putting them down again, his mind empty of anything, except a dulling fog; it was as if he were outside his body, floating somewhere just above it, looking down on a stranger, who was wandering, aimlessly, around the streets of London.

∞

Central London

6.00pm

The sun is still beating down; the city, hot and dry as a furnace. The usually drab streets have taken on an air of celebration; today they are vibrant, colourful. People flit about in search of entertainment: unwieldy groups – dressed more for beach than town, in bright, acid colours – looking like flocks of parrots on the rampage. The stately city squares have, for now, cast off their airs and graces to become little more than common lidos: men and women lie, half-naked, in serried rows on the tinder-dry grass, or lounge on wooden benches. A mass unveiling of flesh. For who knows how long the hot spell will last? Overheated office workers, sleeves rolled to the elbow, dark, wet patches forming on the backs of shirts, abandon their ties and migrate to pubs and bars to drink ice-cold beer from bottles; there, they settle on the already crowded pavements, leaving the dark and cavernous interiors for the few who choose to stay in the cool.

Lee takes the last swig of water from a bottle he brought from the hotel, then throws it into a bin. He is weary; the day has been too long and he wishes it over. He would like to close his eyes, to rest if he could, but that would only bring up ghostly images: of Isabel standing at the door; the flare of her orange dress as she walks away from him.

One day, he thinks, he will be able to remember more than that. He will be able to remember all the good things that have happened: the joy, the passion, the sweet smell of summer on her skin. But for now, all such things elude him.

He has no awareness of where he has been in the past few hours, or what he has done. He hasn't eaten anything, but he doesn't feel hungry. When he looks at his watch, he is relieved to find that it has just gone six o'clock; it is time to make his way to Heathrow. He has just reached the top of Regent Street, near Oxford Circus. If he walks down Oxford Street to Marble Arch, he remembers, he can catch the Airbus. He still has plenty of time. His flight isn't until quarter to ten.

It was fortunate, he supposes, that he had rung the airline that morning, and learnt of the delay to his flight. But four extra hours to kill –

He had wondered, then, whether he would have the strength to hold out for four more hours; or would his already flagging resolve not to call her finally break down? He knew that if he heard her voice, he would tell her that he would stay. He would make a life in London again, so they could snatch a few hours together, from time to time.

His dazed and troubled mind had even latched upon some other thought: that the delay to his flight was a sign, a message from the gods, telling him what to do. For why, otherwise, would they confer upon him four more useless hours – if they were not imploring him to keep hold of what fortune had returned to him?

He glances at his watch once more: almost half past six. She will have left her office by now, he thinks. She will be going home. She may be sitting on a bus, or a tube; and he is saddened to think that he has never asked her about any of this: what sort of journey she has; what it is like when she gets there. There is so much he doesn't know. So much still to learn.

He needs to cross the road, but the traffic is relentless. He will wait until he comes to the next set of traffic lights. He can see Selfridges ahead. He will cross there, he decides, and maybe go inside and buy a card for her. He has her office details now. He can post it from the airport. As soon as he settles upon the idea, he finds within himself a revived sense of purpose; it is a connection with her, a small one, but it will do for now. He almost smiles – something he thought he might never do again. He will repeat what he told her this morning, he thinks, give her faith in the future, give himself faith.

He stands amongst a group of about ten other people at the

edge of the pavement, waiting for the lights to change. An almost identical group stands on the opposite side; they are like bands of outlaws, facing each other down. But as soon as the light turns to green, he knows, they will merely change places, skilfully weaving in and out, yielding one to the other, more like dancers than combatants: an elaborate dance, from another time.

While Lee waits to cross, he looks up at the cloudless sky. There will be a beautiful sunset tonight, he thinks. A bus slides past, a streak of red, the sun glinting silver on its polished metal surface. A moment later, it seems to have lost contact with the ground, lifting into the air with an almost graceful ease. He hears a loud bang.

Lee turns to the person standing beside him. 'What the hell was that?'

For a split second, everything falls eerily silent.

PART EIGHTEEN

Malaysia
June 2007

∞

The street has not changed much since the last time they were here: there is the same crooked row of shophouses; the same racy mix of rotten fruit, incense, spices, fish paste and sewers; pile upon pile of cheap and gaudy plastic goods from China; the same stifling heat. Maybe there are fewer wooden stalls sheltering beneath the colonnades and watched over by diminutive women, with sallow faces as shrivelled and wrinkled as the dried plums they sell in paper packets. Maybe some of the old coffee shops, where men used to sit and smoke and play *mah-jongg* the entire day, have been replaced by newer, brasher versions with glass fronts and tawdry neon lights.

To Isabel's amusement, Tom has used some of his pocket money to buy a green, plastic fly swat, and is currently chasing down the street, swatting indiscriminately at the air. He has got too far ahead of them, she thinks. She will have to rein him in before he annoys too many people.

She uses her free hand to reach into her pocket and pull out a crumpled piece of tissue, which she uses to dab at her face.

'Soooo hot-*lah*,' she says, expertly mimicking the jaunty cadences of Malay-English.

Pau Ling laughs. 'And it isn't even the hottest time yet. But you should be used to it by now.'

'Yes, I am I suppose. But I would rather be by the coast than in the city.'

'So are you going to Muara tomorrow?'

'No, the day after. I thought we should stay here tomorrow, you know . . .'

'Mummy?' Aimee is pulling on her hand, trying to get her attention.

Isabel reaches down and wipes a smear of red from Aimee's cheek. She notices that Tom has stopped jumping around and is waiting for them outside one of the shops. She can see the long, green handle of the fly swat protruding from his pocket where he has carefully tucked it away, for now.

'It will be nice for them to have a little holiday,' Pau Ling says.

'Yes, it will. Tom loves it there – and the orang-utans – and everything. I think he's going to be a vet when he grows up. At least that was what he told me last week.'

'That's good,' Pau Ling says. 'And what about you Aimee? What do you want to be when you grow up?'

Aimee looks up at her, eyes wide, dubious, as if there is a possibility that she is being asked a trick question. 'I don't know yet,' she says. 'I'm only five and a quarter.'

Isabel laughs. 'Some days she wants to be a ballerina. The other day she told me she wanted to have her own *cendol* stall and . . .'

'Mummy?'

'Yes, sweetheart?'

'Shall we buy a car for daddy?'

Isabel glances down at her and smiles. 'Oh, I don't know about that,' she says. 'I don't think daddy likes cars very much.'

'But we are going to get him some money, aren't we?'

'Yes, of course.'

'So he can buy lots of things he likes.'

She feels her throat constrict. For a moment, she thinks her heart is going to burst with love for her precious little girl.

'And a horse,' Aimee concludes, with a firm nod of her head.

They have reached the spot where Tom is standing. He jerks his thumb towards one of the shops. 'This is the one, isn't it? The one we usually go to.'

Isabel reaches out her hand and ruffles his hair, noting with a pang that she no longer has to bend down to do it. He is growing very fast.

'Yes, that's right,' she says. 'This is the one.'

When they come out of the shop, they are each carrying a black plastic bag. Aimee had become tearful when she realized she was not being given a bag of her own to carry; her chin had crumpled, her eyes glistened with tears waiting to spill out. So Isabel had given her the smallest one. Now she is happy again, swinging it around her legs, singing quietly to herself.

Isabel turns to Pau Ling. 'Shall we go for some tea, or do you think we should get back. Maybe your mother will be wondering where we are.'

Pau Ling looks at her watch. 'No, it's fine still. She will be sleeping.'

'All right then. I think we passed a place just down . . .' She stops. There is a man standing in front of her, blocking the way. Isabel looks at him, wondering why he is smiling at her.

'You don't recognize me do you?' he says. 'It *is* Isabel, isn't it?'

The face is vaguely familiar. She thinks she should know who it is. Then something clicks into place. Joseph. Lee's friend Joseph, from Teluk.

He seems taller than she remembers, maybe he has put on some weight too; but it is the same gentle, boyish face, the same spiky crew cut, making him look like a kindly hedgehog. How could she have forgotten him? She smiles. 'Hello Joseph.'

'Wow! What a surprise. What are you doing here? Do you live here?'

'No, just visiting.'

'Visiting grandma,' Aimee pipes up.

Joseph stoops down next to her. 'Hello. And who is this?'

'I'm Aimee.'

'Aimee?' He glances up at Isabel, grinning.

She knows that he has guessed. How could he not have? – as soon as he noticed Aimee's soft, dark eyes, their exotic shape, the tiny button nose, her perfectly straight, jet-black hair? 'And this is Tom,' she says, pulling him close. 'And this is Pau Ling, Lee's sister. Perhaps you two have met before?'

'Er, I'm not sure,' Joseph says, turning to Pau Ling. 'Well . . . Yes, a long time ago.'

'Yes,' Pau Ling replies. 'You were at school with Lee, weren't you? I think we met a few times, but I was a couple of years younger, so . . .' she tails off.

Isabel glances across at her. Pau Ling's cheeks are flushed, and an almost imperceptible crease has appeared between her perfectly arched brows; but her face gives no other clue to what she is thinking.

Joseph's face is lit up; his eyes are sparkling. He looks at Aimee, then back to Isabel. 'You and Lee . . .?'

'Yes,' she replies.

'Ah! I knew it.' He claps his hands together. 'That's great news. I can't believe it. Well, yes, I can believe it. But . . . Wow.' He is beaming at her, and at Aimee. 'I'm afraid that we lost touch after I left Teluk. I moved to Penang. But I did know that he had gone to London.'

The weight in her chest is becoming unbearable. She has to find a way to cut into the torrent of words.

'So how is he? Where is he? Is he here, with you?' He peers over her shoulder, as if he is expecting Lee to pop into sight at any moment. 'Wow! This is great.'

She steels herself. 'Joseph – '

∞

There is an odd expression on her face: anxious, beseeching. Perhaps she wants him to shut up, he thinks. He is talking too much, he knows that, and maybe he shouldn't have become quite so excited – after all, he still doesn't know who the other boy is. But he is over the moon. His friend, Lee, finally married the girl he fell in love with all those years ago. He remembers it all as if it were yesterday. In fact he had been there when it had all started. Lee had been so obsessed with this girl staying at Buah Lodge – it had addled his head – he had never stopped talking about her – on and on, day and night. So they made it, Lee and Isabel. And they had a daughter too. And here they all were –

'We've been shopping.'

The little girl is clutching a black plastic bag, she is holding it up to him, he thinks she wants him to take it.

'Have you?' he asks.

'Yes, we got some money for daddy. And a car. But mummy's looking after the car.'

Curious, he bends down to look into the bag. It is full of paper banknotes: *Koh Ah Bah*, the paper replicas burned for the dead.

He looks into the little girls eyes. She must have made a mistake, he thinks. 'No, not for daddy,' he says. 'Don't you mean . . .'

'Yes, we burn this tomorrow. For daddy.'

He feels Isabel's hand on his arm.

'Joseph . . .' she says.

He senses movement around him, a tussle. He can hear Aimee protesting that she wants to stay with mummy. The little voice is thin, indignant.

Then Isabel is speaking again. It is as if she is standing at the other end of a long, long tunnel.

'Joseph . . .' he hears her say again, 'I'm sorry. Lee died. Six years ago.'

∞

Isabel took the distraught Joseph to a nearby coffee shop. He kept on saying how sorry he was, how he couldn't believe it, how he should have kept in touch – as if that would have changed anything. And he told her again how glad he was that Lee had found her, that they had been able to spend at least some part of their lives together.

On her part, she didn't tell him that it had been just three days: one perfect weekend in which they had shared a love so strong and beautiful that it could have been a lifetime, when they had bound themselves together inextricably, and, to her amazement, had created Aimee. Nor did she tell him the rest of the story: how she had seen Lee's name in the casualty lists after the bomb blast at Marble Arch; how he had died in an ambulance on the way to hospital. And that he never knew he had a daughter.

Since then, there hasn't been a single day when she hasn't thought of him. Sometimes she thinks she catches sight of his face in the street, just like she used to do all those years ago. But then she remembers he has gone. This time, though, she knows where he is.

EPILOGUE

18 June 2001
London

Full circle

∞

Central London
18 June 2001

6.40 pm

For some reason he can't quite fathom, he is lying on the ground. Is he on a beach? He can't remember coming to a beach. He must have fallen asleep. His head is oddly twisted and his cheek is pressed against warm, gritty stone. He wants to go back to sleep, knows he will sleep well – if he could just get more comfortable. He tries to move his head, to turn his face to the sun, but this causes such a stabbing, burning sensation that he lets it rest where it is. He reaches out towards the pain, but his arm simply drifts upwards, his fingers clawing at the air around him.

A moment ago it was so quiet. Deathly quiet. Except for the buzzing inside his head. And now, from somewhere far off, there is another sound: a humming – singing – a tune he ought to recognize. It is getting louder now – louder and louder, bearing down on him – two simple notes – over and over again – like a strange lullaby, willing him to sleep. And someone is there too, leaning over him, blocking out the bright, white light of the sun.

He can just make out a face; the lips are moving, but there is no sound coming from them. The face floats away then comes close again: away, and back, away and back again. Why won't it go? He wishes it would go: he wants to sleep. He must speak to it. Leave me alone, he wants to say, but he finds he can't open his mouth.

He is desperate to sleep. Let me sleep. Please let me sleep.

And at last, he begins to slip into the unconsciousness he is yearning for. But a sudden pain sears across his body. Everything is moving now. He is being lifted into the air. He is flying. And there are people running, running –

www.ingramcontent.com/pod-product-compliance
Lightning Source LLC
Chambersburg PA
CBHW050120030726

47505CB00007B/1963